WRONG HUNT

FANG AND DAGGER
BOOK 1

JS HARKER

For the readers and dreamers

PROLOGUE

Chicago, 1989

"You're late," Dmitri said, the clip of his words hinting at his Russian accent. His voice was quiet, but Roger would have heard him even if the office had been full of people instead of empty.

"I waited five minutes for the elevator before I realized it wasn't coming." Roger traveled down the aisle between the desks. The room reeked of vampires, though the staff had been gone for hours.

After three hundred years, the smell of the grave that lingered among his kind shouldn't have bothered Roger, but every once in a while, it was obnoxious. He slowed his breathing to nonexistent. Ezra and Dmitri had been his closest friends for centuries. There was no reason to keep up human pretenses in front of them.

Roger stepped into the edge of a pool of streetlight illumination that streamed through the window. "Why isn't the elevator working?"

"Because Dmitri is a paranoid bastard." Ezra pushed

away from the wall where he'd been lurking in the deeper shadows. "He turned it off."

"Without the hum, we can hear anyone coming," Dmitri replied.

"We would have heard anyone over the cursed elevator too," Ezra snapped. He'd never bothered adopting an American dialect. His posh English accent was as obvious as his fiery red hair. Gesturing at Dmitri, he continued, "He's checked the bathroom three times. And a plant. Shifters can't turn into plants."

"But a nymph—"

"A nymph isn't going to turn into a bloody office plant!"

If given the chance, Ezra and Dmitri could go around and around for a decade. Roger cleared his throat. "Dawn's coming. I'd like to be in bed before it gets here."

"'Like.'" Ezra snorted and paced. He clenched his fists as he traversed down an aisle the length of a few desks and then came back. His steps were quick but not supernaturally so. But he was close. "I'd *like* Anton to be a pile of bones in the Chicago River. I'd like to rip out his heart, cut it into a million pieces, feed it to a million rats—"

"You want him dead. That's given." Dmitri slid his hands into his pants pockets. As ever, his suit was immaculate, fashioned to fit him and show off his wealth. His movements were smooth, and he stood glacially still. He only did that when his anxiety climbed.

Roger could relate. For the last week, he'd had a ball of nervous snakes growing in his gut. Not real ones, though that might have been more pleasant than the fear coursing through him. If they actually existed, he could have gone to a witch and seen what the hell was causing it. But with feelings, he was on his own.

"I want him more than dead," Ezra snarled. "I want him obliterated. I want to burn him off the face of the Earth and shred every remembrance of him."

Roger fiddled with the gold ring on his left hand. Three centuries had gone past with it on his finger. The etchings on it had never faded. Anton put one on the hand of every vampire belonging to Seamus's coven. When he had placed it on Roger's hand, he'd told him that it would only come off the day he was ready to be his own master.

A week ago, his ring had plopped into the sink while he was shaving. Metal on ceramic, *clink*. He'd told no one.

"You're not the only one who wants him dead," Dmitri said.

"Clearly! Isn't that the whole reason we're here?" Ezra asked.

"Killing Anton won't be simple," Roger said. "There's Seamus to consider."

Dmitri nodded once. "Roger has a point. They've been together for centuries. Seamus will want retribution for Anton's death. We have to rid ourselves of both of them. We need to be careful."

"Fuck careful," Ezra scoffed, and his pacing grew into a longer trail. "You've been selling that shit for centuries. 'It won't be so bad in fifty years.' 'Anton will forget all about you.' 'At least you get away from them.' Here, on the other side of the globe—it doesn't matter. Seamus *owns* us, and the moment we think we might forget it, he lets Anton remind us. I say we walk into the underground tonight and slam a stake through Anton's shriveled heart."

"After what happened, he'll be expecting an attack from you," Dmitri said.

"That's why I invited the golden boy." Ezra waved at Roger. "Though you're standing around more uselessly than usual."

Roger leveled a glare at him and let ice sharpen his words. "I understand your anger, but I am still your sire."

"And what a great fucking one you are!" Ezra grabbed the

edge of a desk and shoved it at Roger, trying to pin him against the next desk.

Roger grabbed the desk on his side and planted his feet. He was stronger than Ezra, always had been. He could shove the desk into him and rip his heart out because of the way Ezra had been acting toward him. Other vampires might have. Seamus definitely would have. But Ezra had always been more bark than bite. Anger had been his companion for two hundred years.

"They killed him!" Ezra shoved harder, but Roger matched him. "They murdered him on stage in front of everyone! And they applauded!"

With a burst of supernatural speed, Ezra grabbed a pencil off the desk and rushed Roger. It was sloppy, and to Roger, too slow. Roger knocked aside Ezra's jab, took him by the throat, and slammed him onto the nearest desk. The desk broke. Before Ezra could recover, Roger put his foot on the center of his chest and pinned him to the floor.

Apparently, he's ready to make that bite fierce. And Ezra didn't even know the worst of what had happened to his lover. Roger glanced Dmitri's way. He knew the truth; they both had learned centuries ago what their sires were capable of.

Seamus and Anton were *eating* vampire souls in order to supplement their own power. If there was an afterlife for vampires, Anton's cannibalistic ritual robbed vampires of that as well as their life. To cover up their horrific practice, Anton animated the corpses, and Seamus made a public display of killing the victims for imagined crimes against the coven. Ezra's lover had been dead before he walked onto the stage.

"Killing" him in front of an audience had been part of Anton and Seamus's ongoing charade, a little farce to keep the average vampire of the coven in check, taunting them with "this happens to everyone who disobeys." Seamus had told Roger the truth one night when Roger was newly made. A joke told in bed that still haunted Roger.

But it was a fate he worked to avoid and one he tried to protect Ezra from.

As Ezra pushed at Roger's foot, his anger broke, and he began to sob. "You fucking let them kill him! Both you bastards! You know Seamus doesn't care about us. You've taught people how to survive Anton, but it doesn't work! One night, a hundred, a thousand—you think you're safe, and then Seamus calls you to court, and Anton does whatever he wants. They break us and laugh about it, and the two of you have stood by for centuries."

Roger removed his foot and stepped back. He didn't have a defense against Ezra's words. Ezra's raw grief numbed Roger's heart. Feelings led to a quick death, and Roger had to survive. Better not to feel.

Dmitri's expression was carefully blank. Not for the first time, Roger wished he could read minds and know what his blood brother was thinking.

"Anton is a mage and a vampire. Seamus is over a thousand years old," Roger said. "This is no simple hunt, and I have no plans to die in this undertaking."

"You desire to make a change," Dmitri said softly. There was an accusation in his words, a quiet murmur of displeasure. "After all this time. They cherish you, and I am supposed to believe you want them dead. Why?"

At first, reasons escaped Roger. Ezra was right to call him the golden boy. Seamus doted on him, buying his affection with money and blood. Roger partied and pretended nothing was wrong in the coven. But he couldn't be more than Seamus allowed, and neither could anyone else. The coven had poison at its core.

Roger spun the ring around his finger. "For the first fifty years, I tried to take this ring off every night. There are times I've hated it more than Seamus or Anton."

Light glinted off Ezra's ring as he waved his hand. "They put one on everyone."

"And when they do, Anton tells them that it will come off when they're strong enough to be their own master." Roger slid his ring off his hand and tossed it onto a nearby desk. Seamus would kill him if he knew he could take it off.

Dmitri gaped at it, and a shiny glint of happiness lit Ezra's gray eyes.

Roger's stomach churned, but he had to keep moving forward. "Why now? Because I'm finally powerful enough to slay the beasts. All I need is a plan."

CHAPTER 1

Rockford, Illinois, 2021

The last few drops of his energy drink were room temperature. Zack shook the can once, caught a couple more drips on his tongue, and then abandoned it in the pile with the others. He tossed two more links into the post he was making and hit send. The HIN—the Hunter Information Network—would have to promote him to moderator if he kept making posts. The research he provided was accurate, and he raced to be the first to answer any hunter's question.

Someone would have to see he was worthy of the Wright family legacy. They just *had* to.

Outside his room, there was a shuffling noise as his family continued packing for their next hunting trip. The legendary Wrights had received a request for assistance the previous night. While everyone else had caught a few hours of sleep, Zack had compiled all their necessary information, double-checked that any necessary toll passes had money on them—Dad believed autopay was a sorcerer's bargain with a demon—and shared a new playlist with his sister, Amber. He'd taken the time to pack a duffle. He'd done everything at an eighth of the volume his family was currently using.

And he wasn't going. Technically. Well, yet. He was going to talk to his parents about the trip as soon as he filled this last request on the HIN.

"Where's my knife?" Cal, the oldest of the three Wright siblings, called out. His voice hacked into Zack's concentration.

"How am I supposed to know?" Amber, the youngest, returned.

The sun wasn't up, but that didn't stop them from shouting. Good thing Zack was still awake. They would've woken him up anyway.

Maybe they'd meant to wake him up so he'd know when they left. While Cal wouldn't bother to say goodbye, he liked rubbing in the fact that Zack had to stay behind.

Amber probably wasn't thinking about her noise level since Cal was being so loud. She was younger than Zack by four years and had spent summer break on the road with the family. At only fifteen, she already had a preferred crossbow.

Their parents had started talking about pulling her out of public school for "homeschooling"—basically more monster hunting and fewer algebra tests. They'd let her choose, like they had Cal.

The Wrights couldn't be prouder of Cal and Amber.

But Zack had finished high school. After one failed trip when he was fourteen, his parents had pushed him into learning mundane stuff. They thought he'd do better in the normal world instead of the supernatural one, and had made him sign up for college. Higher learning in a classroom wasn't his thing, especially not at several grand a semester. So he dropped out. Came home. He knew what he was going to do with his life even if his family didn't recognize his skills.

They would, once he proved that what had happened in Detroit was a one-time fuckup and not who he was.

He just needed a chance.

"I had it during training yesterday." Cal's voice boomed through the wall. Zack might as well have been in the same room as him.

"Okay," Amber replied.

"Well, where is it?"

"I didn't keep track of it."

"Why not?"

"Because it's not my knife."

"You're the junior member of the team. Equipment's your job."

"We aren't on a hunt yet!"

As they bickered, Zack stalked out of his room and to the living room. Cal had been sharpening his knife while Zack was streaming a new episode of *Holy Haunts: Forgotten Churches and the Spooky Tales That Shuttered Them*. It wasn't hard to remember where Cal had put the knife. He'd spent most of the episode waving the point of his blade at the screen and telling Zack what the ghost hunters were doing wrong.

Zack had been through the exact same training as Cal. Their whole lives had been one training session after another. The extra lectures were one of Cal's worst habits. Treating his magical blade like it was any old cutting edge was another.

How he constantly lost the damn thing was a mystery. Zack knew where his dagger was. Besides being more considerate with it, he could feel it. The magic that made it special had been bound to him, like Cal's had been to Cal. But Cal could never find his.

Cal's knife was on the end table. Zack grabbed it and made his way into the kitchen. Cal was searching the cutlery drawer as if anyone would ever put an enchanted, silver, ten-inch knife in with the spoons.

"Here," Zack said dryly.

"You look like death shat on a puppy." Cal took it from him.

Zack folded his arms over his chest, going for a tough stance. He didn't stand a chance at intimidating Cal. In another life, Cal could've played professional football as a linebacker. Though they shared the same shades of brown hair and white skin, they didn't share much else in the way of physical characteristics. Cal was five inches taller and at least sixty pounds heavier. Where Cal had broad shoulders, Zack was narrower. Zack kept hoping for one last growth spurt, but he'd been stuck at five foot eight for a while. Even Cal's knife was bigger, a massive Bowie, whereas Zack's was a stiletto dagger.

Supposedly, a nimble hunter could be as good as one who looked like he could go six rounds with a werebear and win, but Zack never got the opportunity to see for himself.

He couldn't blame his parents. When he was fourteen, the family had taken a mission in Detroit: a vampire nest. Zack had had one job, and he had screwed it up. Every day since, he'd been trying to earn redemption for his mistake. Apparently, he hadn't earned it yet, because Mom and Dad still hadn't invited him along again.

Instead, Zack stayed home. He researched for the family and the HIN and monitored their joint email account for new hunts. Since his parents wound up in places with spotty internet, he balanced the bank accounts and made sure the bills were paid on time. And when he wasn't doing any of those things, he trained with his cousins for the day he'd finally get back out in the field.

He'd been patient for five years. When would waiting pay off?

"I look like shit because I've been up all night chasing down leads for your hunt," Zack told Cal. "The information's sitting in the shared folder, by the way. You're welcome."

"That took you like, what, an hour? What did you do with

the rest of your time?" Cal's grin was lewd. "Get on that vamp porn site again?"

Zack's cheeks heated. "I told you that was one time and it was a mistake."

"Sure it was." Cal laughed. "Don't get your panties in a twist. Beat off to whatever gets you going."

"I don't get off to vamp porn."

"That's not what your internet history says," Amber said sweetly.

"I cleared that!" Zack exclaimed.

Cal looped his arm around Zack's shoulders and patted him on the chest. "Which means there was something to clear." He laughed again. "Wow. Do you actually do anything when we're gone? Or do you spend all day reading those vamp erotica books?"

Zack shoved Cal's arm off. "Those are research. I think a vampire is actually writing them."

"Okay. Sure. Research." Cal snorted.

Zack clenched his fists.

"God, it is too easy to mess with you."

The whirr of the coffeemaker distracted Zack from thinking of a clever comeback. Amber left the coffee pot brewing—practically everyone in the Wright household gathered for a cup whenever the delicious scent filled the air—and took the creamer out of the fridge. After a summer on the road, she had her first noticeable scar on the back of her hand. She had shared pictures of it in the group chat with their fellow monster-hunting cousins as it healed.

Zack had no scars. Yet. One day, he'd get in a real fight and earn one.

"Did you pack the beef jerky?" Cal asked.

"You ate the last of it yesterday." Amber tossed a package of sour candy into the snack box. "That shit stinks anyway."

"You're too young to swear."

Amber rolled her eyes. "If I'm going on hunts, I'm going

to talk like a hunter, which means I can swear as much as I fucking want."

"Fair enough." Cal elbowed Zack in the ribs. "I guess that means you can't."

"Fuck off."

"Such a magnificent way with words. I guess that's why you dropped out of college your first semester."

Cal's mocking tone jabbed at Zack, and he resisted the urge to shove his brother out the back door. Pushing Cal never worked out for him. His older brother was a freaking mountain, and he was a gust of wind.

"You never bothered to go," Zack said, hating how weak the words felt.

Cal snorted. "Because I know what I am, unlike you, pipsqueak."

Zack knew what he wanted to be. His whole life, all he'd wanted was to live up to the legacy of both sides of his family. Grandpa Wright had taken out a Legion demon by the time he was Zack's age, and before he had graduated from high school, his father had helped end a werewolf pack in Southern Illinois that had killed dozens of people. Grandma Wright had been Bonnie West before marriage. Other hunters still talked about her exploits. She was a living legend. And *every* hunter knew the story of the Gladwells, his mother's family. They'd been hunting for over two hundred years.

If Zack voiced any of his anger about being left behind again, Cal would make fun of him like he always did. Zack would wind up feeling bitter. Silence was the better option.

That and sibling-style revenge. There was another package of beef jerky in the pantry. Zack was going to open it the moment his family left the driveway, assuming talking to his parents about going didn't work out.

Tonya, Cal's girlfriend, opened the back door. She had a bag over her shoulder, and she made a beeline for the coffeemaker. While she wasn't a hunter, she was a witch, and her family frequently worked with hunters. Fellow families fighting evil together. In middle school, Zack had had a crush on her, even though she'd been dating Cal. After Cal did something stupid, she'd broken up with him. Recently, they'd gotten back together, and things were going so well she'd gone on a few hunting trips with him.

"Good morning, babe. Come on in. Would you like some coffee?" Cal said in a teasing tone. He kissed Tonya's cheek.

"Less talky, more helping your parents with the trailer so I can get back to sleep faster," she murmured.

"I got it," Zack volunteered. He slipped out the door.

The morning air was cool, but the humidity promised it'd be a hot day when the sun rose. The Wright house was an old farmhouse. When Zack was a kid, they'd torn down the old barn, making serious bank off the old wood in some new-home decorating craze, and built a new one. The family kept their trailer in it alongside three other trailers that belonged to other branches of the local family. The rolling door was open, and Zack jogged over to the entrance. His parents' voices floated on the air, growing louder as he neared them.

"Looks like he finished the upload," Dad said. "He's been busting his ass all summer, Carri."

"I'm aware of that, Thomas," Mom said sharply. The only time she called Dad by his full name was when she was pissed.

Zack ducked in front of the truck before his parents spotted him. Dad was between the truck and the trailer, while Mom was in the trailer. She had to be checking over the supplies, which Zack had restocked when they'd come home four days ago.

"You can't keep holding Detroit against him." Dad wandered over to the open trailer door. "He was a boy."

"Funny how every time I remind you that Amber is still a girl, you say that's not a good enough reason," Mom replied.

"Amber stored a loaded shotgun when the damn thing should have been emptied."

"And Zack let a bloodsucker walk!"

Zack flinched and sat on the ground, his back to the truck.

"Carri—"

"Did you know he's been on those vile sites every time we've been gone? Have you seen what he's been reading?"

Dad grunted. "He's spending time on that because he's bored. If he was on the road with us, he wouldn't have time for it."

Zack closed his eyes and clenched his fists, keeping them on the ground. Mom wasn't supposed to know about the vampire habit. It was just a hobby. Sure, he'd lied to Cal when he said he'd only been on the site once, but it was *research*. He got bored and scrounged around the net for vamp porn. Most of it was fake, but every once in a while, the genuine article popped up. The HIN had places to report the real vampires, and he was in some serious competition with one of the other asshats in the network— an English cousin—to see who could spot the most real vampires.

That's not the only reason you do it, a slithery, nasty internal voice that sounded too much like Cal taunted. A recent vid played back in his head. A moaning, gasping young man, fangs dripping with blood. That one image opened the door to everything else he'd been investigating lately.

Fuck, he had not had enough coffee or sleep to deal with that clusterfuck of an imagepalooza in his head. The last thing he needed was an erection.

Clearly, Mom didn't want him on the trip. He might as well snag some of the fresh brew before everyone else took it. With enough caffeine, he could ignore how heavy his heart felt and how twisted up his stomach was.

"We squared away?" Cal asked as Zack reentered the kitchen.

"Ah, no." Zack forced a laugh. "You know I'm crap at hooking up the trailer. Don't know why I bothered."

"I don't either." Cal sighed. He patted Zack's shoulder on the way to the door. "Thanks for finding my knife, though I guess it's no surprise you know where everything is in the house, huh? When's the last time you went anywhere?"

Cal always knew exactly what to say to make Zack feel two inches tall. Before Zack could summon the words to deflate Cal's ego, his older brother was out the door. Fine. The less he had to listen to him, the better. Tonya followed Cal.

Zack grabbed his second-favorite mug from the cabinet. His true favorite was dirty in his room. At least he had plenty of time to do the housework.

Amber finished scrolling through her phone and slid it into her back pocket. "Thanks for the intel. Were you really up all night?"

"I wanted to flesh out what Fletcher and Eeves sent us. Looks like the vamps are in a feeding pattern, but I think they've grown and split into more groups. You could be looking at as many as three sets. I'd start with the ones west of Tallahassee. Theft reports are up. I think that nest is murderous thieves."

"But the original report was about Pensacola, right?"

"Yes, but if you look at the data, the other group's the bigger threat. The ones left in Pensacola are a suck-n-move operation."

"We'll see what Mom says," Amber replied.

Which meant she wouldn't voice Zack's idea to the family. Why did he keep trying if his efforts weren't going to matter? He poured a cup of coffee, heaped in sugar, and took it to his room. Hopefully, another research request had come through on the HIN, and he'd have something to do.

His duffle bag sat on the end of his bed like an eager puppy looking for treats. *Should never have bothered.* He knocked it off and kicked it into his closet. Then he slumped into his computer chair and opened the HIN website again. After a while, the noise of his family coming and going dropped to nothing.

They were actually going to leave without saying a word to him. Their vampire hunt might take them weeks, and they were just taking off.

He wasn't going to be disappointed. Generations of Wrights and Gladwells had fought demons, faeries, vampires, shifters, hellspawn, and everything in between. Despite all the loud stories and legends, there had to be others who had been like him: the ones left behind who tended to the books. He wasn't going to tear up, because brave hunters didn't cry over something so stupid as being left out.

His eyes were watering from staring at the screen. Yeah, that had to be his problem. He was worn out, not upset. Sure. He turned off his computer monitor and curled up on his bed.

His mother's steps were softer than anyone else's besides his own, but he heard her come down the hallway. When he didn't turn to look at his open door, she knocked. "Zack, we're leaving."

Zack clutched his pillow and continued staring at the wall. If he looked at her, he would break, and he couldn't let her think he was a baby as well as a failure.

"Zack, honey, I know you're not asleep."

"Yeah, okay." Zack's voice broke and he wanted to strangle his traitorous voice box.

Mom came in and sat on the end of his bed, but he refused to budge. She gently shook his leg until he rotated to face her. He had her gray eyes, though when he looked in the mirror, his never had the confident, steely quality hers did. He had her nose too.

Cal teased him that looking so much like Mom made him too feminine—as if there weren't scores of fearless women hunters on both sides of their family. Zack had written a thirty-page report on the subject and shoved it in Cal's face.

Cal had laughed and called him a girl, like that was somehow a bad thing.

Zack should text Tonya and tell her what a misogynist Cal could be. But she'd grown up around him, so his warning probably wouldn't mean anything. *It's not like anything else I've had to say has made a difference.*

"You don't have anything to say?" Mom asked.

"Don't die." Zack thumped his pillow into a better shape and rolled onto it again.

Mom sat quietly for a moment. "You heard your father and I talking."

"No, I didn't."

"Lying is not an attractive quality, Zackery Wright." Mom rested her hand on his leg. "I saw you heading for the house. Cal said you'd been outside for a few minutes before you came back in."

Of course, Cal had ratted him out. Grumbling, Zack sat up. "Okay, I heard you."

Mom looked away from him, and the silence was heavy. Was she staring at the pile of energy drinks? His dirty keyboard that he was totally going to clean now that he saw how nasty it looked? Did she know he kept his *From the Grave* book series on the top shelf of his closet? She was staring at the closet.

He couldn't blame her for the anger. She was the one who had championed for him to be part of the big Detroit operation, and she'd seen him let a vampire go. At the time, he'd thought he'd done the right thing. The girl had been in the missing persons reports he'd compiled for research. She hadn't been a vampire for long. When she'd begged him to let her go, he'd softened. He'd released her because ... *because maybe she wasn't evil.* Zack bit his bottom lip. That thought had been what had gotten him into trouble. He'd made a mistake. He needed to remember that.

"You packed a bag," Mom said slowly.

"I thought maybe I could come," Zack said.

Another crushing silence threw a heavy weight onto Zack's chest. Finally, Mom took a deep breath. "If you think you're ready to commit, you can come."

Ready to commit. Zack closed his eyes and fought off a surge of anger. She was questioning his resolve. Him! Like he hadn't been training as hard as his cousins and siblings. Like he hadn't been doing the research everyone else needed while his family spent weeks at a time on the road. Like he wasn't a Wright or a Gladwell. Every day since Detroit, he'd pushed himself to make up for his mistake, and she hadn't noticed. He hadn't made the team. Bringing him was a burden, an afterthought.

"Never mind," Zack said sharply as he opened his eyes.

"All right, then."

Her tone was so patronizing and dismissive that Zack froze. Unloading his rage on her wouldn't help and would only make him feel like shit in the end. Screaming at her was wrong. She was his mother. She was supposed to know what was best.

But she doesn't know me. Zack clenched his jaw and buried his anger in a ten-foot grave.

Mom stood and headed out of the room. Apparently, searching a few websites—that other members of the HIN were also monitoring—meant he wasn't fit to be a hunter. His time spent training couldn't make up for his mistake. Not to her. She was never going to forgive him for Detroit. Anything could happen to her on the road, and those were her final words.

He stayed silent, letting the chance to say anything more slip through his fingers. Only after the back door shut and locked did he curl up tight and give up his fight against the tears. It had to feel so bad because he'd been up too long. That had to be the reason he couldn't stop crying. He was just so tired.

His excuse didn't apply to the previous four times he'd cried after they left.

Mom almost invited me this time. Maybe next time, she'd see he was ready.

And maybe she would never invite him again. Had he screwed up by saying no?

He'd fucked up. He should've jumped at the opportunity despite Mom's tone.

Except how much harder did he have to work to show he was a hunter like everyone else?

His thoughts twisted, grinding into a deeper swirl of cloying rage. He let himself cry another minute. After it passed, he took a ragged breath and tried to sleep. He drifted without finding restful slumber.

With a loud clatter, Zack's phone buzzed across his desk. He should ignore it, but he couldn't sleep anyway. He grabbed it.

An email had come into the Wright hunting account. Zack rubbed his face clean of the dried tears and shuffled over to his desk. Somewhere—ah, there were his pen and notebook. He flipped it to a fresh page and opened the email.

Callum Wright,

I have a vamp problem that needs a hunter like you …

The protocol was for Zack to take down the notes of the hunt, mark it as new, text Cal about the email, and then start research on the target. According to the map, Taliville was in the Appalachian Mountains, but it wasn't too far off the family's route to Florida. If he alerted them to it now, they could change course and tackle the hunt on their way south.

Or *he* could take the target and then meet up with his family. The email said it was just one vampire. He could handle that. Mom would have to take him seriously if he showed up with a pair of vampire fangs as proof of his first kill. There would be no more jokes, no more getting left behind, no more doubt that he was a Wright.

But hunting was dangerous. Zack would be taking a huge risk.

The email had everything he needed to know. What was he waiting for? Clearly, no one else was going to believe in him until he executed a hunt on his own. He forwarded the email to his personal account and deleted it from the family one. He should take the time to double-check the information on the hunt, but he had read through ones that looked less legit. Besides, he didn't have the time. Cal could have seen the email. If the family scooped Zack's kill out from under him, his plan would be ruined.

He grabbed his duffle bag and his backpack. If he hurried, he could slay his first monster by nightfall and join his family by the next dawn.

CHAPTER 2

Light glinted off the buckle of Zack's hunter's belt. It was currently sitting in the passenger seat, loaded with tools from the family stockpile. He had a pouch of salt, another pouch with a few pieces of chalk, a tiny UV flashlight, a regular flashlight, and his enchanted silver dagger he'd gotten on his tenth birthday. In the trunk, he had a crossbow along with a short sword, his backpack, and duffle bag. Those would be more useful when he joined his family in Florida.

Did he have everything? He was nearly to Taliville, so the point was moot, but he had to be forgetting something. He had the right weapons, enough underwear and socks for at least a week, and he had a few changes of clothes. Charger, check. Tablet and fresh notebooks, check. Laptop—crap, he'd left the laptop at home. He could get by without it. What about his wallet? Zack wiggled his butt against the seat and rocked into the lump in his back pocket. Whew, he had it.

He popped the last bit of beef jerky in his mouth and slurped more of his energy drink. After he killed the vampire, he'd find somewhere to get some actual sleep. He could catch up with his family late tomorrow. That sounded like a great plan.

But first, Taliville's vampire problem was going dowwwwwwn.

"Turn left," his phone's navigation announced, interrupting his playlist.

Shit, he was flying past the highway. Zack yanked the wheel into a sharp turn. Rocks spewed from the gravel beside the road as he righted his vehicle onto the backwoods highway. The road was taking him higher up the mountain, and the forest was growing thick.

Twenty minutes later, a large sign declared, "Welcome to Taliville, Population 7,500," though there was nothing to see but trees. The road curved around the side of the mountain, and the forest broke away to reveal a light downhill slope into the town. Houses and streets were nestled around a clear blue lake. A business area was on the near side, while more spacious neighborhoods and mansions continued around the lake's border.

A massive stone dragon clawed its way up from the lake and into the town park. Zack almost lost focus on the road, trying to get a good look at it. He'd seen some strange statuary before, but the creature was fifty feet long and looked like it wanted to rip the town apart. It didn't mesh with the peaceful small-town vibe. Weird.

A variety of small businesses populated Main Street, and there was a lack of the usual commercial chain stores. The picturesque buildings gave Zack more goosebumps than the dragon statue. Places that appeared "perfect" could hide horrible monsters. Cal would go on and on about the creatures he hunted *and* the bigots and racists he met in bars. Although, thinking about it, Cal had just as many awful people stories set in big cities as he did in small towns. "Sophisticated" businesspeople could be more assholish than a backwoods drunkard.

As if the universe had to admonish him for his bias, both the coffee shop and the bookstore across the street had

Progress Pride Flags prominently displayed. The bed-and-breakfast on the corner, the Sleepy Bear Inn, had a bear covered with a rainbow blanket on its sign.

"Okay, not the worst place on Earth," Zack whispered to himself as he drove by. It didn't really matter how nice the town was. He wasn't sticking around long enough to know the locals. He was driving in, staking the vampire, then leaving to catch up to his family.

A yawn almost made him miss the navigation's next instruction.

Maybe I'll take a longer look at the B&B after I kill the vampire.

His destination was six blocks off Main Street, closer to the lake. He eased his car to a stop in front of the house. It was an ordinary two-story structure, with part of the second floor extended over the garage. A lot of the houses on the street had the same cookie-cutter look, including the one for sale across the street.

His target's house was neither abandoned nor well loved. The grass in the yard was longer than the neighboring lawns but not neglectfully so. More like the neighbors cut theirs constantly, and the vampire hadn't gotten around to it that week. The front stoop had failing garden patches on either side. The house didn't scream *A Vampire Lives Here!*

But the best monsters knew how to hide in plain sight.

Zack turned off his car and grabbed his weapon belt. This was it. His hunt. He could do this. Repeating that to himself a few more times, he stepped out of the car. The summer sun was hot and bright and well on its way out of the sky. Time was running out before the vampire would wake and be at full strength.

He fumbled with the buckle of his belt and accidentally tightened it too far at first. His hunting equipment jostled, and he had to fix the belt, then reposition everything on it. Thankfully, his family hadn't been around to see that mistake. Cal would've never let it go.

His first step was to check for any signs of a human alarm system or a more treacherous magic-based one. While an electronic system would summon cops, magic could throw a lifelong curse on him. He couldn't afford getting caught in either.

After three quick passes around the house, he determined there wasn't an electronic system. Lucky him.

Magic-based systems required closer inspection. Zack wiped his brow as he approached the front door. Damn, it was hot out. Sweat trailed down his spine and made his T-shirt cling to him in places. He was grateful for the sliver of shadow the overhang gave him.

Stretching, he ran his fingers along the top of the doorframe. There were no etchings of any mage marks. If he were a mage, he'd put them in hard-to-reach spots. But that would also make them hard to spell in the first place. He needed to double-check the base better, so he knelt down.

Thoroughness and dedication paid off. A subtle mark was carved into the bottom, right-hand side of the frame. When Zack put his hand near it, it hummed with energy. The mark had a mix of Unseelie and American runes to it. The design was a little complicated, but ones guarding a house tended to be. If Zack's guess was right—and he'd done enough research on the basics of magic to know he was—the mark would zap intruders.

But it wasn't part of a chain reaction, and Zack didn't spy any other marks. Dispelling this one would be fairly simple. He opened his pouch of salt.

In theory, anyone could learn magic. Spells were the application of study, bound by focus, and honed with the belief one could make their will into reality. Like any other skill, some people had a better affinity for it than others. Training and natural talent went a long way to learning magic, but nothing could replace the power of belief.

Zack dipped his fingers into his salt pouch, coating them as best he could. He had practiced neutralizing marks like the one on the doorframe hundreds of times. Out of his siblings, he was the fastest at it. *Not that it matters. I'll never make up for Detroit.*

The thought skewered his focus and brought up a wash of emotions. Doubt hogged the spotlight, playing a drum-solo counter to the calm Zack needed for the spell. Instead of finding a neutral headspace, he was trapped in the cycling clatter. He needed time to meditate, but kneeling in front of a stranger's door on a sunny afternoon was a recipe for disaster. If a nosy neighbor called the police, he'd be in deep shit.

He had another way to dispel such a basic mage mark. It was faster, but it could literally blow up in his face. He bit his bottom lip. There wasn't time to find the perfect balance for a negation spell. The riskier way would have to work.

"Damn it." Zack brushed his fingers off on his shorts and took out his silver dagger.

Every Wright kid received an enchanted silver blade on their tenth birthday. It wasn't just any silver blade, either. A witch, Tonya's grandmother, had empowered additional magic in the blade by connecting it to Zack's soul. The mage marks on it were descended from an angelic dialect, becoming a combination of human with a hint of the divine. The blades always fit the hunter. Zack's was a stiletto: thin, sharp, and meant for stabbing.

The magic in the blade was meant to nullify opposing magics, whether a mage's or a vampire's. It couldn't outright absorb, but it could disrupt. Zack set the tip of his blade at the outer edge of the mark on the doorframe. It buzzed faintly as the magics argued against one another. With a deep breath, he sliced through the mage mark and then threw himself backward.

The energy stored in the doorframe sparked, sending a spray out. A few stray sparks landed on Zack's leg. It smarted, but that was it. No secondary spell went off. Whoever had made the mark had set it for stun, not kill.

Hopefully, that meant there were no traps on the inside of the house.

I'm really doing this! With a grin, Zack slid his knife into its sheath, took out his lockpicks, and scrambled back over to the door. His hands shook. He counted his breaths, trying to slow his heart and calm his nerves. Then he tried again. Cal's old trunk where he stashed his good pot was harder to break into than the house.

The door creaked as Zack opened it. He slipped inside and shut it quietly. The email said that the vampire slept through the day, but that didn't mean it couldn't wake up. He put away his lockpicks and took out his stake and UV flashlight. The little beam of light wouldn't kill a vampire, but it would hurt. One good moment was all he needed to end the monster. He'd take every advantage he could get.

The living room was decorated entirely in purple, from the shade of the carpet to the lampshades. The end table held video game controllers and one for the television. And, oh shit, there was a cat, but it only stared at Zack like the intruder he was.

Despite the color overload, the room was cozy. Vampires didn't *do* cozy. Had he broken into the wrong place? If he had, why was there a mage mark on the door?

The bastard must have a human pet. Zack's pulse sped. He hadn't counted on any humans in the house. While his entrance had been quiet, he couldn't be sure someone wasn't waiting to ambush him. What would he do if he did run into someone? He couldn't hurt a human. No matter what Cal and his family said, a human living with a vampire wasn't necessarily evil.

His only option would be to convince someone that he was doing them and the world a favor by getting rid of the vampire. Maybe they'd even thank him. Maybe they weren't a willing pet.

They probably wouldn't think he was helping them. Zack

really needed to get a move on and finish the job before he got caught.

In the kitchen, Zack discovered a stack of mail on the counter and more dishes than he cared to count piled in the sink. How many people lived in this house? It looked like more mess than one person could make, but then again, when left alone in the house for a week, his kitchen looked this bad. Huh, maybe Mom had a point about making sure he cleaned up more often.

There were four doors in the kitchen, including the one he had come through, and an open one that led to a staircase that went upstairs. Judging from the location, one had to lead to the garage, but that left one more door. Did Zack check upstairs? Or did he look for a basement? The email said the vampire slept in a coffin in the house but not where exactly in the house it would be.

Zack's gut instinct told him to check for a basement first. He went over to the two mysterious doors. One actually led to a pantry, and the other revealed a staircase leading downward. Sunlight barely touched the murky darkness, and his tiny UV beam didn't provide much illumination. What if the vampire was awake? It could kill him, and his family would never know what had happened to him.

It could do worse than kill him. Vampires turned people into vampires all the time. Sires expected their fledglings to obey them for an eternity, and that was one of the better fates. A million horrible ends played out in an instant of Zack's imagination.

Hunters had to work with their fear, not give in to it. If he was going to be part of the family legacy, he had to put his courage to the sticking place and *do* this. He took a steadying breath and headed down the stairs. His UV flashlight wasn't giving him the light he needed, so he swapped to his larger, regular light. The beam was bigger and brighter, and he steeled himself for the horrors he'd find below.

Except … there were boxes of Christmas decorations on one side of the room, a defunct bike leaning against a massive plastic jack-o'-lantern, a set of drums piled together instead of set up, and a line of metal shelves on the right side of the room, stockpiled with human supplies. Toilet paper, paper towels, and … green beans? Seriously, a whole shelf dedicated to green beans. What vampire needed that many cans? It had to be a human.

Or maybe he really, *really* had the wrong house. Maybe someone wanted revenge on Cal, and they were setting him up for an arrest. Zack should leave and go home. No one would even know he'd failed his first solo hunt if he left now. He swept his flashlight beam around the room one more time.

In the back of the room, between a horizontal deep freezer and an old rocking chair, was an odd, long shape under a blue tarp. A pile of junk in the middle of the room made the paths winding, but Zack took care not to trip over anything. He snuck his way across the room. His chest grew tighter with every step. *Breathe, damn it! One, two. In, out. Come on, don't fail the basics.*

Holy shit, he was really going to stake his first vampire!

With a trembling hand, he reached out for the tarp. Too much caffeine and not enough sleep were making him shake. But he could do this. He was already doing this. Sharply, he yanked the tarp off the coffin and batted at the dust that clouded his face.

The coffin was sitting upright, which was a little weird according to hunter knowledge, but not unheard of. Most vampires lived—or unlived, Zack thought—for the drama. This vampire's coffin was mahogany and had a gold crest over the head space. Vampiric heraldry had been one of Zack's interests since discovering a line of supernatural romance novels in high school. Such books were banned in the house, which made them even more thrilling.

His interest in fake vampires had morphed into the practical study, though his family continued to disapprove and suspect his motives. But heraldry was important to older vampires. Around eighty percent of vampires lived in covens, and a crest helped distinguish a vampire from its lessers.

The style of the crest before Zack indicated that the vampire was a few centuries old, somewhere between three and four hundred years. A shark formed the base, and tentacles rose from behind it in what would seem like an incoherent mess to the untrained eye, but Zack spotted symbols for swords, cannons, and the world. This vampire was a seafarer and a warrior. Above the tentacles was a Celtic snake with a crown imprinted on it. Near the head, the snake had a single red band. The shark and tentacles were for the vampire in the coffin, but the snake itself was a symbol of the head of the vampire's coven.

Dread made Zack's blood run cold. Seamus, a particularly nasty vampire, had sired the vampire in the coffin. The single red band meant this vampire was a first-generation fledgling of Seamus and probably held a high rank in the Great Lakes Coven. That group controlled a large territory around Lake Michigan and had been expanding at a dangerous rate over the last two decades.

On top of that, Seamus was one of the vampires the Gladwells had sworn to wipe off the Earth. Killing one of his top fledglings would strike a well-deserved blow against the master vampire.

Zack couldn't afford to waste any more time. He examined the coffin and discovered a series of mage marks at the edge of the lid. They weren't made by the same hand as the one at the door and had more Unseelie characteristics to them than anything else. One looked like it was a locking spell, but the others were harder to decipher. Sleep? That made sense. Knock out any potential disturbances and the vampire could eat the intruder when it woke up.

While the mark series was more complicated than the one

on the doorframe, a focused neutralization spell would do the trick.

Undoing the spell would release energy, which might wake the vampire. But what else could he do? Burn down the house and hope it'd work? People lived there. Someone could still be upstairs. And what if it didn't work? He didn't want a pissed off, flaming vampire attacking him.

He had the advantage, and he had to make the best of it. Speed would be essential. Dispel, open, stab—all before the vampire had a chance to react. It was simple. Easy. Dispel, open, stab. Zack had practiced this scenario in training and imagined doing it dozens of times during his drive. *I can do this.*

After a few deep breaths, he coated two fingers in salt and concentrated on an empty void in his head. There was nothing in the void, no emotion or magic, no fear. It was the absence of existence. A blank spot. He expanded that void and honed it with his will into the spell. As he touched his salt-covered fingers to the mage mark, he said, "Vacuus."

The coffin shuddered with the release of magical energy. Zack jumped back, then swore at himself for being skittish. He threw aside the coffin lid and raised his stake.

Raven-black hair spilled down to the man's shoulders. A gold earring glinted in his left ear, and the tiny embellishment added a roguish quality to his breathtakingly handsome face. His red-plaid shirt was open, and he was muscular in a way Zack had only fantasized about seeing in real life. He had broad shoulders and thick thighs, and even if he wasn't a vampire, he could've snapped Zack in half. He was amazing, and a dozen new fantasies dragged Zack's mind into the gutter and washed him down into a maze of sexual sewers.

Shit, he was getting a boner.

Strike, damn it!

He aimed for the vampire's heart and drove the stake toward it.

The vampire snarled as he opened his blood-red eyes. Quicker than Zack could follow, the vampire grabbed his wrist and yanked his arm wide, throwing him off balance. Zack gasped and tried to sway back. The vampire grabbed him by the throat and shoved him backward as he stepped out of the coffin.

Zack's inappropriate boner hardened. *Worst time ever to find out I might be into breath play.* He dropped his flashlight and scrambled to pull the vampire's hand off his throat. He would have had better luck pushing a glacier. The vampire was endlessly stronger than him.

The vampire's handsome face was still glorious as he opened his mouth wide in a fresh snarl. Time dilated, making the world seem to stand still while the vampire dragged Zack closer. Zack fought back, but his feet slid on the concrete. His sneakers couldn't gain traction. The vampire slid his thumb up Zack's neck and forced his head to the side.

All the time in the world didn't matter. The vampire had him.

Zack cried out as fangs ripped into his neck.

CHAPTER 3

Every fiber of Roger's being burned. Blood filled his mouth, and he drank, but the first few swallows only ignited a deeper fire. His soul felt chapped, as if he'd been out in the sun for merciless days on end. The prey in his grasp squirmed, and he tightened his hold. He needed *more*.

Bright pain in his leg flared through him. On instinct, he shoved his prey away and tried to escape. A brilliant crystalline awareness struck him in a single thought. *What the hell is wrong with me?* He never fed like this. Not on purpose. Not in decades. He controlled the bite and savored the blood taken; he didn't drink like an animal in a drought.

Hadn't he fed last night? Yes. Twice. More than enough both times. He put a hand to his forehead. Why was everything inside him burning? Why was the world sandpaper on his flesh, ripping into his consciousness and shredding his sanity bit by bit? He was better than this. He was no feral creature but a true vampire. A legend. Roger.

There was only a flashlight for illumination, but it was more than enough for Roger to see around the room. Piles of objects filled the space. Was that a Christmas tree? He didn't own one. And the room was cement. He didn't have a place like this in his penthouse. Where was he?

The human floundered in a pile of junk before rising with a clatter that could wake the dead. He growled and lunged at Roger. In his hand was a silver dagger, and the runes on it glowed a bright white light.

God damn it, this was a *hunter*. Roger blocked the knife, but the hunter followed with a sharp jab he wasn't expecting. He rocked back and hurried to counter the next blow.

Supernatural speed should have given him an edge. Reaching for his strength, for the core of his power that made him more than human, he came away with nothing. He simply *couldn't* find the strength to fight. The knowledge made him cold, and the hunger for blood sizzled inside his skin. He hadn't been this weak since his first night.

The hunter stabbed Roger in the side, yanked out the knife, and then aimed for his heart.

I will not die here. Hissing, Roger grabbed the hunter's wrist and twisted. The boy—Roger could see his face more clearly, and while he was a man, he was preciously young—winced, but he moved with Roger's motion. A hard glint in his gray eyes turned them to the color of steel, and he lifted his chin with a defiance that struck an echo through time.

Though Roger had been in more fights in his life than he could recall, let alone count, he knew the number of times he'd seen someone with such a fierce soul. Even among hunters, such a soul was rare. His heart quickened, and a smile eased onto his lips.

You always want the ones that are poison for you, Seamus had teased over the years. Roger had always laughed.

But his sire had a point. This boy was clearly trying to kill him, yet Roger's heart fluttered with a desire to claim him. Wanting him was more palatable than what his hunger longed for. The need to drink ached in his bones. Only blood could satisfy him.

Plenty of the red, delicious-smelling liquid dampened the shoulder of the boy's T-shirt. The wound on his throat leaked. His heart beat a tempo that filled Roger's mind. He should sink his fangs in again and drink. Feed. He'd drain the boy until he was a husk, until death stole his beauty. Damn him, he *needed* too much. He snatched the boy by the shoulders.

Purple light smacked Roger in the eyes. It burned, and he let the boy go to shield his eyes from the beam. His hand smarted where the light hit it. *Resourceful.*

The hunter was clearly trained and had at least one magical weapon and a fighting spirit. He was gorgeous and determined.

A hunter this clever, this handsome, this amazing could be the linchpin Roger had been searching for.

The boy swung his dagger, and Roger dodged it. At last, a bit of his supernatural speed kicked in. The blood he'd drunk was finally taking hold. While he was nowhere near full strength—barely an eighth—he had enough speed to outpace the boy's strikes. He grabbed the boy's wrist and used his momentum to twist the boy's arm behind his back. When the boy struggled, Roger pulled tighter.

"Stop before I break something," Roger murmured.

The boy bucked, and Roger let him before leveraging his arm further. The boy cried out. His scream plucked on Roger's heartstrings, but he couldn't release his hold. Vampires who gave in to their empathy didn't last a decade.

Tears formed in the boy's eyes, but he still had defiance in them as he glared over his shoulder at Roger. "Do your worst. I'd rather die than be your blood bitch."

"And I thought vampires were dramatic," Roger said with a laugh. "'Blood bitch?' When did your lot come up with that?"

"My family will avenge me."

"That'll be hard to do when you're not dead." Roger stretched his senses as far as he could. There was only the boy's ragged breathing and racing heartbeat. He couldn't hear anyone else. No one else was lurking in the basement or in the floor above. "Where is your family? Don't tell me this is a rite-of-passage hunt. I'm worth far more than that."

"You're not worth anything! You're a fucking monster!"

"You tried to kill me in my sleep," Roger whispered in the boy's ear. "What does that make you?"

"That's different! You're a vampire!" The boy flushed a deep scarlet, a good sign considering the bloody wound on his throat.

Roger must not have taken as much as he'd feared. He could take a little more. The bleeding wound was so close. All he had to do was sink his teeth in, and he could drink and drink and drink.

But the boy wouldn't have enough to end the burning in Roger's veins. Dead hunters, especially ones this young and well trained, had family, and someone always showed up looking for revenge. Whole legacies of hunters had been built on the death of family members. Hell, the boy had already claimed his family would strike vengeance. Feeding on him a second time would be a mistake.

The boy was trying to pull something out of a pouch on his belt. With a frustrated groan, Roger hauled the boy backward and twisted him around. He shoved the boy into his coffin, but the boy tripped and landed on his ass. Roger grabbed him by his hair and yanked him upward.

Scrambling, the boy pushed up against Roger. He pulled away instantly, but the moment had been long enough for Roger to feel his erection.

"And you call me the monster," Roger purred. The boy fought a shiver, shoulders staying straight while the rest of him shuddered. Roger didn't need to rely on his magic to seduce him. Apparently, the mundane way of flirts and whispers would work. "Did the chance to kill the big bad vampire get you hard?"

"Gross! I'm not—I don't—I'm not horny."

Roger tugged the boy against him and wrapped an arm around him. The boy's erection was a rock trapped between them. "You can keep lying about it if you want. We could screw all night until your legs are jelly, and you've lost your voice to the pleasure of having me fill you, and you can tell yourself and the world it was just a moment. A fluke. But I can feel you getting harder, boy. I can hear your heart racing, and I smell far more than fear rolling off you."

It took all of Roger's self-control, but he licked one of the bloody trails on the boy's throat. Fuck, the blood was always so much better when lust was added to the mix.

"Jesus Christ," the boy whispered. His bottom lip was wet from where he'd tugged it between his lips. He cleared his throat and raised his chin. Oh, he was worth keeping at one's side. With a huff, he said, "I'm not hard because I'm going to kill you. I got hard because you're ridiculously hot."

Roger raised an eyebrow and pushed the boy back into the coffin. That was the first time a male hunter had freely called him attractive. "You're not a smite-the-gays vampire hunter type. Good to know."

The boy stilled. "Wait, what? You've actually had people come after you for that?"

"I've had my own kind hate our coven for it. A vampire in the 1870s cited that my 'perversion' was the reason I should perish in a house fire. I've lost track of how many hunters claimed I was the worst kind of devil."

A steely look hardened the boy's gray eyes. "Okay, that's awful."

Roger was too old to be fooled by one moment of decency. He kept his hands loose, at the ready, in case the hunter decided to attack. "Says the man who tried to murder me in my sleep."

"You're still a freaking vampire. And you bit me."

"I bit you because you woke me up. You should have ended me when you had the chance."

"I got distracted by how hot you are. Go back to sleep. I won't hesitate again."

Lord, no one had spoken to him like this in forever! Roger laughed. "Oh, I like you."

"Not sure that's a good thing."

"It's keeping you alive."

The boy's breathing was quiet and quick. In the silence of the basement, each puff of air roared through Roger's ears. The boy was copper-scented and steely-eyed. The sweet remnants of his blood tingled on Roger's tongue.

If they were anywhere else, Roger would caress the boy, tell him how handsome he was, and see where the art of seduction could take them. But he had woken in a room he didn't know with a hunter he'd never met. Something terrible had happened, and he couldn't remember last night well enough to know what. His memories were hazy blurs. That was the last time he was going to get drunk on fey wine.

With too many questions and no immediate resources, he needed the boy. Provided, of course, he could convince him to stop trying to murder him.

The room held random belongings, but there had to be something useful in the piles. Keeping one eye on the boy, he scanned the nearby piles. Whose basement was he in? Ezra lived in a penthouse, and Dmitri would never let his place be so disorganized. Seamus wouldn't have let a hunter in so close, and Anton? He wouldn't have let Roger wake if he'd done this to him. Was this one of Candide's places? But she had no use for such utterly mortal crap.

"Where are we?" Roger asked.

"Your basement," the boy answered.

"This could be a perfect dungeon. I wouldn't fill it up with old exercise equipment and Christmas decorations. And I certainly don't have a need for that many green beans."

"Dungeon?" the boy scoffed. "I knew you were a freaking monster."

Ah, there was a jump rope. It'd do. Roger dragged the boy over to the pile of equipment and tugged out the jump rope. "The only men who have been in my dungeons wanted to be there. They always thanked me on the way out."

"Why would they—you mean a sex dungeon."

There was a flash of lust in the boy's emotions. Roger's powers were still weak, but they were there. Feeling the boy's sexual yearning was like finding his hand on a solid rope. He could yank on it, unfurling the sails and guiding them into the wind. But for the moment, simply having his hand on the rope was more than enough. It eased some of his worry. His weakness wouldn't last. All he had to do was feed.

He turned the boy around and pulled his wrists behind his back. "You caught onto that quicker than the last hunter I was distracting. Don't do that with your wrists. I just told you I like sex dungeons. Don't you think I know all the tricks to tying someone up?"

"Yeah, but I'm not consenting. In fact—" The boy started to slide his hand toward his belt.

Before he could move more than a centimeter, Roger grabbed the wound on the boy's throat and dug his fingers into the edge. The boy shouted and his knees buckled.

"Keep your hands behind your back," Roger growled. "If you move again, I will kill you."

Some hunters attempted to fight even when Roger issued that sort of threat. He'd killed people because they wouldn't give up. Smarter hunters bided their time and waited for a better opportunity. Part of Roger hoped the boy would be smart because he could be extremely useful.

His hunger wanted the boy to fight because then he would have a perfect excuse to eat him.

The boy put his wrists together behind his back.

"Good choice," Roger breathed.

"Not much of one."

Roger started to tie the jump rope around the boy's wrists. What had he been up to last night? Drinking, clearly. Fey wine. It was the only substance that could get a vampire truly drunk. There had been a very pretty Unseelie boy buying the drinks. Well, he had looked like a boy. Unseelies could alter their appearance. The club had been a supernatural one, but usually the fey kept alluring glamours on anyway.

"Whatever you're planning isn't going to work," the hunter said.

"My plan is to not get murdered before I know what the hell is going on." Roger finished tying the boy as effectively as he could. A jump rope wasn't ideal, but it should be good enough to prevent him from easily breaking free and attacking again.

Roger reached around the boy and undid his belt. Anyone with that many pouches had too many tools.

"What are you doing?" the boy demanded.

"Disarming you. Don't worry. I won't strip you until you beg for it."

"I'm supposed to believe the word of a *vampire*?"

"Every time I think you're interesting, you decide to sound like a bigot."

"Bigot? You're a centuries-old murderer!"

Roger turned the boy around to face him. Blood on his neck, fire in his eyes, and a clench in his jaw, the boy was spirited and handsome. There was something familiar about the shape of his nose, the set of his eyes. Had Roger lived long enough that faces had started to repeat themselves? Or had he met this boy before?

Questions better left for his next restless day. He had to get through to this boy, or he would have to kill him. He desperately hoped there was something like a conscience in him.

The boy had a glorious righteousness brightening his gray eyes. He believed he was a noble warrior. Or ... at least ...

Wait, there was the slightest tremor to him, an absence of fear, but his lust was a banked fire. He was playing the part of nobility. How far the lies went—whether he was lying to himself as well as the world—was something Roger would have to figure out. That would take time.

I can work with this, though. Roger leaned down so he was more on the boy's level. In a soft voice, he said, "Do you think I chose to become this? One night I was mortal, having the time of my life, and three nights later, I rose with a thirst that's never truly quenched. Have I killed? Yes. Have I enjoyed it? Not every time. As many nights as I have reveled in my nature, I have doubted what I have become."

The boy's head began to dip.

"Your moral high ground is on a sinkhole," Roger continued. "You think 'killing monsters' is a just cause, but who decides what a monster is? You? Your mentors? You mentioned your family. Hunters, I assume. And the family tells you who the monsters are, don't they?"

The boy blanched, but he recovered, and anger tightened his features "I know a monster when I see one."

"What would you call someone who breaks into a home to murder someone in their sleep?"

"It's different!"

"How?"

"You just told me you're a killer!"

"You didn't know that before." Roger put his hand on the boy's shoulder. "You made a plan to murder someone you'd never met."

The boy clenched his jaw. Uncertainty melted the steely quality of his gray eyes.

Roger nodded at the staircase. "Are there humans up there? Did you hurt them to get to me?"

"I wouldn't hurt innocent people."

"So many of your kind do. How can I believe that everyone up there is safe and unharmed? You're a *hunter.*

Hunters treat humans in the proximity of supernaturals like the enemy. Just another foe to fell."

"You're not better than me." The boy puffed up.

"I'm not better," Roger said smoothly. "But you came after me merely because I'm a vampire. That's the only reason. You passed judgment on me for something I can't control. Why do you believe you have the moral authority over me?"

The boy scowled with the fury of the inexperienced and the young. Roger locked him in a staring contest. One of them would break contact first. It had to be the boy. If it wasn't … *Think about that if you don't win. Don't think about draining him dry. Don't think about having to hide the body. Concentrate on his eyelashes, on that tiny fleck of deep blue in his left eye.*

After a long moment, the boy looked away and bit his bottom lip.

It was a slim win, but Roger grasped it.

"If you'll excuse me." Roger searched the boy's pockets quickly without touching him more than necessary. He found a set of keys, a wallet, and a thin device. He held it up. "What is this?"

With a snort, the boy said, "Seriously? I didn't think vampires were that far behind on tech."

Behind? Roger was one of the first in his neighborhood to have a phone in his home, to switch from gas to electric, the first vampire in his coven to own a car. He'd bought a Walkman within a year of its release and had both a VHS player and a Betamax. Other vampires looked to him for guidance on the ever-changing technology humans created.

Hunters weren't usually rich enough to have cutting-edge gadgets in their pockets, and they were too suspicious of mages to employ more than the most essential magic. They tended to look down on new contraptions, didn't they? What was this hunter doing with something Roger had never seen?

And why is he acting like I should know it? Roger pressed a button and the device lit up, illuminating its glass screen from within. The time and date appeared on the screen. August? Last night had been June, hadn't it?

With an increasing sense of dread filling the pit of his stomach, Roger flipped open the boy's wallet. Zackery Wright. Fuck. Good thing he hadn't killed the boy. The Wrights were brutal killers. Roger wondered if his arguments had actually sunk in or if Wright was an excellent liar.

All his concerns were forgotten as he read over Wright's driver's license again.

"This says you were born in 2001," Roger said.

"Yeah? So?"

Roger took a few steps back. *Keep it together. Don't worry about Ezra. Don't think about Dmitri. Don't show for a second that you're worried about Candide or Brad or Cee or, fuck, even Seamus. Get through this moment. Survive.*

"Do vampires vomit?" Wright asked. "Because if they do, don't do it on me."

Roger shoved the device and Wright's wallet into his back pockets and pushed Wright toward the stairs.

"What's with all the manhandling?" Wright teased. "Realized you were hitting on a Gen Z, old-timer? Am I too young for you?"

"You're old enough to know your own mind and desires. Your age isn't the problem."

"Then what is?" Wright turned on the bottom step, defiance lighting a fire in him.

"The problem, boy," Roger said in a deep growl as he leaned in close, "is that yesterday was 1989. Now get up the damn stairs."

CHAPTER 4

Instead of heading for the front door, the vampire pushed Zack around the first floor like he didn't know where he was going. Up until then, Zack hadn't believed this wasn't the vampire's home. But he should have known the front door was to the left and not gone to the right.

The vampire cinched his hand on Zack's shoulder. "Bathroom?"

"I haven't seen one, but I didn't check the second floor."

"Then up the stairs we go."

"Seriously?"

"Start walking."

Zack groaned and headed for the next flight of stairs. Plenty of sunlight streamed through the windows. He could finally see as well as the vampire. There was plenty of space to resist going up the stairs. Having his hands tied was a disadvantage, but he could slip out of the rope if he had a couple minutes to work at it.

But the vampire wasn't going to give him that much time in the middle of a fight, and arguing every step of the way was only going to piss him off. Since discovering Zack was born in the twenty-first century, the vampire's mood had gotten lousy enough. Pushing him wouldn't save Zack in the long run. He needed to play along so the vampire would drop his guard. Then he'd be able to strike a fatal blow.

But would that really be the right thing? asked an internal voice that for once sounded remarkably like himself. Usually, his thoughts were echoes of his parents or grandparents or even Cal. Even the ones that seemed helpful often carried a note of someone he admired more than his own voice.

He hadn't considered his internal monologues before, but the thought was so clearly in his own voice, he couldn't help wondering if all the others had been wrong.

There was one other time I listened to me: Detroit. That night in the alley, that had been all him. *And I fucked that up ... didn't I?*

Reluctantly, Zack plodded up the stairs. The homeowner had decided that the purple living room was such a fantastic color scheme that they'd decorated the bathroom in the same way. The lavender room was relentlessly cheery. Walking into it with blood trailing down his neck, bruises forming all over his body, and a semi hard-on felt wrong, like the universe was telling a joke and he was the punch line.

The vampire dropped the toilet seat lid with a loud bang and then pointed at it. "Sit."

Zack sat. "What are we doing?"

"We need to dress that wound before you go out in public." The vampire dropped Zack's belt in the hallway and then searched through the vanity and in the cabinet under the sink. He pulled out basic medical supplies as he found them.

First the vampire had mercilessly bitten him, and now he was going to take care of him? Zack squirmed. It sounded like something out of *Fresh from the Grave,* the second book in the series he'd obsessed over in high school. But he wasn't in the middle of a romance novel. He had to keep his wits and look for a chance to end the bloodsucker.

But what if he really was just reacting? What if he didn't mean to hurt me?

There was that voice again, the one that had to be him but was giving the vampire too much leeway. Talking and staying in a conversation would be better than the introspection. Zack kept an eye on what the vampire pulled out of the cabinets. "There's not a lot of public around here."

The vampire paused. "We're not in Chicago?"

Don't tell him a goddamn thing, Cal's voice said. That voice was right. Vampires were the enemy. Zack shut his mouth. No matter how much he wanted to ease the obvious confusion on the vampire's face, he had to resist the creature's allure.

But then the vampire glanced his way, and their gazes locked. Zack's own voice whispered, *He looks so damn lost.*

What was the harm in a little information? "We're in Taliville, Tennessee. North of Gatlinburg."

"I know the name," the vampire murmured as he finished digging through the cabinets.

"While we're talking about names, what's yours?"

"Roger." He narrowed his eyes. "You're suddenly very docile."

"You threatened to kill me if I kept fighting. Now you're wondering why I'm doing what you say. Make up your mind."

"As long as you're complying," Roger said as he turned the faucet on and soaked a washcloth. "What year is it?"

"You seriously don't know?"

"Would I ask if I did?"

"It's 2021."

Roger scowled, and his shoulders were tense. He wrung out the washcloth and applied soap to it. When he turned toward Zack, his face smoothed out, becoming expressionless. "This is going to sting."

Zack straightened. "I can take it."

"We'll see," Roger said in a chiding tone.

Dares were common in the Wright family. The annual family reunion usually ended with at least one kid either sick to their stomach from eating a nasty concoction created by their siblings and cousins or someone breaking a bone. Cal had managed to break his own arm with his head once; somehow the monkey bars had been involved.

So Zack would rather be damned than let a vampire see him cry. He stayed as still as possible and breathed through the pain. It really fucking hurt. His eyes watered, but he held his tongue. He focused on Roger's light, comforting touch on his jaw and keeping his head tilted exactly how Roger had moved him. After an excruciatingly long couple of minutes, Roger finished, and Zack let out a shaky, pained breath.

Roger caressed his thumb across Zack's chin. In his deep, purring voice, he said, "Good boy."

The tiny praise made Zack's heart jump. Heat flared in his chest, and he prayed his cheeks weren't turning pink. They felt like they were. Two little words shouldn't have had such a profound impact. Roger was a vampire! This had to be part of his long game. Zack might not have gotten an honest compliment in ages, but that didn't mean he should fall for a vampire's tricks.

"Hold on, it started bleeding again." Roger put the washcloth back on and pressed it to the wound.

Instantly, the soap stung fiercely. Zack took in a sharp breath and then held it. *I'm not going to scream. I'm not going to scream.*

Roger frowned. An instant later, his eyes went wide, and he tossed the washcloth into the sink and grabbed another out from the cabinet. He put the dry one to Zack's wound. "Sorry about that. Did it hurt?"

"Naw." Zack's voice squeaked.

"A tough guy, I see." Roger slid his hand up the other side of Zack's jaw. "Oh, the fun I could have with you."

Zack steeled himself for vampiric magic, but he never felt the press of it against him. All the books—fiction and hunter—said that he should feel intoxicated with a vampire's lust magic. But he just felt hot and horny. His dick was hardening again.

And judging from Roger's knowing grin, he knew exactly what his suggestions were doing to Zack.

"I don't like you," Zack said fiercely.

"You don't have to. You only have to say yes," Roger replied.

"Sure. Just let me get my dagger from the basement first."

Roger chuckled. "You don't know when to give up, do you?"

"Family trait."

"Pity, I was hoping that one was just yours." Roger removed the washcloth and bandaged the wound.

"I'm proud to be a Wright."

"You should reconsider that." Roger slid off his shirt and draped it over Zack's knees. Without hesitating a beat, he undid his belt and slid off his slacks. He put those on Zack's lap as well.

Just as Zack was about to make a comment, he saw the blood and wounds. Oh, right. He'd stabbed Roger in the leg when he'd needed to break free from his bite. Getting mostly naked would be the only way to tend to all his wounds.

Up until that moment, Zack was pretty sure sculptors and Photoshop had always exaggerated how perfect the male form could be. But Roger's skin was perfectly smooth over his muscular body except for the wounds Zack had given him.

Silver damaged vampires more than a regular blade, but even still, Roger's wounds should have healed already. They looked like they'd barely closed. A vampire's magic, which kept the creature alive and gave them abilities like speed healing, was fueled by blood. How low on blood was Roger that he couldn't heal right? How hungry was he?

I'm lucky to be alive. Zack fought to keep his fear in check. He didn't need to make himself smell more attractive to the bloodsucker.

Roger cleaned his wounds. "Keep staring at me like that and I'll have to buy you dinner and make this a real date."

Zack fidgeted, hoping he could slip his wrists free, but he didn't have any luck. Roger really knew what he was doing with rope. *But what's the point in tying me up and caring for my wounds? Why doesn't he just kill me?* "Is that your plan? Date me? Or am I your walking blood bag?"

"I don't keep people against their will."

"Dude, you tied me up."

"Because when you have use of your hands, you try to murder me." Having cleaned the blood off, Roger grabbed his pants and put them back on. "I'm still deciding what the next steps are, all right?"

"I thought vampires always had a scheme."

"A thirty-two-year nap was not part of my plans." Roger grabbed his shirt and buttoned it methodically. Then he rinsed out the washcloths until the blood was gone from them.

When he glanced Zack's way, their gazes locked. The last time they'd entered into a staring contest, Roger's brown eyes had been filled with determination. Now he was too expressionless. His calm had to be a façade, but Zack couldn't guess what Roger was really after. It felt like Roger was assessing him.

Zack lifted his chin. He *had* to measure up. Whatever Roger's criteria was, Zack could pass it. He was a Wright. A hunter. And okay, he'd failed to kill Roger, but he'd survived because he'd fought. He was still alive because he was smart. He was worthy.

Roger clicked his tongue as he looked away. "I need to get to the closest major city. I assume you have a car?"

"Yeah."

"Then the first plan is to take your car. Now, I can steal it, or you can ride in the back and reclaim it as soon as I'm done."

That sounded an awful lot like helping a vampire. Zack said slowly, "Get in my car. With you. Are you serious?"

"Well, I could leave you behind." Roger took Zack by the arm and tugged him to stand up.

They were flush against each other. Roger was taller. On instinct, Zack craned his head back, which put their mouths way too close together. If Roger had been mortal, Zack would have felt his breath. Instead, his own breath bounced back into his face. The beef jerky had been a mistake. He probably smelled like extra good food to a vampire.

"I'm open to suggestions," Roger purred. He softened his grip on Zack's arm and slid his cool touch up his arm. The sly grin on his lips added another layer to the word *suggestions*.

Zack's family was already going to consider him a failure. The only way he could sink any lower was if he slept with Roger. No matter how hot or enticing Roger's offers were, he had to say no. Because he was a Wright, and he had a duty. And he had to ignore the urge to lean in closer and tease Roger in return.

Roger nuzzled in, putting his lips next to Zack's ear. "You could find out what I can do with better rope. We can even play Big Bad Vampire and pretend I'm an evil monster having my way with you."

"Is that different than doing what you want anyway?" Zack demanded breathlessly.

"Very," Roger murmured as he pulled back. He put his hand on Zack's chest. "Deep down you'll know it's only happening because you want it. That you hold control over ending the game with a safe word that you could say at any time, and I would stop."

Zack's throat went dry. His boner returned and became another point of contact, his clothing and Roger's the only barriers between them.

How could I want to be at his mercy? Everyone's right. There's something wrong with me. Zack tried to take a step back, but he ran into the toilet. He lost his balance and started to topple over.

Roger caught his arms and brought him upright. "Think on it."

Then he stepped away, picked up Zack's hunter's belt, and started to guide Zack down the stairs. When they reached the first floor, Roger guided him toward the living room and on to the front door. Zack planted his feet. "Wait, we can't go yet."

"I don't intend to wait around for the owners to get home," Roger said.

"We need my dagger and equipment."

"Oh, I am not arming you again."

"You can hold on to them, but I *need* that dagger." Zack turned to face Roger. The guy was so much taller than him and bigger in every way. But that didn't matter. The dagger did. "You saw how it glowed, right? It's magical. I can't afford to leave it behind."

He left off that it was bound to him. The vampire didn't need to know how connected Zack was to the blade. That sort of magic was rare.

Roger sighed. "I'll be right back."

A whole quiet minute passed with Roger out of the room before Zack realized *he left me alone.* He was wasting a prime opportunity to break free.

Unfortunately, Roger had tied the rope well, and he couldn't easily wriggle out. There wasn't anything in the living room that could cut the jump rope. Roger would hear him if he went into the kitchen, so he couldn't search for a knife. He'd have to settle for getting his wrists in front of him and undoing the knots with his teeth.

Luckily, he'd done that plenty of times. He squatted low and slid his rope-bound wrists under his ass. The next move required a little grace, but he moved his wrists down his legs as he sat. He couldn't get all the way, though, and had to roll onto his back with his legs tucked close to his chest. Finally, he managed to drag his wrists up his legs until they were clear of his feet. With a triumphant laugh, he stood up and examined the knot.

"You've done that before," Roger said, his voice low and soft, vibrating through Zack like a purr.

Zack jumped. Roger was standing in the doorway to the kitchen. His dagger, stake, and flashlights were in their holsters on his belt that Roger kept over his shoulder. However, Roger's expression caught Zack like tree sap. A sticky pity was in his brown eyes.

He's trying to trick you, Cal's voice said. But Zack's voice countered, *He might actually care. Not everything has to be an act.*

Either way, Roger didn't seem to mind that Zack had gotten his hands in front of him. He debated using his teeth to work on the knot. At least the rope wasn't looking at him like it was considering holding him and soothing away imagined hurts. Because Zack wasn't hurt. Not one bit.

"I've had some practice. Someone's got to play damsel when the Wright cousins get together. It'd be totally misogynistic if only the girls got tied up, you know?" Zack examined the knot and then pulled at part of it with his teeth. It started to come loose. An expert knot could be undone in a few quick moves, and Roger had done a pretty good one.

"That sort of skill takes more than a few times." Roger leaned against the doorframe. "Did your parents tie you up? For 'practice'?"

"Naw. We had dolls be the damsels. Wrights aren't supposed to be taken alive."

Roger raised an eyebrow.

"We're not supposed to hunt alone either, so I'm doing the best I can," Zack replied hotly. "So no, my parents never tied me up. A whole group of us cousins live near each other, and we're always staying at each other's houses when our parents are gone. You know how kids are. Get a group of preteens and teenagers together, and you're going to generate a bunch of stupid ideas."

"Like tying each other up for hunter practice?" Roger asked.

Roger's tone was shining a spotlight onto Zack's memories, and if he looked at them too closely, he could see the spots and scars left behind on his soul. His childhood had been fine. Great, even. Nothing all that bad had ever happened to him. Rescue the damsel was just a stupid game they'd played because they'd been kids and liked practicing knots and doing ridiculous shit. So what if the others had picked him for the role of damsel more often than anyone else? He'd always been one of the scrawniest out of the group. It'd made sense. Monsters kidnapped the weak.

And okay, he'd cried more than he wanted to admit. But that was just because he'd been a kid. The first few times they'd played the game, he hadn't known how to get out of the ropes. Cal and the others had left him alone for what felt like hours. By the time he was ten, he could slip out pretty well. After cousin Denny tied him up in the treehouse and kicked him while calling him names, they'd had to stop playing the game altogether.

"We were *kids*," Zack said, forcing his words out. He said it. He believed it. He had to. "We just did dumb stuff."

"Am I right in guessing you're one of the younger ones?" Roger ran his gaze over Zack. "Or you stand out in another way. The only openly gay child? The smart one?"

"I'm pansexual for the record," Zack snapped. "And I don't like your tone."

"What tone?"

The knot came loose, and Zack wriggled his hands free of the rope. "I'm not a sad little monster made from trauma."

"Maybe you are too young for me," Roger drawled as he sauntered past Zack on his way to the front door.

"Yeah?" Zack huffed. He considered throwing the rope around Roger and restarting the fight, but the cat was watching him. Animals didn't usually take the side of the supernatural, but messing up the cat's home might piss it off.

And there was a chance it was more than a cat. It could be a shapeshifter or a mage's familiar. Crap, Zack really should have done his research instead of rushing into this fight. He tossed down the rope and hurried after Roger.

"What makes you think I'm not old enough?"

"Because in the end, everyone has a sad little monster made from trauma in them," Roger said simply. "If you haven't figured that out yet, maybe you're not yet a man after all."

The words were a gut punch to Zack's psyche. Because there had been nothing wrong with the way he'd grown up. Absolutely nothing. Okay, he'd been the weird kid that knew weird stuff, but that was fine. And sure, he knew more about weapons than nearly all of the "normal" kids. So what if no one else had to do drills on taking down a troll or staking a vampire or beheading a ghoul? He was a Wright. And a Gladwell. He wasn't fucked up. His upbringing didn't make him a monster.

You were ready to kill someone in their sleep, his own voice said.

"*Do you think I chose to become this? I didn't,*" Roger had said in the basement.

Did I really choose to become what I am? Zack hated the thought as soon as it entered his head. But his stomach went cold as he realized that thought sounded more like himself. He went colder still as he wondered: *Isn't that the right question to ask?*

CHAPTER 5

Letting Wright stay behind him was a tactical risk, but Roger had to extend some trust. Not all of it, though. He kept his hand on Wright's belt. It was loaded with weapons.

Wright had been prepared for the fight. Roger was lucky to have come out of it with only a few stab wounds. Those wounds were bothering him more than they should, and stepping out into the sunlight smarted. He could feel the sun warming his skin. He wouldn't burst into flames like a younger vampire might, but he was going to slowly burn.

At least he wasn't openly smoking.

If only he had more options, but retreating into the house was no good. Roger had no idea who lived there, and he didn't want to run into whoever had been willing to keep him in a coma for decades until he'd regained his strength. Hopefully, Wright's car would provide enough shade until dark.

"Is that vehicle yours?" Roger nodded at a sky-blue four-door sedan directly in front of the house.

"Yeah," Wright muttered. When Roger had pried into the boy's past, he'd paled, and he hadn't gotten all his color back. There was a chance shock would set in. Roger would have to watch him closely.

Only because he could be useful. Not because I'm thinking of claiming him. Some vampires would have kept Wright as a walking blood bag as he had phrased it.

Vampires did keep humans as pets, caring for them and providing for their welfare. A vampire brandished their status and wealth by having a host of humans. Some vampires preferred their pets to be numb shells. Some treated their pets better than their fellow vampires. Seamus would lock the boy away and break his spirit until Wright was a pliant slave.

Roger had claimed pets over the years because Seamus expected him to. *"A master's captains are a reflection of a coven's wealth,"* Seamus had said over a hundred years ago, the last time Roger had doubted the practice. There was a practicality in having willing blood donors at his beck and call as well. In 1989, he'd had two pets. If they were still alive, they'd be much older men.

Memories began to drift up to his consciousness, like notes of half-remembered songs. He could string together a few details of the last night he'd been awake, but he couldn't connect the whole. He hadn't been to see either of his pets, Brad and Cee. Since making the pact with Ezra and Dmitri, he'd been avoiding them. If their assassination attempts failed, Brad and Cee would be the first to pay the price. *I was their protection, and they had to go on without me. What became of them?*

"What the hell?" Wright ran past Roger to his car and began to circle it.

The light was harsh on Roger's eyes. He put a hand up to shade them.

The car was sitting too low. All four tires were flat, a massive slash through each of them. Wright cursed under his breath, cursed louder, and circled the car again. He paused and stared into his trunk. "Shit! They took my crossbow too."

The sabotage stank of a setup. Roger scanned up and down the street for signs of trouble. The empty house across the street caught his eye. That would be an awfully convenient place from which to launch an ambush.

A shadow shifted.

Roger surged forward, relying on his precious reserve of magic to move him at a supernatural speed. Wright spun toward him and made a grab for the dagger on the belt over Roger's shoulder. With a growl, Roger grabbed him by the T-shirt and yanked him around the car. Their legs tangled, and they fell onto the thin slice of grass between the road and the sidewalk.

A crossbow bolt sailed through the place Wright had been and stabbed into the ground. Wright's eyes widened, and his heartbeat was so loud that Roger almost missed hearing the following gunshots. Flinching, Wright pressed into Roger. Doing so was the practical choice since Roger was the one on the ground, but staying exactly as they were would give their attackers a chance to flank them and strike.

"Off me, damn it," Roger snarled as he pushed Wright off. "Didn't they teach you any tactics?"

Wright rolled and got onto his hands and knees. He scrambled up against the car, putting his back to it. Another few shots sounded through the air and thunked into metal. "You're three hundred years old. Don't you know what to do?"

Roger moved to crouch beside the back end of the vehicle. Blessedly, the car was providing a sliver of shade. Without the burning pain of the sun, he had more energy to think. "Where's your gun?"

"I don't have one."

"You're a *hunter*. I thought guns were your joie de vivre."

"My *what*?"

Roger slammed his fist against the car, denting the plastic bumper. *Hold on, how much of this thing is plastic and not metal?* He frowned as he pulled his fist away, and the bumper half popped back at him, leaving a small crater instead of an imprint of his fist.

"Don't ruin my car. Okay?" Wright leaned his head out around the car.

Roger grabbed him and hauled him backward before bullets went through him. "Don't put your head in the line of fire. Okay?"

"Why do you care?"

"Well, if you want to wind up dead, be my guest." Roger motioned at the street.

Wright frowned at him. "I was just wondering why you care whether I die."

"Clearly you've never been in a firefight before because this is not the conversation we need to be having!"

"Excuse me if I think your motives are sus as hell."

Roger didn't have time to decipher what "sus" was supposed to mean. They needed a plan, and they needed it before their attackers realized how helpless they were. *Or perhaps the attackers are only after Wright. Why should I care if they kill him?* The boy could be useful, but that didn't mean Roger had to protect him. The magical dagger was worth more than the boy, and Roger knew plenty about weapons. He could use it.

He pulled the dagger out of its sheath. The runes remained lifeless, no hint of their white-light glow. *Of course.* "This damn thing is enchanted for you, isn't it?"

"Bound to me, dumbass," Wright snapped.

Roger raised an eyebrow. "Tied to your soul, you mean?" He waggled the blade tip. "Can you feel it if I touch it?"

Wright grabbed for it, but Roger slid the blade back into its holster. Growling, Wright said, "Stop fucking around."

"If you had brought the right weapons—"

"Says the guy who was sleeping away eternity! You don't get to lecture me!"

On their side of the street, the door to the house beside

them opened wide, and a mountain lion bounded out and across the street. The gunfire continued for a few more shots until the mountain lion jumped through an open window of the house shielding the shooter.

Roger risked glancing around the edge of the vehicle. He couldn't see anything, but the big cat growled, and there was the sound of a scuffle. If he were at his full power, he'd run across the street to aid the shifter. But the sun was sapping what little strength he'd gained from drinking Wright's blood. The shifter needed help, and Roger couldn't give it.

But Wright could.

"Prove to me you're not a craven maniac." Roger slung the belt off his shoulder and handed it to Wright.

Flickers of emotions passed over Wright's features in an instant, but he settled into a determined demeanor as he took the belt with a nod. He raced across the street. Roger watched him disappear into the house and prayed that no one, besides the shooter, was about to be hurt.

A man appeared in the open doorway of the house next door. He had a fluffy pink robe over his arm. With understandable caution, he emerged onto his front stoop. "Are you all right?"

"I'm fine." Roger pushed himself up to his feet. The noises in the house were at the edge of his hearing, and it bothered him. He was more used to relying on his supernatural senses than he'd known. Being so close to human was proving to be tiring.

"My wife's been watching that house all day, but I told her she was seeing things. I feel like a complete asshole now."

"Brave of her to shift out in the open."

The man shrugged. "It's Taliville, isn't it?"

His pronunciation of the town name varied from Zack's, with a long *ah* instead of the shorter *a* sound. Roger had heard the name before, from a friend. About a century back …

Chicago, 1921

Smoke clouded the club, the lingering mess of scents mingling into a camouflage for the supernatural. A few humans knew they mingled with vampires and the like. The ones who didn't were more interesting treats. Roger cast an eye around the place for just such an unfortunate. Seamus wanted everyone full up. There was talk of war with some of the other outfits in town. Human gangsters were making the supernatural ones worried. Roger needed blood to keep up his strength.

That night, Roger was in a fine new suit and entertaining a visiting elder vampire, Nell. She was at least as old as Seamus, over a thousand years old. But she wasn't crusty like elders could be. At a glance, she'd fit in with the flappers. Her short black hair was in sleek loose curls, and she wore a vibrant red lipstick that made her dark skin even richer in color. She sported a sheath evening dress decorated with brilliant beads that caught tiny bits of light.

The only giveaway that she was a vampire was the red lurking in her brown eyes. When vampires called on their magic, their eyes turned red, but after a long, long time, their eyes no longer shifted back and forth. The red in Nell's eyes made her brown skin enchanting. Seamus's eyes were starting to undergo the same change, and it wound up making him look mutated.

"I've named it Taliville," Nell said. "Wonderful little town of my own making."

"Far cry from a pirate's ship, then?" Roger asked.

"Far as you can get." Nell sighed contentedly. "It's almost perfect."

Roger leaned in. Places like Devil's Cove were always full

of supernaturals with the ability to eavesdrop. "And what do you need to make it perfect?"

Nell dropped her voice to the barest whisper, and in the din of the club, Roger had to lean in even closer. "The one thing anyone needs. Love."

He wasn't her type as she wasn't his. They'd bonded the few times they'd met over the centuries by picking out hookups for one another. He'd been waiting for the subject to come up during this visit. With a grin, he said, "I've got someone for you to meet."

~

The powerful scent of feline snapped Roger out of his reverie. The mountain lion was making her way across the street toward him and the neighbor. Wright followed, keeping a wary eye on the shifter. He'd haphazardly put his belt back on.

Taliville was Nell's sanctuary, the heart of her coven and diplomatic power. It was a haven for the supernatural. The mountain lion shifting in the middle of the street to her human form proved that. Her husband draped the fluffy pink robe around her shoulders as she finished. She pulled it around her and tied the belt, showing no worry about such a public display of shapeshifting.

The very last being who would be safe in such a town was a hunter from a notorious bloodline. With a few words, Roger could throw Wright to the wolves, somewhat literally because there were bound to be a few werewolves in town.

There was a way to protect him, but Wright was going to hate it.

"He got away," the woman said. "I nailed him, but it's not going to matter for long."

"Shifter?" Roger asked.

"Vampire. Not one I'm familiar with either. Nell makes it a

point to keep the shifter leaders aware of who the new vampires are." The woman gave Roger a pointed glare. "Though I don't know you."

"I've only just arrived." Roger smoothed the lie with a smile. He had to keep tugging the sails into place, adding more lies to keep his voyage going in the right direction. "I fully intend to make the formal arrangements for myself and my boy."

Wright glared at Roger with more heat than the burning sun. "I'm not—"

"Ready for vampire society. I know, boy." Roger put an arm around Wright's shoulders and tucked him in close. He stroked his jaw like he'd done in the bathroom.

Wright bristled, but the caress made him pause. Confusion clouded his gray eyes.

At least the boy wasn't openly defying him. Hopefully, Roger would have a chance to explain, but for the moment, he could continue. He aimed a charming smile at the couple. "We decided beautiful Taliville would be a good place to learn. There are so many rules to remember. Better to do it in some place more forgiving than my coven."

"Which one would that be?" the shifter asked.

Roger winked. "Ah, ah. That information has to go through Nell first. When she approves of my presence, I'm sure you'll hear everything you need to know."

"If you're here to visit Nell, what are you doing at Becks's house?" the man said.

"Thought I'd drop in on an old friend first. We got here before sundown, after all." Roger squeezed Wright's shoulders. "Someone was excited to make his first trip."

"Yeah," Wright said dryly. "Super excited."

That lie didn't go over as well, judging from the skeptical look on the woman's face. "She's out of town, visiting family. Her kid even went."

"I suppose you were right," Roger said dramatically, looking to Wright. "We should have called."

Wright still had a confused look.

We're going to have to work on his deception skills. Roger regarded the couple. "I feel terrible that we need to impose, but clearly our vehicle won't get us anywhere. Any chance you could give us a ride?"

"Aren't you worried someone's called the cops because of the shooting? Won't we have to answer questions?" Wright asked.

The man and woman snorted a few laughs. He said, "Your friend is new."

"Very," Roger said with a purr. He dug his finger into Wright's belt and tugged it undone. It slid off the boy in a quiet slip of leather and light clinks of metal. As Wright opened his mouth to protest, Roger smiled sweetly at him. "Now, now, *darling*. We went over this. A vampire master like Nell has no need for mortal authorities in her territory. We'll appeal to her for our justice."

Wright's eyes widened incredibly. Then he gulped, swallowing down the terror. When he took a breath, he matched Roger's smile. "Oh. Right."

"Where did you need to go?" the man asked.

"The Sleepy Bear Inn," Wright replied quickly. He covered his mouth as he yawned. "It's been a long day."

"That'll be easy to do. Let me go get the keys." The man and woman went into their house.

"Fuck, shit, balls," Wright said under his breath. He turned toward Roger and shoved him. "Why the fuck didn't you tell me this was some master vampire lair?"

"First, this is a nice town, not a lair. Don't call it that," Roger said. "Second, *you're* the one that's been conscious all day. I'm playing catch up."

"Give me my phone. I'll find someone to get me a ride out of this hellhole and—"

"Again, it seems *nice*. Stop insulting it." Roger stepped back when Wright lunged for the pocket where he was keeping the device. "Wait, hold on. I have a proposition for you."

"I'm not becoming your toy for real." Wright reached again.

Roger grabbed him by the wrist. "What if I could offer you the chance to take down two of the most sadistic vampires in existence?"

Wright narrowed his eyes, but he stopped straining for his device. "No promises, but I'm listening."

CHAPTER 6

The car ride to the Sleepy Bear Inn ranked in the top-three most awkward moments of Zack's life. Roger hadn't said anything more about the vampires he wanted to kill, and he rode in the front passenger seat like he didn't have a care in the world. For a second, a fierce anger had lit his expression, an emotion so primal that Zack didn't doubt Roger wanted whoever he was talking about *dead*.

Either it was an elaborate ruse to seduce him, or Roger saw him as a worthy hunter. Zack put his hand on his knee to keep it from bouncing. Roger could be trying to kill him, but he'd saved him twice on the street and trusted him with weapons.

What would Cal do? *Easy. Kill Roger, then this Nell and whoever else he could get his hands on.* Zack had never been able to do things Cal's way. As much as he tried to emulate his brother, no one ever took him seriously as a hunter. But Roger apparently thought he had the skills to hunt down evil. That had to be good.

And there was that nugget of glee again, the warm spot in his chest. It felt a lot like when Roger had called him a good boy. Which made him feel too warm. Which made the silence in the car that much more unbearable, even though the helpful neighbor and Roger were both relaxed.

Finally, after a grueling five minutes, they arrived at the inn. Zack hopped out of the car and dragged his duffle and backpack with him. Whoever had taken his crossbow had nabbed his short sword as well. Roger insisted on keeping his belt, and Zack wasn't sure if that was a bad idea or not. While he didn't have his equipment, he also didn't look like a hunter. A vampire with a few weapons was nothing to notice. A well-armed human in the middle of supernaturals might not be overlooked.

He really should have done his due diligence and checked out the email's information instead of trusting it at face value. Everything had seemed to be there, but he knew better. The chance to become what he was meant to be had tempted him. He'd made a major miscalculation.

Am I making the same mistake trusting Roger? Zack bit his bottom lip as he hoisted his backpack onto his shoulders. No. He wouldn't jump into the hunt with Roger before checking out the details. Since he was pretty much stranded until he got the car fixed—if he even could now that it had bullet holes on top of slashed tires—he'd have plenty of time to double- and triple-check anything Roger told him.

The Sleepy Bear Inn was a three-story building on the corner of Main Street and Second. Judging from the architecture, it'd started life as a Victorian mansion. While the addition had been built in the same style, the newer part of the building didn't have quite the same graceful lines. They approached from the side, and Zack glimpsed a garden with seating that led out to the park next door. The stone dragon and the lake would be in view of most of the rooms.

The inside of the inn was as charming as the outside promised. The owners had leaned into the antique theme but brightened it with as many rainbows as the foyer could take.

Roger went up to the check-in counter and rang the bell.

A tall, round man wearing a dress shirt and slacks emerged from a room behind the counter. At first, he smiled, but his expression faltered and turned false as he rested his gaze on Roger. "How can I help you?"

"We need a room," Roger said.

"Two rooms," Zack corrected.

Roger gave him a sharp glare. Zack glared back. He wasn't sharing a room with a fucking vampire.

"Do you have a reservation?" the man asked.

"No," Roger replied.

"Then I'm afraid I've only got a suite available. Everything else is booked up."

"Crap," Zack said.

"It's all right, sweetie," Roger said as he handed over a credit card.

Roger was either really committing to the act that Zack was his pet, or he was actually trying to claim him. Zack joined him at the counter and narrowed his eyes at him. Calling Roger out in front of a stranger would end the charade once and for all, but Zack was deep in enemy territory. If it got out that Zack was a hunter and a Wright on top of that, then he could find himself face-to-face with an angry horde of supernaturals.

So instead of making a scene, Zack stepped firmly on Roger's foot as soon as the check-in person looked away.

Roger only raised an eyebrow.

Stabbing him had barely slowed him down. Of course, the foot stomp wouldn't do much. *Freaking vampire resistance to pain.* Zack poured all his annoyance into his glare.

Roger winked at him.

Just as Zack puffed up, the man finished running the card and handed it back to Roger along with a piece of paper. Roger slid the paper and pen over to Zack, which didn't make any sense at first. Then Zack realized Roger was putting the credit card away in *his* wallet. He'd put the room on the Wright family account.

Zack sucked in more air. "You—"

"—wanted to know if there was a local wine shop," Roger said. "Thank you for reminding me, sweetie."

Zack grabbed the pen and contemplated shoving it through Roger's throat. His belt was still over Roger's shoulder. Would the guy at the desk help Roger? Zack could probably take the guy, but Roger had beat him on his own. In a two-on-one, Zack didn't stand a chance.

"There is. Corner of Third and March, one block over and two down," the man said slowly. "Is everything all right?"

"Everything's fine." Roger leveled his gaze on Zack, a seriousness in his eyes. "Isn't it, boy?"

Killing Roger would be a lot easier if Zack waited until the vampire went back to sleep. Using more force than necessary, he signed the paper. "Yeah. Fine."

The man swapped the paper for an actual room key. The shining brass key had a metal keychain that was a rose with mage marks on it. It had a slight buzz in it, warming Zack's hand as he picked it up.

"The Rose Suite is on the second floor, toward the back of the house. Stairs are here next to the desk, but the elevator's down that hall, next to the kitchen," the man said. "Breakfast is included in the price of the room. Dinner's extra."

"Good to know." Roger started for the staircase. "Come along."

The pen was right there. Zack could pocket it. It wouldn't kill a vampire, but he'd make Roger think twice about using that bossy vampire tone with him. *I've got better weapons than a pen. I'll get my hands on them again.*

Just as Zack moved to follow, the man grabbed his wrist. "My name's Teddy. If there's anything you need, day or night, give a shout. One of my partners or I will come running, understand?"

That was unusual, wasn't it? Zack had never stayed at a B&B before, but he was pretty sure people didn't make that kind of promise. Maybe they did, though. "Uh, thanks?"

Teddy gently squeezed Zack's wrist. "*Anything*, got it?"

Was the guy coming on to him? Zack gave him as much of a smile and a nod as he could manage before hurrying after Roger.

A beautiful gold rose on the door matched the keychain, so Zack slipped the key in and unlocked it. The suite was a large bedroom, with a bathroom and even a small balcony that looked onto the gardens and the lake.

The color scheme was deep reds and golds, the occasional rose or heart embroidered or worked into the patterns. There was a desk and a couch, along with an armoire. The couch was dark leather and the desk handsomely coordinated. A four-poster, queen-sized bed sat against the far wall. Its comforter was a plush, dark red.

It was the perfect setup for a romantic getaway ... or mind-blowingly awesome sex. A flash of lustful inspiration took form in Zack's imagination. Because there was an amazing bed. Solid walls. A private balcony. A couch. He could really picture having sex anywhere in this room.

"Stay out of my head," Zack snapped at Roger.

Roger frowned. "You do know that mind reading and true suggestion are rare skills among vampires. I don't possess them. I only know of one vampire who does."

"Stop filling my head with crap." Zack dumped his backpack and duffle on the desk. If he could get his hands on his weapons, he could try to finish the job. Except Roger had saved his life, and he had promised to listen to him. *That was before he did mind tricks on me.*

Roger laid the hunter's belt and sword on the couch. He stood between them and Zack, an expression of amusement on his features. "You're seeing specific images?"

"Yes. Knock it off."

With a smug smile and a drop-dead sexy voice, Roger replied, "I'm not doing that. I'm not doing anything."

"Bullshit."

Roger took a step closer to Zack. "You really want to feel what I can do?"

Zack squared his shoulders. "You're already doing something."

"No, I'm not." Roger's eyes turned red.

Taking a deep breath, Zack steeled himself. He should have known better than to challenge a vampire! But he wasn't going to fall under Roger's sway. Whatever magic Roger tried wouldn't dig its hooks into his mind any further. He was stronger than a vampire's charm.

A cool, silky feeling brushed against his body, and the tattoo on his hip warmed. Earlier that summer, Zack had used the money he'd saved up to finally get a hunter's protection tattoo. It was something that the Wrights normally got on their eighteenth birthday before they started taking solo jobs. Zack had waited and waited, but it seemed like his parents were never going to get him the tattoo. So he'd gotten it himself.

He raised his T-shirt and pushed his shorts down just enough to uncover the hunter's mark. The black ink was more vibrant than usual against his white skin. It was working, repelling Roger's attempt to use magic on him.

Which meant that at no point had Roger actually been swaying his mind. It was all Zack's own mind and freewill.

Fuck.

"Is that what I think it is?" Roger asked, amusement plain in his voice.

The silky feeling stopped, and Zack situated his shorts and dropped his T-shirt. The amusement wasn't just in Roger's voice, but in his now brown eyes as well.

"Come on, tell me the truth," Roger chided. "Is that a hunter's mark?"

Zack groaned. "Yes."

"Meaning that you're protected from my ability."

"Yes."

Roger grinned more.

With a deep breath, Zack readied himself for the incoming taunts. He was a hunter who had a thing for vampires. Hiding behind the lie that he was only researching vampires instead of infatuated with them barely worked with his family. He hadn't wanted to admit it to himself either, but the truth was literally staring him in the face. Roger wasn't using magic to manipulate him. His fantasies were his own creations. And this wasn't the first time he'd had sexy thoughts about a vampire.

Zack held his chin up. He had to let Roger's insults and teasing slide off him. They couldn't be worse than anything Cal said.

Roger's salacious grin softened to a gentle smile. He walked past Zack to sit on the edge of the bed. "At least you might stop accusing me of nefarious behavior."

That was it? Roger wasn't going to mock him? Just like that, he was going to let it go? Zack spun to face him, but Roger really looked like he was moving on and abandoning the subject.

A tension that had crawled through Zack evaporated. He hadn't realized it was there until it was gone. He shouldn't relax around a vampire, but this wasn't exactly like being at ease. But he no longer feared the next words out of Roger. They could have a conversation.

When was the last time he'd had a real-person conversation that didn't feel like an exam? Zack bit his bottom lip. Was Roger lulling him into a false sense of safety?

"You said you could offer up two notorious vampires," Zack said. "Start talking."

Roger motioned for Zack to sit in the desk chair. After

Zack spun it around and sat, Roger said, "Anton and Seamus."

Zack felt his jaw drop. He would have hit the floor if he hadn't been sitting. "Anton and Seamus? *The* Anton and Seamus? The rulers of the Great Lakes Coven? Your sire and his oldest fledgling?"

"How did you know that?" Roger asked.

"It was on your coffin," Zack replied.

"I didn't know hunters bothered teaching vampire heraldry anymore."

"Doesn't matter. What matters is that you want to kill the heads of the GLC." Zack leaned forward. "Is this some political bullshit? And how does sleeping away thirty years play into it? Are you just doing this so you can be master of the coven?"

"I do plan on taking control, but that's not why I want them dead," Roger said seriously.

Zack didn't need Roger to have good reasons to go after Anton and Seamus. The Gladwells had wanted them dead for centuries. If Zack could be the one to finally put a stake through both of them, he wouldn't be a hunter, he would be *the* hunter. His reputation would eclipse Cal's, no matter what else Cal managed to accomplish in his life. Zack would be more renowned than Grandma Bonnie. His mother wouldn't look down on him anymore. No one ever would again.

But he'd already walked into one hunt with too little information. Working with Roger could be a setup.

He cleared his throat and put his hand on his leg to stop it from bouncing. "If it's not only about taking over, why do you want to kill them?"

"Because they're monsters," Roger said roughly.

"Didn't you basically advise me I shouldn't let anyone else tell me who the monsters are?" Zack folded one arm over the other. "They're old vampires. What makes them worse than you?"

Roger scoffed as he stood. He stalked to the far corner of the room before turning to face Zack. The shadows there were deeper than the others and Roger's eyes faintly glowed a dim red. Usually, a vampire kept their power contained, and their eyes were humanlike. Was it Roger's hunger that made it impossible for him to hold back the magic? Or was something else going on? The books Zack loved made it sound like overwhelming emotions could turn a vampire's eyes red. Hunters had dozens of theories, but the ones who kept company with vampires didn't pass on information to others.

"Do you know how a vampire is made?" Roger asked.

"A vampire drinks from the victim, then the victim drinks from the vampire," Zack replied.

"Hmph. I suppose I shouldn't be surprised you said it that way." Roger leaned back against the corner. "That's the physics of it. The metaphysics are more complex. What the vampire gives a sireling is more than blood. They give a part of their magic."

"I've heard that theory. The connection of magic is what makes a sire and victim—"

"Sireling," Roger said.

"You told me that you didn't choose this. That makes you a victim." Zack kept his gaze on Roger. They'd made eye contact like that a couple of times so far, and each time was a different kind of battle. Zack had never had anyone stare at him so intensely, and he tried to give as good as he got.

And this time, he wasn't budging.

"Sirelings and victims," Roger said finally, dropping his gaze a fraction. "Some people do choose this."

"Okay, so a vampire gives away part of their magic, and that makes the connection between sires and new vampires. What does that have to do with the reason you want Anton and Seamus dead?"

"You've heard what Anton is?"

Zack stood up. "Why are you asking *me* all the questions?

Am I taking a test? Either I'm good enough or I'm not. Stop jerking me around."

Roger stepped away from the wall, but the shadows seemed to come with him, cloaking him as he moved closer to the light. His eyes remained a deep red, and his white skin became even paler. The scent of earth and blood made the air nauseating. There was a flash of fang in Roger's words. "It is one thing to study the dangers of this world. It is another to *know* them."

All his life, Zack had been put through test after test. The family drilled knowledge into him as much as they made him spar with practice weapons. By the time he was twelve, he'd memorized recordings of exorcisms and journals of seasoned hunters. Facing danger was what he dreamed of. Challenging the vampires who had massacred so many Gladwells was the ultimate dream. But finding reliable information about them was spotty.

He had the family story, though. One repeated through the Gladwells. That told him everything he needed to know.

Taking a step forward and keeping his chin up, he said, "Anton is a necromancer. He'll drain the life out of a child on a whim. He and Seamus have killed families in the pursuit of more power. Knock off the games. I'm a Wright. You can't scare me."

"So it seems." The shadows fell back, becoming less ominous. Roger was still extremely pale, and his eyes stayed unchanged. "A new vampire has a seed of power from their sire. Through the years, it grows. It becomes their own. But there is a time when their magic is stronger and deeply connected to their sire. Anton has perfected a ritual to steal a sireling's magic and reabsorb it. He and Seamus have done it over a dozen times."

Zack took a breath and prepared to snap at Roger that sucking up vampiric energy wasn't as awful as torturing and murdering innocents, but then he froze.

Roger could draw on shadows. He could outpace him in a fight. He could heal. He had a vicious bite. He could influence lust in others, and he had incredible strength—and those were just the abilities Zack had seen him use.

Roger was around three hundred years old and had been out of the world for thirty years, and he was still that strong.

Anton was at least twice that and Seamus even older still. And not only had they been feeding regularly, *they were stealing more power.*

"Holy shit," Zack whispered. "How am I supposed to kill them?"

"A well-placed dagger is better than a poorly swung sword any day," Roger replied. "And I said nothing about you doing this alone. I've been out of the world for over thirty years. I need information. I have to get back into this world like I never left it. With your help, Anton and Seamus will be dust."

Which would put Roger in charge of the Great Lakes Coven. Zack bit his bottom lip. Getting rid of two notorious vampires only to let another one take over the coven didn't sound like a good idea. He wasn't sure he and Roger would even be strong enough to kill such old monsters.

But where would saying no get him? Stranded in Taliville? A lifetime of regret wondering what he could have been if he'd embraced his birthright? He couldn't say no. He had to do this. It was his real chance to show everyone who he was.

"All right. I'm in," Zack said. "What do we do first?"

Zack's stomach growled.

Roger chuckled. "We do something about that, and you start to tell me everything I missed."

"What's the last date you remember?"

"June 18th, 1989."

Zack made a face as he grabbed a fresh shirt from his bag. "Ugh, catching you up is going to take *forever*."

CHAPTER 7

Charming the waitress into serving Wright alcohol was the easiest feat of Roger's day. The boy stuck to beer, while Roger had a whiskey. Two glasses in, Wright's face was flushed, and his news updates grew increasingly quick and unconnected. The waitress brought a third beer for Wright, along with the pizza he'd ordered.

Wright's drunken grin could light up a disco ball. Despite Roger's best efforts and the incredible shocks he was being dealt over and over, he caught himself smiling in response. Having dinner with his would-be killer wasn't a common occurrence. At least Wright was handsome, and he had an appealing demeanor when he wasn't trying to murder anyone.

"I can't believe that man was president," Roger said. "He was a cheat. He couldn't run a business."

"Turns out, he couldn't run a country either." Wright took a large bite of pizza and only swallowed half before he continued talking. His manners needed improvement. "I was too young to vote in the first election, but it divided my high school anyway. You wouldn't think 'hey, maybe we should treat all people like they're human beings and not legislate hate' would be a controversial topic in the twenty-first century, but apparently it is."

"There is some hope." Roger nabbed the last piece of garlic bread from the appetizer basket. While human food wouldn't sustain him, the buttery warm bread would fill his taste buds and distract him from thinking about blood. "For most of my life, loving another man was considered illegal in this country."

Wright had taken another bite. He made an impatient noise as he chewed, waving his hand in excitement until he swallowed. "Oh! I forgot! You were asleep for it. I was in middle school when it happened, so it feels like forever ago. But there was a Supreme Court ruling, and same-sex marriage is legal in the US."

The announcement would have dropped Roger to the floor if he hadn't been sitting down. *Marriage*. He had cast aside the shame people tried to force on him while he was still alive and banished it completely when he became immortal. But so many of his lovers and friends hadn't been able to do the same. Centuries of struggling in the shadows, of finding discreet ways to be seen when out in human society, of carving out tight-knit communities only to have them destroyed by time or bigots—and then the worst, watching history rewrite his loved ones without their love—had finally *changed*. Marriage! Rings and wedding cakes, houses and mortgages, rights and lives intertwined, and they could be publicly celebrated. Be witnessed. Be written into history with legal papers and public records. And if that had happened in the human world, then the supernatural one must have finally started to right itself. The groups of mages and vampires who had tried to impose their hateful agendas across the globe might no longer hold a powerful sway over the politics on the continent.

"We've still got a long way to go," Wright said as Roger tried to regain his grasp on his spinning thoughts. "There's some real bullshit standing in the way of true marriage equality, and some people want to revoke same-sex marriage. But it's a huge push in the right direction and … Roger, are you—your eyes."

Roger grabbed a napkin from the table and quickly wiped away his tears. They were a watery red. When he was at full strength, his body would react more like a human's, and his tears would have been clear. In his current state, he was lucky he'd been able to revert his eyes to brown and hide his true nature from everyone in the bar. Not that he was the one who needed to hide in Taliville. In fact, he could stand to call a little more attention to himself.

Without the tears on his face, though. He continued dabbing at his eyes.

Wright set down his pizza. "Are you okay?"

"I am."

"You're crying."

"I am fine."

"Blot your eyes again because the waitress is coming."

Roger sheltered his face with his long hair and dabbed the corners of his eyes. There wasn't much more to dry.

"You two doing all right?" the waitress asked.

"We're okay," Wright replied. "He could use another whiskey."

"Make it a double rum instead," Roger said.

"Can do. Anything else you might need?"

The mountain lion shifter had mentioned Nell, so Taliville and the surrounding territory were still hers. But Roger didn't have her phone number, and he didn't know where she lived.

There were ways he could make himself known. A breach of protocol would get him killed in some areas. Unless Nell had changed, that wouldn't be the case in her small town.

Roger slid to the edge of his seat and fixed a smooth smile on his lips. He tilted his head slightly, letting his hair fall more to the side so that he could make eye contact with the waitress. Throwing his voice lower, he said, "Well, I wouldn't mind a moment alone with you."

The waitress's smile wavered. "Is that so?"

Roger put a gentle burr in his voice. "That's so."

"And this moment alone ... you want to ..." She mimicked a vampire bite.

Dear Lord, Nell must have truly worked on this town if a human felt that comfortable in calling him out as a vampire. He grinned. "If you're interested."

"Uh." The waitress flicked her nervous gaze at Zack, clearly looking at the bandage on his neck. Her heart began to race. She was educated enough to know how dangerous vampires could be to her kind. When she glanced back at Roger, resolution filled her expression, and she clenched her hand. "Wait right here."

She marched off in the direction of the bar.

Wright leaned in and lowered his voice. "Could you be more obvious? Maybe just announce it to the whole bar."

"Oh?" Roger knew exactly what the boy was on about, but the opportunity to rile him up was too juicy to pass up. "More obvious about what?"

"Wanting to eat her, duh." Wright grabbed his table knife. "I won't let you hurt anyone."

"Relax," Roger said under his breath. "I don't enjoy nonconsensual feeding."

"My neck says otherwise."

"That was need, not enjoyment."

The waitress was on the phone, and a moment later, she hung up. She flashed a smile at the bartender who asked if she was okay. Then she told him not to worry and to fix the vampire at table six a double rum.

"I don't care what it was. You fucking—"

Wright's manners were going to get them both killed at some point. Roger was sure of it. In a stern voice, he broke in,

"Behave yourself. Save your moral high horse for when we're alone. Besides, I'm not going to drink from her."

"Really?" Wright deepened his voice in a clear imitation of Roger's. "'I wouldn't mind a moment alone' isn't supposed to be some vampire come-on?"

Hearing someone mock me shouldn't be so damn cute. Roger nabbed the pizza off Wright's plate, completely ignoring the half a pizza between them. "If I didn't know better, I'd say you're jealous, boy."

Wright grabbed the pizza out of Roger's hand and bit into it. Mouth full, he said, "I'm not jealous."

"Mmhmm."

"I'm not!"

The waitress returned with Roger's drink. Her smile was forced, but her heart had slowed closer to normal. "My break isn't for half an hour. You'll wait?"

"All night if I have to," Roger teased.

"Heh, it won't be that long." The waitress grabbed Roger's and Wright's empty glasses.

As she walked away, Wright hissed, "I should have fucking stabbed you when I had the chance."

"Alas, I'm just too pretty to kill." Roger blew Wright a kiss.

Wright clenched his hand around his table knife like he might try cutting Roger's heart out in the middle of the bar.

While Roger was having fun, he couldn't work with Wright like this. Vampire society was a delicate dance, and if Wright kept on this way, he wouldn't be useful. In a more serious tone, Roger said, "It's too easy to wind you up. You have to work on that."

Wright blinked. "What?"

Roger lifted his piece of garlic bread and stared at it aloofly. Wearing an emotionless mask was too easy at times, but he found himself struggling in front of Wright. The boy had already seen him at his weakest, and he was so refreshingly human. Playing at being a big bad vampire was fun yet unnecessary. The façade was exhausting, and he didn't have the energy to spare.

"Everything in vampire society is a test," Roger said. "The strength not to react is as important as how you react. You have to know when to strike, when to laugh, when to hide your anger."

"Just now … you were testing me?" Wright narrowed his eyes. "It looked a lot like flirting and making fun of me."

"Tests can be deceptive." Roger popped the bread into his mouth. Wright was watching him, waiting for his next words. He was getting through to the boy. Good; that bettered their chances. "Those of us who make it past a century have learned how beings will hide their true intentions. Testing everyone constantly becomes a survival tactic."

"So you don't mean any of it?" There was a fragile note to Wright's voice despite his frown. "The flirting and teasing's just bullshit?"

"You made your position quite clear, little one." Roger raked his gaze over Wright. A nagging familiarity dragged across his mind. He must have seen someone like Wright before, but then he'd always liked dark-haired men more than others. "When you change your mind on what you want from me, I'll be happy to oblige."

Wright's cheeks pinked, but he held Roger's gaze. It was tempting to push magic toward him, to inspire lust. Wright's tattoo would block it, and he'd likely be aware of the attempt. Besides, Roger didn't need to use magic when he was getting somewhere with his natural charm. But the moment passed as Wright grabbed his beer and gulped half of it down.

"What else do you need to know?" Wright asked.

"I suppose we should get back on track." Roger wiped his fingers off on a napkin. "What about HIV? And AIDS?"

"We haven't cured them, but we've got better treatments and PrEP."

Roger motioned for Wright to continue. From that launching point, he jumped into more societal updates: Black Lives Matter, the fight for trans rights, mass shootings, ICE and immigration, the year 2020, the COVID pandemic. Roger drained his glass and ordered another. The world was good and bad, full of hope and despair. It was too much; it was an utterly foreign place; it was exactly the same as it'd always been.

The soft, steady noise of the other patrons' talking suddenly died away. Roger glanced over his shoulder to the front door.

Josefina looked as lovely in a three-piece tailored suit as she had in a gingham gown. Her black hair was pulled back into a bun, and her makeup heightened the beauty of her brown skin. A brush of death—a smell of the grave and a chill in the air—came with her. But it would; she was another vampire. Not the one Roger had been hoping for but the one he should have expected. Her face was set in a scowl as she scanned the room. When her gaze fell on the waitress, the waitress pointed to Roger.

A flicker of recognition crossed Josefina's face as she made her way across the room. The thump of her boots against the wood floor was a drumbeat threatening to become a dirge.

Without a hint of subtly, Wright grabbed his knife again.

I have to teach him to talk first, hit second before he gets us killed. Roger gave Josefina a bright smile as he stood. "Josefina. You're still working for Nell? That's wonderful."

Josefina's stern expression didn't change. "Roger. You're alive."

"You know her?" Wright asked.

"An old friend," Roger replied. *Hopefully.*

"You've crossed into Nell's territory uninvited." Josefina clenched her left hand into a fist. "My love doesn't tolerate unsanctioned feedings."

"Love? I knew you and Nell would make—"

Josefina punched Roger in the gut, knocking the air from his lungs. He doubled over and grabbed onto the table with one hand for balance. She took hold of his hair and yanked him toward the back door.

Wright was on his feet with the table knife in his hand.

"Sit down, *boy*," Josefina snarled.

Wright puffed up.

Dear Lord, how am I supposed to protect him from the dangerous ones? Roger rasped, "Listen to her."

With a startled blink, Wright deflated. "Huh?"

But Roger didn't have time to explain because Josefina dragged him out of the bar. She shoved him through the door before her. Roger braced for the pain of the sun, but night had come.

Free from her grip, Roger turned and raised his hands. One punch for show he could take, but a beating was out of the question. "Josefina, let me explain—"

Josefina broke into a smile and tucked her hands into her pockets. "Relax, Roger! I had to play the part in front of the others. I can't afford for them to think you could get away with attempting to have an unsanctioned feed. We protect our townspeople."

Roger sagged against the building. "Thank God. I'm in no mood for a fight."

Josefina stepped in front of him, her shoulders squared. Her stance was tense. Though her hands were in her pockets, she had supernatural speed. She looked healthy, which meant even though she was almost two hundred years younger than him, she could outmatch him. In a fight, in his current state, Roger would lose to her.

Everything's a test. Roger kept his hands loose.

"Assuming, of course, that you only tried to feed in an attempt to make contact," Josefina said carefully.

"Of course," Roger said lightly. He would fight as hard as

he could if it came to that. Until she swung, he'd keep on a civil mask.

"No one's heard from you for thirty years." Josefina continued to act too calm. Roger knew her—or at least he had —so her play at a peaceful exchange was layered with tension. "And you pop up here?"

"You saw my new boy. Seamus would rip him apart in an hour. I've got to train him better before I take him to the GLC."

"Is he even old enough?" Josefina asked.

"He's almost twenty," Roger replied.

"Practically a child."

"Who isn't to an immortal?"

Josefina took her hands from her pockets, and one definitely had something in it. She noticed his interest and opened her palm to show a closed switchblade. "I take the security of my love's domain seriously, Roger."

"That's the second time you've called Nell your love. I knew you two would make a great couple." Roger straightened and shook his finger at her. "I think I should get at least a night's worth of credit for introducing the two of you."

"Why are you in Taliville?"

"I've always wanted to vacation here," he replied. "The Appalachians remind me of the Cambrians."

"That would be much more nostalgic if you actually *liked* England. Weren't you threatening to go back and burn down Parliament the last time I saw you?"

Ah, fuck, they'd seen each other that recently? Wait, no, not recently to her, and a few years for him. Josefina had been at the same party he'd attended in … Ohio. That was right. Roger could recall the Unseelie's party. A winter party in 1984. He cracked a smile, "I believe I was threatening to do the same to Congress at the time."

She flicked the blade open in his direction. "Stop avoiding the question."

Why is everyone intent on waving silver in my face today? Roger feigned ignorance. "What question was that again?"

Josefina narrowed her eyes.

"Are you still asking me why I'm in town? I told you. I've always wanted to see it, and my boy needs training in a safe environment," Roger replied. "See? I've already given you your answer."

"There's only one problem with your answers." Josefina tensed, a bit of light from a streetlight glinting off her blade. "I don't believe you."

CHAPTER 8

If Josefina was planning to stake Roger behind the bar, Zack should celebrate. But some part of him couldn't stand by while Roger was in trouble. He wanted to blame the buzzing in his head for the confusion. Clearly, drinking had been a poor choice.

Wouldn't the world be better off if Josefina killed Roger, and then Zack caught her off guard and ended her? Two vampires gone from existence had to be a good thing.

Except Roger seemed … nice. He'd actually cried when Zack told him about the progress made in the last three decades, and he'd seemed equally appalled by the things that hadn't improved. Zack had already agreed to be his ally, so what would Roger gain from faking those emotions?

Maybe there was such a creature as a good vampire.

And that thought wriggled and nestled into Zack's conscience like a tick.

"Damn it," he snarled under his breath. His weapons were back in the inn room, so he took the table knife with him. It would be a shit weapon against a vampire, but if he moved with the element of surprise—well, he was definitely still going to get his ass kicked. The knife wasn't silver, and it wouldn't obliterate a vampire's heart. But he had to do something.

Didn't he?

He thrummed with energy as he made his way to the rear exit. The floor threatened to sway under him, but he kept his balance. He reached the door without stumbling. It was open a fraction, so he paused beside it to listen.

"See? I've already given you your answer," Roger said.

"There's only one problem with your answers. I don't believe you," the woman—Roger had called her Josefina—said.

Well, shit. That didn't sound good. Zack tightened his grip on his table knife. It was a dull thing. He might be better off finding something in the alley.

"I'll remind you that I'm almost two hundred years older than you and a good friend of your love. Staking me in an alley for a minor transgression isn't about security. It's grinding an axe I'm surprised you want to stick in my back. I'm hurt."

"The boy," Josefina said sharply.

"What about the boy?" Roger asked. He was trying too hard to sound like he didn't care.

The door flew open. Before Zack could move, Josefina grabbed him by the T-shirt and dragged him outside. Instinct kicked in, and he rocked back, then took a step forward. The sudden slack caught Josefina off guard. Zack slammed the knife into her gut.

Or he would have if she were slower. Instead, Josefina grabbed his wrist. He rotated and yanked free through the weak point of her grip. Vampires couldn't win against physics and anatomy. She slapped him across the face, and his teeth cut the inside of his cheek. Dazed, he slashed toward her, but her hand latched on him again. Her grip was a vise on his thumb, and when she twisted, his wrist threatened to pop.

Zack dropped the knife and went to his knees in an

attempt to take the pressure off. He squeezed his eyes shut and fought to keep the scream lodged in his throat. Giving in to the pain would show weakness to a vampire, and he wasn't about to do that. Her hand was warmer than Roger's. The sensation was a focus, and he could block out the bulk of the pain.

"The boy," Josefina repeated.

"I haven't had a chance to train him," Roger said, his voice aloof. He seemed relaxed, but his eyes were red.

"Someone has trained him and not to be a pet."

"I've had pets that would have gotten the knife into your chest."

Josefina snorted. "Seamus would never let you keep someone that dangerous."

"Who said Seamus knew?" Roger stepped closer. "Let him go, Josefina. The boy is under my protection."

There was an edge to Roger's voice that might have been thrilling if Zack wasn't worried that he was about to lose his hand.

"Tell me who you are, little boy," Josefina said.

Giving a vampire his name would be a death sentence. Zack ground his teeth together and shook his head. She twisted further. It was a name or his hand.

"Zackery Blight!" Zack hated the pitch of his voice, but the lie came easily enough.

"Are there any more of your kind around, little Blight?"

"My kind?"

"*Hunters.*"

Shit! She had him figured out. Didn't she? Zack bit his cheek and winced. There was blood in his mouth, and biting made more of it. Mom claimed lying wasn't a good thing, but it was the only way he was going to survive.

"I'm not a hunter!" Zack choked out. "I've never hurt anyone!"

"Then where did you learn how to attack like that?"

"Self-defense class at the gym!" Zack gasped as Josefina let him go, and he sank backward onto his ass. His eyes were too full of tears to see clearly, but he could use them. Turning tears off and on was a trick he'd learned during those times he'd been the damsel in the games with his cousins. He let his voice shake with a sob. "I ... I met Roger on the internet. And I thought it'd be smart to"—he blinked hard so the tears would start to fall—"to know some stuff in case Roger wasn't what he said he was."

"So you thought you'd stab me?" Josefina glared down at him.

Fuck, she was intimidating. Her no-nonsense demeanor was downright terrifying.

But he'd grown up with Cal, who'd been bigger and stronger than him his whole life.

"You grabbed me!" Zack looked down to the ground. "I got scared!"

"He has a point," Roger said dryly.

Josefina stepped away. "And the true reason you disappeared for thirty years?"

"I got tired of Seamus's shit. I've been taking it for centuries." Roger knelt beside Zack and put a hand on his shoulder. When their gazes locked, there was a hint of warmth in his eyes, but his body language remained stiff, inhumanly still. He examined Zack's wrist like he was inspecting a piece of fruit. "Three decades was long enough to get bored with lurking. I thought I'd reacclimate to the world in a quieter place, but I didn't know how to contact Nell."

"And reacclimating is where the boy comes in?"

Roger slid his thumb across Zack's chin, like he had when he'd called him a good boy. Was that a signal? Were they doing signals now? Zack brought his wrist back to his chest and dropped his gaze again. Vampires thought humans were beneath them. He needed to escape notice.

"I can't very well show up to Seamus's court like a

pauper," Roger said. "My boy needs to learn what vampire society can be like. I thought we'd wade into the waters instead of diving into the ocean with a weighted belt."

"Next time, announce your damn visit." Josefina put her switchblade away. "Honestly, Roger, would it have been that hard to send an email?"

"I didn't know where to send it," Roger replied.

"We'll have to change that." Josefina sighed and scooped up the knife Zack had dropped. "How's your boy's hand?"

"Damaged, but he should heal."

"I'll cover your meal as an apology." Josefina began to walk away.

"Wait," Roger said. "When can I see Nell?"

Josefina hesitated, and her pause became a long silence. Zack dared to look her direction. She was solid as stone, radiating a statuesque, deadly beauty. "Our donor house is on the corner of Crawford and First. She'll be there from midnight until two. I'll tell her to expect you."

"Thank you, Josefina."

Josefina nodded once and then walked through the back door of the bar.

Zack stared upward and willed his tears to stop. Unfortunately, a few more spilled out, but they slowed.

Roger sank to his knees in front of Zack and drew his hand out away from his chest. "Can you move it?"

Zack wiggled his fingers.

"Good. If she'd broken something, I'd have to break a few of her bones," Roger growled.

Hearing Roger's protectiveness was nice, even if it wasn't about him. Zack managed a weak smile. "Can't let another vampire get away with hurting your 'pet,' huh? That'd be a blow to your pride."

"Fuck pride. There was no reason for her to hurt you like that in the first place, let alone break any part of you." Roger brushed back Zack's hair and trailed his hand down his jaw. "Are you going to be all right?"

"We can go. No worries." Zack pushed himself up with his good hand.

As they walked back to their inn room, the adrenaline from the fight wore off, and Zack's tears dried, leaving his cheeks stiff. He scrubbed his good hand across his face. His bad wrist radiated pain up his arm. That was going to suck later on because it was his dominant hand. His cheek had stopped bleeding, but it was sore too.

Two fights with vampires and he'd lost both horribly. Maybe his family was right to leave him at home. *They normally tackle vampires only a few decades old as a team. I went up against older ones on my own. And I'm alive. Take the win.*

That thought was actually comforting. Zack tugged the room key out of his pocket and unlocked the door. He flicked on the light switch as he stepped into the room. The lamps provided a soft illumination that only heightened the saccharin romantic feel of the décor. He put the key on the desk and kicked off his shoes.

Roger shut the door quietly. His eyes hadn't reverted to brown. In a soft voice, he said, "We should get our story straight. What you told Josefina, how believable is it?"

"That we met on the internet? Pfft, people would probably be more weirded out if we didn't meet that way." Zack flexed his hand. Pain flared up his arm. His wrist was more fucked up than he'd thought. Damn it. "There's a website for anything and an app for everything else. Just be vague and refuse to give up the specific site name, and no one will be able to dig for info that isn't there."

"Clever."

The one spoken word seemed to brush against Zack's spine, even though Roger was across the room from him. He wished he could blame magic, but Roger's powers didn't work on him, because of his hunter's tattoo. Sometimes having a libido sucked. After he dropped out of college, he had barely socialized outside the family and rarely beyond other hunter families. Being the black sheep of the local hunter community made it hard to date, never mind hooking up.

That had to be why Roger turned him on so easily. Just the right kind of rain after too long a dry spell. Zack needed some sleep to regain his energy, and then he wouldn't even think about Roger's silky voice or majestic black hair.

Zack started for the bathroom. He ought to check the bandage, and then he'd be able to swap into his sleepwear and sink into bed.

Into the *one* bed.

Halfway across the room to the bathroom, he froze and stared at the four-poster queen bed. It was a good size. And there were lots of pillows and a headboard. And freaking curtains that could be dropped down to turn it into an even more intimate fuck space. Roger had *centuries* of experience as a vampire, and he'd boasted about having a sex dungeon. He was probably really, really good at fucking.

And Zack would have to share a bed with him.

"What's wrong?" Roger asked.

"There's only one bed."

"That doesn't sound like a problem to me," Roger whispered in his ear.

Zack jumped and spun to face Roger. They were less than an inch apart. He hadn't even heard Roger close the distance, When Zack took a step back, Roger took one forward. So Zack took another step, but Roger followed again. He was wearing a sexy smirk that warmed his red eyes.

Okay, it was time to put his foot down. Zack motioned between them as he continued walking backward. *"This* isn't happening."

"This?" Roger raised an eyebrow while he kept in step with Zack.

"We're pretending about this whole pet thing. I'm not actually fulfilling any 'duties,' got it?"

"And your research has told you what those would be, has it?"

Little Red Riding Hood had an easier time with the wolf. Zack sputtered for words because he did *not* want to say anything about sex because he wasn't thinking about sex because sex needed to be the farthest thing from his mind. And he wasn't going to start describing duties because he didn't need to. Roger knew much more about this topic than he did. Not reacting was better than reacting—wasn't that what Roger had said? Zack kept backing away.

He ran into the edge of the bed with enough force that he fell backward. Flailing his arms, he landed with a loud thud, and his wrist smarted with another wave of pain.

Before he could move, Roger climbed onto the bed, one knee between Zack's legs. He leaned over Zack. His long hair trailed down over one of his shoulders, and the ends tickled Zack's cheek. In a deep, purring voice, he murmured, "Did your research tell you about *my* duties as master?"

An incredibly hot man was on top of him, and they were on a really comfortable bed. The word "research" didn't make sense at first, but "master" did. Clips flashed through Zack's mind, vivid imaginings and recently rewatched porn filling up the space where coherent thoughts usually formed.

Family teachings and lectures pressed in. The weight of their knowledge dragged his exuberant wishes down into cages. Vampires kept humans as pets, but they didn't care about them. The romantic stories Zack secretly read were propaganda to make humans more susceptible to seduction. Nothing good came from vampires.

According to family lore, I should already be dead or enchanted. I'm not. Maybe the family was wrong.

"Y-your duties?" Zack was too warm, and he should shove Roger away, but he didn't want to.

"A vampire has to care for their pet." Roger ghosted his knuckles down Zack's cheek. His light touch was a cool chill, refreshing against the blazing heat of Zack's skin. "Shelter them. Feed them. Clothe them. Provide the necessities for body and mind. A good master cares for their pet's happiness, and I have always prided myself on being a *very* good master."

There was no mistaking Roger's meaning. Sex wasn't just implied in his words; it was promised with the curve of his lips and the glee in his eyes. Zack's chest felt tight, and the feeling increased as Roger slid his finger to Zack's chin.

Roger pressed upward, closing Zack's mouth. Zack hadn't even realized it was open. With a chuckle, Roger said, "Careful. I might think that's an invitation."

This was ridiculous! Roger had to be leading him on, but even if he wasn't, Zack couldn't sleep with a vampire! Growling, he pushed Roger with his good hand and shoved him back to his feet. "Knock it off."

"Knock what off?"

"Toying with me." Zack pushed again, and Roger moved the rest of the way off him. "I've had a long, weird day, and I don't need any more bullshit."

"It's not bullshit. I'd be quite happy to prove it to you."

Zack met Roger's gaze. People lied, and undead people had more reasons to lie. Roger had seen more years than Zack could hope to comprehend. All that history coursing through him, and he found something worthwhile in Zack? Yeah, right. He was just trying to sucker Zack in more so he could keep the advantage.

"Don't you have a local coven master you're supposed to meet? You know, so Josefina doesn't hack us into pieces for existing."

Roger shrugged, and his playful demeanor dropped. He took the key off the desk, letting the metal scrape on the wood. "I do. Lock the door after me. I'd hate it if someone got around to debauching you before I had a chance."

"What does that even mean?"

"It's better taught than told."

Zack was definitely too warm. He stood and pushed Roger toward the door. "Just go do anything that is not staring at me in the room."

"Oh, all right," Roger said with a dramatic sigh. "Try not to stab me when I come back."

"No promises," Zack replied with a growl.

Roger was chuckling when Zack slammed and locked the door on him. Zack turned and slumped against the door. His dick was hard, and thinking over the last few minutes only made him harder.

The simple get-in-and-get-out mission had gotten so far off track that Zack wasn't sure he had ever been on the right path. He was lost in the woods without GPS, and his dick was offering to be his compass, pointing right to Roger. Just because he was attractive.

It's more than that. Zack let his head thunk against the door. No. It wasn't more than that. He didn't like Roger. All he had to do was masturbate and sleep. Tomorrow he'd be able to concentrate on the real hunt. In a few days, he'd bag Seamus and Anton, and he could say goodbye to Roger.

Yeah, masturbation was the answer. He could get the kink out of his system and put it behind him.

Ah, fuck me. Why'd she have to wreck my good hand? Zack sighed and headed to the bathroom.

CHAPTER 9

Midnight was hours away according to Wright's slim device. However, staying out on the street was an invitation for whoever had tried to kill him and Wright to try again, so he slipped into a shop while he fiddled with Wright's phone. It was a fascinating thing. During their dinner, Wright had claimed it had all the power of the internet, but finding anything on it was challenging.

Suddenly, the screen was filled with a dark-haired man with red eyes, and Roger dropped the phone. It tumbled toward the floor, but he grabbed it before it hit. As he slowly straightened, he looked at the image again.

That's my face. Roger ran his fingers along his cheekbone and turned his head to the side to see his gold earring. He tilted his head further and aimed the camera down his neck. Scars were hard to find on a vampire. When the magic healed a vampire from death, it repaired much of the body. Roger had had a few scars on his hands from working on ships that were now nothing more than faint lines only he could find. No one had ever been able to find the mark where Seamus bit and drained him.

Roger couldn't find it either. He knew the place on his

neck, and he checked around it too, in case his memory had failed him. But no, the magic had healed it centuries ago.

Staring at himself began to feel indulgent and conspicuous. *But I can see why I'm too pretty to stake.* Roger chuckled and attempted to clear the screen of his image. Touching different places on the device changed things but didn't bring back the other screen.

Instead, an image of an old book appeared. When Roger dragged his finger across the screen, attempting again to clear the pictures, he thumbed through more images. Wright had mentioned that not only could the device be a camera, but that it could show pictures instantaneously. Clearly, photography had changed while Roger slept because Wright had photo after photo of books, a yard, and empty soda cans.

Then there was a picture of Wright standing in front of a mirror. He was shirtless, the thumb of his free hand hooked into his waistband and dragging his jeans down. The tattoo on his hip was bright black against his pale skin. His gray eyes had an element of the steel Roger had seen during their fight. There was a softness to his expression despite his attempt at an aloof coldness. Lips in a firm line, staring down his own reflection, he seemed to be saying, *Fuck me or fight me.*

Wright had strength, courage, wits, and a love of books. His blood had been hot and filling. Roger could entertain a future where Wright was happily his. It wasn't going to happen—Wright had made that painfully clear—but the fantasy was more than pleasant.

"Can I help you?" a woman asked.

Roger slid the phone into his pocket. He'd walked into the shop far enough to be out of the way of anyone entering or leaving, but he hadn't taken in any of the details of the establishment. The lighting was gentle as if taking in the needs of supernaturals instead of humans. Shelves went from the floor to the ceiling through most of the space, and a beaded curtain in the back had a sign over it saying "18+." The musty scent of incense filled the air, even though its display was toward the beaded curtain. Other shelves held books and components for spells, everything from crystals for new-age novices to devil's bane for the seasoned exorcist.

The woman had a tiredness in her smile.

"Are you closing? I'm sorry, I'll leave," Roger said.

The woman waved at him dismissively. "It's Taliville. I'm open until two, same as everyone else. What brought you in?"

"Just killing time until an appointment."

"All right." The woman started to step away but paused. "You should know, I report any powerful sale to Nell, including succubus lashes."

Eyelashes from sex demons could be made into an aphrodisiac that would lower the inhibitions of anyone, even Wright. Roger had never used the potion, but Seamus had. The thought of it churned Roger's stomach.

Nell was right to keep an eye on such a sale in her territory. Roger nodded once to the woman before drifting among the shelves. He shouldn't approach Nell without a gift, but the goods in a magic shop were tricky. Anything worth purchasing would either be a component or beyond Roger's meager means. He only had four hundred dollars in his pocket, assuming his wallet was intact.

Cursing himself for not checking sooner, he dug it out and skimmed through the bills. All of it was there. And he still had Wright's wallet. Using his credit card to procure the room was one thing; taking Wright's money for his own purposes went against Roger's code. *He* ought to be the one paying for everything, but his credit card was wildly past its expiration date.

Nothing in the shop would suit his needs. On his way out, he wished the woman a good evening.

Taliville's Main Street area had a collection of shops: a bookstore, a thrift shop, a secondhand store, a high-end clothing boutique, and more. The park's stone dragon loomed over the area like a reluctant guardian. Vampires and shifters weren't the only supernaturals in town. Roger caught the scent of a few faeries and even a demon as he wandered between the stores.

Except for being painfully limited on funds, shopping was relaxing. The thrift store had a dress shirt and jacket that were more appropriate for a meeting with the master of a coven. The manager even accepted his old shirt in trade and didn't blink when Roger insisted on cutting off the bits of his blood still in the material. Apparently, the youths of the town liked to buy clothing with the intention of wrecking it further in their "vids" for "that fang app," whatever that was. Roger would have to ask Wright.

The wine shop was on Third and March, just like Teddy the innkeeper had said. When Roger perused the shelves, an employee approached him. With their help, he picked out a wine that was one of Reed's favorites. Nell and Josefina didn't drink much wine, but their pet, a man named Reed, according to the employee, loved the red wine Roger bought. It'd have to do. He didn't have the money to spend on anything expensive enough to suit Nell's station.

Not long after midnight, Roger arrived at the corner of First and Crawford. The mansion occupied a lot beside the lake around a slight curve on the water from where the Sleepy Bear Inn and the park were. It had a large porch, and a handful of beings were out enjoying the cooler night air.

Bracing himself for the worst, Roger headed up the stairs for the front door. If any humans lived in the house, the door would repel him until he had an invitation. Everyone on the porch turned their attention toward him as he opened the door. He stepped through the threshold without a problem. *At least one thing has gone right tonight.*

Lighting was brighter in the donor house than it had been in most of the shops. The smell of the grave was in the air, along with the scent of sex, but there were more threads, making a complex weave. Coffee and candy, alcohol and barbeque. Voices in conversation created a gentle murmur of a song occasionally punctuated by soft and distant moans of utter pleasure.

Immediately upon entry was a foyer. A young woman at a desk stood when he walked in. She had a device in her hands, like Wright's phone but much larger, and she wore a sleek black dress. Her heels clicked on the granite floor as she approached Roger. "Are you here to see the Master?"

"I am. My name is Roger. Josefina told me she would be here."

"She is," the young woman said. She pointed to the paper bag in Roger's hand. "Is that a gift?"

"It is."

"Put it on the desk, please."

Roger nodded and did so. As soon as he'd stepped away, the young woman twisted her hand and muttered a word. Her eyes flashed deep blue before returning to normal.

Nell had a mage working the reception area. *She and Josefina don't screw around with security. I could learn something from that.*

"It's clear," the young woman said.

Roger thought she was talking to him until he caught motion out of the corner of his eye. Another young woman stepped out of the foyer and into the nearest sitting room. She had the smirk of a wolf when her gaze crossed Roger's. Had she been behind him when he came into the house, waiting beside the door? Or had she snuck in?

"You can present your gift to the Master, sir," the young woman said. Once Roger picked up the bag, she continued, "If you'll follow me, please. The Master is expecting you."

She led him down a hallway to the back of the house. On the way, he glimpsed a half-dozen rooms, most filled with humans and shifters that were partying, watching television, or playing video games.

There was one room, near the kitchen, that was clearly for feeding and fucking. The lights were lowered, the sofas bigger. Everyone in that room was preoccupied with their partner or partners. A general, warm buzz vibrated against Roger's mind. Lust without fear. It was intoxicating. One handsome vampire was biting into the neck of a gorgeous young man, fully nude. Roger almost forgot to keep walking. He hurried his step to keep up with the girl and follow her outside.

Strings of tiny lights hung between wooden poles around the perimeter of the brick patio. While there were many seats and a few tables, Nell and a man standing behind her were the only ones out there.

The man was another handsome specimen of humanity. A faint bite scar marked his neck just below his black leather collar. A metallic round tag dangled from a loop on the collar. It had Nell's crest, a mermaid stretching upward, her locks floating behind her. Nell had made her reputation on the seas before settling on land, and her crest reflected that. Her pet wore slacks and a dress shirt, attire that was uncommon for a pet.

Nell wore a tailored suit of red and a lipstick that precisely matched it. She'd let her hair grow since the 1920s, choosing a style of long locks in tight curls that went to her shoulders. With a sharp smile, she waved to the seat across from her. "Roger. Have a seat."

Roger placed the bag on the table as he took the seat she motioned to. "You have a lovely town, Nell. I'm in awe of it."

"Go on in, darlings," Nell said.

The young woman who had escorted Roger out to the patio immediately turned on her heel and headed for the house. The man beside her took his time walking around the table, slowly making his way behind Roger. For a pet, he wasn't following an order very quickly.

Nell took the bottle from the bag and examined it. She

raised an eyebrow. "Reed's favorite. You have been getting to know people."

"You know me," Roger said with a grin.

"I do." Nell dropped her smile and motioned with her hand.

Roger had a fraction of a moment to wonder what the metallic sound behind him was before something white-hot looped across his neck. He started to reach for the silver chain, but Nell lunged forward and caught his hands. She was stronger than him on a good night, and this was one of his worst. Sputtering, he tried to slip from her grip. Her hands locked down harder.

Her pet wasn't even yanking on the silver. He kept it taut against Roger's skin, and it burned into him. Roger's resistance was so low that it hurt far more than it should have.

"You disappear for thirty years, and you suddenly appear in my domain pretending to be a friend," Nell growled. "I can't believe Seamus thought I would fall for it. I am not some fledgling. I am a *master*."

"Seamus doesn't know I'm here!" Roger choked.

"You haven't been able to scratch your ass without asking for his permission since he turned you." Nell's eyes were a deep red. The shadows around her deepened and wrapped around both of them. Ice-cold fear came off her hands, roiling up Roger's arms.

She was trying to influence his emotions, and her magic was stronger than his. Panic began to set in. The silver on his neck would eventually slice through him, all the way through if the human tried hard enough. Nell could reach into his chest and pull out his heart. She could—

He was stronger than the fear. With a cough, Roger leaned his head back, trying to get the silver off but failing. "Check my hand."

"You have a right and a left. For the moment."

"Look at my left!"

Suddenly, Nell released him and snapped her fingers. Her magic stopped slithering inside Roger, and the chain vanished from his throat. She was still staring at his hand when he managed to drag his gaze back down from the sky. "Your ring is gone."

"Yes," Roger said.

"Seamus might let you off the leash to prowl neighboring domains, but Anton would never break an enchantment." Nell held her fingers poised to snap. "You are going to answer my questions honestly, or Reed gets to play with his toy. Understood?"

Speaking to an elder vampire was never simple. Roger shouldn't have counted on their friendship to protect him. There was no such thing between vampires, especially ones without any blood connection. He wasn't in her coven, and he wasn't her sireling. She not only didn't have to protect him by the rules of vampire society, she had every right to treat him like an invading enemy.

Wright and his dagger wouldn't have done much, but Roger would have felt more comfortable having backup.

Rubbing at the raw place on his throat, he said, "As you desire, Master."

Nell leaned back in her seat and crossed one leg over the other. Her position didn't matter. If she wanted to catch him off guard, she could. She'd just proven that. Roger didn't even blame her. *It's something to remember when I become master of the GLC. Show of strength to dominate the enemy.*

"You told Josefina that you grew tired of Seamus and went into hiding for thirty years. Now you plan to go back to him, but you're training your boy here because my land is 'shallow waters.'" Nell fixed a cold glare on him. "She suspected it was bullshit, and I think that story reeks more than a werewolf after a rainstorm."

"Are you pissed because I called this forgiving territory?" Roger drew his hand away from his throat. The line across it had to be red still. "Lesson learned. Don't fuck around with your people."

Nell smirked. "You've always been a pretty face with pretty words. Don't tempt me to ruin you."

"You didn't ask a question. My comment was sincere. You have built your domain effectively, Master," Roger said, letting awe fill his voice. Vampires weren't known for their sincerity, but he needed Nell to believe him.

"Where have you been for thirty years?" Nell demanded.

The truth would expose his weakness. A lie would damn him and Wright.

Nell had always been one of the better vampires he'd known. The first time they'd met, she'd been captain of a small fleet of ships in the Caribbean. She was a rival of Seamus's. Since they shared a sire, everything between them was a competition. In those nights, the challenges had been full of laughter.

Somewhere along the line, that changed. Nell stopped visiting Seamus's territory before the 1930s, staying to her territory in the Appalachian Mountains. Seamus no longer sent anyone as a diplomat to keep relations open. A full-blown war between them could have happened while Roger was asleep, though he doubted he would have been sitting before her.

Someone would have to rule the GLC after Seamus was gone, and it wasn't going to be Ezra or Dmitri. Ezra's temper was too hot, and he was too young. Dmitri was cold and paranoid. Roger had been the popular one, and he had to reclaim that. But he also needed to lead. Seamus embraced horrific practices, slaughtering anyone who displeased him and absorbing the energy of his sirelings. He was a terrible example.

Roger needed to be his own man. And there needed to be a place for unvarnished, imperfect truth in his life.

"I was in a magical coma," Roger said. "I only woke earlier today and not by my own means."

"You woke in my town?" Nell asked.

Roger nodded.

"Becks's mysterious coffin guest," the man behind Roger—Reed—said.

"It appears so."

"You knew about me, and you didn't do anything?" Roger said.

Nell tilted her head. Her glare was regal and calm. An owl swept out of a tree in the distance, the noise the only sound besides Reed's breathing and heartbeat.

Should I apologize? Roger had only questioned Nell's failure to act. He hadn't insulted her, had he? The second-guessing worried him. Knowing exactly what to do around superior vampires was difficult.

"When Rebecca Glum moved into town, she made me aware of her unique problem." Nell laced her hands together and rested them on her knee. "It seems she had made a deal with her Unseelie kin. Her part of the bargain was to hide your coffin. She didn't know what it contained, if anything. She told me about it out of fear of what might happen when the coffin finally opened." Nell gave him a genuine grin. "Honestly, of all the possible outcomes, I'm happily surprised it's you."

Roger motioned between them as he said, "Are you? Because this treatment seems extreme."

"I have to protect my people. Visitors never escape my notice or that of my captains."

"Does that include people who shoot at your visitors?"

Nell narrowed her eyes. "Tell me more."

Quickly, Roger went over the details of the incident outside of Becks's house. He included being saved by a neighbor mountain-lion shifter but left out how he'd been too weak to do more than send Wright in as backup.

"I will have this investigated," Nell replied.

"Fantastic. I believe that concludes our business for the evening." Roger started to stand.

Nell shoved him down in his seat in such a quick motion that he didn't see her move. His senses were duller than he had thought.

"We're far from done," Nell said. "The boy."

"What boy?" Roger glanced over his shoulder before looking at Nell again. "Reed's a very nice boy. Well done."

"Your boy."

"Oh, *my* boy?" Roger laughed, trying to lighten the mood between them.

Nell was not moved. Her previous grin was long gone, replaced by her icy, queen-like glare. "What arrangement did you make that you woke and have already claimed a boy? Have you made a contract with the Unseelies for him? A favor paid forward?"

"It's not like that. You know me, Nell. I'm not that complicated."

"Tell me about the boy."

"No."

Nell snapped her fingers. Before the sound could finish, Roger brought his hand up. He managed to grab the silver chain that Reed attempted to loop around his neck again. Holding it firmly in his hand, he allowed it to burn him. It stung and sizzled against his skin.

"The boy is under my protection. You don't need to know anything about him."

"Josefina said he moved like a hunter. You're claiming him?"

"He is my ally."

Nell laughed. "You don't have allies. You have pets and men you bed. If Seamus discovered you were doing anything so grand as making *allies*, he'd—"

"Cleave my head from my shoulders. I'm aware," Roger

replied. He yanked on the silver chain, and Reed released it. Roger dropped it beside the chair. "I know the part I've played for the last three hundred years. But it's time for a change." He lifted his hand, showing it empty of Seamus's ring. "I'm strong enough to become my own master."

"Out to make your own coven?" Nell said with amusement.

Speaking the treason aloud to Nell would give her an excuse to execute him on the spot. But something had gone wrong between her and Seamus long ago. Roger folded one leg over the other. If he was going to do this, he'd have to start taking risks. Sitting back and letting life happen had been a way to survive, but he needed more than that.

At least if Nell decided to kill him, she'd make it quick.

"I'm out to take the GLC."

Nell raised an eyebrow. "You would have to kill Seamus first, and I doubt Anton would allow that."

"Seamus and Anton are vicious parasites that need to burn," Roger said coldly. "Someone put me in an enchanted sleep before I could finish my plans. I have to start from scratch. The boy will be useful."

"Because he's a hunter," Nell said.

"Because he's a Wright."

Nell grimaced. "Fuck's sake. Tell as few people as possible about that. Which Wright?"

"Forget which one," Roger said. "I told you I plan to commit treason against one of your peers."

"Mm, you did." Nell leaned forward, a glint of glee in her eyes. "Seamus and Anton have been blights on our kind and on our continent. So I only have one question left for tonight. How can I help you take the bastards down?"

Roger smiled. Sometimes the truth paid off after all.

CHAPTER 10

Rain soaked Zack to the bone, but he kept running. The stench of rot was overpowering, clawing through him until he gagged. The alley went on and on ahead of him, the worn-down buildings encasing a channel. Puddles splashed underfoot. He was cold. Running should have made him warmer, but he was *cold*.

All of a sudden, the alley broke away to a street. Despite the rain, a building across from him blazed. Flames spiked higher and higher. Zack put up an arm to block the light and backed away. Burning the building hadn't been the plan. Something had gone wrong. His family was in danger.

A girl emerged from the flames. Red tears streamed down her cheeks. Zack chased her. When he caught up, he grabbed her and slammed her against another building. She was his age. He wasn't sure how he knew, but he knew. Her eyes glowed redder than the fire, and she bared fangs when she snarled at him.

Vampire.

He had to stab her. That was the job.

But she was just like him. So young.

Dagger in hand, he hesitated.

"Come on, little brother," Cal chided. "Do it. *Do it.*"

How was Cal here? Where was here? It didn't matter. Zack clenched his hand around his dagger and started to move in.

The girl whimpered. Zack was older, himself now, and the girl was Amber's age. She wasn't any older than his sister. He dropped his dagger and backed away.

"Tch, tch. Wish I was surprised," Cal said with disgust.

Zack spun to face him. Suddenly the mouth of the alley was dozens of feet wide. He was saying words, only they weren't coming out. Then a sharp pain spiked into his neck. Fangs. The girl had bitten him. She latched an arm around his waist, only … that wasn't the girl's arm. That was Roger's arm. Zack twisted and came face to face with the man.

Roger ran his thumb over Zack's chin. With a devilish gleam in his brown eyes, he murmured, "Be a good boy now."

As he bit Zack again, he ran his hands over him. Zack's clothes vanished, and he fell onto his bed. The walls of his room felt like déjà vu, like he should know them, but he had never seen them before.

Roger kissed him and trailed more kisses down Zack's neck. The bedsheets slithered around Zack's wrists and pinned him to the bed, making him helpless for Roger. Somehow, Roger was sucking his dick and draining him of blood at the same time. Zack moaned. Release was so close, but he didn't deserve it. Was never going to get there.

Cal was at his shoulder, lying in bed next to him as Roger continued. Thankfully, he was dressed. "Dude, you're fucked up."

Zack couldn't form words, but he wished Cal would go away. Cal's presence should have thrown a bucket of cold water on him. Maybe that was why he couldn't finish. Because this was super weird.

In Roger's voice, Cal said, "Wake up."

Zack frowned and tried to roll away from Cal, but there he was again. Cal slapped his cheek. "Wake up."

Blinking, Zack groaned and latched his arm around a pillow. Roger tugged it back out of his hold and tossed it off to the other side of the bed. "About time."

"What?" Zack opened his eyes further. He wasn't in his bedroom. Everything was red and gold, and there was a rose on the canopy of the bed overhead. Where was he?

The previous day roared back like a vid jumping forward as it uploaded. He was in the Sleepy Bear Inn. Cal wasn't in Taliville. Seeing him and reliving his Detroit mistake had been a dream.

Zack flopped back against the bed. "Oh, thank God."

"Thank God when you're gone." Roger pushed Zack toward the edge of the bed.

"Huh?"

"Get dressed and go."

Bewildered, Zack tumbled out of bed and stumbled over to his duffle bag. In his sleep-addled state, he stripped off his pajama pants before he realized he still had a hard-on. And oh, great, his dick was in plain view for Roger.

Their gazes met. Roger smiled in his sexy, devilish way, and that was *not* going to help Zack's erection go away. He hurried to get clothing on before Roger decided to say something about his nudity.

The world was beginning to make sense again, and what Roger had said sank in. Zack frowned. "Wait, you're kicking me out?"

"I am."

"You can't toss me out of the room. I'm paying for it." Zack tugged on a tank top.

"We established yesterday that I'm stronger. I will toss you off the balcony if I have to."

"Hey, I hadn't slept in over twenty-four hours before

yesterday's fight." Zack raised his hands, mimicking a fighting stance. "Want to try it?"

"I want to sleep," Roger said roughly. He grabbed Zack by the shoulder and turned him toward the door. "Come back at three."

"It's like barely seven. What am I supposed to do for all that time?"

"I don't care."

"Someone tried to kill us yesterday, remember?" Zack turned, walking backward in time with Roger's steps.

"I also remember that you tried to kill me in my sleep."

Zack bumped into the door. "This isn't fair."

"There is a way you could stay." Roger smiled slyly, mischief dancing in his eyes.

He gently took hold of Zack's wrists. Slowly, he drew them up, putting them in a position that echoed where Zack's wrists had been in his dream, and pinned them with one hand. Their chests were less than an inch apart. Zack lifted his chin and scooted back as much as he could. If Roger found out that this was only keeping him hard, he was bound to make fun of him.

I shouldn't have let this happen. Zack swallowed hard. Something had to be clouding his head, the dream or Roger's magic—except he didn't feel his tattoo. All he felt was a pulsing need to get naked with Roger, and that was his libido leading the way in the feelings department again.

Roger's grin grew more handsomely wicked, and he stroked Zack's jaw with his free hand. "Of course, I'd tie you up on the bed so you could be more comfortable. All I need is some rope." With a deep chuckle that tickled Zack's balls, he continued, "A lot of it, since you're apparently an escape artist."

Bondage and vampire kinks were uploaded side by side on many of the sites Zack visited, and they rolled into one kink on others. The one site he'd gotten in deep trouble for surfing—he'd been technically too young for it, but he'd been too curious to look away—had a vid preview of a man on his knees, ass red from a spanking, collar around his throat, hands tied behind his back. And the vampire bit him, and Zack had totally clicked on something he shouldn't have and had seen the whole thing. The spanking, the begging, the fucking. He'd learned how to clear his browser history after his parents lectured him on it.

But his mind didn't clear as easily, and the vid played back from time to time. His throat went dry as he updated the visuals to feature himself and Roger. He'd always assumed he'd be the one to tie up a partner. Even a vampire could be into submission.

His dick jumped, and his heart leapt into his throat at the idea that Roger would be in charge. The dream teased the edge of his consciousness, slipping away to fog the longer he was awake but leaving an impression of longing behind.

He's screwing with me. He's not serious. Zack glared at Roger. Anger and suspicion were easier. Another kind of heat, one that felt like strength, flowed through him. He yanked his wrists free and swallowed the groan from hurting his injured wrist. Then he shoved Roger back a step with his good hand. "Stop using your vampire tricks on me."

"We established that you'd know if I used my magic on you, boy," Roger replied.

The way Roger said *boy* made it sound like an intimate compliment. It was a whisper in Zack's ear even when Roger happened to be across the room. At the moment, Roger was only a breath away.

"Fucking asshole." Zack shoved Roger again, but this time Roger only moved half a step.

When Zack went to push Roger a third time, Roger side-stepped him, and Zack fell forward a few steps. Roger took the opportunity to open the door, and then he started to force

Zack out of the room. "All right. I've had a long night. I'm done screwing around."

"Stop. Hold on! I don't have my shoes. And I need my tablet. And my wallet and my phone, which you still have, prick. And my dagger."

"No."

"Someone *shot* at us, remember? I need defenses!"

"Fine. You have until the count of five to grab anything else you might need." Roger handed over his phone and wallet. Then he stepped aside and put his hand on the door. "One."

Zack scrambled over to his backpack. First he dumped anything he wouldn't need into his duffle bag. Then he crammed his charge cord and dagger alongside his tablet and notebooks. Meanwhile, Roger continued counting. Zack managed to grab his socks and shoes and get out the door just as Roger declared, "Five."

"Ha!" Triumphant, Zack turned around. "Did it."

Sexy smirk firmly in place, Roger leaned in and purred, "You're a very good boy. I'll see you back here at three."

Shock stunned Zack long enough for Roger to shut the door in his face and click the lock shut. Heat rose through him. He wasn't Roger's play toy. Working together didn't mean Roger was his boss. "I'll come back when I feel like it."

From the other side of the door, Roger said, "You'll be back at three, or I'll spank you."

"No you fucking won't! Because I will cut your fucking dick off if you do."

"Careful. Naughty boys don't get rewards."

Zack dumped his things on the floor. He didn't have the room key to get in and kick Roger's ass. "I don't want whatever 'reward' you think you have."

The door unlocked, and Roger threw it open. He grabbed Zack by the tank top. In a low whisper, he growled, "Do you want to say that a little louder for everyone else to hear? Maybe tell Josefina that my boy is an insolent pest?"

Zack puffed up his chest and narrowed his eyes. "I am not *yours*."

"If you want to survive this, act like you are." Roger's eyes were a deep red again. "You have to play the part, especially in this town, before everyone decides you're free game. Now, be back here at three so I can start teaching you how to survive vampire society."

"Why do I need to know that?" Zack demanded.

Roger groaned and let go of him. "I'll explain later. Leave already so I can sleep, you heathen."

"Fine."

Roger shut the door again.

"Wow, 'heathen.'" With a huff, Zack sat on the floor and put on his socks and shoes. "Old-ass vampire thinks he can boss me around."

"Young brat thinks he can survive on his own," Roger growled on the other side of the door.

"I heard that!" Zack called back.

"Good!" Roger snapped.

Just as Zack opened his mouth again, the door down the hall opened, and a woman stepped out. She didn't even look Zack's way, but she served as a reminder that despite appearances, they weren't the only ones in the building.

Zack was making a fool of himself by talking back through a door. Later, when he had some privacy, he would show Roger he wasn't a pushover. With his dagger if he had to.

A quick search on his phone revealed that Taliville didn't have anything close to a car-repair shop, although not much from Taliville apparently had a webpage. Zack chewed on his bottom lip. His car definitely needed new tires, and he hadn't stuck around to see what damage the gunfire had done to it.

And Roger expected him to be okay with walking around town without the protection of a vehicle.

Zack reached the first floor of the inn. There had to be some way to get his car fixed. But what was he going to tell his parents about the repair bills? Maybe he'd never have to mention it. If he put it on the right credit card, he could get it paid off before they ever saw the amount. Dad might notice the odd account balance, but Zack could try bluffing his way past that.

The smell of waffles and bacon brought him out of his worries. The dining room was empty, except for a couple sitting next to a sunlit window. As Zack stood, wondering which table he should sit at, the waiter emerged from the kitchen and headed straight for the couple. The waiter had blue-and-pink hair, and one of their ears had three piercings, while the other had only one, and they wore black slacks and a white shirt.

"Sit anywhere you want," they said cheerily as they passed Zack for the couple.

Zack picked a spot next to the empty fireplace. Everything on the menu sounded good, though there were only a couple of choices.

"Hello there," the waiter said as they came to Zack's table. "I'm Kit. Hope you don't mind me asking, but is that a vampire bite?"

"Does everyone know about the supernatural in this town?" Zack blurted out.

Kit laughed. "Pretty much. We've got some people who believe our interest in the supernatural is a weird small-town quirk instead of the truth and the occasional out-of-towner who summers here and doesn't have a clue, but otherwise, yeah, everyone knows."

"Oh."

"So?" Kit tapped their neck, mimicking the spot of Zack's wound.

Was there any shame in admitting a vampire bit him in a town this open about the supernatural? So far, no one had seemed to care. Instinctively, Zack touched the edge of the bandage. "Yeah. Vampire."

"If you're not a vegetarian, I recommend the Picnic Omelet with a side of bacon hashbrowns. If you are a vegetarian, I suggest that be your last vampire bite. Unless you happen to be a shifter. I'm not saying it's impossible to keep your iron levels up without meat, but it's not easy."

"I hadn't thought about that," Zack said quietly.

"Most newbies don't. You have a regular vamp daddy, or is this a scratch-a-kink kind of weekend?" Kit motioned at themselves. "I'm debating it myself. What's a little blood if you get to live in penthouses and shit, right? Oh, sorry. I'm not supposed to swear around customers."

A man leaned out from the kitchen. "You're not supposed to talk their ears off either."

Kit waved dismissively, but the kitchen door was already swinging shut again. "What'll you have?"

"The waffles smell too good to pass up. Can I get bacon and coffee with that?"

"You don't want our coffee. You want to grab it from Sugar Moon when you're done here," Kit replied. "Have an orange juice instead."

"Uh, yeah. Okay. Orange juice."

"Good call." Kit patted Zack's shoulder on their way to the kitchen. "New blood wants the—"

Their voice faded away as the door swung shut, and Zack concentrated on his phone instead. He'd have to get the password for the Wi-Fi later because he had limited data service. Sites like the HIN homepage weren't loading right.

As soon as he was finished with breakfast and had squared away a tip for Kit, he made his way out of the inn and down the street to the coffee shop, Sugar Moon. Zack dodged a particularly large guy on his way through the door, a cheerful bell ringing as the door opened.

The floor was black-and-white tile, and the tables were widely spaced from one another. It had an old-school soda shop feel, complete with a counter where customers could sit. A display on the end showcased tempting pastries and cookies. There was one woman at a table in the far corner and a man at the counter, but otherwise the shop was empty of customers.

The employee behind the counter looked like she was around Zack's age. She had dark-purple hair, but the pink scars across her pale face drew Zack's attention. After she had finished filling the man's coffee cup, she moved over to the register. "Can I help you?"

She had to be a shifter with scars like that. Taliville really was a haven for dangerous supernatural creatures.

And shit. Roger's right. That sounds like a bigot. Zack clenched his hand on his backpack strap. *Shifters aren't always evil. I know that.*

"Are you going to order anything?" she asked.

"Yeah. Just a sec." Zack glanced at the chalkboard menu off to the left, but his gaze kept falling on the girl and her scars. He was starting to stare, and that was rude. Clearing his throat, he said, "The Nighttwister, please."

"Size?"

"Biggest you got."

"Here or to go?"

"Here," Zack said. "Wi-Fi password?"

The girl pointed at the chalkboard. The password was at the bottom. "Cash or card?"

"Card." Zack paid and then took a table by the window near the door. From his position, he could get a good look at the street.

Zack opened his notebook and connected his tablet to the Wi-Fi. By the time the girl dropped off his coffee, he was neck-deep in answering an HIN research request. Some new hunter didn't know that sirens were a saltwater-only creature, and that what he had to be dealing with was a nymph. After answering such a basic question, Zack jumped into his own research, starting with Roger.

Which led him precisely nowhere. While the HIN had information about the Great Lakes Coven vampires in its own subsection, it seemed to have nothing on Roger. The internet at large led in useless circles about vampire lore in general, and his name didn't pop up on the other three sites Zack used for his research. That made sense if Roger really had been in a coffin for over thirty years.

So Zack moved on to the next name. Seamus. *That* name he could find plenty of references to, but figuring out what was truth and what was vampire boasting was going to take some work.

Every once in a while as he worked, Zack had to give his sore wrist a break. He would look up from his notebook and glance toward the counter and the girl working behind it. She wore her hair down, hiding her scars, but they were clearly from claws. A bear? Or a wolf? Or maybe even a mountain lion. Some kind of bigger predator. Zack started a list in the margin of his notebook.

Customers came and went. Zack took a note or two about them when someone interesting walked in. He was pretty sure at least one of them was part fey, but he couldn't figure out whether they were Seelie or Unseelie.

About three hours and two coffees later, Zack was truly in the research groove when a blond-haired white guy came into the shop. He was in slacks and a dress shirt, looking a little more upper class than the others who had been drifting in and out. He also had on a black leather collar. Zack scribbled a few notes about his appearance and started a rough sketch while skimming the next page of research.

The guy and the employee chatted quietly, and the notes

of their voices pinged Zack's mind as odd. Those weren't happy notes. He did his best to discreetly look up from his notebook.

The guy was staring right at him. And he had a metal disk hanging from his collar, marking him as a vampire's pet.

Oh shit. Zack dropped his attention to his notebook and continued writing. His wrist ached from the bruise and the effort, but he bit his lip and kept going.

"I've got this," the guy said.

"Reed, don't," the girl said.

Coffee cup in hand, the guy sat down across the table from him and blew noisily on his hot drink. When Zack looked up, the guy was pointedly staring at the bandage on Zack's neck. And he kept staring.

"What's your problem?" Zack demanded.

"Is it uncomfortable if someone stares at your injuries?" The guy slurped.

"It's rude."

"Then why have you been doing it to Blake?" The guy nodded toward the girl behind the counter.

She turned red and began wiping an already clean spot off the counter.

Zack could feel the heat flaring up his neck and through his cheeks. "Sorry."

"I'm not the one who needs to hear it."

The guy had a good point. Though Zack hadn't meant any harm, he'd caused some. He needed to own it. He closed his notebook and crossed the room to the girl, Blake. "I'm sorry for staring. I didn't mean to."

She shrugged.

"My name's Zack."

"I know Reed made you come over here, but seriously, let's pretend none of this happened." Blake tossed her rag into the nearby sink and started to tuck a strand of her purple hair behind her ear. She stopped and reversed her motion, pulling more of her hair in front of her face.

"Yeah. Okay." Zack went back to his table.

The guy, Reed, was still sitting there. He had to be a few years older than Cal, putting him closer to thirty. The metal circle on his collar had a mermaid stretching upward. With approval brightening his voice, he said, "That's better. Try not to do that to anyone else."

"I didn't mean—"

"I don't need your justifications. I was up late last night, and now I'm up early, and one cup of coffee is not going to be enough to get me through my bullshit day as it is." Reed took another sip. "Wonderful as it might be. God, I could live on this stuff."

"You do," Blake said from across the room.

Zack glanced around. At some point, they'd become the only ones in the coffee shop. "I seriously didn't mean to stare." He raised his bruised wrist. "I probably wouldn't bother looking up at all if this didn't hurt like hell."

"Did Roger do that?" Reed asked, a quiet seriousness to his words.

It reminded Zack of the way Teddy had told him to call if he needed *anything*. Was Reed worried about Zack like he'd been protective of Blake's feelings? They'd just met. But then again, the mountain lion had come to his aid when she didn't need to, and Kit had suggested a breakfast based off his involvement with a vampire. People in Taliville looked out for one another, even strangers.

"Josefina did," Zack replied.

"This morning? She's not up."

"Last night."

Reed rolled his eyes. "And no one thought to send you to Dr. Micah. Jesus Christ, they're so thick sometimes."

"They?"

"Vampires. They get old and forget that we mortals don't

heal as fast as them." Reed grabbed Zack's notebook and flipped open to the last page. He began to write. "I'm giving you Dr. Micah's address—that's Dr. Micah Wermager—and I'm writing a note that this goes on Josefina's tab, so don't worry about filing health insurance."

"You can speak for Josefina?" Zack asked.

"I'm both Nell's and Josefina's. I'm their head pet and run the donor house in town." Reed finished the note and slid the notebook over to Zack. "I'd offer to walk you over to the doctor's place, but I've got a list of tasks better done during regular business hours. Come by the house in a few days, and I'll give you a tour."

"We're not going to be here that long."

Reed paused as he stood up. He slowly said, "You are."

"It shouldn't take me that long to find a car to get us to Chicago."

"You're staying here for at least the next two weeks. Didn't Roger tell you about the party?"

"Party?"

"The one to announce he's not dead."

Zack frowned at him. "What are you talking about?"

Reed finished standing and waved his hand. "Forget I said anything. Talk to your master and come by when you're ready."

Zack clenched his fist as Reed left the coffee shop. *Two weeks? Party?* Roger's insistence on vampire society lessons made sense. Roger had said something about getting back into the world like he'd never left it, but Zack had assumed that meant catching up on the latest iPhone. They were going to socialize with *vampires*? His family would never approve.

I might stake that motherfucker after all.

CHAPTER 11

Before settling into bed, Roger set the clock on the nightstand for two thirty, and he scheduled a wake-up call for five minutes after that. Though getting up before dark was challenging and unpleasant in a number of ways, Roger managed to make himself rise. Sunlight threatened the edges of the curtains, creating a halo of painful light. It wasn't direct, and it wasn't on his skin, so he could work around it.

Unfortunately, he didn't have a spare set of clothes, and Wright's clothing was too small to borrow. He redressed in his only outfit. By three o'clock, he was lounging on the bed, alert and ignoring the hunger in his stomach.

At four o'clock, Roger rose and paced the room in slow steps. He had clearly said three when he spoke to Wright. Had he been abandoned? Moving forward without the boy and his dagger was possible, but having Wright at his side would make killing Seamus and Anton easier. That silver dagger was enchanted. Finding another one like it wasn't out of the question, but it would take time. And in that time, Seamus might figure out Roger meant to kill him, and the whole plan would fall apart.

Assuming, of course, it hadn't already. Nell had said that

Ezra and Dmitri still lived but hadn't revealed more details than that. Besides, Nell didn't know Seamus anymore. She wouldn't know if Seamus knew that Roger was planning on killing him or not.

At five o'clock, Roger hauled the desk chair to the middle of the room and sat facing the door. The would-be assassin could have hurt Wright. The boy could have pissed off one of the local supernaturals and gotten himself in deep trouble. He might need help. But the sun was still up, and Roger was too weak to spend any time in the daylight. Yesterday's short journeys into the light had hurt, and he'd only been allowed a minimal feeding at the donor house. Regaining his full strength would take weeks on his current allowance of local blood, but it was doable.

Provided he didn't do anything stupid like chasing after a hunter in broad daylight.

But he was beginning to think it was necessary.

What if he's disobeying me, and there's nothing wrong with him? Roger leaned forward, lacing his hands together. Wright had made his position clear; he didn't want to be Roger's pet. Perhaps he was trying to prove his point in a stubborn way. While their alliance was based on a shared goal, that didn't mean he believed Roger should be the leader. The recalcitrant boy was convinced he knew plenty about vampires.

"He knows enough to get himself killed," Roger muttered to the empty room. He stood and paced around the chair.

People listened to him because he often spoke for Seamus. As one of the captains of the GLC, underlings didn't buck him out of fear of what would happen when he told Seamus about any insubordination. Other vampires were so scared of Seamus, Roger never had to exert authority over them.

His not-recent-but-recent-to-him pets, Brad and Cee, hung off his every command. Master was a role he could use on them, and punishments were a game between them. They liked obeying him, or they wanted the lifestyle he provided them badly enough to pretend they did.

But he didn't have any of that leverage with Wright. He wouldn't technically have power over anyone when he took over the Great Lakes Coven. Oh, in theory, he would. Vampires operated on a policy of claiming the estates and privileges of those they killed. That unspoken rule was why sires kept firm hands on their sirelings and why Seamus was so paranoid of those under him. When Roger claimed the title of master of the coven by killing Seamus, the vampires in it *should* obey him, but they didn't *have* to. No one had to listen to him.

He couldn't make a mortal boy show up on time. It was an inauspicious start to his rise to power.

At six thirty-one, there was a knock on the door. Roger opened it, the air moving fast enough to rustle his hair. "Where the hell have you been?"

Wright's gray eyes went wide as he took a step back. Then he glared at Roger, lifted his chin, and pushed his way past him into the room. "Oh, fuck you."

Roger slammed the door. "I told you—"

"I have had a shit afternoon thanks to you, you son of a bitch." Wright dropped his backpack on the floor beside the bed. He whirled toward Roger. His injured wrist was wrapped, and the scent from it was pungent. "My day started out okay. Nice breakfast, good coffee. I ran into this guy, Reed, and he pointed me to Dr. Micah to get my wrist looked at. By the way, apparently I'm lucky I don't have a fucking break in my wrist from defending you last night."

"I—"

"I'm talking!" Wright snapped. "The doctor's a witch because *of course* everyone in this fucking town is fucking magical. But while I was there, I thought, 'hey, I should do something about my car.' Dr. Micah gave me the number of the local tow-truck guy, and I decided to meet him by the car.

So I go to where I left it, jumping at every fucking noise because someone shot at us yesterday, only to find out that it's not there!"

Roger folded his arms across his chest. "I had it towed last night."

"I know that *now*." Wright stomped forward. "But I was standing around, freaking out because, you know, someone tried to shoot me, and now my car was stolen. And it's not like there are any cops I can call because there are no cops in this town, and what would I say anyway? It's not like I have any idea who stole it. The tow guy shows up and tells me that he towed it, and he can give me a ride to the junkyard. He smelled like sulfur. His whole truck smelled of the crap. Which means I got a ride from a demon. *Yay*."

Very few beings spouted rage at Roger like this. Only beings superior to him or his equals ever dared to show this level of disrespect. *And Ezra, my ever-petulant sireling*. Wright didn't seem to care that Roger was older, wiser, and a vampire.

"So we go to the junkyard, and you know what I find out? It's run by freaking gremlins, and they've stripped it for parts!" Wright was less than an inch from Roger. He was flushed with anger, and he stank of human sweat on top of the herbal compound from his wrist.

"They weren't supposed to do that," Roger said.

"Well, they did, and they informed me that they put the money into my *master's* account." Wright clenched his fists. "It wasn't even paid off yet! I owe thousands on it! And they broke it and gave you the money!"

"I think the bullets broke it," Roger replied.

"Not the fucking point!"

Rage rolled off Wright in an almost palpable aura. The lust and fear that had earlier flavored his emotions were completely absent. Though Roger could try to influence him with magic, his tattoo would protect him, and Roger wasn't strong enough to overcome it. There was no cheating the situation. Wright was pissed, and no amount of intimidation or screaming at him was going to change it.

Seamus could get like that, but all Roger had to do was smile, say he was sorry, and then offer himself up. A little sex, the right victim to feed from—appeasing Seamus was an art Roger had down to a science. All Ezra ever needed was the chance to vent his feelings. He eventually broke into sobs.

But Wright was solid as a rock.

"I will pay off the car," Roger said. "And buy you a new one."

"How the fuck am I going to explain that?" Wright puffed up. "And how the fuck am I going to explain being in this town for two weeks? We can't stay here on my parents' credit card for that long! I need to get back to the house and mow the yard. I have to train with my cousins. Everyone is going to freak out when they realize I'm not home. And I can't be seen socializing with a vampire! My family will lose their shit."

There was that word again. Family. Everything Wright did seemed to revolve around them. Now that Wright's initial outburst was over, the shock of being shouted at was dying. Roger had his own anger pulsing deep at his core. He smothered it. Unleashing it wouldn't fix anything. He had to be the level-headed one, dancing two steps ahead of the moment. Always.

"This is going to take a lot longer than two weeks," Roger said sternly. He stepped away from Wright, needing the distance to draw up an air of command, and slowly began to walk around the desk chair. "Seamus and Anton are old, paranoid creatures. I don't know what defenses they might have made in the last thirty years. Hunters like to be martyrs, but I would hope you plan on surviving their assassinations."

Wright frowned and turned to continue facing Roger. "Well, yeah."

"'Well, yeah,'" Roger mocked. "We aren't eradicating a nest of fledglings. We are hunting two of the most powerful vampires in existence. You need more conviction then *Well, yeah*."

"I have conviction."

A bright anger burned in Wright's gray eyes, and he still had his chest puffed out, trying to make himself bigger. His heart raced, steady but quick. He was vibrantly alive.

Looking at Wright was like discovering a stowaway in a secret hold Roger hadn't known existed in the ship of his heart. He was used to finding something to like in just about anyone, whether their blood or their smile. But Wright was … special. Roger wanted to shatter his defenses and coax the man inside to finally reveal himself in full. There was courage in Wright, more than some people had in their entire lives, but that was different than conviction.

Roger trailed his fingers along the back of the desk chair. "You failed to kill me. You were distracted."

"I told you to let me have another shot at that," Wright complained.

"We'll only have one chance with Seamus and Anton. As soon as our attempt is made, we only have two possible outcomes. Their deaths or ours, along with the deaths of any other allies we may find and our loved ones. Seamus does not forgive. He punishes." Roger gripped the desk chair in both hands. "We have to smile and pretend until we are in a position to slide your dagger in his heart. It's going to take deception and patience. If you can't commit to that, then we'll find you a ride out of town tonight because I will have no use for you."

At the last sentence, Wright clenched his jaw and straightened his shoulders. A swell of hope rose in Roger. He'd found the weak spot in Wright's psyche. The flaw was now so painfully obvious that Roger wanted to kick himself. Pride mattered to the boy but not nearly so much as *purpose*.

Roger could work with that. He might even admire it if he allowed himself to open his heart to the boy.

"How long will it take?" Wright demanded.

"Months, maybe as long as a year."

"And the whole time I've got to play at being your pet?"

Roger leveled a serious gaze at Wright. "You've got to do more than play. You have to convince everyone around us that you are."

Wright met Roger with another staring contest. "So what's the difference?"

"If you were my pet, I'd have the right to spank your ass for showing up three and a half hours late without a word," Roger said. "And for speaking to me like you did."

"Wow, you're an abusive asshole," Wright replied.

"Let's throw out some of your preconceived notions already, shall we? Even if you run out that door, maybe you will finally learn something about me and my world." As he spoke, Roger sauntered toward Wright. "There are those who like rules, who embrace being told what to do, who enjoy having someone else make the decisions. And there are those who like to fight every restriction tooth and nail until someone finally makes them bend. And there are some who truly want nothing a vampire has to offer." Roger pushed Wright hard enough to send him two steps back against the door. "I treasure exploring a man's limits, but I respect boundaries. If I didn't, you'd be on your fucking knees wondering whether you were always fated to be mine."

Wright's heart pounded, and he flushed a deep scarlet. He kept his gaze locked with Roger, determination warring with his arousal. Clenching his good fist, he sucked in a deep breath. "How am I supposed to explain any of this to my family?"

"What do I care? That's your problem." Roger shrugged. His dismissive gesture broke the steel of Wright's expression, and the boy ended their staring contest. *And that is the weak-*

ness that needs patching. God, he is too easy to read. With a sigh, he continued, "Don't tell them anything until you need to. Perhaps they'll admire your determination."

"Yeah. Maybe they'll be able to help."

Wright barely sounded convinced of the idea. Roger wasn't going to put any stock in it. "Maybe."

A long silence enveloped them. Wright glanced up from the floor, and he searched Roger's face. Whatever he hoped to find must have shown through because Wright nodded and released a pent-up breath. "All right. You've got a year. What do I need to learn?"

A smile curled up from Roger's core, finally reaching his lips. "Oh, only *everything.*"

CHAPTER 12

"You're doing it wrong," Roger said for the umpteenth time.

Fucking bullshit. Zack groaned as he straightened. Sit-ups were part of his workout routine, and he considered his abs to be in decent shape. Making practice bows was causing his stomach to ache. "What did I do wrong now?"

"You're doing it sarcastically." Slowly, Roger walked around Zack, posing like someone judging a fashion.

"How can you even do that?" Zack demanded.

"You make the face you keep making." Roger motioned for him to bow. "Do it again."

"We've been at this forever."

"It hasn't been twenty minutes. Again."

"Come *on.*"

"I'll continue saying it until you do it. Again."

Zack sighed heavily.

"And you already need to start over," Roger said.

"Dude—"

Roger raised an eyebrow. Just the one, solitary motion. Otherwise, his features were devoid of emotion. He was playing the part of the aloof vampire because apparently that was what Zack would see when they were in public.

Zack clenched his teeth. As part of "lesson" time, Zack had to follow the rules. Since he would have to call Roger "master" in public, he was supposed to do that during their practice sessions.

It sounded like an excuse to get Zack used to the title so Roger could pounce on him later and claim him as a pet. Cal would never have stood for this kind of treatment, and his mother would be *pissed* if she found out what he was doing. But if he didn't blend in, he might not make it out of Taliville.

At least Roger had promised that he wouldn't touch Zack without asking permission first. Also, Zack could ask any question he wanted. They'd also decided that if either of them reached a breaking limit on teaching or learning, they'd stop. The agreements hadn't seemed like a big deal at first, but having those slivers of power gave him some control. They were the only reason he'd pushed through this long.

"Master, is bowing that important?" Zack said. "Maybe people don't even do it anymore."

"Seamus has had pets doing this for two and a half centuries. He gets joy from having everyone be subservient to him. Bows are part of our culture. You'll have to do it. So. Again."

Zack swallowed a sigh. Finding a point on the distant wall, he kept his gaze on it and relaxed his face to a neutral, uncaring non-expression. He kept his bad wrist at the small of his back, elbow bent gently.

That was the easy part.

Next, he held out his good wrist, fist clenched, knuckles pointed toward the floor. Then he tilted his head to the side. Only slightly because too much was a sloppy invitation. He bent at the waist slowly, and he continued until he was practically bent in half. He kept his attention on the floor as Roger walked around him.

"And up," Roger said.

Keeping his head tilted at the correct angle—too little was

an insult—was a challenge. Zack struggled to keep his gaze empty. He wasn't entirely sure how to do that, except anytime he thought too hard, Roger seemed to know. Apparently, he showed his anger and annoyance easily. But pets weren't supposed to show emotion during a presentation.

Stepping into resting pose meant keeping his head tilted and slightly bowed, putting his good arm at his side, and keeping the other one behind his back. He was allowed to have his feet shoulder-width apart.

Roger circled and inspected his form. Having someone judge his stance wasn't a completely new experience, but usually Zack was ready to fight when an instructor critiqued him. Showing this level of passivity made his shoulders itch. Zack fought the urge to break form.

"A little slow, but much better," Roger said. "We can move on for tonight."

Zack sagged. "Fucking finally."

Roger paused, shooting him a look that said *try that again*.

As much as Roger was acting like the boss, they should be a partnership. With the fakest sincerity he could muster, Zack smiled. "Why, thank you, Master. How fantastic that we can do something else that will drive me absolutely bonkers. I'm thrilled to my toes."

Roger *almost* smiled. Zack saw the twitch of his lips. However, he settled into a cold scowl as he faced Zack. "If you pull that shit in public—"

"I'll have my ass handed to me, probably by you." Zack stretched, trying to ease the tension in his stomach. "I heard you the first thirty times."

"You better hope it's by me. I'll pull my punches. No one else will give you any slack."

"I wouldn't expect them to, oh great master of suck."

Roger put his hand to his own face.

Zack grinned. Annoying Roger was fun so long as it didn't anger him. He'd run into that line earlier when he'd come back late, and Roger had shouted at him. But after cutting through the crap, Zack thought he could see where Roger was coming from. Yeah, Roger should have told him about the car, but Zack could have tried to call the hotel to check in with Roger. And *maybe* Zack's shouting hadn't been necessary. Zack had been on edge from looking over his shoulder the whole time he was out of the room. The shooter could have fired on him at any point.

Had Roger worried about him when he hadn't been on time? Did he care? Was that why he was upset when Zack came back later than he was supposed to?

After a moment, Roger dropped his hand. His mouth was a tight line, but he lacked any fire in his voice as he said, "Do you have it in you to start another subject tonight, or should we review everything we've discussed?"

Before Zack could answer, there was a light knock on the door. Zack was closer, so he started to reach for it. Roger used his vamp speed and beat him to it. When Zack opened his mouth to complain, Roger held up a hand for quiet.

Considering there were rules on how to sit in the presence of a vampire, there was probably something about who opened doors for what. Zack stepped back and folded his arms over his chest as Roger opened the door.

"Master Nell wonders if you'll take advantage of the house this evening," a voice said. Zack couldn't see the person past Roger's muscular body.

"I will. Tell her that I will be there shortly, and I thank her for inviting me." Roger started to shut the door.

"A moment, sir," the voice said. "She asks that when you come, you bring the boy. She wants to meet him."

Roger stiffened. "He's not trained."

"She knows that, but she says she can hardly allow one such as him to roam freely in her community without an understanding between them."

"Then I'll be happy to do as she asks. We'll be along soon," Roger replied.

Zack waited for Roger to close the door and turn around before he said, "'One like him?' What's that supposed to mean?"

Roger went to Zack's duffle bag and started going through it. "Don't overthink it."

The audacity. Zack clenched his fists. "What are you doing?"

"You're dressed terribly. Don't you have any reasonable clothes?"

"Says the guy wearing last night's outfit," Zack grumbled.

"*I* don't have anything else to wear. This is all T-shirts and shorts. Not even a full pair of pants, much less a dress shirt." Roger sighed and put a hand to his forehead.

"Sorry I'm not up to the dress code, oh great one." Zack grabbed his arm. "Now tell me what 'one like him' means?"

In a quiet, tense voice, Roger said, "She knows you're a Wright."

"She *what?*" Zack walked away, throwing up his hands. "What is the fucking point of training me if everyone's going to know I'm from a hunter family? I thought this pet act was supposed to protect me, but if she knows, there's no fucking reason to hide."

Roger turned toward him and adopted that too-patient, steady glare he used when he was waiting for Zack to stop talking. The look was so patronizing that Zack shut his mouth out of anger, which Roger took as a sign he was done. "She had silver around my throat and a willingness to end me if I didn't answer honestly. Besides, people were bound to learn your name at some point. We need to convince them that you came to me willingly."

Which means I shouldn't tell my family about any of this. Cal can't keep a secret to save his life, and Mom will never understand.

The thought circled a few times as he tried to imagine what his family's reaction would be. Zack tugged a corner of his lip between his teeth. The best way to keep a secret was to tell no one. They'd either think he was lying to himself or spread it through the family, and that could spread it outside the family, and that would get him killed.

He had to play the part. And he had to do it well.

"Do I have to bow to Nell? Because you said 'better,' not 'good,'" Zack said.

"Show respect and don't swear in her presence, and you should be fine." Roger straightened the cuff of his shirt. "I think."

"You *think*?"

"I like Nell, and she seems to like me. We agree Seamus is a problem. That doesn't mean courtesies will extend to you."

"Well, this keeps getting better and better." Zack stepped closer. "Am I getting murdered tonight?"

"No. Unless you provoke her, Nell won't kill you. The last thing she wants is your blood spilled in her domain."

"Why?"

Roger snorted. "Seriously? Because you're a Wright. Your family has a certain reputation. You are aware of it, aren't you?"

Zack folded his arms over his chest. "We're determined hunters who smite evil."

Roger stepped close enough that Zack had to look up to meet his gaze. Any hint of playfulness disappeared under Roger's serious expression. "They're killers. Your brother's known as the Butcher."

"Of course supernaturals would see us that way," Zack said. "We keep them in check."

"We don't give epitaphs to every hunter. Your brother is the only Wright with one at the moment." Roger lowered his voice. "Do you know why?"

"He gets the job done," Zack replied quietly. Standing still was hard to do with Roger focusing his immortal seriousness at him. His anxiety had nothing to do with hearing about Cal's reputation. Nope. Not a bit.

"He doesn't care about a supernatural's behavior. He doesn't care about their age. A teenage werewolf who shifted for the first time is the same as Seamus to him."

"You don't know my brother. You don't even know what's been happening for the last thirty years."

"Nell and I had a long conversation last night. I have learned plenty." Roger looked down at Zack. "Are you claiming you had no idea of his reputation?"

People have been calling him Butcher on the HIN. Zack couldn't look up anymore. His family preached no tolerance for supernaturals. That was why letting the vampire go in Detroit was a sin to them. They hadn't cared that the girl had to be a new vampire. They hadn't cared she was the same age Zack was. No amount of pleading would have worked on them. And Zack had broken with one soul-crushing *please.*

Please wouldn't have stayed Cal's hand.

Any argument would be hollow. Zack held on to his arms and stared at the floor between their feet.

"There is evil in the world that needs to be stopped," Roger said softly. "Not everything they taught you is wrong."

"Sure," Zack muttered. He stalked over to his bag. "I think I've got a polo. Maybe."

He changed his shirt silently. His head buzzed with too many questions and all the wrong answers. *But haven't I always known something was off with the way we talked about stuff?* Zack shoved his feet into his shoes and tied them.

"We'll have to work on our wardrobes at some point." Roger opened the door.

"Ah yes, wouldn't want to be unfashionable, oh great one," Zack said.

"That behavior stays in the room."

There's that line. Zack knew where misbehaving with his family got him. His mother's disapproval had ground deep grooves in familiar patterns on his psyche. Both his parents would heap on responsibilities, and Zack would do anything to get back on their good side.

Ever since Detroit, that hadn't been possible. Nothing ever seemed to be fixed between them.

But what would Roger do to him? He deserved to know. Zack puffed up his chest. "There's no way every human behaves one hundred percent of the time. And I bet there are vampires who like it when their pets act up in public."

"There are," Roger said smoothly. *Too* smoothly. His voice was a sultry reminder that he had centuries of being a sexy vampire under his belt. "Their pets also like public punishments. Do you want a spanking with an audience, boy? Is that when you'll finally behave?"

An image of bending over Roger's lap flared bright in Zack's imagination. Molten-hot lust pounded in his veins. Just as quickly, his heat froze. Cal had walked in on him masturbating once. *"Dude, I had to check on you. Sounded like a cat dying."*

Embarrassing himself at home was awful. No way could he stomach a roomful of vampires judging him for moaning. Not that a spanking had to be erotic, but the way Roger looked at Zack made him think spanking was some kind of code. But people might look at him. And would that be so bad?

Mean words circled around in his head, almost all of them carrying Cal's voice.

None of that could matter. Not now. Zack needed to stay in the moment. "Behave myself outside of the room. Got it."

His legs felt wobbly. His lungs hurt so badly he worried he was breathing in something acidic, but he realized he was hardly breathing at all. What was wrong with him? *Nothing. Nothing can be wrong. I'm fine.*

He made it all the way out the inn's front door before he remembered that he didn't know where the donor house was.

Roger stepped out beside him. "Are you all right?"

"I'm great. Lead the way." Zack gestured at the street. When Roger didn't budge, he started down the steps and onto the sidewalk. Was the donor house to the right or left? Was that where they were going? The voice had only mentioned a house. Were they supposed to go to Nell's house?

"This way," Roger said, suddenly less than an inch from Zack's shoulder.

Zack's pulse thundered so loudly in his ears he was surprised he could hear anything, but Roger was finally taking the lead. Zack fell into step behind him. He expected that they'd travel in that fashion, but Roger slowed down so they were even.

Walking down the street was kind of nice, now that Zack's heartbeat was returning to normal. Taliville was beautiful at night. The dragon statue in the park didn't seem scary.

"Are you a virgin?" Roger asked.

And just like that, Zack's heart pounded hard again. Any of the other people on Main Street could be supernaturals. They'd be able to hear their conversation from great distances.

Zack shoved his hands in his pockets. "Can we talk about that later?"

"We can." They walked on for half a block before Roger asked, "Do you know what goes on in a donor house?"

Zack had to catch himself before he said it the way his family had taught him. *Undead bastards drink from blood-bitch addicts.* He rubbed his temple. That saying had never sat right with him.

Taliville didn't have a vibe like that. Reed had scolded Zack for being a jerk and then given him help with his wrist.

Dr. Micah had been kind. So had the tow truck guy. People in town seemed to genuinely care about others.

"Vampires pay humans so they can feed from them," Zack said.

"They do more than feed." Roger put a weight on his words; the subtext was potent enough to be a pop-up ad.

"Sex."

"Yes."

They were about to visit a donor house. Zack was supposed to act like a pet. What if there was some kind of hazing thing or claiming ritual Roger hadn't warned him about? His lungs froze. "We don't have to … We're not going to—should I go back to the room?"

"We don't have to do anything." Roger stopped and gently took Zack's good wrist in his hand to pull him to a pause as well. His touch was so light, it was like a ghost was holding on to him. "I would never do something a partner wouldn't enjoy. *Never*."

Sincerity warmed Roger's eyes, and Zack relaxed. He'd worry the calm was some trick of magic, but the tattoo on his hip was dormant. Vampires weren't known for putting people at ease either. Roger was being kind.

"Oh."

"Other people will be having sex, though," Roger said.

"Pfft, I've seen porn. A lot of porn. Probably more than is healthy. The internet was made for it, and I've been alone all summer." Zack bit his tongue before he continued to ramble. He didn't need to sound pathetic in front of Roger.

"That's nothing like people having sex in front of you."

"I'll be fine."

"Will you?"

"I'm not a virgin, okay?" Zack snapped. "I'm not an innocent who's going to die from a nosebleed around people doing it, and I'm not going to be an asshole and assume I can just jump into sex with anyone I see doing it." He started to take a step.

Roger gently tugged on his wrist, bringing his attention back. He rubbed his thumb in a slow circle. "You're stiff with fear. I can smell it rippling off you. What's wrong?"

Zack bit his tongue harder. Roger didn't need to know anything about his personal life. That wasn't the deal between them. What good would it do anyway? They were partners on a hunt, nothing else. Handing over a confidence about his sex insecurities was extending trust Roger didn't deserve.

Except ... Zack didn't have anyone to talk to about sex stuff. What few friends he had also knew Cal. Talking to his parents about the subject was too mortifying to contemplate. The only time anyone in the family brought up the subject, they were telling him he was reading the wrong books and visiting the wrong websites.

Roger was never going to talk to his parents. And he didn't seem judgy.

With a heavy sigh, Zack sagged. "I'm not good at any of it."

"Any of what?"

"Sex." Zack shoved a hand through his hair. "I sit in my room and research all day. When I'm not doing that, I'm at fighting practice. I tried dating in high school, but it was high school, you know? So I figured, hook-up apps. I had the house to myself, so why not? But I wasn't exactly successful."

Roger trailed his fingertip along the underside of Zack's jaw, encouraging him to look up. "I hardly believe no one would find you interesting."

For a breathless moment, Zack believed him. He wanted to keep doing that, but he had data from the real world. "I had some interest. Just not good sex. Kind of how-fast-can-we-get-naked-oh-we're-done-already sex."

"Ah." Roger shifted his weight so he was closer. The

world seemed to fade away until there was only his face in front of Zack's. "You've never had someone unravel you with pleasure, and you long for that."

Zack could feel his dick getting hard, brushing against Roger. "Yeah."

Slowly, Roger stroked his thumb across Zack's chin. "Hm."

Then Roger stepped away and started down the street again.

Horny and yearning, an electric scream caught in Zack's throat. He shoved the welling disappointment down. He wasn't supposed to want Roger anyway. Roger was a convenient path to what he truly wanted: the respect of his family. Nothing more. He couldn't be anything more.

Zack's hands hurt. He had to shake them loose from the fists he hadn't noticed he'd made. An ache pulsed deep inside him, from his heart to his dick and back again. Roger was an undead creature of the night who survived by sucking blood out of people. He was evil.

Only he wasn't, and Zack knew better. An evil man would have killed him a dozen times over by that point. An evil man wouldn't accept when Zack disobeyed him. An evil man wouldn't bother teaching him how to survive the supernatural world.

As much as Roger had pushed him in the short time they'd known each other, he hadn't shoved. He was showing real consideration for Zack's feelings.

The best monsters hide in plain sight, Cal's voice said.

What could be in plainer sight than family? Zack rubbed his palms, trying to make the fingernail marks disappear. But they lingered like his doubts.

Roger stopped and half turned to face Zack. He'd gotten a few feet away while Zack was stuck in thought. The breeze swept up his hair, and he ran his hand through it, sweeping long locks from his face. With a soft smile, he said, "Aren't you coming?"

There was a crack in Zack's soul. He hadn't felt it until that moment, but the fissure went through his core. His life was lacking, and even if Roger wasn't the answer, he might be the way toward one. *Or the way to my death.*

But maybe he'd get to live first.

"Yeah," Zack said. "Yeah, of course."

CHAPTER 13

Wright was rattled, and Roger itched to take him back to their room and pin him to the bed until he relinquished all his secrets. The confession Wright had made earlier in their walk —that he longed for a good partner—seeped into Roger like a gentle wave creeping up a shoreline. Moment by moment, Wright was growing on him. He had beauty in him.

And dangers. Roger needed to remember that they were partners in crime, not lovers. The mission needed to come first.

When they reached the donor house, Roger slowed on the front walkway until Wright stepped even with him. He put his hand on Wright's back and walked in pace with him. Wright stiffened under his light touch, but he didn't pale or pull away.

Roger leaned in close to murmur, "Whatever you see in here, don't interfere. If you believe something nefarious is happening, point it out to me."

"What will you do?" Wright asked.

"I'll do the best I can in the situation," Roger replied.

Wright stopped, bringing them both to a halt, and glared up at him. "Is that fancy talk for *nothing*?"

People on the front porch could see them, and a few might be able to hear them. What Roger said could be monitored by them, but it would matter more to Wright.

Technically, he had no authority in Nell's lands. Causing a scene on behalf of a human or shifter could get them kicked out of Nell's domain and ruin his chances at a much-needed loan. He had no power to interfere.

Wright wouldn't want to hear that. He might not accept it.

And Roger couldn't blame him for that. Standing by, feeling powerless—neither had sat well with him in the past. He had witnessed pain and suffering caused by other vampires, unable to speak out for fear of his own life. Staying docile was like having a blade stuck in his throat. Always cutting, always hurting. For the first time, he was free of Seamus. He could act how he saw fit. He could make a stand.

Nell and Josefina, along with the dozen or so other vampires who lived in Taliville, could kill him in a heartbeat. But if he couldn't find his feet in this place, he stood no hope of doing so in front of Seamus.

"I'd investigate and report everything to Nell. This is her domain," Roger said.

Wright puffed up. "And if Nell said, 'Hey, let someone kick the crap out of that human?'"

"If it's a nonconsensual crap kicking, then I'd figure out what to do. But I don't think that will be a problem here."

"No one would ever consent to a crap kicking," Wright replied.

"My dear boy, you know very little about what people will seek," Roger said. "It might surprise you that some people like pain."

"And you expect me to do nothing about rape?"

"I expect you to *tell me*. If we're going to go down fighting, we should at least be back-to-back when it happens." Roger put his hand up before Wright could speak. "But as I said, Nell doesn't tolerate that in her donor house or in her territory. She's created a paradise, and we need to respect her rule. So be on your best behavior."

Wright shifted his weight back and forth before nodding. He headed up to the door, leading by a half step. That was part of the protocol Roger had taught him during their lesson. Human pets should open doors for their masters, then trail behind once they were inside. Hopefully, most of what they had covered would stick with Wright. The sooner he learned everything, the faster they could go to Chicago. *And then the real tests begin.*

The girl was at the front desk in the foyer, and she stood as soon as they entered. "Master Roger, Master Nell is expecting you, but she isn't here yet." She handed Roger an orange chit. "You are welcome to your allowance while you wait."

Roger took the chit and closed his hand around it. The little circle represented one feeding. Anyone could turn him down if they wanted. The first person he'd approached the night before had. Orange chits didn't pay as well as red ones did, and the donors in the house knew it.

Nell was doing him a favor by letting him have living blood. Some masters would make visiting vampires feed from blood bags, a practice that would have kept Roger starving in his current condition. A vampire could survive on blood bags, but not well. It didn't carry enough of a person's essence after a few days, and that was what truly fueled a vampire.

"Thank you," Roger managed to say.

"Allowance?" Wright asked.

Roger glanced over his shoulder at Wright, shooting him the lightest glare. Asking questions exposed Roger's foolishness as a master. Hadn't he told Wright that?

"I heard you were new to this," the girl said. She stepped to the side so she could make eye contact with Wright. "Master Nell permits vampires in her territory the opportunity to purchase an allowance of blood each night from the donor house. Feeding without a chit inside the house's premises is against the rules and will result in swift punishment. In Master Nell's domain, feeding is only allowed within donor houses, at parties with enthusiastic participants, or from a vampire's willing pets. Anything else is unsanctioned and punishable."

"Vampires stick to that? They follow those rules?" Wright said.

"They do. In turn, Master Nell provides safety from hunters, social relations with other supernatural groups, and business alliances that generate considerable income. Taliville has existed for over a hundred years, and it's a wonderful place."

Wright opened his mouth again.

That's not going to work for me. Roger grabbed him by the arm and tugged him past the girl toward the back of the house. "Thank you for your time."

Wright had the decency to wait until Roger pulled him into one of the living rooms before yanking his arm free. The motion caught the attention of a few of the others in the room. Roger smiled at them, trying to placate their spontaneous audience, but Wright's face was clouded with anger. People were watching them.

"Control yourself," Roger whispered through his smile.

"You're the one manhandling me," Wright snapped under his breath.

"I wouldn't have to if you hadn't interrogated the first person you met."

"I'm supposed to be learning this crap, aren't I?"

"From me," Roger snarled. He had Wright cornered against the wall, and the boy smelled of manly sweat and summer sun. His heartbeat was elevated, his skin flushing from anger. The tiny shifts were tantalizing.

Roger put his hand on Wright's collarbone. His thumb rested near the hollow of Wright's throat. He could feel the twitch of Wright's pulse. The world narrowed to that solitary feeling, to the whisper of his breath and the hum of his heart. *I could drain him. No one would notice until it was too late. No one would blame me when they learned who he is.*

And. I'd. Finally. Feel. Good.

But he needed Wright. And he was growing fond of him. And he didn't like killing.

But he was so *hungry*. Every bone in his body ached. Every muscle was dormant, barely following the simplest of orders. He was weak. He couldn't afford to be weak. And Wright tasted so good. The last feed from him had been a merciless quick suck with no pleasure in it for either of them. Necessity. That was it.

Maybe he could have just a sip. Maybe Wright was strong enough for that.

Roger's hand trembled.

Wright reached down low and cupped Roger's groin. Welcoming his boldness, Roger shifted so he'd have an easier time. Sex wasn't as good as blood, but it was good. One could lead to the other. Wright slid his hand down further, searching, seeking.

Then he locked his fingers around Roger's balls and *squeezed.*

The pain bit through the hunger, driving Roger's focus away from Wright's throat and back to his own body. He closed his mouth in time to muffle the yelp and then buried his head in Wright's shoulder. Wright wasn't letting go. Roger put his hands on either side of Wright on the wall.

"You in control?" Wright hissed.

"Yes," Roger groaned.

Wright twisted. "You fucking sure?"

"Yes. Fuck. Let go."

Slowly, Wright released Roger's balls.

Roger sucked in a deep breath and raised his head. He met Wright's gaze, expecting anger. A fierce fire lit Wright, but it wasn't rage. As they locked sight, he softened for the fraction of a second before hardening.

"Great," Wright whispered. "Now go suck on as many necks as it takes to get your red eyes to go away."

"I only get the one." Roger held up the orange chit.

Wright blinked at the chit. "Vampires need at least three to four pints a night to be in their prime. And you're centuries old. You need more than that."

"Is that concern in your voice?" Roger purred. "For little old me?"

"How many pets do you normally have?"

"I typically keep two and frequently hunt outside of that." Roger fought to keep his hands on the wall. If he moved them, he might fall into the trance of Wright's pulse.

"You need to feed from more than one person a night," Wright said. "Nell has to understand that."

Some answers couldn't wait until they were alone. Roger leaned in close to lower his voice to where hopefully only Wright would hear him. "I've been declared dead. I don't have access to my accounts. Nell is doing me a great favor allowing me this."

"Okay. Then we pay for one or two extras. It can't be out of our price range."

"An orange chit is two thousand dollars."

Wright gasped and then sputtered. He pushed Roger back enough that their noses brushed and then a slight bit farther. "What?"

"I thought you knew everything about vampires," Roger teased. Because teasing was better than the weakness, and his knees threatened to buckle unless he found an outward focus. "Look around the room and tell me what you see."

This living room had multiple leather couches, all in wonderful condition. Roger didn't know what all the various devices in the room were, but he was willing to wager the flat-screen televisions and gaming equipment weren't cheap.

At the far end of the room were two pool tables. The vampires at each of them were dressed in the effortless look of having spent a small fortune to appear richly casual.

Even among the humans and townspeople, Wright stood out in his shorts and polo. While the mortals' clothing wasn't always as expensive as the vampires', what they wore helped accentuate their bare arms, their necks, or seemed either easy or fun to remove.

"Vampires are filthy rich," Wright whispered.

"I think the phrase is 'no shit.'"

Wright glared at him. "I wasn't sure if that was vampire propaganda or not."

"Propaganda," Roger drawled. "Fun little syllables."

Wright narrowed his eyes. "You need to find someone to drink from. Now."

"Since I'm only having one tonight, I am going to enjoy myself. Rushing into it won't help me."

"Dramatic vampire pain in the ass," Wright whispered.

Roger shifted his weight so he leaned more against the wall beside Wright and turned toward him. He scanned the room again. A few of the patrons had collars with crest tags on them. Those individuals were off-limits.

Nell's donor house served as a social hub like the vampire clubs in Chicago did. There were so many interesting people. Trying to narrow down his choices made the hunger burning in Roger roar with renewed flame. He closed his eyes for a moment and concentrated on swallowing down the hunger. It had never been this bad before. He couldn't trust himself, but he couldn't refuse to feed.

"How about you pick for me?" Roger asked, the words rough in his throat.

Wright bristled. "You want me to choose who you're going to suck on?"

"Yes."

"Why?"

Roger opened his eyes. He didn't try to hide the helpless feeling in his veins. The need for help. Because if Wright didn't help him, he might sink into the hunger, and *that* would damn them. "Please."

The tenseness in Wright's brow changed from annoyance to deep concern. He folded his arms over his chest. "Okay. Fine. That woman on the couch wearing a collar."

"Does her collar have a tag?"

"Yeah."

"Then not her. She belongs to someone."

"Pretty much everyone in this room does. Or is hanging on the arm of a vamp already."

"There are other rooms." Roger motioned. "Lead the way."

Wright nodded and walked out into the hall. Roger trailed behind him. Memories played at the edges of his mind. Different places, different people. One laugh echoed into another, into a song, back to the present. The past overlapped reality, slipping and grinding. Blood was everywhere. Dozens of heartbeats, tiny wounds, sounds of biting, feeding, fucking. He put a hand on the wall to steady himself. Was it wallpaper or paint under his hand? Paint. It had to be paint. That wallpaper belonged in 1873. To a burned house.

"Hold it together," Wright said as he put a hand on Roger's shoulder.

"I'll manage."

"Good. Because I found someone." Wright pointed into the room. "Them."

Roger followed his direction. There was a young person sitting on the edge of a couch. They had pink-and-blue hair, combed in a fetching style. When they saw Roger staring in their direction, they rose from their seat and crossed the room.

"Is this your master, Zack?" They ran their gaze over Roger, down and then up again. Hunger was in their eyes, but not a blood lust. Sexual appetite. "Are you looking for someone tonight?"

"I am." Roger's throat felt like swallowing seawater after broken glass. The world was spinning on without him. He held up the orange chit.

"Is there somewhere private?" Wright asked.

"Is he okay?" Kit whispered to Wright.

Wright pressed his lips tight and stared at Roger. They entered one of their many staring contests. Then he reached into his pocket. "He *needs* to feed. But pain brings him out of it. If you get in trouble, use this. Don't hesitate."

Wright tried to hand off something small to Kit, but Kit yelped, and it dropped. The bright silver bracelet lay on the floor.

"What the fuck?" Kit demanded.

"Sorry. Sorry." Wright scooped it up. "Protection."

"I appreciate the thought, but I'll scream instead." Kit put his hand on Roger's shoulder. "Why don't you come with me, baby?"

"Don't call me that," Roger said.

"Yes, sir." Kit looped an arm in Roger's, and they headed for the stairs. "We'll be back in a bit, Zack."

Roger leaned into Kit and went with them to a quiet place upstairs. He would feed, and the world would be balanced. And he wouldn't overthink how Wright had come to his rescue.

Or how much he owed him for his act of mercy.

CHAPTER 14

A bathroom was surprisingly hard to find, but Zack spotted one toward the back of the house and off one of the many living rooms. Thankfully, the door locked, and he could be alone. He turned on the cold water and splashed his face a few times. His family was right; he'd spent way too much time watching vampire porn. That had to be why he was obsessed with imagining images of Roger biting Kit when he should be worried about Roger. For a minute there, Roger had nearly given in to blood lust, and *that* was dangerous.

How long could a vampire operate on as little blood as Roger was getting? Was Kit safe with Roger? What kind of being was Kit? They had to be a shifter. Vampires didn't drink from undead, and fey were allergic to iron, not silver.

The cold water on his face warmed quickly, so he splashed some more on. Roger wasn't his problem. He couldn't be. He was over three hundred years old; he didn't need some kid watching his back. Except … that was exactly what their partnership was about. Zack had figured that meant literally watching his back in a fight, not looking out for him and choosing donors.

Donors. Cal would hate that. They're victims. But were they?

The people in this house were chatting. Laughing. Playing freaking video games. Someone might be hurting for money —someone was always in need of quick cash anywhere in the world—but no one seemed *desperate*. No one seemed like they were in a rush for a vampire's attention. There was no overpowering pressure of vampiric magic bewitching people.

Zack caught a glimpse of himself in the mirror. The bandage on his neck was getting wet from the water splashes. He peeled it off and tossed it into the garbage.

Zack had caused more aggressive hickeys—although without the scabbing. But he'd definitely had and made worse bruising on people when he was making out with partners. More teeth than Roger's fangs had bit in. Zack would probably have a scar. His first hunting scar. And he hadn't finished the job.

And it was clear that he didn't want to. Because if Nell was as protective as she sounded, Zack could have called for help when Roger was losing his control. He could have abandoned Roger to the blood lust, and the others would have put him down as a feral. Vampires could lose their minds that badly, even older vampires like Roger. Other vampires never tolerated it for long. They couldn't afford to.

Instead, he'd helped get Roger under control and picked out someone for him to feed from. Roger was probably fang deep in Kit, and it wouldn't be the harsh bite Zack had experienced. He'd probably use his magic. The bite would feel good. Roger would lock his arms around Kit and …

Zack wiped a hand down his face. The surge of jealousy was like a cat scratching his arms; sharp and quick and stinging way more than it should. Roger didn't belong to him. He didn't belong to Roger. They were nothing more than two men with a similar goal, and *it had to stay that way*. His family was never going to understand otherwise.

Zack turned off the water and found a paper towel.

Drying his face helped. That was something he could feel and focus on. His face felt fresher. "Pull it together. You got this."

The pep talk sounded hollow. He slammed the paper towel into the trash and left the bathroom.

He had no idea how long Roger needed to spend with Kit. The bite had taken only a minute or two when Roger had drunk from him, but if he was doing it right, it could take a lot longer. At least, Zack assumed it could. Feeding slowly had to be better for the donor, right? He glanced around the room, but no one was actively drinking from a donor in the room where he was.

There was a bar, though. He approached and waited for the bartender. "Bottle of water, please."

"A pretty boy like you should have a little fun." A man leaned against the bar beside Zack. He had dark-blond hair that hung halfway down his back. He was a white guy, and while he looked like he was around Zack's age, he smelled like dirt. It made Zack's nose tingle the same way Roger did.

And if the smell wasn't obvious enough, the man smiled broadly to show off his fangs.

"Drunk doesn't equal fun," Zack replied.

"I suppose that's true." The vampire leaned in and brushed his hand over Zack's shoulder. "There is plenty of fun to be had without alcohol." He started to slide his hand down.

Zack stepped away. "I've already got a master. No thanks."

As Zack went to grab the bottle of water the bartender had put out for him, the vampire slammed his hand on top of Zack's wrist and pinned it to the wood. Fresh pain throbbed out from Zack's already bruised wrist. The vampire's grin grew more predatory as he leaned in again. "A master who doesn't give you a collar isn't doing his duty."

Zack struggled to bite down on the shout of pain caught in his throat. He'd grabbed for the drink with his bad hand out of habit—and he could have held the bottle in it—but the vampire's grip aggravated the injury.

"Anyone could grab you and claim you," the vampire whispered in Zack's ear. "Maybe that's what you want."

"Let me go," Zack said, proud of how strong his voice felt despite the pain.

"When I'm ready." The vampire closed in on Zack's neck.

Suddenly, the vampire bashed his head against the bar. Only on the second whack did Zack's mind catch up to the speed of events. A black woman was on the vampire's other side. She wore a deep-red suit with a black silk shirt, and her eyes were a deep ruby-brown color. With effortless strength and speed, she slammed the other vampire into the bar a third time and cracked the wood. Zack was free of the grip, so he slid another foot away.

"What is my rule?" the woman demanded.

In a chorus, the room replied, "Only the willing."

The woman nodded once and then knocked the man to the floor. "You've forfeited any chits you purchased for the night, Quinn of the GLC. Break my rule again, and your visitor's pass to my domain will be revoked. Permanently. At a dawn of my choosing. Do you understand?"

The man on the floor, Quinn, nodded and hurried from the room. He even used a burst of vampire speed to get away.

Zack rubbed his wrist gently but still winced. Then he made the mistake of looking directly at the vampire who'd saved him. He wasn't supposed to be making eye contact with superior vampires. From the way she spoke, this woman had to be Nell. Dropping his gaze, he said, "Thank you, Master."

"Mm. Are you Roger's boy?"

"Yes."

Nell pointed to a door. "Outside with me. Now."

"Should we tell—"

Nell snapped her fingers and pointed at the door again.

Right. No questioning the master vampire where everyone can hear. Or ... ever. Zack walked out the door. A chill crept across his back. The air around Nell was colder. Zack had read about the effect that older, more powerful vampires could have on the environment around them. Most hunters who met one never lived to talk about it, but there were a few stories. Really more legends or myths.

The ending never went well for the hunters.

Zack stepped out onto a well-furnished brick patio with plenty of late-blooming flowers and comfortable furniture. No one was taking advantage of the beautiful night. Maybe this was considered her personal space. He turned to face her.

Nell swung a slap toward his face. He barely dodged out of her reach. Her next attack hit and sent him back three steps. But he didn't lose his balance.

He couldn't hope to match her. While her reach was no longer than his, she moved so much faster than him. Weaving and countering the best he could, he still took a few hits and landed nothing in return.

While trying to back away, he tripped on the brick. He flailed as he started to fall. Nell grabbed his arm, halting his imminent crash. Then she released him. He thudded onto the ground with only a few new bruises.

His pride was less intact. He'd been training his whole life, and he hadn't stood a chance.

Nell didn't have a hair out of place. She folded her arms over her chest and stared down at him. "Not much for a Wright. Even less impressive for a Gladwell."

Zack shoved off the ground. He was the same height as Nell. After looking up to meet Roger's face, having someone the same size as him was disorienting. He had to fight to drop his gaze again and then decided not to bother. She'd attacked him, and he couldn't risk being caught off guard again.

"Who said I'm a Wright? Or a Gladwell?" Zack asked.

"Roger told me your last name. As for your mother's

maiden name, your brother has bragged about it for years," Nell replied.

"You've never met my brother."

"Of course I haven't. If I had, he'd be dead." Nell began to walk around him. "You don't think hunters are the only ones capable of connecting over the internet, do you?"

"I've never found anything," Zack said.

"Because we're very, very careful, Zackery." Nell stopped beside a chair and put her hands on the back of it. "But I needed less than a day to find out plenty about your family. Your brother, Callum Wright, has been following in your ancestors' footsteps with a religious zeal matched only by his mother. Your sister, Amber, has been spotted over the last few months doing the same. However, there is remarkably little about *you*. Why is that?"

"I'm a researcher." Zack felt his throat tighten. Why did he have to defend his role in the family to a master vampire? He straightened his shoulders. "And the best reputation in our business is no reputation."

Nell laughed. "Dear child, reputation is everything, and the only ones without one are the ones who don't matter."

"I am a Wright. And a Gladwell. And I will live up to that," Zack snapped. "I'm not a weak human."

"Worse, you're an inexperienced child with delusions of grandeur," Nell said.

"I'm an underestimated monster slayer who isn't afraid of any bloodsucker."

"You realize you're attempting to intimidate a twelve-hundred-year-old vampire, yes?"

Fuck. Fuck, fuck. Fuck me. Fuck Roger. Fuck! Ignoring the sparking fear crackling through him, Zack cleared his throat. "Yeah. Well. You started it."

Nell laughed again, but her tone shifted to a lighthearted one. With a graceful movement, she stepped around to the front of the chair and sat in it. "All right, that's enough grand-standing. Please, have a seat."

Uneasily, Zack took one near her. "This was some kind of test?"

"What Roger plans to do is challenging," Nell said. "Though I do like him, he's not proven himself to be the best judge of character. I wanted to see for myself what kind of person he was dragging into this war. I see he's more convinced you than seduced you into it."

"It's an assassination, not a war."

"We shall see." Nell lounged in her chair, seeming completely comfortable. "Why aren't you as well known as the rest of your family? You're of the age that Wrights and Gladwells start making names for themselves, but most of my sources weren't sure you existed."

Zack bit his bottom lip. Amber had only been hunting for a summer, and people already knew about her, but they didn't know about him? "I'm a secret weapon."

"Roger certainly hopes so."

Silence stretched between them. Roger had to be done with Kit. Would he know where to look for Zack? Zack held his injured wrist closer to his body and shifted his weight. If Nell attacked again, he still didn't have a prayer, but he wanted to be in the best position to defend himself.

Questions plagued him. Nell was over a millennium old. Besides the intricacies of the present, she had lived through fascinating eras of time. And Roger considered an alliance with her to be key. Annoying her wasn't a good way to cement that relationship. She'd dragged him outside, and they were sitting. Humans weren't supposed to start conver-sations with older vampires. However, Nell seemed to consider humans and vampires equals. So maybe she wouldn't get angry if he opened his mouth.

And then there was Roger to consider. Zack did his best to keep still in his seat. Vampires were preternaturally still, and he knew his imitation would never equal the undead, but he tried.

If Nell wasn't going to interrogate him, Zack could get down to business.

"Roger needs a bigger blood allowance," Zack said.

Nell arched an eyebrow. "Is that so."

Zack slid to the edge of his seat. "I'm going to drop the bullshit. You could gut me anytime you want to. I can't beat you. Roger can't either. We're here as your guests, and he needs more blood."

"He can't afford it," Nell replied.

"You can't afford for him not to get it," Zack said.

Nell folded her hands in her lap. "That's a bold assumption."

"I'm not sure why you're siding with Roger, but you're considering it, or we wouldn't be here. I'm guessing you make plenty of money, so holding out on him isn't about the cash. You're keeping him in check for some reason. Maybe you don't trust him yet."

"A captain of another coven and a hunter walk into my land. A little precaution is in order," Nell said.

"We just established you're too strong for us."

Nell's demeanor grew cooler. "The best assassins hide in plain sight."

Exposing Roger's weakness was against the rules, but if Zack couldn't convince Nell, they would run into more trouble. He pointed at the wound on his neck. "Roger wasn't in control when he did this. I had to use silver to get him off me. Barely fifteen minutes ago, he nearly gave in to his hunger again. For the safety of your territory, he needs more blood."

"I could kill him. That would make me safe."

"I don't think you'd bother testing me if you were considering that," Zack replied.

"Oh?"

"It wouldn't make any sense. You want Roger to succeed."

Nell raised her folded hands so that she could rest her chin on them. "Why would I want that?"

Rumors said Seamus didn't get along with other masters in neighboring territories. While there were technically a few covens separating Seamus's and Nell's domains, the land was a thin corridor. The masters governing them were weaker, younger vampires. With the absorption of one or two, Nell and Seamus would have a border in common. Add in that Seamus's rule sounded like the antithesis of Nell's philosophies, and she'd have every reason to dislike him.

But over the last few years, another rumor had started to surface. Once upon a time, vampires had been solitary creatures. Vampire nests had always existed, but they never lasted very long. The bolder vampires had lived on their own with only one or two sirelings. In the 1500s, they'd started forming courts. Those groups would swell and drop in size.

Over the last century, as human populations boomed, so did vampires. More prey, more predators. Covens continued to grow in size. There was talk that the masters were solidifying structures, unifying into larger and larger domains. Up until the last ten years, that had been dismissed as a conspiracy theory.

Zack sank back against his seat. The ideas were connecting, and the realization numbed him. Because if he was right, then everything was more dangerous than he'd already assumed.

"Seamus wants to be the vampire king of America," Zack said quietly.

He wanted her to laugh at him and tell him he was a stupid human.

Instead, she grinned with delight. "Ah, you are a clever one. Good. Roger will need that."

"He needs blood."

"He seemed in control last night, but you are the one closest to him." Nell lowered her hands. "All right. I will increase his allowance. You will be on your best behavior. If I find that you instigate a single fight, I will throw you out and cancel Roger's loan."

"I can't instigate, but I can defend," Zack said.

"You're catching onto the wordplay, child. That's good." Nell nodded. "Defense is always permissible."

"I, um, have one more request." Zack cleared his throat. "Can I train with you? Roger's teaching me everything I need to know to survive society, but that won't matter if I can't land the dagger when I need to. You're about Seamus's age. Older? Training with you would give me the edge I need."

Nell smiled again, warmth lighting her eyes and broadening her lips. "Thinking ahead. In time, I might train you, but you'll start with Josefina."

"Thank you, Master."

Nell made a dismissive gesture.

Zack stood and bowed half-heartedly.

"You have to work on that before Seamus sees it," Nell said.

I have to work on everything. Zack swallowed his response, nodded once more, and headed back into the house.

CHAPTER 15

The rush was hard to give up, but Roger pulled away from his deep drink. Kit leaned back against the couch they'd found in a private corner upstairs. Their eyes were hooded, lust clouding their focus. Roger closed his eyes. His magic continued to coax Kit's lust. They'd wanted it to ease the pain of the bite. The act was over, so Roger swallowed his power down. His head was clear again, and Kit's would be too. He opened his eyes.

Kit grinned at him lazily. The bite mark on their wrist was already closed. In no time, it would disappear. That was the advantage of shifter healing. Kit noticed him watching the spot and rubbed their thumb across it. "Your handiwork won't stay for long."

"Some believe that a blessing," Roger said. Speaking felt easier. His throat was relaxed. It was like a switch had flipped in his mind. Suddenly, there was brightness where everything had dimmed. Coherent thoughts strung together in long lines.

Which brought regrets. Doubts.

He gave Kit his best smile as he put his arm across the back of the couch. Running off to find Wright would be bad form. Even among the donors, he had a reputation to protect. He held up the orange chit in his left hand.

In a smooth motion, Kit clasped their hand around it and took it from Roger. They scooted closer. "I don't have anything else to do tonight. I could show you around town. Zack, too. I wouldn't mind the three of us getting closer."

"You are lovely, but I'm not considering associations in that way," Roger said.

"You and Zack aren't … associating?" Kit asked.

"That's a private matter."

Kit danced the chit around their fingers in a show of dexterity. "Is he your only pet? Don't you need more?"

"That sounds incredibly like an offer," Roger replied.

"I am offering anything you want, sir."

Roger leaned in. "With the wrong vampire, that is dangerous."

Kit leaned in in return. "That kind of vampire doesn't let their human walk around with silver on them."

Roger held back that he hadn't known Wright had silver on him. He hadn't even thought to double-check Wright for his enchanted dagger. The boy could have snuck it into the donor house. If he used it on anyone, Roger would be to blame. The silver was bad enough.

"He's cautious," Roger said. "I appreciate Nell's domain, but he is new to the life."

"I know." Kit motioned between them. "To drop talking around it, we're not fucking, are we?"

"We're not."

"Then I'm going to see if my usual booty call is interested before this sex buzz wears off." Kit held up the chit. "Thank you."

"Thank you for sharing," Roger replied.

"Keep me in mind. Not right away, but I'd be willing to do it again." Kit stood and headed away from the couch.

Roger took a long moment to center himself. The sounds

of the nearby people were easier to filter through. The second floor was quieter than the first as vampires fed on the willing. Soft moans and the occasional sucking noise were common.

He had almost lost himself to the blood lust. Wright had saved him. Did that mean something? Did Wright care? He could have been rid of Roger without any effort on his part. Instead, he'd helped him.

Never mind. I have more pressing concerns. Like where he is. Roger wiped his lips. A few drops of blood. Nothing too messy. He headed down the stairs.

Quinn Turner was walking out the front door of the house and into the night.

Roger had made only five others into vampires, in part because of what Seamus did to those in his bloodline, but also because each time seemed to end in disaster. Ezra had a rage that was never quelled, James hated him, Phoenix was more an accident than intentional, and Roger had forgotten the name of the first man he turned. His first sireling had been a pirate, and either Seamus and Anton had consumed him like they had others, or the sireling had escaped and spent the last three hundred years out of sight.

But none of them, not even James's hatred, filled Roger with regret like Quinn. Thinking back to that time in his life was like a crack in a bone. Every time he thought himself healed of it, the slightest pressure in the wrong way proved how fragile he was.

Because, other than Seamus, the one man in Roger's long centuries that had taken advantage of him had been Quinn Turner.

A growl rumbled low in Roger's chest, and he rushed down the stairs. He was hardly moving faster than a human. Using his energy like this would burn up the gift Kit had given him if he wasn't careful, but he couldn't lose Quinn. He hurried out the door. It couldn't be a coincidence that he'd lost decades, and his traitorous sireling was close at hand.

His moment of shock had cost him precious time. Quinn was already climbing into a car as Roger emerged from the house. Shouting was not a thing a master vampire did, and Roger didn't trust his voice to stay level. As fiercely as the fire of hunger had burned through him, rage boiled and threatened to melt him.

If he were stronger, he could have raced in front of the car. He could have slammed his hands down on it and forced it to stop. He could have lifted it off the fucking ground. But there was a lack in his body. A weakness that became numbness, making his movements sluggish. It'd been like that since he awoke. He needed more blood. That would require promises. Permissions.

Nell has to see reason. She just has to.

Roger crossed the threshold into the donor house once more. The girl working the reception desk was speaking to another vampire. The hour was late enough that Nell should be somewhere on the premises. And he had to find Wright too. He started going from room to room. The third time he stepped into the hall, a firm hand landed on his shoulder.

Josefina.

Before he could say a word, she nodded at a door down the hall. He opened it, finding a dark landing at the top of a set of downward stairs. Just as he opened his mouth to speak, she kicked him square in the ass and sent him tumbling. Bones cracked on wood, and more broke as he hit smooth cement.

"Josefina—"

She picked him off the floor and slammed him into the wall. A concussion wouldn't have been possible if he was at full strength, but he was so far from it that reality started to slide away. Darkness threatened to envelop him. In his blurry vision, Josefina looked like the mortal girl she'd once been.

She'd been a quiet girl. Kind. She'd only spoken Spanish before she was turned. Roger hadn't known her long as a mortal. A passing on the street. Some other sireling of Seamus's liking her too much. Changing her. Like Roger, she hadn't chosen to become a vampire. Like Ezra, the change had brought out her anger. But where Ezra was a torrent of emotion, Josefina was a diamond sledgehammer.

"You *lied* to me last night," Josefina hissed. She slammed him against the wall again.

Blood was slicking the back of his neck. He cried out, not from the pain but the loss. Bones mended as quickly as they could, and he couldn't make his magic heal him slowly. Couldn't beg it to wait. He wasn't a wizard. He couldn't command what was innate. So his body healed and started to drain itself of what little magic it had. Power was slipping out of his fingers.

Roger put his hands on her shoulders. While he hadn't made many vampires, he'd taught many of them to be what they were. Josefina was one of those. One he'd treasured. One he'd saved by getting her out of the coven, and she was breaking him into pieces. The betrayal stabbed into his heart, twisting an invisible knife.

Then he saw the fear in her eyes. Felt it pooling in her veins. "Josefina ..."

"You want to drag my love into a *war*. You don't have the strength to stand, and you want to bring *them* down?"

Roger gripped her suit jacket tight. His knuckles turned white. Blood dripped from his mouth, but he had a grip. She couldn't slam him again. He pulled her in as tight as he could. Because if she didn't have the leverage, she couldn't hurt him. He'd learned that in moments he longed to forget.

"I have to," Roger gasped.

Bloody tears streaked Josefina's cheeks and dripped off her jaw to speckle her collar. "If Seamus finds out, he will bring ruin to us."

"There are dozens of supernaturals upstairs."

Josefina pushed him up against the wall. "This basement

is soundproof. I *love* her, Roger. I would never endanger her. I would never be so careless."

"Do you have any idea what I saved you from?" Roger snarled. Centuries of placating, of smiling and pretending that nothing hurt, had made him a nest of sharp wires, twisting and cutting. Josefina's fear was real but not as deep as the one he'd buried over and over again. He pushed away from the wall, driving her steps back. He was older. If he gave in to his magic entirely, he could beat her for a moment. But he would succumb to hunger again.

He had to get through to her. Had to make her understand.

"Abuse. Death. I will always be grateful, but—"

"*Oblivion.*" Roger held on to her. The fabric was starting to give. The genial façade he cultivated dropped. His voice was rough, no longer hiding the coarse English sailor's voice he'd had in life. "You had a glimpse of their horrors in the few decades you spent at their side, aye. But you were a bauble to them. I got you out. *I got you out.*

"They devour the energy of others. They feast on it. Laugh about it. Then they parade the bodies out and make an act of killing them as warnings. All for power. So they can continue raping and murdering and plundering. They hold control over the coven so that none can rise. None can leave. You become useful, a toy or food. And they will eat until the world ends unless someone stops them, and I have to. I can't live like that anymore, Josefina. I can't. I won't. And if I can't live in their shadow, they will snuff me out. I want to live. I want to have joy they can't touch. *I have to kill them.*"

Josefina's eyes widened. Her grip slackened. "What do you mean devour?"

"Anton uses his magic to draw the power from the young of Seamus's bloodline and drags it into them. Anyone too unhappy. Anyone unattached. The unloved." Roger's strength began to wane. The momentary push had been too great. But he stayed on his feet and in control of the rising hunger. "You were nearing forty years as a vampire. Anton snickered that you would make a great meal. Introducing you to Nell was all I could do."

Roger's knees buckled. Josefina changed her hold on him to brace him. Wonder filled her voice. "You always seemed happy."

A bitter laugh broke free of him before he could catch himself. "What else can you do when the Devil has his foot on your throat?"

"Roger ..."

"And I find myself here," Roger murmured. He felt hot, and he was sinking to the floor. Josefina stayed with him, easing him down. "Thirty years gone. No idea how. Wakened by a boy who tried to kill me. I did lie. So did he. He is a hunter. But I need him, Josefina. I need him to drive his blade into Seamus's heart because it is one of the few things on this Earth that could kill him. And he's willing. He's smart and beautiful and God above, my dream will put him in danger, but I don't know where else to turn. I need help. I need Nell. I need you. I need him. Please forgive the lies. Have mercy."

"Roger—"

"I don't wish for war. But I have nothing. Nell agreed to get me on my feet. Money. Blood. Enough to barely stand, and I will have to face the Devil." Roger put his head on her shoulder.

Stiffly, Josefina wrapped her arms around him. "I always knew you delivered me out of hell. But I thought you chose to stay. I should have known better. Of course, I'll help. Whatever I can do."

The impact of her promise lulled the screaming fears of his mind into a quiet rest once more. Giving out his trust created a bridge he wasn't sure would last. He didn't want to test its strength, but he had no other choice. He gave himself one minute to relish the feeling that someone might actually care if he suffered or thrived.

Then he lifted his head, cleared his throat, and put on a half-hearted smile. He was more his modern self, not the broken man who was hiding. But the jagged scars of his past were not as healed as he pretended. A few centuries of lying to everyone made it easier to lie to himself.

"Can I get another drink? I think most of the first is coating the back of my head," Roger joked quietly.

Josefina touched the back of his skull and swore under her breath. "You aren't controlling your eyes."

"Are they red again? It's been a problem."

"We'll get you another drink." Josefina helped him to his feet. "No more lies, Roger. Not to me or Nell."

Roger nodded. He'd break that promise if he had to, but he'd keep it as long as he could.

CHAPTER 16

Four days later, Zack dug his heels into the carpet as Roger started to push him out of their room. The clock on the wall said it was barely past seven in the morning. "I got like four hours of sleep."

"You had six and a half."

"For the record, I don't kick you out when I go to sleep," Zack replied. "This is bullshit."

"Behave for three more days, and I'll consider amending our arrangement." Roger picked up Zack's backpack from the floor and shoved it and a folded piece of paper into his hand. Something made the paper feel thick. "Nell's loan came through. I have a list for you to complete. Appointments to make, supplies to purchase. That sort of thing."

"You're giving me *errands*? On top of the research you asked for? I've got lessons with you and training, and you want me to spend all day running around?" Zack demanded.

Roger leaned in close. "It's almost like you have to be an adult and get shit done."

"Hey, I know how to adult just fine. I've been doing it all summer without vampires ordering me around." Zack held up the paper. "How am I supposed to pay for this stuff anyway?"

"You have the card in your hand."

Zack unfolded the paper, and the plastic card fell to the ground. He scooped it up. "This has my name on it."

"How else do you expect to use it?"

"You put me on your account?"

"Of course. That way you can run errands for me like a good boy," Roger said.

Zack narrowed his eyes. It wasn't fair when Roger, who had somehow gotten more serious and therefore ridiculously hotter, used words like that. Something in Zack always melted when he did. The few nights on a bigger blood allowance at the donor house had given Roger more vitality. He was still an undead creature of the night, but now his eyes remained a deep brown with a hint of gold at the pupil. He stood straighter; his movements were effortlessly graceful. And there wasn't a hint of pain in his smile.

Sometimes annoyance or—as was currently true—smugness changed the tug of his lips, but that was hot too.

Not fair. Zack sucked in a deep breath. "If I get all this done and I don't complain through tonight's lesson, I get to sleep in tomorrow."

Roger raised an eyebrow. "And we put your dagger in the room safe."

Putting the dagger out of easy reach would give Roger the upper hand. Zack could break furniture to make a stake, but it wouldn't be easy or quiet. But if Roger was going to kill him, he would have done it. Zack had to give trust to get it.

"Deal," Zack said.

"Deal," Roger agreed.

Then he finished pushing him out of the room.

"I need my shoes," Zack shouted as Roger started to shut the door.

Roger chucked them out the door and then shut it.

Zack sighed. At least he'd get to sleep in the next day. He sat on the floor, put on his shoes, and went downstairs for breakfast. His morning went as the last couple had: food, coffee, research while drinking even more coffee. Instead of having lunch at the sandwich shop on the way to the library before doing more research, Zack started on Roger's errand list. Among requests for more clothes and making appointments at a couple other shops was "books published in the last thirty years." The very bottom of the list also had "anything you think you need."

"Bookstore first," Zack said to himself.

The summer sun was hot, but the inside of the bookshop was pleasantly cool. Zack had browsed through the store on one of his other exiled days, so he skipped past the cookbooks and other craft books. Fiction was broken into several categories, and nonfiction had several sections too. Roger hadn't specified what he wanted to read other than something newer. Zack ran his hand through his hair. There was a lot to consider. What would Roger like to read? Did Zack care?

He wandered into the nonfiction section. If he'd been out of the world for thirty years, he'd want to know everything. As much as he tried, he didn't know all the important events from Roger's missing time. The nineteen nineties had been pretty long ago. Books on that era should be in a history section. Roger had asked about the Cold War. The internet said that ended in 1991, after Roger was asleep. Zack scanned the titles as he went.

Turning a corner, he nearly bumped into Blake. He stepped around her and continued down the row. They were in a reference section about supernaturals.

Zack paused. A shifter should have a pack or a mentor. She shouldn't need the books on supernaturals. *You think I chose this? I didn't,* Roger had said. Not all shifters chose to become supernatural either. He'd spent hours upon hours in the coffee shop. Blake didn't talk to anyone she didn't need to, except for Reed. But Reed seemed capable of getting anyone to open up.

She seemed nervous and lonely, and Zack didn't have anyone to talk to except vampires who bossed him around.

"Hey," Zack said.

Blake tilted her head so her hair was a curtain over the portion of her face closest to him. "Hi."

"What are you looking for?"

"Nothing. Never mind." Blake turned.

Zack dashed in front of her. "Wait. I didn't mean to spook you. I've read pretty much everything on those shelves. I just want to help you find what you want."

Blake folded her arms tight over her chest, but she was holding on to herself rather than inflating with bravado. "What, ah, bit you?"

Out of reflex, Zack put his hand on the healing bite wound. He'd have a scar from it. "Vampire."

"So you know about all this … supernatural stuff," Blake said.

"Yeah."

She let out a soft sigh, and a tension in her shoulders eased. "I spent my summers here, but I always thought it was small-town superstition." She motioned at her face. "Found out the hard way last spring that it's not. And now I have these questions, and I don't want to sound like an idiot."

"Questions about what?"

Blake swung her left foot, then tapped her toes behind her right. "About what I am."

She didn't choose either. Zack nodded and turned to the shelves. There were a lot of good choices. Most were legitimate sources of information, and the couple that weren't at least had good bits. "Here we go. *Richmond's Guide to the American Lycanthrope.* She made the title flashier for sales. She explains werewolves and then uses those definitions to talk about other shifters. There's a section on the different pack structures and social dynamics."

"That sounds exactly like what I was hoping to find." Blake took the book from him. "You're Zack, right?"

"Yeah."

"Thank you, Zack."

"No problem."

They went their separate ways. Zack picked up a couple nonfiction titles before heading into the fiction section. He grabbed a copy of *Gone Girl* because his mom had loved it so much she had made his dad read it. For a moment, he considered picking up the first of a book series he'd read as a kid. The magic in them was completely nonsensical, but there'd been movies based on them. Zack didn't know if the supernatural community talked about them as much as the regular human world did. They probably didn't, and the books had long been tarnished for him. How someone could create a huge magical world while hating and misunderstanding such a vital part of the real world was a complete mystery to him. Millions of other books had been published. He'd find something else.

As he made his way into the paranormal section, he ran into Blake again. She gave him an awkward smile that he did his best to return. They perused the shelves and wound up on the same bookcase together. Blake pulled out *Over My Grave*, the latest book in the *From the Grave* series.

"That finally came out?" Zack leaned in closer, then realized he was invading Blake's personal space and dodged back a step. "Sorry. I've been dying to find out what Pierce's deal is. The author's been super cagey about it on social media, but it's been six books. There has to be some reason he's always pissed off. And clearly he and Michael used to bang."

"You read these?" Blake asked.

"Love them. I've actually been trying to figure out if a vampire is writing these."

Blake's eyes widened. "Oh my God, really? You think a vampire would? Because that would make these more awesome than they already are."

"I can't prove it yet, but yeah. Probably. The lore in them's pretty close to accurate."

"Awesome." Blake scrunched her nose. "Darn, they only have one copy in stock."

"And I can't buy digital. Crap."

"How come?" Blake asked.

"My family doesn't approve," Zack said. "We share digital libraries, and my brother's always snooping through my computer shit. Somehow, he's not smart enough to just check for books in the bottom of my closet, but that would require him to stop looking down his nose for five minutes."

"Screens have been really hard for me to look at since I got …" Blake mimicked a claw motion. "Still getting used to werewolf vision."

"I'd never thought about that before. Must suck."

"I mean, colors are way more fascinating than before. Like, did you know you've got the faintest auburn streaks in your hair? I bet if you spent time out in the sun, they'd get red or blondish."

Zack fussed with his hair. "That used to happen when I was little. I thought it was all boring brown now."

"Definitely not boring."

Did Roger see his hair in interesting colors? Zack bit his bottom lip.

"I know what we could do!" Blake said. "You spend so much time at the coffee shop, I can get it, and you can read it while you're there, and I can read it when I'm off work, and then we can talk about it. We can have our own little book club."

And Zack was finally going to be able to stay in the room during the day if he kept his deal with Roger. *That doesn't mean I have to stay. I can still get coffee. Coffee is life, after all.* "Sounds great. I've never had anyone to talk to about these. Some internet posts, but, ah … the crowd wasn't that interested in them."

"Cool!" Blake was genuinely smiling. "Not cool if people were shitty but cool if you want to share."

"Are you doing anything today? I've got a bunch of errands to run and could use the company. I'm betting you know where I can find everything on this list."

"Sure. It's been a while since I've just been out."

Just like that, his long to-do list didn't seem so long.

CHAPTER 17

"Her name is Blake, and she's from Chicago," Wright was saying from the bathroom.

Roger continued sorting through the shopping bags Wright had unceremoniously dumped onto the bed before heading into the bathroom. He'd been out past sunset. Apparently, Josefina had texted him and rescheduled their training session for earlier in the evening. Wright had come back smelling like a man who had worked up a great deal of sweat.

Even now, the scent came off the clothes he'd piled outside the bathroom door. It was driving Roger to distraction. Trails of sweat would have curved down the hollow of Wright's throat. His pulse would have raced. Groaning and panting, he must have gotten that determined look in his eyes at least once. Roger could imagine it.

If he stepped to the right more, he could see through the sliver of open door and perhaps catch a glimpse of naked, wet —although showered—Wright. The soft sounds of shaving promised that he wasn't fully dressed.

But that would be leering. Inappropriate. Roger hung up another dress shirt instead. What Wright had bought him would be functional, but he'd have to see a tailor. Alterations would flatter him, and he needed custom suits as well before he rejoined vampire society.

"She's a werewolf," Wright said as he emerged from the bathroom. He had on a pair of jean shorts. His T-shirt was in his hand.

"You won't be wearing that tonight," Roger said.

Wright froze. "We agreed, I'm not actually fulfilling duties."

"Private duties. Which you won't be." Roger pointed to a pair of slacks and a blue dress shirt he'd laid out on the bed. In addition to purchasing more clothes for him, he'd told Wright to pick up a better wardrobe for himself. "Tonight we're going to see how well you can follow. No interrupting, no speaking—"

"No murdering," Wright interjected.

Roger glared at him. "What did I just say?"

Wright rolled his eyes and dropped his T-shirt onto the bed. "Fine. Fine."

Roger made himself look away as Wright undid his shorts and dropped them to the floor. In a few moments he was ready, and the two of them left the inn. Although Roger hated the need, they made a quick stop at the donor house, and he took his blood allowance from willing donors.

Then they headed for the house Roger had slept in for thirty years.

The living room light was on, so they weren't going to disturb the entire household's sleep. As they approached the door, Roger put his hand on Wright's shoulder. "Remember, you're mine. You observe. I don't believe this person is responsible for putting me to sleep, but this Becks had something to do with how I was kept that way. Your job is to watch our backs. Can I trust you?"

The chip Wright had had on his shoulder since they'd left the inn crumbled. He straightened his shoulders and nodded once.

Roger shot him a quick smile. "Good boy."

By the time he turned back to the door, his expression was stoic once more. He rang the doorbell and waited.

The girl who opened the door was dressed in layers of black. Her hair was inky black, and thick eyeliner and eyeshadow continued the trend. Her eyes, though, were a shade of aqua that weren't possible without supernatural heritage. A faint hint of crisp juniper mingled with human tang.

"Great. It's the vampire. Mom!" The girl called out as she walked over to the front staircase. She shouted up it. "Mom! It's the vampire!"

"I'm coming!" a voice from upstairs responded.

The girl glared over her shoulder at Roger and Wright. "I guess you can wait in the living room."

"Thank you," Roger said smoothly. He stepped into the house. At some point, he must have been invited in—most likely when his coffin first entered—because he crossed over the threshold without issue. Wright followed behind him.

While Roger took a seat on the couch, Wright moved to the far corner of the room, nearer to the kitchen entrance. They were on opposite sides of the room from each other, and Wright was close to a plethora of items he could use as makeshift weapons. He'd made a decent choice. Roger would have to congratulate him when they were alone.

A few minutes later, a woman in a purple robe entered the room. Her short hair was in springy curls, and she wrung her hands as she stepped into the room. The girl walked in behind her and plopped into an armchair. She crossed her arms over her chest, tossed her leg over the arm of the chair, and glared at everyone in the room equally.

"Sapphire, maybe you should go upstairs," the woman said.

"No," the girl replied. "I have a feeling I'm about to get some answers."

"You know who I am?" Roger asked.

There were social techniques vampires cultivated over their immortal lives. Young vampires tried too hard to emulate the mannerisms of older ones, but Roger had practiced his habits. Flirting was generally more pleasant. People liked to be flirted with. This woman had kept his coffin in her basement for decades. He wasn't in her home to make friends but to find out the truth. He pulled on a mask he seldom used: the blank, overwhelmingly confident vampire. The lack of emotion could be intimidating. Roger would rely on that.

The woman shot her gaze to her daughter, then back to Roger, and then to the floor. She continued wringing her hands. "I learned your name the other night. I-I didn't know before that. I swear I didn't."

"You expect me to believe you?" Roger said coldly.

With a tiny moan, the woman squeezed her eyes shut.

The girl, Sapphire, softened, and she shifted her position so both her feet were on the floor. She straightened her shoulders, and though she still had the appearance of a teenager, her demeanor changed to one far more serious. Not like an immortal, though. She was older than she looked but not in the way a pureblood fey would be.

"She made the deal to have me," Sapphire said.

The woman's eyes flew open. "You knew?"

"Mom, I'm almost thirty, and I look like I'm fifteen. I figured out the pieces a long time ago. I just don't know how everything fits together." Sapphire motioned at herself. "Clearly, I'm not all human. And I don't believe for a second that Uncle Gavin is my uncle."

The woman sat in a chair closer to her daughter. "Oh, but he's not your father either, dear. I think he is your uncle. Or a cousin. But not your father."

"Then who *is* my father?" Sapphire demanded.

"I don't know," the woman replied.

"Don't you?" Roger said softly.

The woman spun her attention between Roger and Sapphire before settling on Roger. She flinched as she met his gaze. "I don't know his name. Sapphire is right. I … I made a deal. My husband and I were trying to have a child, and it wasn't working. Fertility treatments are expensive, and he didn't think we should bother with them. I wanted a child so badly."

Roger rested his hands on the arms of the chair. "I believe I've heard you called Rebecca or Becks. Which do you prefer?"

"Rebecca from you if you don't mind," the woman said. She dropped her gaze to her lap. "Stupid, I know. I basically held you prisoner for decades, and I didn't know it."

"Rebecca," Roger said, letting his voice purr with her name.

She looked up, fear plain in her eyes.

"I don't think you're the one I am truly angry with, but I have to know more. Tell me the story of how I came to be here, and, assuming you played no malicious part, I will leave without claiming any offense from you."

Rebecca bit her lip and squeezed her hands.

Wright stepped closer to her and put his hand on her shoulder. He leaned in to speak quietly to her. "Roger will be true to his word."

"All right," Rebecca sighed. She nodded once. "I grew up in Taliville. It's not a secret here that there are vampires and faeries and demons. I never had any talent for spells. So I went to college, met my husband—ex-husband—and tried living my life. But I wanted a child, and we weren't conceiving. I … I grew desperate. On a trip to visit my mother, I spent more time searching the woods than with her. I was afraid of what a demon might want, so I found a fey. An Unseelie. He was so handsome. Sapphire looks a little like him. Especially since she's taken to goth makeup." Rebecca managed a faint smile. "The Unseelie man offered to help me have a child if I did him a favor. I didn't care what the favor would be so long as I had a child of my blood that I could keep. I knew enough about faeries to be specific in what I wanted. And being with him was like a dream. I wasn't sure it'd actually happened until I was pregnant with Sapphire. And even then, I thought maybe my husband and I had gotten lucky.

"Then the Unseelie man and your coffin showed up on my doorstep. I was six months pregnant. He said I had to hide the coffin and never open it. If I went back on the deal, I would lose the child. But he didn't need to threaten me like that. By that time, my marriage was showing more and more cracks. I'd thought a child could fix it, but that wasn't meant to be. And honestly, Sapphire, honey, learning that your father was the Unseelie man and not the man I married was a relief. My marriage was over, and moving back home with a baby and coffin in tow, well, that wasn't so strange for Taliville." Rebecca met Roger's gaze. "I didn't tell anyone about the coffin, I mean. Other than Nell, who I thought had the right to know. And my mother. Because when I first came back, we moved into her house. I eventually bought this house and moved you in with me. Sapphire discovered your coffin when she was little, but none of us opened it. That was the deal struck."

"Your mother, Nell, and your child. That's all you told about my coffin?" Roger asked.

"Yes. I swear it. I had it wrapped up in a tarp so when the movers handled it, they just saw a large package. I told them it was a boat. I'm not sure anyone believed me, but that's what I said."

"Has anyone ever come looking for me? The Unseelie man, perhaps?"

"No," Rebecca said firmly.

"That's not exactly true," Sapphire said. She cleared her throat. "I, uh, hang out at the donor house a lot."

"Sapphire!" Rebecca said.

Sapphire shrugged. "It's a safe place to hang out. I don't take any chits. But there was a guy poking around, asking about coffins. He was being sketchy about it too. Like he was making sure no vampire would hear him, and he spoke mostly to humans. I avoided him because something seemed off."

"Can you describe him?" Roger asked.

"Blond white guy. Narrow nose. Under six feet tall. Huge ego problem. You could tell he wanted people to think he was cool, but he had no confidence about it."

Quinn. Roger clenched his jaw and fought to keep his hands still on the armrests. Not reacting was the better path. If he showed he was upset, then that was information given away. "He asked about my coffin?"

"At first he was asking about Unseelies. Their court doesn't have strong ties in Taliville, so that was a little weird to me," Sapphire said. "After a couple nights, he started asking if anyone had seen a coffin hidden away in their house. He was slyer about it than that, but since I knew what he was after, it was pretty obvious to me. I didn't say anything."

"I appreciate that," Roger said. "Rebecca, is there anything you can tell me about the Unseelie man? Or this Uncle Gavin?"

"Gavin started checking up on Sapphire when it was clear she wasn't aging as fast as a human ought to," Rebecca said. "I think he's a friend of Dr. Micah's. I was worried that she wasn't growing like she should and confided in the doctor. Not too long after, Gavin made his first appearance. Said he could help fill in blanks for her as she grew."

"And the man?" Roger asked.

"He was breathtaking," Rebecca said with a sigh. "Long dark-blue hair, alabaster skin that shimmered like starlight, eyes deep as midnight, and a smile that made me think of shadows and a flickering fire. He was everything I'd ever dreamed of."

"That's all?" Roger said.

"Other than, like I said, Sapphire looks a little like him."

Roger took in Sapphire's sharp features again. She looked more like her mother than Rebecca had acknowledged. Nothing about Sapphire surfaced a memory for him.

"Thank you, ladies, for your time tonight and for guarding my coffin as well as you did," Roger said.

Wright left the house with him.

"It might be nothing, but this guy, Quinn, tried to take a bite of me while you were with Kit the other night," Wright said. "Nell put him in his place."

"It certainly doesn't ease my suspicions."

"Where do we go next? Dr. Micah's to find out more about Gavin?"

"No. Never approach a fey with questions and no gifts. They'll see it as a challenge to wrangle anything they want out of you. For now, we keep on behaving like nothing's changed for us. I'll figure out our next step and tell you when it's time," Roger said.

"Sure," Wright said.

The tone of Wright's voice was harsh, but Roger echoed his frustration. Rebecca had provided answers to a few questions, and more propagated in their wake. Why would an Unseelie put him to sleep? Had he angered one? Why put him in a coma instead of trapping him in the fey realm? Or killing him? Was Sapphire's father an enemy or a friend?

Either way, I have to watch my back from yet another angle. Roger slid his hands into his pockets and cleared his throat. He wouldn't linger on the anxiety. Too much was riding on Wright's education and he needed to continue filling the gaps. He began to walk back toward the hotel. "All right, boy, tell me what you're supposed to do when …"

CHAPTER 18

Technically, Zack was hogging three seats at the counter, but Blake hadn't told him to make room for other people. Hardly anyone hung out in the coffee shop. A workout studio had to be somewhere on Main Street because a stream of people came in midmorning every day dressed in spandex or loose clothes. Zack was in his usual seat at the counter by that time.

During the week and a half that he'd been in Taliville, Zack had filled an entire notebook with research. While Roger no longer kicked him out at dawn, he got out of the room before noon most mornings. Roger wanted updates on a dozen names. Though the internet was vast, vampires knew how to hide. In some cases, like with "Cee," Zack didn't have a real first name or a last name. How Roger had maintained someone's livelihood without knowing their name was a mystery, but it had been the eighties. Maybe there had been some way to do it writing checks that wasn't really plausible in the digital age. Zack wasn't sure. He only knew the theory of how to write one out.

Other names on Roger's list were too easy to find. Ezra Gladwell had four separate social media aliases. Since that was the vampire who had helped Seamus and Anton murder

Mary Gladwell's family and had begun Zack's maternal line of vampire-hunting legacy, he already knew a fair amount about Ezra. For the last twenty years, Ezra had lived in England. Cal had marked on his calendar when he was sure Ezra would move back across the ocean. Zack had a bet on the HIN.

But since he was trying to locate Ezra for Roger—which led to questions Zack didn't dare ask yet—he took a closer look at Ezra's social media profiles. Two of the accounts had gone dormant. No posts over the last three months. One continued to post pictures, but Zack hunted for landmarks, signs of weather, and times of year. The tone of the posts implied the pics had been taken that day, but they weren't matching up. Ezra was bluffing his location.

Zack picked up his coffee cup and found it woefully empty. "Uh, Blake?"

"We're going to have to invent a limit because of you," Blake said jokingly. She refilled his cup.

"Eh, I'm helping you keep it fresh for everyone else."

"Speaking of—looks like the yoga class is over. EWE is coming in."

Zack swiveled his attention to the door. A group of four was coming in. Behind them, a couple more people were trailing in with Reed at the rear. Zack closed up his research, shoved it into his bag, and then joined Blake on the other side of the counter. Since their run-in at the bookstore, he'd started helping during rushes if he was around. The exchange was coffee and baked goods, which was fine with him. Roger claimed the credit card had a fifty-thousand-dollar limit—and it was only one account he'd managed to open with Nell's loan. Blake promised she'd get her aunt to throw him an actual paycheck if he wound up helping a lot, but for now the exchange was enough.

After washing his hands, he took over grabbing baked

goods and running the register. Blake focused on making the drinks.

Among the small crowd was an unfairly attractive man who wore biker shorts and a tank top. The tight shorts showcased just how big his dick was. Blake had dubbed him EWE —exceptionally well endowed. Zack had to do his best not to stare, especially since EWE had fang marks on his inner thigh.

How shit, that's somewhere vampires actually bite? Zack swallowed hard, then stumbled over his words with the person he was helping.

But the next customer was EWE. A blush crept up Zack's neck. Once started, heat flared through him. EWE had a chiseled jaw and a bright smile, and as he turned his attention on Zack, he gave him a long once-over. When he dragged his gaze up, his smile became sultry. He leaned on the counter, hands clasping the edge so his arms became taut. His muscular pecs threatened to bulge out of his loose tank top.

"Hey there," EWE said.

Speaking was a thing he was supposed to do, right? Zack opened his mouth, forgot what he was supposed to say, and closed his mouth again. Getting naked and sweaty with EWE was about the only thing on his mind, except for the thought that Roger could bite him in the same place EWE had been bitten. Did Roger have a big dick? Did it matter? Roger had to know what he was doing. *A guy who's had multiple sex dungeons should.*

"Who did that?" EWE motioned at his own unmarred neck.

Zack's brain continued to short-circuit, but one part came screaming back online. He cleared his throat. "A vampire."

"Obviously," EWE purred. "Which one?"

"Roger, my master." Zack fought the urge to clench his jaw. Roger had been explicit in his lessons about vampire society. If someone asked, and they were in the know about the supernatural, Zack had to claim Roger was his master and not grimace about it.

"Master? Where's your collar?"

"I'm earning it."

"By working in the coffee shop?"

"This is helping out a friend," Zack replied. "Were you going to order anything?"

"Yeah, yeah." EWE looked over the menu. "Give me an extra-large Long Night. Oat milk instead of creamer."

"Got it."

As they were finishing out the transaction, EWE took a napkin and wrote out a number. "If you want help proving to your master that you're worthy, I'm willing."

"Help how?"

"You are new to this, aren't you?" EWE grinned more and leaned in. He lowered his voice to a hushed whisper. "I find that vampires like seeing their pets come. Sometimes you need an extra body to put on a good show."

He's offering to fuck me and have Roger watch. Zack could feel sweat beginning to bead along his temple. It wasn't the worst idea, but it was awful. EWE probably pictured some amazing home-brew porno. Zack wasn't that sexy. He made weird faces and weirder sounds, and Roger wouldn't think he was worth watching. Invasive thoughts—sounding more and more like Cal—jeered at him.

"One Long Night," Blake said as she slid past Zack to deliver the drink. She nudged him.

Right. Zack needed to stay in the present. Cal had been wrong about a lot of things. And the one time Cal had overheard him masturbating had been a weird time anyway. And years ago. And before he'd ever had sex. And …

Blake put her hand on Zack's shoulder. "I think I've got it from here if you want to sit down."

"Okay." Zack went back to his seat at the counter. Instead

of pulling out his research, he folded his arms on top of the counter and leaned on them. He was caught up in his different imaginings of the future. In some of them, Roger was laughing at him. But in a lot of them, he wasn't.

Reed took a seat beside Zack. "Are you all right?"

Zack opened his mouth but remembered that too many people in Taliville were supernatural. Admitting weakness in a crowd was a bad idea. He glanced around the coffee shop. Somehow, it'd cleared out, so it was only Blake, Reed, and him. That usually happened after the yoga rush, but hadn't there been more people? Or had he been that out of it?

The last thing he wanted was a stranger worrying about him. Zack faked a smile and tugged open his backpack. "I'm fine."

Reed rotated so he was facing Zack. "I've seen more than a few folks struggle in their new life among the supernatural. I can spot a liar. What's bothering you?"

"Nothing."

Slowly, Reed reached forward and closed Zack's backpack. Zack still had his hand in the bag. Reed said, "Look me in the eye and say that."

Lying was something he could do. He'd been doing it for years. So he sucked in a breath, blanked out his expression as best he could, and met Reed's gaze. "Don't worry about me."

Reed raised an eyebrow. "That's a far better imitation. If I hadn't seen you glazed over and pale, I might even believe it."

"I don't know what you expect me to say, okay? I got distracted."

"You were panicking. I know how to spot that too. Is Roger forcing you to do something you don't like?"

"What? No. This isn't—it's not about Roger. Not really." Zack slid his backpack to the floor. Blake was listening, but she was a friend. If she was a shitty friend, better he learned that sooner rather than later. "Do vampires like threesomes? Is public sex a requirement to be a pet?"

"Have you talked about this with Roger?"

"Sort of."

"What did he say?" Reed asked.

Zack ran his thumb around the bottom of his coffee cup. "He said he'd never do something a partner wouldn't enjoy."

"He said enjoy? Not want?"

"From the way Roger is, in order to enjoy it, you'd have to want it," Zack said.

"Then you don't have to worry about this pressure from him," Reed said. "That's good."

"Okay, but. Seriously, do vampires have orgies all the time? Is getting bit that much of a turn on? You're head pet to two vampires. Is it about the sex?"

"Not for me." Reed took his coffee when Blake offered it. "Thanks. I used to get the feeding and lust conflated. Nell and Josefina have no interest in sleeping with men, but they like to watch. When I was your age, I thought that was the only way to make a good impression. That wasn't what helped me become head pet, though."

"What did?" Zack asked.

"Becoming more myself. My confidence went a long way. There is a power in freely giving blood to a vampire. Emotional, not magical." Reed poured another sugar into his coffee. "When they use their power on you, it can be over-whelming. But the lust comes out of them as much as out of you. Feeling wanted that badly, knowing you're giving them life, seeing what they can do with the power you give them ... it's a rush. I realized how much I enjoyed that sensation, stopped acting like someone I wasn't, and a relationship with Nell and Josefina grew."

"You're dating?" Blake said.

"Dating's a very human term for it. We're committed. I've discovered along the way that while I like feeling horny, I'm not fond of sex. I get all the cuddles I want. They like having me warm up the bed. It's good."

"Sounds nice," Zack murmured.

"It works for us. You'll find what works for you and Roger." Reed picked up his coffee cup. "If you've got a moment, could you walk with me?"

"Uh, sure." Zack zipped his backpack shut. "I'll see you later, Blake."

"Bye."

Zack and Reed headed out into the bright noon sun. Reed winced and stepped into the shadows of the storefronts as they walked along the street. "I can't wait for summer to be over. Winter's so much better."

"I guess," Zack said. "Did you want to talk about the weather?"

"No." Reed tugged down his shades and sipped his coffee. "Do you know how old Roger is?"

"More than three hundred years."

"And in your training, have you covered how much blood a vampire that age needs?" Reed asked.

"Is Roger not getting enough? Because Nell said—"

Reed smiled. "I'm glad you're worried about that. I guess my concerns about whether you're using him and don't give a shit are unfounded." He sighed. "I owe Josefina money. Damn it."

Zack frowned. "But about the blood—"

"He's fine for now." Reed came to a stop at the end of the block. There was some foot traffic, but people seemed to be minding their own business. "Eventually, you'll go to Chicago. A vampire of Roger's age and status should have more than one pet."

"How many should he have?" Zack asked.

"Besides me, Nell has five and Josefina has three. Seamus has been known to keep as many as fifteen."

Zack's eyes widened. "What?"

"Vampires use their pets to show off their status. Those who can't keep one or can't give them a lavish lifestyle are looked upon as poor. The higher up the hierarchy, the greater the expectation of wealth. It's why pet status matters. There are social climbers who will jump at a chance to make a pet look bad so they can take their place." Reed glanced both ways along the street.

Zack did as well and crossed with him. "Wait, that guy earlier who offered to help me … he wasn't really interested?"

"Carver bangs every pretty person he can, and you qualify for that," Reed said. "But he's also been kicked to the curb by his latest master. He's not vicious. I doubt he'd embarrass you on purpose, but his motives aren't altruistic. He'd help you out if it helped him out."

"Everyone's playing a game," Zack said.

"Even the humans."

"Thanks." Zack frowned more. "But what's your game? Why are you telling me this?"

"Because you're in a position of responsibility. I'd like to hear that Roger builds the kind of coven Nell has, but it'll take more than him. He'll need you."

But it's just supposed to be an assassination, and then I'm out. A year, tops. Zack scratched his elbow while his mind spun. The threat had always been vampires. He hadn't thought he'd have to watch his back from other mortals. He should have realized that. The vampire world was more complex than he'd known. Had he bitten off more than he could chew? *I can make sure whoever becomes Roger's head pet is a good person.*

That was the right plan, but Zack instantly hated it. He didn't want to think about anyone else working closely with Roger, looking out for him if his hunger got out of control. Besides, although he trusted Roger, wouldn't it be better if a hunter was close to him? To make sure he didn't become the monster that Seamus was?

Mom would say I'm making excuses. Maybe I am.

"Thanks again," Zack said.

Reed nodded and continued on his way down the street.

Unfortunately, the library was in the other direction. Zack quickly checked the street and started back. By the time he'd reached the end of the next block, he was deep in thought. He glanced around for safety's sake but barely slowed his steps before crossing. The path was familiar. None of the cars were anywhere close to the danger zone.

Until suddenly, one was. Zack caught a motion from the corner of his eye and heard the acceleration of a car far too close. Relying on instinct, he dove forward and continued into a roll like he had in practice since he was a kid. He made it to the other side of the street, scrapes on his skin already smarting.

A truck with heavily tinted windows barreled up the street. It careened around a corner and out of sight.

The street had been clear before he crossed. *Hadn't it?* Zack doubted his own memory. Had he been so used to the streets he hadn't taken enough care? Slowly, he stood and took stock of his injuries. Nothing major, only a few superficial cuts and bruises. His training had saved his life.

Hunter training. Like Cal had. Because Cal was a hunter, and *he* was the one who was supposed to have answered the email. Someone had sent that email, and someone had shot at Zack and Roger when they left Rebecca's house. After a quiet week and a half, Zack had assumed they'd been after Roger and left town after failing.

But someone had just tried to run *him* down in the street. And Quinn had tried to get him alone. Vampires usually slept through the day, but they could stay awake if they wanted. Quinn must have been the one who tried to hit him with the car. But why?

Zack needed his knife, which was in the safe at the inn.

And he needed more information. Roger had stiffened when Sapphire mentioned Quinn's name. While it'd been a subtle reaction, Zack had caught it. Something about Quinn bothered him.

It's time to put our little alliance to the test and hunt a vampire.

CHAPTER 19

Devil's Cove, Island in the Caribbean, 1682

On Roger's first voyage, the endless expanse of blue waters captivated him. The most water he'd ever seen before that was the thread of a river outside his village. Sailing was a curse that became a blessing. He grew used to the hard work and found a peace in the rhythm. Lapping waves and the creak of wooden boards were as musical as the shanties. When life's monotonous constants threatened to drive him mad, he found new ways to make his lover, Dmitri, moan in dark corners of the ship. Dmitri was his latest lover on his most recent ship, but there was a companionship between them he hadn't found elsewhere.

Though he loved his newest home, reaching land remained a joy. The sandy beaches of the island were different than the muddy fields of his birthplace. After making his way off the dock, he looped his arm around Dmitri and tugged him down the shore. "Come on, let's feel it."

"You feel it every place we go," Dmitri said, accent

making his voice thick. Months together had given Roger practice in understanding him. He'd picked up some of Dmitri's tongue, though no one else bothered. Russian wasn't common, so they had a code all their own. Roger liked that.

"A man's allowed his joys." Roger pulled him along until they found a place on the beach for themselves. It wasn't far, and it wasn't much—they had no privacy since the docks were well within sight. He went to his knees and dug his hands into the sand. He had to work at it. The sand was packed from the tide. "Don't just stand there."

"You're a fool." But Dmitri joined in. He squished a few mounds of sand between his fingers and sighed. "I miss snow."

"I don't." Roger sat on his ass and took in the sea. Looking out at the water was strange after being on the ship for weeks. Not feeling the waves as they moved made him long for the gentle rocking.

There hadn't been much gentleness the last few nights. A storm had roughed up the ship. They'd limped into port, lucky to find one close to where they were. It wasn't on any of the maps, but the navigator knew of it and cautioned them to stay on the ship.

Caution would have kept Roger at home in a house full of loud siblings and louder parents. Caution would have kept him chained to a life he hated. Thus, Roger sank caution to the depths as frequently as he could.

Besides, they were on land! There was drinking and carousing to be done. A solid bed—or floor or wall—to use with his lover. He drank deep of the salty air and relished the shade of a passing cloud.

Dmitri sat beside him, shoulder against him. "I don't like this place."

Roger intertwined his hand in Dmitri's. "We've been here but an hour."

"The name is bad."

"A few trying to sound tough, that's all." Roger nudged Dmitri. "I'll keep you safe from the riffraff."

"You *are* riffraff."

"Aye, so I'll be able to spot it from a distance."

Dmitri snorted and leaned his head on Roger's shoulder. Roger chuckled and squeezed his hand.

Neither knew how broken Roger's promise would become.

~

Taliville, 2021

Blood. Presence. Open air. Danger. Gripping. A pulse under his fingers. A breath brushing down his arm. The tang of fear on his tongue. A slam against his jaw. Another. He caught the wrist attached to the fist hitting him. Knee in his groin. Light. Too much light. He turned his head away.

Wright's ragged breathing on his cheek. *Wright.*

Roger released his grip and stumbled backward. He hit the edge of the bed and sat.

Wright stayed against the wall. Fury burned in his steel-gray eyes, and he held a hand loosely at the base of his throat. Small cuts and bruises were on his arms, his cheek, and his legs.

"What the fuck was that?" Wright rasped.

The primal fear screaming inside Roger wasn't easy to quell. He slid his hand through his hair. His touch was solid. Real. He was in Taliville. With Wright. Nothing was wrong. Old means of soothing his nerves came back to him. He began counting backward in Russian in his mind.

"Roger," Wright snarled.

The anger in Wright wasn't like Seamus's. Wasn't like Anton's. It came from a place of fear. Roger could taste it on the air between them.

"I need a moment," Roger whispered.

He expected more outrage, but Wright frowned and scrutinized him. The stink of his fear started to fade. Wright slid along the wall, stepping from shadow into sunlight. He pulled the balcony curtain open wider, and Roger said nothing. Because Wright deserved to better protect himself. His neck was red from where Roger had grabbed him.

But Roger had no blood under his fingernails, and the scratches on Wright's skin weren't consistent with a human hand. The blood was old enough to have stopped seeping. A couple of the cuts had reopened, and tiny drops of blood formed along them. Those wounds were from something—or someone—else.

"What happened to you?" Roger asked.

"You attacked me." Wright clenched his fists at his sides.

"Other than me. Where did you get those scrapes?"

"Since you tried to kill me, I'm getting answers first. What. The. Fuck."

He's angry. A tremble worked up Roger's arms and into his hands. He smoothed his hands over his sleep pants. The feel of cotton under his fingertips gave him another point of focus. *He's scared. He's angry and scared, and he should be. I nearly killed him.*

How could he explain his body's reaction when the man before him was little more than a boy? One who had lived a sheltered life?

How can I expect him to trust me if I don't extend trust to him?

His hands continued to tremble. He folded them together and stared at the floor at Wright's feet.

"Roger?" Wright asked, a note of trepidation in his voice.

"Asking you to stay out of the room wasn't only about my

safety." Roger felt hollow, like someone else was speaking through him. *The haunted, broken man I ignore.* "From time to time, I have attacked those who try to wake me. It happens in times of great stress. When I'm terrified. I was afraid that with everything going on, I might lash out at you."

"Why didn't you tell me?" Wright asked.

Roger glanced up with a crestfallen smile. "Because I didn't want you to look at me like I was a sad monster made of trauma. I've hidden it away for centuries. Buried things deep enough that I have likely forgotten plenty of it. But the subconscious is tricky. Sometimes it remembers on its own. I have never consciously attacked someone I care for. Someone I consider an ally. But in that space between asleep and waking? It happens on occasion.

"I am sorry. I am so deeply, truly sorry. I should have told you that it was a risk to you."

Slowly, Wright unclenched his fists. He released a long breath, and the tension in his shoulders eased. "Okay. If I ever have to wake you up in the middle of the day, I'll use a giant stick from across the room."

"Let's hope you don't need to." Roger relaxed. "Why did you this time?"

"Because someone tried to run me over in the street."

"What?" Roger stood. Instinct wanted to check Wright over for serious injuries, but he was still standing in the sunlight. "Are you all right? Anything broken?"

"Naw. Banged up but okay." Wright went over to sit on the couch, which was at the edge of the sunbeams coming through the open curtains. "Hunter reflexes. Saw something out of the corner of my eye and dove hard and fast. I assume it was Quinn. Who is he?"

Everyone else in Roger's life knew the story. Ezra and Dmitri had been close enough to witness the repercussions firsthand. Roger had never dared to put words to the betrayal before. Not to a stranger. He folded his arms over his chest and let his expression go blank. "A vampire of the GLC."

Wright narrowed his eyes. "Give me the full answer."

"I don't think there's anything else you need to know."

"I need to know why he wants me dead."

"I doubt that has anything to do with my history with him."

"I knew you had a personal connection." Wright pointed at Roger. "You've got that too-bland, bordering-on-brooding-master look. That means you're hiding something. You got the same look when Sapphire mentioned him."

"My past has nothing to do with you."

"Considering we don't know why he wants me dead, I'm not ruling it out. I need more information, Roger. Before the lack of it kills me."

Roger paced away from Wright. The dark corner of the room was inviting. He could hide in it and wait out the day. But he couldn't keep Wright's interrogative spotlight away so easily. Worse, Wright had a decent point. Until they knew Quinn's motive, any knowledge was valuable.

He hasn't run. He hasn't held on to his anger at my mistake. Though Wright had judged him for being a vampire, that had been ignorant intolerance. Over the last week and a half, Wright had shed more and more of his family's ingrained prejudices. He was trying.

Roger leaned against the wall. "I learned early on what Seamus was doing to the vampires in his sire line. It terrified and disgusted me. By the early 1800s, I had only made two others into vampires. Making a vampire takes power from the sire, so I behaved as if I was weaker than I actually was. I made that my excuse not to turn others more frequently. Seamus pressured me, but I told him that I could either create another weakling for him or fight by his side against his enemies. He had a lot of enemies at the time.

"But Seamus has a way of getting what he wants. He conspired with Quinn Turner.

"When he was mortal, Quinn worked at a donor house. I took him on as a personal pet. He was handsome. Charming. He craved life and living like I did. I thought we'd fallen in love. His tuberculous grew worse, and he begged me to change him. He was my everything at the time."

"I'm sensing a giant 'and then everything turned to shit,'" Wright said.

"It did. While I was waiting for Quinn to rise, Seamus joined me at his grave. He boasted how much he'd paid Quinn to be my lover. He'd taught Quinn tricks on how to seduce me. The whole thing had been a setup. My lover's affections were faked. I confronted Quinn when I could. He admitted that Seamus had told me the truth. If I hadn't turned him, Seamus would have. His immortality was guaranteed before we ever met."

Roger tilted his head back. Memories seeped forward. Seamus's laugh. Quinn's pleas. Roger sighed. "I was hurt. I didn't care about what happened to him, but I didn't want Seamus to gain more power. So I've fostered a grudge for the last two hundred years. It's been easy to do. It's kept him alive and kept Seamus from one more source of power."

"How does you being pissed at someone keep them alive?" Wright asked.

"Seamus loves power. Favoring Quinn from time to time forces me to deal with the wound of his betrayal all over again. Snubbing him drives him to commit horrific acts in an attempt to grovel his way back into Seamus's good graces." Roger pushed away from the wall and finally brought his gaze down to rest on Wright. "Had I forgiven Quinn and loved him, then his death would have hurt me. Sometimes the best thing for a pawn is to remain a pawn."

A long silence stretched out between them. Wright appeared lost in thought. Watching him work through the information took away the sting of having spoken the story. Roger waited.

"You're right. None of that explains why he's trying to kill me. I'd get it if he was after you. But if he is the one who shot at us outside the house, then he had to be the one to send the email. If he did that, he knows what I am and that we're not that connected," Wright said.

"An email is the new version of a letter, correct?" Roger asked.

Wright gave him an exasperated roll of the eyes. "*Yes.*"

"I only wanted the clarification because it leads to my next question." Roger walked over to the edge of the light. "A letter has to have an address. How did he know yours?"

Wright scratched the back of his head. He could be a magnificent liar, but other times he telegraphed his anxiety. "It's not hard to find the address he used. It came into the family account. We have it posted in a couple locations so people can send us tips."

"What are you hiding?" Roger said.

"Me? Nothing," Wright replied, a fake innocence driving his voice higher.

Roger steadied his glare, ready for another staring contest. But Wright continued his *Who me?* act.

"We're trying to discern Quinn's motives. I showed you my hand. You need to show me yours."

Wright held up his right hand. "Here it is."

"You read, and you're smart. You know that I meant to stop bullshitting me."

With a huge sigh that deflated him, Wright said, "The email was meant for Cal."

Cal the Butcher. Roger wiped a hand down his face. If he had been the one in the basement, Roger would have been dead. Only … "That doesn't make sense. If Quinn wants me dead, why would he be going after Cal and now you?"

"He may have been rolling the dice about you. Cal is the

professional, but I'm better at magic. I know a few dispelling charms, and I used one on your coffin," Wright said. "Our daggers have an enchantment that lets them cut through wards, but it's more like it releases the spell in one burst. My method caused it to shake the coffin, dispersing the impact. Knowing Cal, he would have used his blade. While he would have been prepared for the blowback, he wouldn't have been up on your coffin either. You might have been able to grab him." Wright put his arms over his stomach. "I'm going to stop following that line of what-ifs because I really don't want to think about either of you dead on the ground."

"We don't need to extrapolate further," Roger said. "I wouldn't be surprised if Quinn simply didn't care if I survived or not. Either outcome would have suited him. He was waiting in ambush in case Cal was the one who made it out from the basement."

"And he used the email to lure him because Cal's constantly moving around. It was his way to make sure he knew where Cal would be." Wright bit his bottom lip. After a long moment, he sucked in a loud breath. "But I'm not Cal. He has to know that by now."

"I'm afraid we won't know the true cause until we talk to him."

"We've got a couple of hours until dark. When it hits, I'll take my dagger, and you grab that fancy sword you got for the party and—"

Roger held up a hand. "We're not going after him tonight."

Wright's eyes went wide. Then his face turned red, and he stood up with fists at his side. "The bastard tried to kill me!"

"I am a guest in this territory. I cannot afford to piss off Nell by starting a fight. Neither can you."

Wright huffed and then began to pace past the edge of the sunlight and back. Several times he stopped, spun toward Roger, and then groaned in frustration before continuing to pace. Finally, he stopped with a look of triumph in his smile. "You're his sire! That gives you certain rights and expectations. He went after your 'property.' We can take him out."

"I'm glad you're paying attention to our lessons. Now, what proof do you have?" Roger asked.

"Shit, fuck. Damn it. *Fuck.*" Wright flopped onto the couch. "That shifter! She saw him in the house."

"At the time, she said she didn't get a good look."

"We can't sit around and wait for him to come after me again."

"I didn't say we would."

"You just said we couldn't go after him."

Roger smirked and walked back to his dark corner. When Wright didn't click the pieces into place on his own, Roger said, "We need to find our advantages, or at the very least remove his, and keep our reputations pristine in our host's territory. Can you think of how to accomplish that?"

"This is some kind of test, isn't it? You already have the answer."

Roger's smile grew. "I've been alive a lot longer than you. I have all the answers."

"Suuuure you do." Wright leaned back and let his gaze drift up to the ceiling. He really was a handsome man, especially when he relaxed. An idea had to have clicked because he bolted upright, his mouth hanging open and a brightness in his eyes. He grinned at Roger. "We make him attack me at the party. Maybe get the mountain lion shifter close enough to him to smell him. She might not recognize him by sight, but she might know his smell."

"I like the second part as confirmation. But yes, if he's eager to hurt you, and we can demonstrate that in front of everyone, Nell will rule on our side, and we can put him down."

"You're okay with that? Us killing your sireling? Because

not that long ago, you didn't want me killing vampires just because they are vampires," Wright said.

"He's not the man I knew, and there isn't much you can do to a vampire to make them stop a vendetta besides put them in the ground," Roger replied. He went to the desk and found a hotel stationary pad. "Nell and I have been going over the arrangements for the party. I know the layout. Let's make a plan."

CHAPTER 20

The day of the party, Roger had declared Zack needed a break from the lessons, and Roger needed to watch a movie to help him catch up on pop culture. To better protect Roger from the last couple hours of sunlight, they had drawn the curtains of the four-poster bed. The darkness made the colors of Zack's tablet stand out while they watched the movie. During the course of the film, Zack had wound up leaning against Roger. His skin was cool, and his unique blend of earthiness was less overwhelming and more a familiar element.

Roger had looped his arm around Zack's shoulders, but that didn't mean they were cuddling. Because they weren't. Getting that close to each other just made it more comfortable to share the tiny screen.

"I deserved a warning," Roger murmured. His voice rumbled in his chest, a far too pleasant feeling.

Zack tossed his tablet to the side. The movie was over, but the screen gave off a light illumination. He should scoot away from Roger, but he didn't want to seem like he was distancing himself. The last couple of nights had been … strange. Roger was quieter. He practically whispered during their lessons on vampire society.

With that quiet came a calm. All his masks were abandoned. Seeing him like that felt like a special treat, like Zack had unearthed a pirate treasure no one else knew existed.

Part of him wanted to stay curled up against Roger no matter how much the tiny voice in his head that sounded like Cal complained.

"Warning?" Zack asked.

"I think my eyes might bleed from watching that."

"I'm sure you've seen worse."

"They *sparkled*. In *sunlight*."

Zack playfully thwapped Roger's chest. "Hey, that was one of my favorite movies growing up."

"That? How? How were you allowed to watch it?"

"I wasn't. That was half the fun." The light from the tablet dulled as it went to sleep. Zack was left in the dark in the arms of a vampire. "I was eleven and realized I had the biggest crush on Robert Pattinson. Only one other boy in my class did at the time. Of course, it was another thing Cal teased me about. Waifish boys and chick flicks."

"I hate the movie. I liked sharing it with you. Let's not ruin the moment by talking about your brother."

"For the record, I was talking about me, jackass." Zack moved off the bed, fumbling with the heavy bed curtains as he went. He left them open wide. The sun had set, and darkness had settled in. He made his way across the room and flipped on the overhead fixtures.

A spill of light penetrated the bed, bringing illumination through the gap Zack had left in the curtains. Roger was leaning against the pillows and dark wood of the headboard. He had schooled his features into the careful, concerned expression he used when telling Zack about vampire protocol. Like he was afraid Zack would shatter with one wrong word.

"I was sharing something that happened." Zack folded his arms over his chest.

Idly, Roger traced one of the grooves in the headboard's floral etchings. The undead bastard refused to wear a shirt because the only casual clothing he'd bought was a pair of sleep pants. He didn't want to "create extra work" by wrinkling shirts when he lounged. So he was relaxing on the bed with his abs of steel in plain sight.

Abs that were a lot softer to the touch than they looked.

Zack focused on the flare of anger he'd felt rather than the impulse to find out if he could warm up Roger by kissing his way up, down, and across his chest. "How can you put up with me if you hate my family that much?"

"I don't hate them."

"Liar."

"Fine. I do. But you can hardly blame me."

"Because they're hunters?" Zack snorted. "Careful, that sounds a lot like bias."

Roger sighed and finally met Zack's gaze again. He dropped his hand down from the headboard. After a long staring contest, he slid forward to the end of the bed. His eyes were red, but there was a softness in his gaze that made Zack's breath catch in his throat. It was different than the sympathy he'd had the first time.

"Because of what they've done to you," Roger said softly.

"To *me*?"

"You can't possibly see what I see," Roger continued gently. "You're on the inside. I've been on this side many times. Not all families deserve to be cherished."

Standing still wasn't working for Zack. He tried to walk away from Roger. The party was in less than an hour. He could get ready for it and avoid talking about his family. But the urge to prove Roger wrong was like a spider crawling up his back. He needed to get rid of it, but he couldn't reach it. Words were hard. *Because maybe he has a point.*

Bullshit. It has to be bullshit.

Doesn't it?

"I'm not … My life is *fine*," Zack snapped as he turned around. "Everyone has shit to deal with. And my shit is nothing. My family loves me."

"Then what's their opinion on our plan?"

"I—ah." Zack bit the inside of his cheek. He hadn't texted them in over a week and when he had, he'd lied. "I haven't told them."

"You don't trust them to understand the truth about what we're doing."

"It doesn't help that you keep questioning how they raised me."

"Am I wrong?" Roger asked. "You clearly know what you're doing when it comes to a hunt. Why aren't you on the road with them? What sin would be so great that you continuously struggle for their approval?"

This wasn't a conversation Zack ever wanted to have. Especially not with Roger. But Roger kept his attention focused on him. A quiet patience filled his expression as he waited for Zack to speak.

Zack closed his eyes and let out a shaky breath. *Maybe he'll finally see how weak you are*, Cal's voice whispered. His own replied, *Maybe someone will see I did the right thing*. When he opened his eyes, Roger had slid to the edge of the bed. There was no judgment in him, only expectation that Zack would spill the beans.

"You're not my first hunt," Zack said. "My family got wind of a nest network in Detroit. We planned a big operation. I was fourteen. My first job was to help compile data on where the nests could be located. I wound up going through missing persons information trying to figure out who could have become a vampire victim.

"When it came time to strike, I was positioned outside with my mom. The building we were focused on started to burn during the attack. Vampires started fleeing. Mom ran after one and sent me on another. I caught up to her.

"She was just a girl. A terrified girl. I'd seen her missing persons flier. She'd only been missing for two weeks. She hadn't been a vampire very long, and she was my age." A place on the carpet between them was far more fascinating than watching Roger's red eyes. "She begged me to let her go. I hesitated, but I had her pinned against the wall. She wasn't struggling against me. Just pleading for her life. Crying so hard I could hardly understand her.

"I let her go." Zack clenched his fists so hard his fingernails began to cut into his palms. He'd never talked through it before. *I did the right thing. And they've been punishing me ever since. It's not right. It's not fair.* He let out a shaky breath. Those were the things he told himself, but his family said differently. "My mother caught me doing it. I got in her way so she couldn't catch her. The girl ran. She got away. Every kill she's made since then is my fault."

"Have you tracked her? Used the internet to find her like you did the people I knew?"

"I tried. She's stayed off the grid."

"Then you don't know what she's done. She could be helping people."

Zack laughed bitterly. He'd made that comment to his father once, and Dad had scolded him for an hour. His grandparents had never looked at him the same. No one in the family had. "Sure she is."

Roger slid off the end of the bed and neared Zack. He hooked his finger under Zack's jaw and made him look up. "Compassion is not a sin, Zackery. Mercy is a virtue. You are not responsible if she's repaid your kindness with death. We can only be responsible for our own actions."

The logical part of Zack's mind told him the same, but that logic ran counter to everything the family taught him. *He's trying to make this okay.* Zack whispered, "She might have tricked me."

"Is that what your heart tells you?" Roger asked.

"No."

Roger smiled gently. He brushed Zack's hair out of his face. "You're a clever, good-hearted man. Have a little faith in yourself."

This is worse than cuddling. This is trust. I trust him. Zack stepped away and wiped at his eyes. "We should get going to the donor house if we're going to make it before the party."

"The donor house is closed for the night," Roger replied.

"Then we'll make a run to the butcher shop or grocery store. Asking for animal blood can't be that weird in this town."

"It wouldn't have the potency to do me any good." Roger went to the armoire and opened its doors. Whenever he didn't want Zack to see how fragile he was, he turned his back. Zack had caught onto that a few nights ago.

"Your eyes are already red." Zack motioned at the balcony and the park beyond. "Go catch some squirrels or a deer or something."

Roger chuckled darkly under his breath. "Why do hunters always approve of slaughtering animals instead of drinking from consenting humans? An animal doesn't have the capacity to approve."

Zack rubbed the back of his head. "I never thought of that."

"It's all right."

"But you need blood."

"I'll manage."

"Drink from me," Zack blurted.

Though the words escaped on their own, once they were out, Zack didn't regret them. He'd been thinking about the bite marks he'd seen for days. While the first time Roger bit him wasn't a fond memory, he understood what had happened. Roger had been starving, and to be fair, Zack had been trying to kill him. It'd been the fight response of a predator.

But this situation was different. Roger was in control—for the moment—and he needed to eat before his willpower deteriorated.

Roger remained motionless at the armoire, hand paused as he reached into the depths. After a long, quiet minute, he replied in a distant voice, "No."

"No?" Zack's voice jumped in pitch and volume. "*No?*"

"That would be what I said." Roger took out his costume's coat and hung it on a hook on the inside of the door.

Zack grabbed Roger by the shoulder. Trying to move him was like shoving a boulder uphill, but he managed to slide between Roger and the armoire. "Can you make your eyes brown?"

Roger motioned at his face. "This is a sign of age, you know."

"Not for you. I see them go back and forth all the time. They're only like this when you're hungry."

"I won't drink from you." Roger stepped back with tense precision.

"You go from complimenting me to rejecting me? What the hell?" Zack latched onto Roger's arm. "I have what you need. Take it."

With a flash of fang and a brightening of his red eyes, Roger took him by the shoulders and whirled him onto the bed. He remained over him, one hand on Zack's chest to pin him down. A hungry snarl curled his lips. In a ragged voice, he said, "I could kill you."

That had always been a possibility. The way Roger said it made him sound like he hated himself for thinking about it.

"You won't," Zack replied. "If you weren't stronger than your blood lust, I would be dead already."

"Because I haven't started to feed."

"You have to drink something."

"I'll survive."

"This party has to go smoothly. Our plan has to work,"

Zack said levelly. "You can't be at your best if you're fantasizing about ripping open every viable blood source. If you show up like this, you'll look weak."

Roger grinned and a faux malevolence twisted his features into a monstrous expression. "You're only thinking of saving face? Of the fight ahead? You don't want anything else from me?"

Slowly, Roger dragged his fingers up Zack's chest. He ran his thumb over Zack's throat, tracing an artery. Zack's heart leapt into his throat. His pulse pounded and he could feel it thudding against Roger's thumb.

"If you're trying to scare me into saying no, it's not going to work," Zack whispered. "You can play Big Bad Vampire, but I know you're full of shit."

Roger's façade cracked and fell away. His grip softened. "I've been fighting my want of you for hours. Once I start, I might not be able to stop."

From killing me. And he doesn't want to. Zack put his hand on Roger's wrist. "Then let me have my dagger. It drove you off before."

"And if you had to kill me to stop me? Could you do it?"

The question demanded silence. Zack held Roger's gaze, but he could still see his fangs. Those teeth could kill him. But Roger wasn't a heartless killer. Deep down, he was a good man.

"I don't think I'll have to do it," Zack said softly. "You might want my blood, but you don't want me dead."

Roger brushed his fingertips along Zack's hairline, his touch a gentle slide. The coolness of his skin eased the heat flaring through Zack.

"Then grab your dagger," Roger said. He sounded ancient, a distance in his voice like he was speaking across time. With unnatural grace, he moved off to the side and let Zack up from the bed.

Zack's dagger was in his backpack. Since Quinn had tried

to run him down, they'd agreed he should carry it again. He pulled it clear from its sheath. The runes shone with a pale light. They should be brighter. *They would be if I thought I was in danger.*

"I may not be able to control my power. I'm too weak to hold it back. It might bring you under the sway." Roger had wide, hungry eyes as Zack approached the bed.

"I have my hunter's mark tattoo." Zack climbed onto the bed beside him.

"That stood against my magic when you made an effort. Allowing me to bite you will connect us in a deeper way. I will be surprised if you're not overwhelmed."

Zack glared at him. "You think I'm weak-minded?"

Roger gave him a half smile. "I think even steel can bend when heated. I would hate for us to regret what happens."

"Then we set up another precaution." Zack took out his phone and opened an app. A loud noise had distracted a character in the *From the Grave* series and ended a vampire's pull. "I'm setting a timer for seven minutes with the most unsexy sound I've got."

"You could bleed out that fast," Roger said.

"If you were ripping into a main artery, sure. But you're doing a controlled nip."

"You trust me that much?"

Zack shouldn't, but he had a hard time seeing Roger as the enemy. His gut said he was doing the right thing. "I think you're a good person too." He shot him a crooked smile as he settled in beside him. "Well, good for someone who's over three hundred years old. I'm sure you've done some fucked-up shit I don't want to know about. But honestly, I'm learning that I need to let go of my biases. I should judge people on what they show me. And you've been patient and trusting."

Roger smiled, gentle and genuine. Zack's heart melted into a puddle.

Carefully, Roger took Zack's left hand. His touch sent a

pulse of lust through Zack. The hunter's tattoo on Zack's hip warmed, but the pleasure came in strong waves. He rode through it without getting lost in how good Roger's cool touch felt. When Roger looked at Zack with a question in his eyes, Zack hit the timer, then grabbed his dagger again and gave a tiny nod.

Roger bit him and sealed his mouth around the wound.

Liquid heat coursed through Zack, seeping from his core into the rest of his body. In an instant, he was harder than he'd been in his entire life. He gripped the hilt of his dagger so hard his knuckles turned white. A moan ripped out of him, and letting the sound loose only brought more joy. Roger's hands cinched on his left arm, locking him in place.

The noise Roger made while he sucked should have been repulsive, but Zack couldn't help wondering if he made better sounds sucking dick. The lustful image combined with Roger's magic threatened to make him come.

Zack had to keep himself in check. Roger was drinking from him. Someone had to stay aware of the situation for both their sakes. As much as Zack didn't want to die, he was certain Roger wouldn't forgive himself if he killed him.

Shaking, he forced his eyes open and watched Roger drink.

Fuck, Reed was right. This is too fucking hot. Panting, Zack focused on what was happening rather than what he was feeling. Every detail should go into his journal so he would never forget the intensity of Roger's magic, or the shape of his lips, or how a few mouthfuls of blood brought color to his cheeks. Roger's hands were less like ice and more like a chilled blanket. And he didn't keep his fangs buried in Zack. And even though he was careful, a drop of blood ran down Zack's arm until it touched his hand near Zack's elbow.

Pleasure continued to pound through him. He wanted friction. Skin on skin. Cool against hot. *God, his cool fingers would feel incredible on my dick. In my ass. Anywhere. Everywhere.*

But underneath the thoughts was a wooziness that made Zack's head spin.

Hand firmly on the hilt of his dagger, he rasped, "That's enough."

Roger opened his eyes. The red was bright enough to actually glow. For a split second, he seemed not to hear Zack, but then he broke the seal he had around the wound. He licked the bite mark clean in sure, confident strokes.

The action was indecently hot; the slide of Roger's tongue stoked the rising fever in Zack. Slowly, Roger released him.

Ending the contact broke the magic coming from Roger but did nothing to ease the building primal want. The urge to strip and ride Roger remained.

Why was he wasting so much energy keeping Roger at arm's length when he clearly wanted him? Zack dropped his dagger to the floor and straddled Roger's lap. Their mouths were so close he could smell his blood on Roger's tongue. *That shouldn't be hot, but it is. Fuck.*

"You're such a good boy, Zackery." Roger wrapped his arms low around Zack, creating a comfortable weight against his ass.

Zack threaded his hand into Roger's hair and tugged his head back sharply to make him look up. Roger parted his lips, and a coil of tension uncurled in Zack. Having Roger underneath him like this felt amazing. Being wanted, having someone need him, was intoxicating.

All his life he'd been scrambling for approval from his family to no avail. But without Zack being anything more than who he was, Roger looked at him with warm acceptance. His cocky smile cranked Zack's heart up to a thundering rate.

With a purr, Roger said, "Do what you want."

Groaning, Zack kissed him, thrusting his tongue deep. Roger slid his hands under Zack's T-shirt, and the contact made him want to burst into flames. He ground down into Roger, needing more friction on his dick and not finding satisfaction. A frustrated moan slipped out of him. He pulled his T-shirt over his head. His breath caught when he saw Roger marveling at him.

Roger tugged him closer and kissed him. Heaven had to feel something like this.

Just as Zack was getting lost in the second kiss, the most awful, heinous scream blasted in the air. Startled, he jumped off Roger, half spun onto the bed, lost his balance, and then fell onto the floor off the end of the bed.

Laughing loud enough to compete with the alarm, Roger rocked backward.

Embarrassment endangered Zack's joy, but Roger's laugh was so lighthearted that Zack pushed aside his shame to see things from Roger's perspective. If their positions were reversed, he wouldn't be able to contain himself.

Laughter bubbled out of Zack, and it felt so good he leaned into it. The goat-scream alarm added to the ridiculousness of the moment. Right when Zack thought they were going to stop, they started all over again.

Eventually, Roger tossed the phone to Zack. He still had amusement in his voice as he said, "Make it stop before my ears bleed."

Zack thumbed off the alarm. "Note for the future, that works."

"For the future?" Roger asked.

The unintentional meaning of the words sucker-punched Zack. He made the mistake of catching Roger's eyes. Despite centuries of what had to be a long and exciting life, there was a hint of insecurity in Roger's smile. He had a questioning sincerity that stretched out toward Zack in a way Zack had never seen. No one had ever cared about his judgment. They certainly didn't worry he'd reject them.

"We might do that again sometime," Zack said under his breath. But he knew Roger could hear him perfectly.

Roger stood and offered his hand out to Zack. Without

straining, he helped Zack to his feet. They wound up chest to chest. Zack held his breath, hoping for another kiss.

Instead, Roger slid past him. "We need to dress for the party."

"Fine," Zack grumbled. He was only feeling the tiniest bitterness about not getting a kiss. Like, a smidge. Not at all like ordering a pizza and waiting three hours longer than it should have taken and winding up with cold disappointment. He nabbed his costume from the armoire. "I'm getting dressed in the bathroom."

"Trying to hide your hard-on?" Roger teased.

What was the point in lying? Zack stepped into the bathroom and shut the door. "Yup!"

CHAPTER 21

"Do you prefer Zack or Zackery?" Roger stood beside the bathroom door with his arms crossed over his chest. He'd finished dressing in his costume, complete with a sword on his hip. The party's theme was pirates, and he looked the part of a captain. The outfit was impractical for life on the seas but was apparently all the rage these days.

"How is this a question you're asking now?" Wright's voice came through the bathroom door.

"How are you taking this long?" Roger replied. "My outfit is three times as complicated as yours, and I'm waiting on you. Do you want me to call you by a nickname or not?"

"Whatever's fine. And someone's been telling me for the last two weeks that a pet has to look appetizing. That takes a lot of work for me. I'm almost done."

Roger opened his mouth to respond but halted when Zack opened the door. Then he forgot what he intended to say.

Initially, Roger had balked at Nell's idea of a pirate-themed party, but she was the one holding it and sponsoring him. While Roger had paid for Zack's outfit, he hadn't been present for the fitting. The tailor had limited nighttime slots, and Zack had daytime availability. Roger had sent him on with the credit card and hadn't given the costume a second thought.

Pirates as a theme doesn't seem like such a bad idea anymore. Roger ran his gaze over Zack again. While his vest had too many laces and buttons to be historically accurate, he'd found a way to sinch the laces on the sides so they accentuated his lithe frame. He'd buttoned the three bottom buttons down the front. His breeches were too tight for a man who needed to work on a ship but fantastic for someone who wanted to show off slim legs and a tight ass.

And then there was his makeup. Oh, Zack had embraced it, and Roger wondered who'd taught him to make his cheekbones look sharper. He had on mascara and black eyeshadow that leant him an air of stark beauty. Through the magic of hair products, his brown hair was attractively messy.

"Unbuttoned would be better, huh?" Zack quickly undid the three vest buttons. The vest hung open only a little, exposing more of Zack's upper torso and hints of his lower abdomen. He had pecs and a flat stomach. A thin line of light-brown hair started above his navel and thickened as it went lower. He had the muscle tone of someone who worked out seriously but who wasn't a bodybuilder.

"Unbuttoned is better," Roger said slowly.

"I thought I knew all the faces you make. I've never seen that one." Zack went across the room and dug out the pair of boots that belonged to his outfit.

Get it together. Roger cleared his throat. "Faces?"

"The different masks you hide behind. You know, Aloof Vampire, I-Think-I'm-Sexy Hot Guy, Annoyed-But-You're-Clever Teacher, Close-to-Pissed-Off Authority Figure, and Please-Leave-Me-Alone Immortal." Zack finished putting on his boots. He frowned at Roger. "I'm not sure what this one is."

It's wonder. Roger pulled his features into check, adapting what Zack likely believed was Aloof Vampire. "Don't worry about it. And try not to make a face when I give you this."

Roger approached him and held out a small box. Zack took it. Inside was a gold-chain necklace with a two-inch medallion molded with Roger's kraken crest.

"This is your sigil." Carefully, Zack took the medallion out of the box. The chain fell out behind it, dangling from his hand.

At least he hadn't thrown it across the room. Roger slid his hands into his pockets. "It would be dangerous for you to go without it."

"I was wondering when we were going to talk about this." Zack ran his thumb over the kraken. "I thought you'd insist I wear a collar."

"Wouldn't go with your outfit."

Zack continued to stare at the medallion. "But I'll have to start wearing one."

Typically, when Roger presented his crest to a man, he made a night of it. There was good food, fantastic wine, and a wonderful time in bed. He had whispered sweet promises to dozens. Considering his long life, precious few had worn his crest. Romance—or sometimes seduction—was always a large part of his connection to a pet. He'd never given his crest to someone he wasn't already bedding. Many put on his crest and professed love, and he'd done his best to care for them in return.

But he knew that to Zack he was a dangerous undertow. Society's morals had made many a man question whether Roger used his magic on them or not. More than one lover had broken off their affair with claims that he was the Devil and was sending them to Hell. The fear and regret had torn tiny pieces of Roger away. Over time, he'd kept his heart guarded behind more and higher walls. Easier to pretend he was in love than to give in to it.

Somehow, Zack had wiggled through the cracks in his

defenses. A rose was blooming through concrete. Roger wanted to sweep him off his feet. Perhaps he could truly fall in love after three hundred years of pain. But Zack's confusion was as obvious as a sunset on a cloudless sea.

Zack's hesitation was based in his family's rejection of him. Roger had walked men through that fear to both good and bad results. *I couldn't take it if he turned me away. It'd break me. And I can't afford that.*

But he wouldn't cause this wonderful man any more pain than he needed to. In the end, Zack would need to return to his family. He'd need to be able to look himself in the eye and feel comfortable with everything that had happened. Enough trauma existed in the world. Roger wouldn't be a source of more.

Roger sat beside Zack. "There are ways around wearing a collar."

"I'm not getting a kraken tattoo, though I'm sure we could find a killer artist." Zack picked up the chain and looped it over his head. The medallion rested above his heart. "Welp, I'm now one of a dozen guys who've put this necklace on."

"That's not true."

Zack raised an eyebrow. "I know you've had lots of pets. You've told me."

"True." Roger kept his gaze on the medallion. He didn't want to see Zack's reaction. "But I commissioned this piece for you."

"You did?"

Was that happiness in his voice? Roger dared to glance up.

Zack had the softest of smiles, though it was fleeting. His expression turned cynical. "I figured you had dozens of these lying around."

"I only give them to people who are special to me," Roger replied.

"Is that something other people know?"

"I've never made a secret of it. Why?"

Zack brushed his thumb against the medallion on his chest and bit his bottom lip. His brows knitted together. After a moment, he let out his breath and brightened. "No worries. You've got my dagger?"

On one side of Roger's belt was a cutlass. Although technically part of his costume, it was a real weapon. Zack's dagger was on his other side. Unfortunately, it was in its actual sheath rather than one that matched the rest of Roger's outfit. But it was black and sleek, and Roger's coat was black. If anyone looked closely, they wouldn't see the dagger in the first place.

"I've got it," Roger said.

"And you're sure you can get those in?" Zack asked.

"Vampires carry weapons on them frequently, even in Nell's territory. These help me look the part. No one's going to think twice about them."

"Let's go over the plan one more time." Zack walked over to the desk.

Drawn like a magnet, Roger followed him. After their conversation about Quinn, Roger had drawn the basic layout for Nell's party. A large rectangle stood in for Nell's mansion. A small one behind and to the right represented a free-standing hall. Nell's grounds were near the lake, so between the hall, the mansion, and the lake was an expansive garden.

"We arrive at the party," Roger said.

"Which is happening over there." Zack pointed to the smaller rectangle. "Why isn't it in the main house?"

"A security measure. Vampires never host large gatherings in their own homes. There's usually a separate building; that way, they don't have to invite other vampires into their private residences."

"A vampire needs an invite to a vampire's home?"

"No, but a vampire with a large home typically has

humans living with them. Because of them, an outsider vampire can't simply walk through the door."

"But what's the point of having a huge house if you don't show it off, so they make the secondary building," Zack said.

"Exactly."

"Okay. We arrive at the party." Zack lifted his finger from the map. "Where we will be charming and establish to the vampire world that you're not dead. We know Quinn's invited, and since even the regulars at the coffee shop couldn't shut up about it today, we also know everyone in town wants to be there tonight. He won't want to miss out."

"And he'll be hoping for the opportunity to get you alone," Roger said.

"Yup. So around midnight, I head out to the garden by myself. If anyone asks, it's so I can get some fresh air. Because I'm so new to this." Zack raised his wrist to his forehead to fake a fainting gesture.

He flashed the fang marks Roger had given him an hour ago.

He tasted sweet. Not an ounce of fear in his blood. I feel stronger than I have in weeks. Because of him. Roger almost missed what Zack said next.

"If Quinn's hunting me like we think he is, he won't pass up the chance to follow me outside. Then you grab Josefina or Nell and follow us outside. I goad Quinn into a fight."

"Or try to keep him from killing you until I arrive with Nell or Josefina," Roger said.

"Yeah. When he thinks he has a shot, he's not patient about attempting murder." Zack frowned at the map. "I don't like that we don't know the layout of the gardens. You have to have some respect for the fact that Nell's managed to keep this place off Google Maps, but it would have been nice to know. Your vamp hearing will have to do."

"I'll be there."

"This is a pretty basic plan."

Roger slid Zack's notebook over the sheet of paper. "Elaborate schemes fall to pieces in the first step. We'll do fine with our simple plan."

"I hope so. Because not fine means—" Zack drew his finger across his neck and made a gagging sound.

The sudden flash that the beautiful man before him could end up dead on the ground drove a coldness into Roger's heart. He didn't want the image and hated that it was a possibility. *Not if I do my part.* "You'll be more than fine."

"I'll settle for not dead." Zack sighed loudly and headed for the door. "Off to mingle with hundreds of pretty people."

"Shall we dare to enjoy ourselves before murdering a threat?" Roger teased.

"That sounds weird."

Roger opened the door for him. "Only because you haven't been to a vampire party."

"Putting it that way doesn't ease my mind." Zack went out into the hall.

"Then do what I do. Smile anyway." Roger locked the door behind them and slid the key into his pocket. "The goal is to never let them see you sweat. If they don't know how to get under your skin, that's one less weapon in their hands."

Zack was watching him closely. His brow was scrunched and his eyes narrow. It was one of his thinking faces, one he did when he was assessing what Roger had said.

Roger gave him a warm smile in return. *Don't let him see the cracks. Not him.*

"What's wrong?" Roger asked.

"Nothing," Zack said quietly. "You just reminded me of a meme for a second."

"Meme? What's that?"

Zack groaned as he headed down the hallway. "Every time I think I've managed to catch you up, you ask something like that. It is going to take me *forever.*"

Roger remembered what a meme was, but distracting

Zack and watching him walk away allowed him to ignore the pain in his heart. Because for a moment there, he was sure Zack had figured him out.

And if Zack did that, Roger might not be able to stop himself from falling in love.

CHAPTER 22

The limo pulled away, leaving Zack and Roger outside the gorgeous mansion. Other guests were arriving around them. Some walked up from parked cars, while a string of limos continued dropping others at the door. The front lights of the mansion illuminated the night, but everyone headed for a cement path that led around the house. Roger started on that path, and Zack followed a step behind him.

The path continued through a corner of the massive garden. Tiny lights brightened the mazes of plants. At first, they seemed like flashing decorative lamps, but at times the colored lights changed or suddenly went out. A burst of light would dash from one lamp to another.

They're pixies. Zack marveled at the tiny faeries laughing in delight as they raced each other from platform to platform. Deep in the garden, a multitude of colors shone out into the night. An enchanting mix of music drifted out from it.

Louder music with a nautical feel spilled out from the large building at the end of the path. Welcoming light poured out from the hall's giant windows. Nearer to the entrance stood the girl who ran the reception desk at the donor house. She had a wand in one hand, and she swept it over guests.

Beside her was an equally attractive man. He held an electro-magnetic wand.

"Shit," Zack whispered. "They check for magic and metal?"

"Don't panic," Roger said softly.

"Why not?"

Roger glared over his shoulder.

Right, Zack wasn't supposed to question his "master" in the presence of others, even if said others appeared to be too busy with their own business to notice. It was one of the many annoying rules he'd have to abide by.

The girl motioned for one of the guests at the front of the line to step over to a table with additional security personnel. The next didn't make it past the electromagnetic wand. Both of them moved off to the side, where their items were more thoroughly inspected. After a moment, one guest was allowed to reclaim the pistol, while the other had to leave the ring behind.

But how did Roger expect to get Zack's dagger through security? Zack drummed his fingers against his leg.

They were next. Roger stepped up first. The electromagnetic wand buzzed, but the girl with the magic wand said nothing. Roger only had to go through the mundane side of security, where he pulled out the sword and dagger for inspection.

"Are either of these silver?" the guard asked.

"The dagger," Roger replied.

The guard furrowed her brow as she examined the dagger. "It has runes. Check it again for magic."

The security guard beside her pulled out a wand and ran it over the dagger. He shook his head. The first guard put the dagger on the table and took up the sword.

"You're clear to go inside," the girl at the door told Zack.

Zack hadn't even paid attention as the wands were swept over him. "My master's still over there."

The girl sighed in exasperation and pointed to a waiting place just inside the door.

After talking to the guards, Roger put the weapons back in their sheaths and headed through the door. He continued forward like he was expecting Zack to fall in line.

Which Zack did. How had the dagger passed the check for magic? The runes had barely glowed the last time he'd picked it up. Had letting Roger feed from him broken the dagger's enchantments? Was it possible to ruin the blade? Was that why his family discouraged his interest in vampires? Were they only trying to protect the best tool he had for fighting monsters? He whispered, "They let it through? Why didn't the dagger—"

Roger spun, taking hold of Zack and gently pushing him up against the wall. Other guests filtered past them to join a line at the end of the short hallway that led into the large hall. "Careful what you say, boy."

Mission first. Don't think about how nice it is to be up against him again. Zack fought the surge of heat in his cheeks, but he didn't have control over it. "Master. Please tell me why the dagger was allowed."

Roger glanced around them and then nodded down at the dagger's hilt. In a voice so soft Zack barely heard him, he said, "Go ahead and pull it out. Not all the way. Just to the first rune."

Given their current position, Zack was able to slide the dagger up without anyone else seeing. As the first rune cleared the sheath, soft white light flashed against the inside of Roger's coat. The magic worked. Zack exhaled a sigh of relief. "I don't understand."

Roger put his hand over Zack's and slid the dagger to rest in the sheath. "When I took it out of its sheath, it was lifeless. I guessed that its magic lies dormant except in your hands. A clever bit of camouflage so it can make its way into places like this."

"Why didn't I know that?" Zack whispered.

"Because your family is bent on annihilation, not infiltration. Now, shush. We need to get in there."

Zack bristled and clenched his jaw as Roger stepped away. But they'd had long conversations on the importance of a neutral expression in supernatural company. With a deep breath, he stowed his anger and questions. Roger had taken a big risk, and it'd paid off. Zack had taken the dagger and its magic for granted. He'd have to research the runes when he had time.

Person by person, sometimes group by group, guests were announced to the room beyond. Roger and Zack rejoined the procession into the party. By the time they reached the front of the line, Zack had to fight the urge to go up on his tiptoes to see over Roger's shoulders. Then the last guests in front of them made their way in.

"Roger, Gentleman Pirate of the Seven Seas, Highwayman of the Unwatched Roads, Tempter of Forbidden Desires, and Captain of the Great Lakes Coven," the caller announced.

Roger walked on, and Zack continued to follow. They entered an enormous ballroom. A massive chandelier hung in the middle, giving off the bulk of the party's light. The center of the polished wood floor was open for dancing, though no one had started yet, while clusters of seating arrangements were scattered around the sides of the room.

Everyone was in costume. According to vampire custom, pets wore fewer clothes than everyone else, and vampires wore elaborate outfits that covered most of their skin. Few wore collars; most pets had a medallion like Zack's, with their master's crest.

Either the whole town had turned out for the party, or Nell had invited her entire domain and more. Zack estimated there were three hundred people in the room, and more were coming in. The bulk of the crowd paused mid conversation as Roger's name was called. Some immediately returned to what they had been doing, while others watched Roger move through the room.

He is worth watching. Roger smiled, shook hands, and continued moving through the group until they were to the far side of the room. Zack kept an eye out for Quinn, but there were so many people. He hadn't been in a crowd this big since he'd left high school.

When Roger had said vampire society, Zack had pictured a couple dozen individuals at most. He'd figured the party wouldn't be more than a hundred people. Taliville only had a few thousand citizens. While the supernatural was celebrated here, there couldn't be that many shifters, faeries, and vampires living in town, could there? How was he supposed to fool these people into believing he was Roger's pet? Was the GLC bigger? Roger spoke like it was. Someone was going to figure out he was lying.

Roger slid an arm around Zack's waist and drew him closer. Other masters and pets were doing the same, so Zack welcomed Roger's closeness. Roger's familiar scent of earth and musk helped Zack breathe deeper.

"You're panicking," Roger murmured in his ear.

Supernaturals would be able to smell that. Zack took another deep breath and swallowed his fears. He had a part to play. If he could get away with lying to Cal about stealing his pot, then he could manage this. "Maybe I'll tell you why later."

"Fair enough." Roger kissed his temple and started to release him.

Zack held on to his arm. "Wait, what does 'Tempter of Forbidden Desires' mean?"

"Flashy vampire way of proclaiming I'm gay." Roger flashed him a grin with a hint of fang. "I've been out and proud for centuries."

"You still have to declare it?"

"Nell and I went over my titles. Admittedly, if you listen,

most of the vampires are going to have that one or a version of it. Especially here. Now, are you all right? Because we're becoming conspicuous, and people want to say hello."

"Let's do this."

Roger nodded once, then drifted away from him. His expression shifted back into Carefree-Sexy Vampire. Zack did his best to adopt his own neutral mask as he followed.

Over the course of the last two weeks, Zack had seen examples of the vampires' wealth—including Roger's borrowed money—but the party put money on full display. A seafood bar was set up outside the back doors. Inside, three open bars served a variety of alcoholic and nonalcoholic drinks. There was a buffet of savory food and one of sweet. Everything was labeled for cultural, religious, and allergy needs.

Waitstaff circled the ballroom in tailored uniform costumes with trays of food and glasses of rum. Another group of people had on different uniforms, and they offered their wrists when vampires motioned for them to come close. In one corner, a live band played jaunty music.

Zack had never seen anything like it. And still more people were pouring in. An hour into Roger shaking hands and saying hello, Zack nabbed a passing glass of rum.

Before he could take a sip from it, Roger paused his conversation with two other vampires, took the glass, and drained it dry. "Thank you, boy."

Zack sucked in a breath.

Roger slid close, putting his mouth against Zack's ear. "We discussed this. Lesson four."

That had been over a week ago. What was the protocol about drinks? *Never take a drink you didn't see made.* It was standard common sense, and yet Zack had forgotten it. He whispered, "*You* drank it."

"I'm not human," Roger replied. "And I've got you to wake me up if someone puts me to sleep again."

Roger trusted him to do that? *He trusts me?* Zack grinned. "Damn right you do."

"Quinn Turner, Rider of the Open Plains, Nightmare of the Trenches, Reveler of the Disco, Member of the Great Lakes Coven," the caller announced.

Zack spun toward the main entrance. Quinn was dressed like a pirate captain, though his coat wasn't as extravagant as Roger's. Even from across the room, his grin was malicious. He moved into the crowd on the opposite side of the room.

"He's still using his last name," one of the vampires near Roger said. "How ridiculous."

"He's claiming a *disco* title. That was never in fashion," her companion whispered.

Zack took a step away from Roger.

Roger put a hand on his arm and pulled him back. "Wait. Give him a few minutes before initiating the plan."

"How long?"

Roger's gaze went distant. He was looking past Zack.

"Dmitri, Gentleman Pirate of the Seven Seas, Scourge of the Ton, Seducer of Guileless Men, and Captain of the Great Lakes Coven," the caller said.

Zack spun and spotted a pale man with short dark hair walking into the ballroom. His features were severe, cheekbones sharp enough that he looked gaunt. He wore a darkred coat, but the rest of his wardrobe was black. Like Roger, he had a sword on his hip, and he had a hand on it. He scanned the room with the intent gaze of a predator. Immediately after turning his head in Roger's direction, he began making his way toward them.

Dmitri. Was that one of the names Roger had asked Zack to look into? There had been over a dozen names. Zack would have to consult his notes. He whispered to Roger, "Who is this guy?"

"Oh, only the last man I loved as a mortal," Roger whispered. "And my blood brother."

"Seamus turned you both? At the same time?"

"Technically, Anton made him, but we came out of the same grave," Roger replied.

The zillion other questions populating Zack's mental processors had to go on hold because Roger turned on a bright, playboy smile and moved away from Zack to greet the approaching Dmitri.

Those two had centuries of history, and Roger hadn't mentioned a word of it. That shouldn't hurt Zack. And the cat-scratch jealousy making an ugly appearance in his thoughts was completely unwarranted. Just because Zack had kissed Roger, and Roger seemed into it, didn't mean they were anything to each other. The medallion around Zack's neck was a lie, not a promise.

But Zack was glad both men were too busy greeting each other to notice the frown he couldn't erase.

CHAPTER 23

If Roger's heart could beat, it would have quadrupled its speed when he hugged Dmitri. The last two weeks suddenly felt like an escape. Despite the political maneuvering he'd had to do with Nell and Josefina, the illusion of safety had condensed into reality. Even Quinn's attempts on Zack's life hadn't broken the spell.

Dmitri was the reminder that the GLC waited for him. Seamus was waiting.

But that was a different night and Roger didn't need to borrow future pain. He smiled and clapped Dmitri's shoulder. "I was hoping you'd make it!"

"Were you?" Dmitri said softly.

Always dismissing my joy. "I am the one who put you on the list."

"But you didn't come to me." Dmitri's shroud of coldness had only strengthened over the decades. As vampires grew older and more powerful, they acquired new talents. By the 1980s, Dmitri had had a constant chill in the air around him. The heat of the crowded room didn't diminish his aura and the more intense chill he'd developed.

The world had moved on without Roger. Hearing about

changes had been hard, but taking in Dmitri's differences firsthand made Roger's smile brittle. The dozens of daggers and needles of intrigue he'd avoided over the centuries hung at the edge of his memory. There were bound to be dozens more schemes he didn't know about.

Focus. Roger said, "Still taking stock before I make my grand entrance."

Dmitri glanced past Roger. "Who is that?"

"I'm guessing you've spotted my new boy." Roger gestured for Zack to come closer.

Zack did, and he kept his gaze on the floor.

Dmitri picked up the medallion on Zack's chest and then let it swing back and thump against him. "I wish I could say I was surprised. Roger, we need to speak. Alone."

"Of course. After the party—"

"*Now.*"

"I can hardly disappear from the party. Nell is hosting it in my honor," Roger replied.

"I won't take long."

He's a pushy bastard. Some things never change. Roger motioned toward an exit on the east wall that led into a hallway. "There are private rooms that way. It's early enough we may be able to find one."

Dmitri motioned for him to lead the way. With a nod, Roger began to cross the ballroom.

When they were twenty feet from the hallway, Dmitri put his hand on the center of Zack's chest and made him stop. "I said alone, boy."

"I go where my master tells me, *sir*," Zack replied sharply.

Dmitri glared over his shoulder to Roger. *Handle him* was what that look said.

"It's all right," Roger said smoothly. "Go find Reed, boy. We'll be quick."

"As you wish, Master," Zack said. He returned Dmitri's glare before walking away.

He and I need to come up with codes so we can talk in public. Roger headed for the hallway. The first doors led to bathrooms, and then the hallway split. One path led to the kitchen, and waitstaff traversed in and out to the ballroom. The other route led to a series of smaller rooms. The first three already had guests enjoying the lack of noise and stimulation from the crowds.

As soon as they had stepped into the fourth room, Dmitri tossed a rod at Roger's head. Roger caught it effortlessly. The gray metal was cool in his hand, and he took a sniff of it to confirm his suspicions. "Iron? How on earth did you get this into the party?"

"Asks the man with steel on his hip," Dmitri replied.

"Mine will give a fey something akin to a sunburn. This could burn through their flesh."

Dmitri folded his arms over his chest. "I am considered Seamus's representative, here to assess that you are who you claim to be."

"And because I've been 'dead' so long, you thought I might be a fey." Roger pressed the iron bar to his cheek, then bounced it between his hands. He tossed it back to Dmitri, who caught it and returned to crossing his arms. "I'm afraid I'm no more fairy than I've ever been."

"If the iron test wasn't enough, your attempt at a joke would be," Dmitri said.

Roger gave a nod of acknowledgement and then slid his hands into his pockets. Leaving Zack alone in the main room stretched his nerves in an unpleasant way. He had hooks in his stomach, twisting and yanking him into knots. None of his worry showed, though. He could keep his smile light, even though it felt so false it might carve through him.

Dmitri was too calm. He never truly furrowed his brow, especially when he attempted to hide his anger. Instead, there was only the slightest pull across his forehead. The corners of his mouth turned down ever so slightly. Cold fury deepened his blue eyes.

Seconds ticked by. A minute. Two.

"You wanted to talk," Roger said.

"I have been imagining this moment for thirty-two years and seven weeks. I am trying to decide how to begin," Dmitri replied, voice thick and deep with the emotions he was hiding.

Had they been in the prime of their relationship, Roger would have wrapped an arm around Dmitri and coaxed a smile out of him. Over the centuries, they had tried to be together again, but the last attempt had been in 1913. That had been short and had gone poorly.

I'm not able to dance around his problems. I don't have to do that with Zack. The realization roared like cannon fire through his consciousness and blasted another hole in the wall around his heart. For the last two weeks, he had simply been himself. After Zack had agreed to help him, he'd accepted Roger. He was reasonable. No one was ever reasonable with Roger. *How long has my life been so fucked?*

The answer was a chilling *too long*.

"How about we start with something easy?" Roger said lightly. "How have you been, Dmitri?"

"Who is the boy?" Dmitri snapped.

"He's not relevant at the moment."

In a blur, Dmitri rushed him. Roger had regained some of his strength, but Dmitri was his equal, and he wasn't ready for the attack. He had no sooner readied a paltry defense when Dmitri slammed him against the wall and used the rod against his throat. Dmitri pushed until Roger craned his head upward to relieve the pressure. And then Dmitri growled and shoved a centimeter further.

"Where the fuck have you been?" Dmitri snarled.

"Here!"

"Nell's been hiding you? She wouldn't be so stupid."

Roger gulped. He didn't need the air to breathe, but he needed it to speak. Scrambling, he found Dmitri's face and shoved his thumbs in the corners of his eyes.

Dmitri hissed and released him. When he tried to corner Roger again, Roger dodged him. He weaved around the room, using the limited furniture to gain space from Dmitri.

"Nell didn't know I was here," Roger said. "I was in an enchanted sleep."

"Of all the pathetic lies you have told in our long lives, I have never heard you utter one that asinine."

"Because it isn't a lie. Until two weeks ago, I was in a coffin in a basement. That last night in June, when you saw me at your club—for me, that was practically yesterday. I swear to you."

Dmitri clutched the iron rod in one hand. Roger considered going for Zack's dagger. He couldn't activate its magic, but it was silver. It would give him an advantage. Dmitri pointed the rod at Roger. "Look me in the eye and tell me the truth. And remember, I've known exactly what kind of man you are since we met on the docks in Port Royal."

I lied to him that day, and he called me out on it. Roger kept his hands ready to grab the rod if Dmitri threw it at him. "That night in 1989, someone laced my drink. The next thing I knew that boy out there was opening my coffin."

"He hardly looks of age. There's no way he was alive then," Dmitri said. "I was close enough to know if he is something other than human. He's not."

"He is human, aye. And he is young." Roger glanced at the doorway. There was no door to close. No one would be able to get away with behavior against Nell's codes, but there was no true privacy either. Switching to Russian wouldn't work. Any number of other supernaturals might know it, and there was something called Google Translate that Zack had shown him. "He dispelled a curse on my coffin that had kept me asleep."

"How did he know where to find you?" Dmitri demanded.

"Quinn emailed him."

"*Quinn?*" Dmitri scoffed. "Why would Quinn want to help you? He hates you."

"We think it was more about trying to kill the boy. Well, the boy's brother," Roger said.

Dmitri shoved the iron rod into his coat pocket. "This is quickly becoming ridiculous. What reason would Quinn, of all the useless vampires in the world, have to kill some random boy's brother?"

"Because he's not a random boy." Roger mouthed his next words: "He's a Wright."

Dmitri widened his eyes, then snapped his attention to the doorway. At first, Roger worried someone had been listening, but Dmitri backed further into the room instead of chasing after a potential eavesdropper. When he looked back to Roger, wide-eyed fear and comprehension were plain in his features. "You're sure?"

"I've seen his driver's license myself. And this is hard to forge." Roger pulled the dagger from his hip, flashed it in the light, and then slid it back into its sheath. "Quinn's tried to kill him twice more."

"And we've left him alone in the ballroom with him. Damn it." Dmitri rushed out of the room.

A chill worked up Roger's spine, and he hurried to follow Dmitri. They went into the ballroom. The party had swelled by another hundred at least. Roger swept his gaze over the crowd. Earlier, Nell, Josefina, and Reed had been near one of the buffets. Now, Nell and Josefina were dancing, and not too far from them, Reed danced with Kit.

Where is he? Zack's costume wasn't special enough to stand out in the crowd. Countless other pets were wearing vests without shirts. And his hair was light brown, with hints of auburn. In a room full of color, that didn't stand out either.

Roger grabbed Dmitri roughly by the collar. "What do you know? Why does Quinn want him dead?"

Dmitri took hold of Roger's wrists but didn't fight him. He met Roger's fierceness with levelheaded, clear eyes. "Three years ago, the Butcher slaughtered Quinn's pets *and* his tribute to Seamus. Quinn's had the security footage as proof the whole time, but Seamus refuses to engage the Wrights."

And now one was walking among the supernaturals in a territory controlled by someone outside the GLC. *If Zack dies in Taliville, it could bring a hunter war on Nell's head. Quinn will get revenge and back into Seamus's good graces. But he wouldn't do it in here.*

Roger released Dmitri. "Tell Nell exactly what you've told me. I'll check the gardens."

"What if he's still inside?"

"Then stay by his side until I return," Roger snapped. Then he ran for the back doors.

He didn't give a damn how many odd looks he got. He had to save Zack before he failed another person who trusted him.

CHAPTER 24

Finding anyone at the party was an epic-level challenge. Zack was around average height for the guests, which meant he didn't have the advantage of looking over people's heads. And there were a *lot* of people. Plus, the band shifted music styles, and the middle of the room began ballroom dancing.

"Screw this," Zack whispered to himself. Instead of finding Reed, he'd post up somewhere he could watch the hallway and rejoin Roger when he emerged from the private rooms. There was an open seat in a cluster near the hallway entrance. Zack plopped into it.

"Excuse you," one of the guests occupying another seat in the cluster said. "Who said you could sit with us?"

"It was open," Zack replied.

"It's talking back to me. The gall," the guest said to one of his friends.

Another guest motioned for Zack to vacate. With a scowl, he climbed out of the seat and continued circling the party.

A heavy hand clapped onto Zack's shoulder. It was harsher than Roger had ever been with him, but his heart swelled with hope as he turned.

Quinn twisted his lips in what could pass for a smile—

provided the definition of smile changed to a gesture of intense displeasure and murderous intent. In a sickeningly sweet voice, he said, "I have been looking all over for you."

This was the perfect opportunity to lure Quinn outside, but Zack had no idea where Roger was. Going outside without backup or his weapon was suicide. He slid out of Quinn's grasp. "How interesting, sir. Why?"

"You wouldn't want anyone else to hear why. Let's go outside."

"I'm supposed to wait here for my master," Zack said.

Quinn leaned in. When Zack attempted to back away, he put his hand on the small of Zack's back with lightning speed. He snarled under his breath, "You're going to walk outside right *now,* or I am going to tell everyone in this room who you really are."

That couldn't end well. Zack gulped and nodded. His feet were lead as he made his way across the ballroom. The grand party turned into white noise. There had to be a way out of his current situation, but he didn't see anyone he knew. The closest he got was EWE, who was outside by the seafood buffet grabbing a plate of food. He made brief eye contact, but EWE only frowned around a mouthful of shrimp.

Quinn nudged Zack down a garden path. The flower beds stretched several hundred feet ahead of them, with a multitude of gravel routes between the varieties of plants. Zack tried to steer the doomed march through the shorter plants, but Quinn steered him into an alcove surrounded by hibiscus and delphiniums.

Zack had no advantage. *But I'm not helpless.* He whirled and spread his feet in a ready stance. "I know you shot at me and tried to run me down."

"No one's ever accused a Wright of being stupid," Quinn said. His eyes blazed bright red, and he made no attempt to hide his fangs as he spoke. The air around them was chillier. The pixies that danced between the lamps clustered in threes or fours at the nearby tiny structures. Weird, multicolored light bathed the area, blues and greens casting nerve-racking shadows.

"I'm not Cal," Zack said.

"I know that," Quinn snapped.

"Then why are you trying to kill me?"

"Because if I can't have him, you'll do. What I can't figure out is how Roger is controlling you."

"He's not. I have my own will."

"A Wright who likes to fuck vampires. No wonder no one ever talks about you, *Zackery*." Quinn's grin grew, but it had the warmth of an icicle. "I don't have to kill you. Why don't you drop Roger as your master and come with me?"

"Why don't you walk into the sun?" Zack returned.

"See, that's the talk I expect from one of your kind, hunter. Full of bravado, pissing into the wind."

"All I'm hearing is a vampire acting like a badass." Zack snorted. "You still use a last name. What kind of vampire does that?"

Quinn rolled his hand. "Keep talking. I want to hear everything that makes you think you're better than me."

Icy dread seeped into Zack. "Why?"

"That way, this will have more impact." Quinn threw a phone at him.

Zack caught it. A video played on the screen. It was in a green color scheme, and there was no sound. *Security footage.* A lump caught in his throat as a man onscreen made his way into a bedroom. He had a knife in his hand, and he moved with stealthy precision.

Two people were asleep in the bed. The man grabbed one sleeper by the head and slit the person's throat. From the angle, it was impossible to see the blood spilling out onto the bed, but the jerk of the knife had been quick.

The other person in the bed began to wake. And scream. And the man smothered her cries with his hand and stabbed her seven times. He climbed off the bed and turned to leave. The camera caught his face.

Zack already knew who it was. He knew the knife. He knew the walk.

But seeing Cal's face on camera turned the icy dread into an electric jolt. Zack dropped the phone and stumbled away from it. Killing monsters was the family's mission. *But you don't slit a vampire's throat. You don't have to stab anyone seven times.*

"Those were my pets. Declan and Sasha," Quinn said in a quiet voice. "He didn't stop there. He murdered my sireling that night too. Do you know what people have done about your brother?"

Zack's hands were shaking. He had to gain control of himself before Quinn attacked. If he didn't keep his head, he was dead.

"Nothing," Quinn snapped. "Seamus says we can't pick a fight with your family. That it's not worth the war it'd start. And he wouldn't let me turn this over to the mortal authorities. He didn't want them mixed up in our business. I showed this to your mother in Dallas. Do you know what she said?"

Dallas ... the last job in Dallas had been over a year ago. Zack gulped. There were no weapons around. Nothing he could use to protect himself from Quinn's long-boiling rage.

"'The blood bitches got what they deserved,'" Quinn hissed. "Then she tried to put a knife in me."

I really wish I had my dagger. But it's far. Roger, where are you? Zack raised his fists. "I'm not the one you want."

"No. But you're the one who came. You'll have to do." Quinn snarled and lunged forward.

Zack swept his first attack out of the way and followed with a solid kick to Quinn's side. Josefina had emphasized using a vampire's strength and speed against them. *You'll never outclass them. Think ahead. It's your only chance.* Zack shifted his weight. To a sloppy fighter, his left side seemed completely open.

But he was prepared for the punch Quinn aimed at his left shoulder, and he grabbed Quinn's wrist and executed a perfect flip. Quinn smacked into the gravel. Zack backed away. His instincts said to run, but Quinn was faster than him. His best hope was to parry and dodge until Roger arrived with his dagger.

If he arrives. Zack breathed through the fear. He had to hold on to his trust. Roger would have to come.

He was dead otherwise.

CHAPTER 25

Three vampires and a shifter actually tried to greet Roger despite the fact he was running past them. One stepped directly into his path, and he nearly collided with them. By the time he reached the doors leading outside, he was ready to rip the next well-meaning guest's hand off their arm.

There was no sign of Zack immediately outside the back doors. The party's music and general din of noise was louder than earlier, and Roger took a few steps away from the doors. Was he outside? Inside? Roger didn't know.

A handsome man abandoned a plate of food on a patio table and started to approach Roger. When Roger glared, baring his fangs, the man halted. But then he lifted his chin and continued forward. "You're Zack's master, right?"

"I am," Roger snapped.

The man pointed at a garden path. "He went that way. With Quinn. He didn't look happy about it."

Roger could have kissed the handsome stranger. He memorized as many details about him as he could. "Thank you. Tell Reed, Nell. Josefina. Any who will listen."

Then he ran, not bothering to check if the man obeyed him. Fifteen feet down the path, he heard the rustle of gravel, grunts, and flesh hitting flesh. A fight. But if they were fighting, then Zack wasn't dead. He had a chance. Roger turned the corner.

Zack was panting, and he had a few red welts. One eye was beginning to swell. But he was on his feet. He had his attention fully on Quinn, who was scrambling up from the ground.

Roger skidded to a halt. Gravel danced out from under his feet, skittering a new percussion into the fight's melody. He pulled the dagger from his belt. As he lunged forward to grab Quinn from behind, he shouted, "Zack!"

He tossed the dagger.

With an effortless grace, Zack caught it, spun it around in his hand, and changed his stance to incorporate the weapon. As soon as the hilt made contact with Zack, the runes on the dagger flared bright white. Roger stored the moment. He could enjoy the details later.

Staying in the fight, he tossed Quinn into the nearest plants and moved so he was at the ready if Quinn should spring at him.

But Quinn took his time standing up. He dusted pollen off his arm. Then he smiled with a perverse joy. "Didn't I tell you? Didn't I say that Roger knew what the boy was? He hasn't been gone thirty years by accident. He's been plotting against our kind!"

Five more vampires stepped out of the taller plants. Each wore an angry snarl and had embraced their nature, which turned their eyes blazing red.

"Whatever Quinn's said is a lie," Roger shouted. He moved so Zack was at his back but not flush against him. They needed their space to fight. Because if he couldn't stall, then they were in trouble. "My thirty-year absence wasn't my choice."

"Then it's worse," Quinn snarled. "Hunters found a way to poison you. Control you."

"When did you lose your mind, Quinn?" Roger demanded. "Mind control isn't real."

"Brainwashing is."

Roger weighed the reactions crossing the vampires' faces. "I am not on the side of hunters. But this one is mine. Attacking him means attacking me. You have no grounds for this. Stand down before we put you down."

"They can't take us," one of the other vampires said. "Roger can barely control himself. He's weak. I've seen it."

Zack let out a long, soft breath. Roger had heard it once before from him. He was preparing for the incoming strike.

Roger closed his fists.

The vampires attacked.

Combat was a dance with a unique tempo and goal. Roger had found his sea legs in a day, but he'd gained steadiness in a fight quicker than that. From drunken brawls to swinging from his ship to the enemy's deck, he had been in countless battles before ever becoming a vampire. And one did not become a captain in Seamus's coven without thriving on violent altercations. Roger had fought pirates, gangsters, so-called gentleman, soldiers: humans, shifters, witches, and vampires alike. Even a Seelie one time in a contest.

But he was sluggish. His lack of speed kept the fight balanced in favor of the group.

Or it would have if Zack wasn't a marvel in his own right. His technique had flaws, but Roger covered those holes. When an unexpected strike came for Roger's side, Zack slashed his knife through the attacker's forearm, causing the vampire to howl and relent. Roger flashed Zack a grin as they spun past each other to counter attacks and lash out against the enemy.

They weren't winning, but they weren't dying either. Roger searched for the gap that would give them the advantage. He snapped one vampire's neck. It wasn't a killing move, but it would take the vampire a few minutes before she could rise again. *Four attackers and Quinn.*

With a furious scream, Quinn soared over Roger's head and landed in front of Zack. He quickened his moves, driving Zack backward against Roger.

Maintaining stamina in the fight became the challenge. Roger could feel his strength beginning to wane. Two vampires grabbed his arms and hauled him away from Zack. He broke the hold one had on him but had to fight the other.

Zack drove his dagger into Quinn's gut, pulled it out, and then slid it upward into Quinn's heart. Immediately, Quinn's skin began to turn gray. The silver was burning him. If the dagger wasn't removed, it would burn out his heart and kill him.

He brought it on himself. Roger pushed away the memories of the man he used to know. Holding on to them would only hurt. He wasn't willing to sacrifice the present or Zack to a ghost.

Zack twisted the dagger, working it further into Quinn's chest. Only when the red blaze of Quinn's eyes had turned to dull emptiness did he yank it free from Quinn and let the body drop to the ground.

"What the hell is going on?" Nell demanded. She was in full pirate-captain regalia, though her hat was gone. She reminded Roger of the first time they'd met on the boards of her ship.

Her shout ended the fight. The four vampires on their feet immediately ran. Two seconds later, Dmitri and Josefina arrived, both with a fleeing vampire in each hand. One of them pointed at Zack and said, "He's a hunter."

"He's protected," Nell snapped.

"But he's a Wright!" another said.

"I do not care if he's the Butcher himself. I have granted him protection in my realm. He bears the crest of one of my guests. Unless he has attacked one of you, then you have no grounds to attack him," Nell said.

The first one to speak up pointed at the body. "He killed Quinn!"

"I was attacked," Zack said.

"Multiple times," Roger added.

Nell's sternness broke for only the briefest of seconds as she shot Roger a look. But it was fleeting. "I have seen Quinn try to drink from this boy without permission with my own eyes. I don't doubt he started this ill-conceived attack. The five of you are exiled from my domain for the next ten years."

"Exiled!" one of them shouted.

"Or you can spend forty years in a stone coffin. Pick your punishment," Nell growled.

The vampires looked between themselves. At least the ones who were standing did. The fifth was starting to come to consciousness. The first to speak, who seemed to be taking leadership of the small group, stepped forward. "We'll take the ten years. But don't be surprised if we don't come back, Master."

"If you want to renounce claim of my coven, fine. But you'll renounce my protections as well." Nell leveled her glare on each in turn. "You have until dawn. If I hear of you in my domain after that, I will put you in stone."

The lead vampire assisted the fifth off the ground and the five of them left. Josefina trailed after them, likely making sure they didn't interfere with the party.

Lacking the fight's distraction, Roger could take in the details around him. Zack was out of breath, and he had a few more cuts and bruises. Otherwise, he looked unharmed. When Zack's gaze fell on a phone lying on the ground, a brush of panic flowed out from him. He stomped his heel down on the glass screen, but a haunted look had seeped into his eyes.

Roger went to his side and put his arm around him. The

brightness of the runes on Zack's dagger were dimmer. Carefully, Roger took the blade from him, surprised when Zack released it without a word. Zack put both arms around Roger.

He's never killed before. Roger stroked Zack's short hair and kissed the top of his head. "You didn't have a choice."

Zack squeezed him tighter.

Nell and Dmitri neared Quinn's body. Nell had her hands on her hips, and she tsked loudly. "I wish you hadn't killed him on my grounds."

"We didn't choose where he attacked," Roger said sternly.

Nell glanced over her shoulder, eyebrow raised in a perfect arc. She tilted her head at them, then graced Roger with a soft smile. "I understand that. But this will be a disaster to untangle with Seamus."

"It won't be," Dmitri said. "I'm here as his representative. Quinn's desire to go after the Wrights is well known. I'll settle the matter with my master. Considering the nuisance Quinn has been the last few years, Seamus might even thank you."

"That almost makes me more nervous," Nell murmured.

Despite the heat of the evening, Zack shivered.

"Nell, I appreciate the lengths you've gone to in order to host this party, but I need to take Zack back to our hotel. I should stay with him," Roger said.

"Take care of your boy," Nell replied. She waved at the hall. "They've seen you, and a party is good for morale. You were just my excuse to throw one."

Roger nodded. "Dmitri, you and I still need to talk—without anger."

"Yes, yes. I'm staying at the Sleepy Bear Inn."

"So are we."

"Then that will make it easy. I'm in the Moon Room. Knock on my door after dusk tomorrow night."

"I'll see you then." Roger wiped the remnants of Quinn's blood off the dagger and onto his pants. He slid it into its sheath. Zack stumbled along beside him as they walked.

Once they were around the corner from Nell and Dmitri, Roger swept Zack into his arms and carried him onward. Zack buried his face in Roger's neck. His warm breath was pleasant. Roger only wished the situation was better for him. He cradled him closer. Zack's compliance worried him, but he wanted to be back in the room before they spoke.

If Zack was going to break, he should have the opportunity for privacy.

Even if, when he shattered, he demanded that Roger leave him alone and abandoned their mission to end Seamus.

Roger wanted the best for him. *And that may not be me.*

CHAPTER 26

Roger hadn't said a word since they left the garden. The quiet stretched into a silence that threatened to cut Zack into a million pieces. But talking would bring a sledgehammer down onto the glass bridge he'd built with Roger. If he told Roger what Cal had done, then he was admitting his brother was a killer. Not just to Roger, but … *but to me. If I say it, it's true.*

Not saying it doesn't keep it from being real, though. Zack clutched onto Roger a little tighter.

When they reached the door to their room, Roger set Zack down on his feet and took the key out of his pocket. The sliding bolt sounded like a cannon. Zack held his arms tight across his chest.

Roger walked into the room first. He flipped on the lights and shed his coat. As he tossed it onto the couch, he glanced over at Zack. "I'll run you a bath."

That wasn't what Roger was supposed to do. He was supposed to be pissed that Zack had killed his sireling. He should be angry that Zack hadn't done what he told him to do. That he'd gone outside into what was clearly a trap.

With a frown, Zack met his gaze. "What?"

Roger reached toward him but stopped short of touching him. "You're covered in blood, Zackery."

"I'll get the bathwater bloody."

"But it's easier for me to bathe you in a bath than a shower. Unless you don't want my help."

The words didn't make sense. Theoretically, they did. Zack understood their meaning, but he didn't know why Roger had said them. He dropped his hands and clenched his fists at his side. "How can you want to be near me?"

Roger blinked and stared at Zack as if he were speaking an unknown language.

His confusion sparked the waiting bonfire inside Zack. The shamble of a house that had been his morals had collapsed when he saw the footage of what Cal had done. It had been falling since he let Roger live, but the remainder was pulverized rubble.

"Everything my family taught me was a lie," Zack said. "We're not the heroes. We're not even good people! We're murderers. No. Worse. *We're* the fucking monsters. Invading homes. Killing people in their sleep for no reason. Hunting harmless people. S-s-stabbing them in the heart."

Tears started to roll down his cheeks. A torrent flooded out of him. He started to fall to the floor.

Roger caught him by the shoulders. His brown eyes had their own fire. "You are not to blame for what happened."

"Cal—"

"Forget about your blasted brother," Roger growled. "Quinn was trying to kill you. He would have. He didn't give you a choice."

"Maybe if—"

Roger changed his grip so he had Zack by the upper arms instead of at the shoulders. "Do not play through the what-ifs. Quinn organized an ambush to come after you. He wasn't going to stop. He had vampires lying in wait in case you won the fight. You understand that, don't you?"

Zack nodded. Speaking through the tears was too hard.

"Let me run you a bath. Help you get clean."

"Why would you want to help me? Why do you care?" Zack demanded. He knocked Roger's hands away and stepped back. Slamming a hand on his chest, he continued, "I'm the fucking monster. Don't you get that? I'm just like them!"

"You are *nothing* like your family," Roger replied.

"You don't know them!"

"I know you. You are clever and caring. Beauty makes you pause, and doing the right thing matters to you."

"They raised me!"

Roger took Zack's dagger out of its sheath and spiked it into the floor. The hilt stuck up between them. When Zack's frown deepened, Roger motioned at it. "Go ahead, then. Be what they raised you to be."

"What?"

"Their teachings said you should kill me, didn't they? That's what you came here to do. So do it." Roger ripped open his shirt and vest. "Shove it in my heart—because if you keep on like this, it's going to break anyway."

Zack ran his hands through his hair and stumbled away from the blade. The last thing he wanted to do was hurt Roger. There was no touch of magic to it. No vampiric sway. Roger was everything he'd ever wanted in a partner. Kind. Attentive. Wise. And being incredibly hot was the icing on the cake.

And he was standing there, waiting for Zack to pick up the silver dagger. Giving him the chance to kill him. *Because I could break his heart?*

"Are you in love with me?" Zack asked.

"I think I could love you if given the chance," Roger said.

A sob caught in Zack's throat. This perfect, immortal man —who had known thousands of people in his life—could love him? He could matter to someone with so much experience? Who would live forever? Zack sank to his knees.

"I won't hurt you," Zack whispered. "I could never hurt you."

Roger went to a knee in front of him and put his hands on Zack's shoulders again. "That's how I know you are different." He slid his touch down so he held Zack's hands together in his own. "I don't know what it's like to be part of a family. My mortal father was a prick, and my immortal master is a bastard. But I know *people*, Zackery. You have a courage few possess. You have it in you to be your own man. I saw that in you when we met."

Roger's touch was cool, and Zack felt too hot. He leaned forward, putting his forehead into the crook of Roger's neck. He wanted to wrap himself in Roger's words and comfort, but doing so would mean fanning the flames of his internal bonfire while hoping that even the ashes would vanish. And he couldn't abandon his family. He was still a part of it. Maybe they didn't know what Cal had done. Maybe Cal didn't realize he'd killed humans.

Don't keep lying to yourself. Zack squeezed out more tears.

"Come on," Roger whispered. "Let's get you clean."

"All right," Zack murmured. "But I don't want a bath. I want a shower."

"Do you want my help?"

"Does that mean you'll get naked with me?" Zack asked.

Roger pulled Zack up and looked him in the eyes. They entered the gentlest and briefest of their staring contests. Roger broke first, sliding his hand through Zack's hair and brushing it back. "If you'd like."

"Yes, please."

They shed their clothes quietly. Zack dropped his few pieces into a pile, but he didn't feel naked until he joined Roger in the bathroom. The tub was a huge clawfoot model, and it had a showerhead with five settings. Roger brought a stack of washcloths over.

He was gorgeous and graceful.

"Zack?"

Zack blinked. "Sorry."

"For what?" Roger asked with a grin.

A blush heated Zack's cheeks. "Uh. Nothing, I guess." He started to reach for the faucet.

Quinn's blood was on his hands. He froze, unable to take his eyes off it. The moment he had driven his blade into Quinn played over and over in his head.

Roger put his hand over Zack's and leaned over to turn on the shower. "You survived. Focus on that."

"How many people have you killed?" Zack whispered.

"I've lost count." Roger warmed one of the washcloths and began to wipe the blood from Zack's hands. "That happens when you live in violence for centuries."

"Did you ever do it for fun?"

"For fun? No. Did I have fun killing some awful people? Yes." Roger paid close attention to a drying spot. "Did you have fun?"

"*No*. I … I didn't even think."

"He was going to kill you if you hesitated." Roger motioned at the shower. "Test the water. Climb in if it's fine."

Zack put his hand under the spray. It was too hot, but the heat was punishingly good. He hissed when he stepped into it.

Roger gave him a cold frown and turned the temperature down before stepping in. "Don't hurt yourself."

"I was about to turn it down."

If Roger realized that was a lie, he didn't call him out on it. Instead, he began to wash Zack. A protest bubbled up in Zack, but he swallowed it down. Roger's touch was gentle but thorough. He shampooed Zack's hair. Then he carefully cleaned the makeup off his face. In between, when Zack was rinsing shampoo or soap from his body, Roger took the opportunity to clean himself.

The tenderness was the balm Zack hadn't known he longed for. He took the washcloth from Roger and caressed a spot on Roger's hip that still had blood. Water poured down on them, running in streams over Roger's chest.

They were chest to chest, their mouths so close.

The world had felt so right when Zack kissed Roger. He leaned up and pressed a tentative kiss to his lips. Roger put his hands on Zack's shoulders.

"Give me something else to focus on," Zack said.

"Zackery," Roger groaned with pent-up frustration. "I'd be happy to, but I don't know if we should."

"Please," Zack whispered between the light kisses he pressed to Roger's lips. "Please. I want to be what you see. I want to be clever and sexy. I want to forget everything else. *Please*."

"I don't want you to regret this." Roger stroked Zack's cheek down to his chin. "Your head is clouded right now."

Zack held on to Roger's hand and pressed his face into his palm. "The only thing that's been clear to me for weeks is how much I want you. Please, Roger."

"Mm, if you keep asking that nicely, I may have a hard time saying no." A playful smile lit Roger's brown eyes.

The tiniest laugh bubbled out of Zack. "Well then, *please*, Roger. Please kiss me."

Roger bent down and kissed him. Making out with a vampire and not scraping his tongue on a fang was hard. Zack winced as one of Roger's fangs drew blood, but the lust-filled groan Roger made was worth the slight pain. Lungs burning, Zack wrapped his arms around Roger's neck and pressed flush against him. The water had warmed Roger, but he was still cooler against Zack. Roger reached down, gliding his hand over Zack's ass.

In a break for air, Zack panted, "Finger my hole open, Roger. Please, please, please."

"That word has never been that erotic before," Roger said. "I don't know how you've twisted it into something so wonderful."

"I'm going to have to figure it out in other languages if you don't touch me more."

Roger chuckled. "Hold on. I want to, but this is not the place. Last thing we need is to fall over and give you a concussion."

Roger reached past Zack and turned off the shower. They climbed out of the clawfoot tub and grabbed towels for each other. Zack wiped the streams of water off Roger's shoulders, pecs, and abs, then followed the touch of cotton with his mouth. Roger's skin was cool and hard. Zack lapped at one nipple until Roger wrapped a towel around him. Then he sealed his mouth around the nipple and wrapped his hand around Roger's dick.

"Oh, you're sneaky." Roger lifted Zack up. With a mischievous grin, he hoisted Zack over his shoulder and carried him into the bedroom. "Keep your head down."

Zack almost protested, but by the time he caught his breath, Roger was tossing him onto the bed. The moment of weightlessness lasted for a fraction of a second, but it made Zack's heart soar. He laughed and stretched out on the bed.

Roger stood at the edge of the bed, watching him.

"I think you mentioned debauching is better taught than told." Zack put his wrists over his head and grinned at him. "Please debauch me."

With a sexy growl, Roger climbed onto the bed over Zack. He hovered above him, one knee between Zack's, one hand beside his head. He kept his lips just above Zack's. The closeness without contact was torture. Zack leaned his head up and caught Roger's mouth in a kiss. Roger put his other hand on Zack's wrists and pinned them to the bed. His tongue slipped between Zack's lips and plunged into him. Then he pulled his tongue out to the tip. Zack whimpered, and Roger plunged his tongue in deeper.

Zack felt like coming just from the kiss. He shivered and whined from the pain of holding out.

Instantly, Roger ended the kiss. He caressed Zack's face, his gaze sweeping over him. "What's wrong?"

"Keep kissing me like that and I'm going to come," Zack whispered.

Roger smiled at him. It felt like taking shelter in shadows on a sun-drenched day. "Darling, debauching you means making you come until you're too exhausted to get it up." He caressed down the center of Zack's chest, brushing the few light hairs. He kept sliding downward. "If you're all right with that."

More than once? With Roger? "Yeah. Please. Let's try that."

"Don't hold back," Roger murmured against Zack's ear. He gently wrapped his hand around Zack's erect dick. Ever so carefully, he stroked his thumb across his tip. "I want to feel you. I want to drink down your moans."

Then he went back to tonguing his mouth as he slid his hand up and down Zack's length.

Zack had no control over his hands because Roger still had them pinned to the bed. Having them there, not having to think about what to do with them, erased dozens of Zack's worries. He moaned into Roger and arched his hips toward his hand. Roger formed a circle with his thumb and forefinger. Zack bucked into him, and a deeper, shattering moan pulsed up from his core.

"Did we find something you like, darling?" Roger shifted on the bed. "Put your knees up. Use the leverage."

"Keep kissing me," Zack panted.

"I will, baby. I will. One second."

Zack moved into the position Roger had suggested. He kept his eyes screwed shut. He couldn't stand to look at Roger in case … in case … *in case he thinks I'm shit at this.*

Roger put his hand around Zack's tip. "Push up. Tell me how that feels. Then I'll kiss you."

Zack did, feeling Roger's hand caressing and gently squeezing. His ass was in the air, and the chilliness went up his spine. "Fuck, that's good."

"Then keep doing it." And like he promised, Roger kissed him.

Freedom and confinement. Fucking Roger's hand while Roger tongue-fucked his mouth. Feeling Roger moan into him while he was losing himself in pleasure in return.

Zack came in a stuttering burst that lengthened into white noise. The world was gone. He was nobody. And then Roger wrapped his arms around him and held him. The orgasm wrung him out. He was a noodle against Roger.

A minute could have passed. Five hours could have. Zack wasn't sure time had any meaning. But he was breathing more normal and he was back in his body.

Roger nuzzled his cheek. "There you are."

"That was amazing."

"That was just the beginning." Roger nipped Zack's ear. "Unless you're too tired."

Zack rolled onto his side. Roger was a wonder. *And he's all mine. At least for tonight.* Idly, he traced Roger's collarbone. "I need a couple more minutes."

"Okay." Roger kissed his forehead. "Do you have lubricant?"

"No. Try calling the front desk."

Roger raised an eyebrow.

"What?" Zack asked. "Teddy did say I should ask for anything we need. If his answer is no … then put on some pants. This town has to have an all-night sex shop."

Roger laughed happily. "I think I've been fooled. I think it's you who's going to debauch me."

"Only if you ask nicely." Zack kissed him.

CHAPTER 27

Every worry Roger had that Zack would leap from bed and denounce what they'd done evaporated when Zack gave him a sleepy smile as he woke. Even better, he snuggled in closer and kissed Roger. They spent the remainder of the day—what little there was as Zack had slept in as well—in the room, primarily in bed. Zack showed off how to order pizza on his phone and have it delivered to their room. After that, they turned on a movie on Zack's tablet. Zack snoozed, his head resting on Roger's chest.

It was the most blissful day Roger had had in decades. He hated when dusk finally came.

"I shouldn't be long." Roger finished buttoning his shirt. "Dmitri and I need to catch up. Discuss business and next steps."

"I'll get a change of sheets while you're gone. Maybe shower again." Zack stood and winced. "Ow. Make that a bath."

"Are you okay?" Roger hurried to Zack's side and helped him stand.

"I love that you're concerned, but seriously, Rog. I've never had anyone pound my ass like you did last night. I wouldn't trade a second of it, but yeah, I'm a little sore. Nothing I can't handle." Zack tilted his head up and pursed his lips.

It was his *quick, kiss me* gesture. Roger gave him a light peck. "All right. I'll be just down the hall."

"Moon Room. I heard Dmitri."

"I won't take long."

"You said that already. Geesh." Zack gently pushed Roger toward the door. "Go so you can come back."

"I'm going, I'm going." Roger snuck in another swift kiss before stepping out into the hall.

The rooms in the Sleepy Bear Inn were nature based, and only the inn's owners could make sense of their organization. Roger searched his floor and found the Moon Room at the front of the building. He rapped three times, paused, and then twice more.

Dmitri swung the door open wide and stalked off without another word.

He's pissed off. Again. Roger sighed and walked into the room. After he swung the door shut, he said, "What could I have possibly done in the last twenty hours?"

Dmitri was still getting dressed for the evening. He took a dress shirt off its hanger and slid it on. His movements were precise, expending only the minimum effort. No one had ever made dressing as tense an activity as Dmitri could.

Refusing to rise to the bait, Roger sat on the couch and stretched out. When Dmitri glared his way, he smiled brightly and said, "I'm waiting on an answer."

"I stopped by your room last night to check on you and the boy. I didn't knock on your door because I heard how busy you were." Dmitri finished putting a cufflink in. "How long have you been fucking him?"

"Not that it's any of your business, but last night was the first time."

"You're dragging a Wright into the middle of our coven,

so it is my business." Dmitri struggled with his second cuff-link. With a snarl, he gave up and glared at Roger. "What the hell are you thinking?"

An insinuation tightened Dmitri's voice, drove it lower and angrier. Since the day they'd met, Dmitri had treated Roger like he wasn't capable of thinking ahead. Year after year, century after century, Roger had endured it because Dmitri was the "smart one," and Roger was the "pretty one."

Things had to change. Roger traced a winding silver design on the couch's armrest. Once the silence had stretched on long enough to be dramatic, he said casually, "Are you done berating me without knowing a damn thing about what I'm planning?"

"You? A plan?"

"I know I've been out of the picture for thirty years, but I thought you might want to finish what we discussed in 1989."

A small smile crept across Dmitri's lips. "You want to go through with that?"

"Don't you? It was hardly a new idea for you back then. I can't believe you've given up on it."

"Is that why you haven't come back to Chicago?"

"I woke up weak. I wasn't about to show that to Seamus."

Dmitri joined Roger on the couch. "Where does the boy come into it?"

"You saw Quinn's body. Zack's blade did that." Roger leaned forward. "His dagger is enchanted."

"Then we take the dagger."

"It's bound to him. It won't work except in his hands."

"Shit."

"You should have seen him last night. If he'd had it on him when the fight with Quinn started, he may have been done with them before I reached him."

"You've found a dangerous plaything. What a surprise." Dmitri ran his hand over his chin before sighing and shaking his head. "Seamus has grown more paranoid. He wouldn't engage the Wrights when Quinn asked. He may want you to get rid of him."

"He'll take one look at him and pretend he doesn't want to claim him for himself." Roger folded his hands together. Thinking about what Seamus would want made him nervous, but if he was going to outsmart his enemy, he'd have to indulge a few thoughts in his mindset. "Seamus has always … desired the attention of handsome young people. Especially young men like Zack."

"Your plan is to offer Zack up to that monster and hope the boy puts his dagger in Seamus's chest before Seamus does something terrible to him?" Dmitri asked.

"Fuck no. I won't let Seamus touch him."

"Then what?"

"I don't have a full plan yet. I don't know what Chicago is like these days. All I know is that we need to penetrate Seamus's defenses, catch him off guard. Maybe get rid of Anton first. You can't tell me that Zack wouldn't be an asset in our scheme."

"That dagger is useful. I've never seen the heart burned out of a vampire so thoroughly. But Seamus could be old enough to survive the damage to his physical body."

"Then we need to find a way to test the limits of the dagger. Or research them. I'm sure Zack would like to know them as well."

"Zack, Zack, Zack. Two weeks alone with him, and you're obsessed," Dmitri scoffed. "How typical."

"What is that supposed to mean?"

Dmitri narrowed his eyes. "Seamus isn't the only one who likes pretty young men."

"Jesus Christ, Dmitri. I have a sex life that doesn't include you. Get over it."

Dmitri stiffened.

Roger didn't ease his glare. Dmitri had always been the one to end their relationship after it restarted. Twice, Roger had been close to calling it off himself, but he'd hesitated. Too much hope had long been a problem of his.

"That was uncalled for," Dmitri said woodenly.

"So is your judgment." Roger held his tongue to avoid making insults. Delving into old wounds wouldn't bring either of them peace. A good leader rose above petty squabbles; they didn't punish allies for ancient history. "You haven't watched Zack blossom these last two weeks, and it's only the beginning of what he can do. He has a presence and a cunning that are hard to ignore. And he's not afraid."

Dmitri put his knuckles to his forehead and muttered under his breath in Russian. The bits Roger could understand sounded like a prayer. "There's no talking you out of it, and you have a good point. Zack's dagger is far more powerful than anything we've uncovered while you were gone."

"Glad to know I can bring more than my pretty face to the table." Roger turned to face Dmitri. "What happened to Cee? And Brad? Phoenix? Ezra? There's only so much on the internet."

"Cee goes by Savanna these days. Ezra sired her in 1991, and she transitioned not long after that. I don't see Brad much. He nurtured that latent talent for magic and married into one of the mage circles. He has a wife, kids. Looks miserable every time I see him, but we are usually in a crisis when the wizards and the coven have to talk." Dmitri sighed. "Phoenix is ... Phoenix. He constantly experiments with new colors and looks and actively avoids Seamus's eye. Rumor has it, he's making friends with Unseelies, but since I'm part of the leadership, he avoids me to avoid Seamus."

"And Ezra?"

"Ezra. Ezra is becoming the bane of my fucking existence. He won't return to the coven even though Seamus has cordially invited him back. Claims he's dismantling his English nobility for good, which of course makes Seamus and Anton absolutely livid."

"Given what I've learned about the modern era of selfies and constant uploading, I'd think ridding himself of the title is a good thing. If we don't want humans to rediscover us, we have to be careful," Roger replied.

"That would be a fantastic argument if Ezra wasn't currently holing up in his English manor finishing his next vampire book."

"Ezra's a writer?" Roger laughed. "I've got to get my hands on his books."

"You may not want to. A version of you is in them. Me as well. He's cannibalizing coven members' histories, tweaking details here and there, and then throwing everything into a personal 'what-if.' No one has discovered his identity yet, but I see his accounts, and the books are selling. And he ended the last book with the character Nolan suddenly coming back after forty years."

"This ... Nolan—and Ezra has to be aware how much I would loathe that name—does it explain where he was for forty years?" Roger asked.

"Not a hint. Throughout the series, the characters have wondered where he's gone from time to time, but they're too caught up in fucking each other to give a shit," Dmitri replied. "It's aggravating drivel."

Roger nudged Dmitri's knee and grinned at him. "Who did he pair you with?"

"The two of you think sex and romance matter that much," Dmitri grumbled.

"Come on. Who? If you don't tell me, I'll find these books for myself and read them."

"It is an unflattering, inaccurate satire of me, and I am going to put a stop to it the next time he comes home," Dmitri replied.

Roger tapped his chin as he thought of the vampires he knew, both in the coven and out. He hummed to himself. Inspiration struck. "He put you with Nathaniel, didn't he!

That sireling of his, the blacksmith."

"The blacksmith owns a bar called the Last Deal," Dmitri said sourly. "And yes. He has me groveling, debasing myself for that man's attention."

"Have you—"

"Finish that sentence, and I will find out for myself if I can kill you with Zack's blade," Dmitri growled.

Roger held up his hands in surrender and tried not to laugh. "Consider the matter dropped. Back to my business, you mentioned seeing Ezra's accounts. Do you still watch over mine?"

"You were gone, Roger. We absorbed your accounts into the coven's finances in the mid 90s."

"You didn't keep anything back in case I returned?" Roger asked.

"Do you have any idea how many vampires drop off the face of the earth, never to be seen again?" Dmitri replied. "In our coven? I have been waking in a cold sweat for three decades, scared that Anton found some way to harvest you after all this time and was about to do the same to me."

Roger stood and paced. His plans needed money. While Nell's loan was worth millions, it was a *loan*. He had to find a way to pay it back before the interest kicked in. "I don't have a dime?"

"Your pet did kill Quinn, which makes him your kill. And you were his sire. I wasn't handling his money personally, but I'm sure it's substantial. He invested in technology at an early stage and started selling off the art he stole during the World Wars. He was probably worth upwards of fifty million."

"I was worth almost a *billion*," Roger snapped.

"I'm aware of that." Dmitri stretched out on the couch. "If you truly want to sidle up to Seamus, you'll consider that money gone. A tribute to apologize for your sudden absence unless you plan on telling him someone knocked you out for thirty years."

"Without money, I'll look weak."

"Once Seamus is gone, his money will be up for grabs. That's nearing ninety billion and growing by the second."

Roger paced across the room and back a few times. The options weren't fantastic, but Quinn's money would keep him afloat even in wealthy vampire circles. "The penthouse?"

"I sold it. I think an actor lives there now."

"Do I have *anything*?"

"You were dead to us, Roger," Dmitri said sternly. "One night you were partying as usual, and then you were gone without a word. We waited weeks. Then months. I convinced Seamus to give you three whole years. I know that you feel like it wasn't that long ago, but your new plaything was born well after you disappeared, and he's a man. Do you understand that?"

"I understand that you need to stop referring to him as a plaything. I don't want to hear that from you again." Roger finished pacing and ran his hand through his hair. He'd forgotten to brush it in his hurry to leave the room, and he struck a knot in it. With a hiss, he tried to untangle it, then gave up. Nothing was working out like he had hoped. *Except Zack.* "All right, Dmitri. I have a little reserve I've managed to procure. I can make it work until Quinn's accounts are formally mine. How long do you think it will take?"

"I'll have to see the state of his affairs, notify Seamus of his death. There are channels to move through."

"Then let's start discussing the timetable for my return to the GLC." Roger sat down beside Dmitri. "I think it's time I work on leaving Taliville."

CHAPTER 28

"Yes, please. This is exactly what I need," Zack moaned. He brought the cup of coffee closer and held his hands around the mug. Warmth tingled in his fingertips. The weather outside was blistering hot, but he was sitting inside the cool air-conditioning of Sugar Moon. The stool was uncomfortable.

Well, sitting in general was a little uncomfortable at the moment. After three more nights of sex, training, and discussing the move to Chicago, Zack was exhausted, and his body was sore. He'd gotten out of the room early because Blake had been texting him. Even Kit had made a comment that he should get out and see the sun.

"Did you finish it yet?"

"I literally just got the coffee," Zack muttered against the lip of his mug.

"I meant *Over My Grave*. I need to talk about that twist with you."

"It's kind of hard to read it when it's still under the counter."

"Oh!" Blake set it on the counter in front of him. "You can borrow it from here. I finished it two days ago. I thought I'd already handed it off, but I forgot you haven't been in since then."

"I've been busy."

"Busy boinking, from the gossip I hear." Blake grinned.

Zack's face felt as hot as the mug of coffee. "Gossip from who?"

"Kit. They said something about dropping off food for you in the morning and letting Roger feed the other night."

Dmitri had stressed that Roger needed another pet during their planning session before he took off for Chicago. While Roger had claimed he didn't want to drag anyone else into their problems, Zack couldn't help wondering if having someone else around wouldn't be better. Both older vampires were paranoid about everyone in the GLC. *Wouldn't it be better if we brought someone else with us and didn't have to watch our backs from the inside?*

"What do you think of Kit?" Zack set his coffee cup down.

"They're nice. There was some drama a couple years ago. Some kind of dating mishap where it wasn't quite poly but it wasn't exactly not. I wasn't paying close attention. But they come in for coffee on the regular and tip on occasion." Blake grabbed a slice of coffee cake and split it on a plate, sliding part of it over to Zack. "Thinking about expanding Roger's harem?"

"Not a harem. An entourage. I don't have enough blood to keep him fed, and Kit seems to like him. But Reed gave me this talk on being careful about who gets to be Roger's pet."

Blake popped a piece of coffee cake in her mouth. "Honestly, I'm pretty sure Kit sees Roger as their ticket out of small-town life."

"Have you thought about going back to Chicago?"

"Hoo boy, no. I don't know anyone in supernatural circles there."

"Roger and I will be there."

Slowly, they ate their coffee cake. Blake scowled in

thought as she took bite after bite. When they were done, she sighed, "I do miss seeing different faces. Taliville is nice, but it's not the same."

"We're not leaving for a couple of weeks. Maybe a month," Zack said.

Blake chewed on her bottom lip. "I might be ready to move back around then. I've been sticking around here because I didn't know what it would be like to handle all this supernatural stuff on my own, but if you guys are there, then I'm not solo, right?"

Zack felt a swell of hope at the thought of having a friend in the city, but it quickly faded into worry that he was steering her in a dangerous direction. The risks were real and potentially fatal. Would Blake be safe if she wasn't directly involved with their plan? Should he warn her? Wouldn't he be safer with more people he could trust?

"Okay. What have you got on your face? Besides cinnamon," Blake said.

"Eh, it's complicated." Zack wiped the corners of his lips and found the bits of coffee cake.

"Hold that thought." Blake motioned for Zack to be quiet as she tilted her head toward the large front window. "I think a customer's coming in."

Striding down the sidewalk, in the full summer sunlight, was Cal. Zack wished he were confusing a stranger for his brother out of some desperate desire to see his family, but no one could imitate Cal's casual saunter. Ice clawed Zack's throat and crept up his veins. He'd managed to push the video Quinn had shown him out of his head. Seeing Cal brought it back.

And now I've fucked a vampire and have his crest around my neck. What will Cal do to me? Zack's instinct was to run. There was a bathroom. He could hole up in it until Cal passed. *But that leaves him free to wander the town. What will he do to others? To Roger? To Blake?*

"He's a hottie," Blake said.

"He's my brother," Zack whispered.

As Cal reached for the coffee shop door handle, the cold turned to an intense burning fear. Zack shoved *Over My Grave* off onto the floor beside Blake and slipped his medallion under his tank top. When she started to reach for the book, he grabbed her wrist and hissed, "Don't say anything about the supernatural around him."

"Nonbeliever?" Blake asked.

"*Hunter*," Zack replied under his breath.

Startled, Blake stepped away. The shop's bell tinkled brightly, and Cal meandered inside. He pulled his sunglasses off and hooked them into the collar of his T-shirt. His warm smile only made Zack's guts freeze further.

"There you are! Been looking all over for you. Freaking innkeeper wouldn't tell me if you were still in town," Cal said. He crossed the room.

Each thud of his boots felt like the slam of a nail in Zack's coffin. Zack put his hands around his coffee mug. "Here I am."

"So you are." Cal took a seat beside Zack. "Hey, precious, can I get a cup of coffee? Black."

"Sure," Blake said nervously. She turned away and focused on making the coffee, as far away from Cal as she could get.

The other few patrons in the shop slid out as quietly as they could. Assuming Quinn hadn't told anyone other than the vampires who'd ambushed Zack, then it was clear that he'd given away his secret. But his stomach roiled at the thought of Blake trying to get along with Cal.

His stomach continued to churn. The bite mark on his neck was obvious, but it was on the side away from Cal. Was the mark on his left wrist visible? Not if he kept his arm rotated. On top of that, he still had bruises from his fight with

Quinn. He could try to say the bite marks were from the same battle. Would Cal buy that?

"What are you doing here?" Zack asked.

"You don't sound happy to see me," Cal replied. "Little tip, if you don't want someone coming after you, don't tell the extended family you're with us and then tell us you're at home. Uncle Pat texted Dad three days ago asking how long he had to take care of the lawn."

"Then why didn't you text me?"

"We did, numbskull. You didn't answer. You got everyone freaking the fuck out."

Zack pulled out his phone and thumbed through his messages. He'd responded to Kit and Blake, and to Reed, who'd been making sure he was all right as part of his duties looking after humans in Taliville. He had a chat going with Roger, though that was just letting Roger mess around with texting so he could figure it out. Below that, he had a message from Cal that he'd ignored and another one from his mother. And Uncle Pat. And Amber.

"Fuck," Zack groaned.

"You are in deep shit, little brother." Cal took the coffee from Blake. "Hey, can I get a muffin too?"

"You know that stuff costs, right?" Zack said sharply.

"Why don't you just put it on whatever you've been using the last week and a half? You must have some way of paying since you stopped using Mom and Dad's card," Cal replied. "By the way, again, if you don't want people finding you, don't use cards other people have access to. And if you are using other people's accounts, *keep using them*. I am overjoyed you're sitting here roughly the picture of perfect health, but Mom is going to be pissed once her relief wears off. Speaking of. Hold on."

Cal pulled up his phone, and it made a picture sound.

"Why did you do that?"

"It's called proof of life. Have you forgotten everything we taught you?"

Blake dropped off the muffin. "I'm going to see if my aunt needs help. Call me if someone comes in."

"No problem," Zack said, his mouth feeling far too dry.

Once Blake was through the door, Cal continued talking while shoving muffin in his mouth. "The rest of the fam is heading back to Rockford. We went through most of our supplies on the Florida nests. You should have told us to head to Tallahassee first. Took us the better part of two weeks to find the Pensacola nest, and by then, the Tallahassee one had swollen. Dad's on the mend from getting a piece of rebar through the stomach in case you care."

"I care," Zack said. "And I told you to go to Tallahassee first. I put it in the files, and I told Amber."

"You should've mentioned it to Mom." Cal popped more muffin into his mouth. "What brought you out of the house? And how've you paid for anything the last week and a half without using any of the family cards? You got an account we don't know about?"

"I don't," Zack said. "And I ..."

The truth almost spilled out of Zack's lips, but Cal glanced his way. There was a hardness in his eyes that Zack had seen his whole life. He'd believed it was just Cal's suit of armor. An older brother's hard, protective shell against the world.

But Zack's voice caught in his throat, and a wave of relief washed over him. Because Cal wasn't going to understand what Zack was trying to do. That hardness in Cal's soul that shone through his steady, assessing glare was what everyone else in the family had. What Zack lacked.

Roger's right. I'm not like them. Zack emptied his coffee and put the mug nearer to Blake's side of the counter. He couldn't abandon Roger, not when they were making the first steps on their hunt for Seamus. While he could try to tell Cal to fuck off, he knew his brother wouldn't listen. He had to keep Cal close to protect the supernaturals in Taliville.

"I took a debit card from a vamp I killed," Zack replied. "Been using that instead of draining the family's accounts. I've been working on a bigger hunt. Gathering intel. We can talk about it in my room across the street."

"Look at you! Coming up in the world." Cal laughed and patted Zack's shoulder with all the camaraderie Zack used to dream about. "Let me finish my coffee, and we'll go."

Silently, Zack prayed Cal would take the whole afternoon and the next forever to finish drinking it. Maybe by then, he wouldn't feel like throwing up because of Cal's approval.

CHAPTER 29

Slamming onto the floor and into a patch of bright sunlight woke Roger from his deep sleep. He'd been having a strange dream, one where Zack and Dmitri were making out. While a pleasant fantasy, the oddness of reality left a bitter taste in his mouth, and he shifted away from the burning light. Was the clock on the nightstand correct? It was barely past noon. What on earth was Zack thinking?

And what was he saying? As Zack dropped the side of the mattress he'd lifted—apparently having rolled Roger out of bed instead of risking closer contact—he seemed to pick up in the middle of a monologue. Mental fogginess clung tightly to him, and Roger only realized Zack was speaking to him rather than himself when Zack threw a shirt at his face. Underwear and pants flew at him next. He gathered the clothing and crawled to the darkest corner of the room. *Mm. That's better.*

"We're running out of time." Zack grabbed the new suitcase and started shoving clothes into it. "Didn't you hear anything I said?"

"We were up past dawn, and I haven't had any blood, and

the sun is still up. I am lucky to know you're speaking English," Roger grumbled. "What the hell is going on?"

"Get dressed. I don't have time to go over it again."

Waves of fear were pouring off Zack and tainting the air with an electric smell. Roger staggered to his feet, clothes in one hand, and leaned against the wall. "I'm not doing anything until you tell me why you're panicking."

"Look, I know this has to be confusing on your end. But please, just put your clothes on."

There were footsteps in the hall. Zack's eyes went wide with terror, and he slammed the suitcase shut and zipped it tight. After glancing wildly around the room, he cursed and shoved the suitcase under the bed. "Roger, clothes. Now!"

Fumbling, Roger dropped everything but his shirt. He slid his arms into it, trying to move faster, but he was sluggish.

The door started to open and Zack raced over to it. He slammed his hands on it and attempted to push it shut. "Not yet!"

"Dude, I don't care what freaky shit you've been up to," a voice replied.

The door continued to open. The man who entered the room had to be in his mid-twenties. He was broad-shouldered, dark-haired, and bore a striking resemblance to Zack. He had a duffle bag over one shoulder, but the gun and knife on his hips caught more of Roger's attention.

This had to be Zack's older brother, Callum Wright. The Butcher.

No wonder Zack was panicking.

"Zack, you sly dog. Didn't realize you'd been slutting it up."

Zack backed up to the edge of the bed and shrank in on himself. He buried his face in his hands and muttered, "Fuck my life."

Roger was sorry he'd played a part in bringing him such anguish. He was tempted to cross the room and knock Cal on his ass, but that would cause more problems than it solved. Quickly, he picked up the clothes Zack had tossed at him. "Excuse me while I get dressed."

While Roger didn't need privacy to get dressed, he was afraid of what he might do if he stayed in a room with Cal. He went into the bathroom.

As soon as the bathroom door was shut, he heard Cal whisper to Zack, "I can see what you've been doing with your spare time. Is he how you're paying for shit?"

"Um, sort of."

Cal laughed, and the sound dragged on Roger's nerves like a knife sawing through rope. "No wonder you were walking funny. Man's a fucking powerhouse. Your twink ass must be wrecked."

"I wasn't walking funny," Zack mumbled.

"What'd you say?" Cal asked.

"Could we talk about anything else?" Zack said more clearly.

Roger focused on putting on each article of clothing as calmly as he could. Cal's arrival was a wrench in their plans.

"We'll get down to business as soon as your sugar daddy's gone."

"Oh my God, Cal, it's not like that."

"You said he's paying for stuff. Wait, just what is he paying for?" There was a gleeful-tormentor quality to his voice that rivalled Seamus's. "Is hooking your side hustle? Have you been doing this all summer? Trying to earn a little extra cash?"

"Cal, stop, okay?" Zack said.

The pained note in Zack's voice made Roger clench his teeth hard enough that his fangs pricked at his gums. In the middle of a fight for his life, Zack had never sounded so hurt. And until four nights ago, Cal was the brother Zack had idolized. The exalted child, the sibling who could do no wrong.

Cal's current attitude was not new. Roger knew that tone

of voice. He knew Zack's. He'd heard both tones more times in his life than he could count and far more than he wanted to think about. Such pleading always fell on unsympathetic listeners.

Somehow, the cruel child was the favorite, and the wonderful man Roger wanted to whisk off into the sunset was the black sheep of the family. *This is why I hate families. Blood means nothing.* Roger yanked on his pants' zipper and felt it jam at the top. He'd caught his underwear in it. Luckily, he hadn't caught anything else. Unworking it and redoing it took focus.

"Hey," Cal said in the other room, "if people are willing to pay you for it, I say go ahead. You're only going to be cute for so long. I mean, I don't see it, so probably not much longer, huh?"

"I'm not a hooker," Zack said.

Cal laughed again, a sound that stung like jellyfish. "Okay, okay. Geez, calm down, will ya? I'm just teasing. Can't a big bro have a little fun?"

It's nothing serious, Seamus had said over and over, when in fact he had been completely serious. And Roger had pretended the words hadn't hurt him and had ignored the pain others were steeped in.

God, he had so much to make up for. An eternity wouldn't be long enough to absolve him of his sins of callousness and cowardice.

After he dressed, Roger opened the door to the bedroom. Cal stood near the balcony door, a joker's grin on his lips. Zack sat in the same place he'd been, at the edge of the bed. The misery clouding his features was obvious to anyone with a heart.

Seeing the crack in Zack's armor and remembering the way he had shattered after Quinn showed him the truth of what Cal had done hardened Roger's resolve into steel. No matter what happened between him and Zack, so long as Roger was alive, he would make certain Zack never had to go anywhere near his family if he didn't want to.

But sometimes they choose to go home. Sometimes fear keeps them from finding a life elsewhere. Roger clenched his fist tight enough that he could feel the sting of his nails and the wetness of blood in his hand. He longed to kick Cal off the balcony and follow through until he was nothing more than a stain on the grass. *Get yourself under control before your eyes turn red.*

Upon seeing Roger, Zack leapt up from his spot. "Cal, I need a moment in the hall with … my friend here."

"You want another quickie for the road, then I can clear out for what, ten minutes?" Cal said, the leer in his eyes as well as his voice. Roger could feel a flicker of lust in Cal, directed toward him. Zack's lust was a warm welcome; Cal's was a sickening, cold hunger. "Or do you only last five?"

"A minute in the hall because it's not about sex, asshole." Zack hurried for the door. "Roger?"

"Coming." Roger kept his hurt hand clenched, though once he eased his grip, the wounds healed. He nabbed his phone from the bedside table and followed Zack.

Once the door clicked shut behind them in the hallway, Zack whispered, "Look, I understand this is fucked up. I'm not happy about him being here either. But I—"

Roger dropped his phone to the floor and swept Zack into the wall across the hall. Words would never be enough. He pressed a needy kiss to Zack's mouth. When Zack parted his lips, Roger slipped in, kissing him as deeply and thoroughly and ruthlessly breathtaking as possible. Every trick and tease he'd learned went into that kiss. Zack clutched his shoulders, and his heart raced.

Mid kiss, Roger broke it off. A kiss like that had a magic all its own. Zack had his head tipped upward, his face flushed and his lips quivering. No trace of the doubt or shame Cal had caused lingered in his expression.

He was glorious.

Pressing his lips together, Zack gently pushed on Roger's shoulder. "As much as I liked that, it's not why I brought you out here."

"Do you have your phone? Wallet? We could run," Roger said.

"We can't."

"Zack, I know you think you need your family—"

Zack's gray eyes hardened. "We can't leave Cal wandering Taliville on his own."

The courage and conviction in Zack broke through another of Roger's cracks. Zack was right. A hunter like Cal would wreak destruction on whomever he felt justified in attacking. In Taliville, that could be anyone.

Roger traced Zack's chin. "The Wright family name isn't worthy of you."

Zack grinned at him. "Eh, maybe not."

"Do you have a plan?"

"I think we should go with your first idea for me," Zack said. "Tie him up, toss him in the back of his truck, and drive out of town. Figure it out when we get to Nashville."

"It's too soon to go to Chicago."

"It might be. But Cal's already told my family I'm in town. If I stay, that could bring more of them here looking for me. They won't understand this place. We can't risk Nell's people. They deserve better."

Roger didn't like it, but he could contact Dmitri. A few of their old friends might have a place for them to hide so Nell and her people wouldn't be at risk. "There's the problem of sunlight."

"I can keep him distracted until dusk. Then we book it out of here."

"All right." Roger kissed Zack. "Text me if you need to."

"Stay safe," Zack murmured.

Roger put his forehead against Zack's. He couldn't bring himself to move away, not yet. His own heart had stopped beating centuries ago, but he swore it was racing. He whispered, "If he lays a hand on you, I'm ripping his arms off."

"Is it fucked up that's the second sexiest thing you've said to me?"

"Depends. What's the first?"

"'Are you okay?'" Zack sighed. "Yup. I just heard that myself. I am definitely a sad little monster made of trauma."

"I don't think that at all." Roger kissed him gently.

Zack groaned and broke off the kiss. He nudged Roger's shoulder. "Seriously. Go. Come back at dusk."

"I will. I will." Roger snuck in one last kiss before heading down the hall. He glanced over his shoulder before he turned the corner.

Zack stood at the door with his hand on the knob. Roger watched while he took in a deep breath, and his demeanor shifted. Gone was the confident man; the embarrassed little brother had returned.

Which was the true Zack?

The confidence. You can't fake that. He has more than I've ever had. Roger made his way downstairs, trying to dismiss his worries. Fretting for the next seven hours wouldn't do him or Zack any good.

Unfortunately, Dmitri had taken off the night before. Roger's planning sessions hadn't progressed past catching him up on the coven news. While he'd hoped for more time, Dmitri had responsibilities that couldn't wait in Chicago.

Teddy was at the desk. Without much hassle, Roger procured another room. Although it was smaller and on the first floor, it would work for the day. Roger closed the curtains and lay down on the bed. Sleep wasn't going to happen even though he needed it. Countless visions of Cal lashing out at Zack played through his mind.

Roger brushed his fingers across the screen of his phone. It lit up. After fumbling through a long text, he sent Josefina an update on their situation. He included their plan to take Cal out of town as soon as possible. Minutes went by without an answer. She had to be asleep. He would at least pretend he was too.

CHAPTER 30

"Now that we're alone, we can have a real conversation." Cal dropped his bag on Roger's side of the bed.

Zack fought the urge to push Cal's bag off the bed. Having Cal in the room he'd shared with Roger was a walking nightmare. Over the last three weeks, Zack had convinced himself that he'd never have to answer to his family. He hadn't thought of a story to tell them because he hadn't been sure how long it would take for them to notice he was gone. He should've prepared for them like he was readying for battle with Seamus.

"What brought you into Taliville? Other than some serious dick." Cal opened his duffle bag and drew out his messy leather journal.

What few notes he took and his daily recounting of what he'd done all went into the same journal for Cal, and he was only on his second as a hunter even though he'd been hunting for almost a decade. Zack was on his fourth journal, and he kept the bulk of his supernatural lore separate.

Cal rooted around in his bag and made a sniff of disappointed annoyance. "You got a pen?"

"Somewhere," Zack said.

"Got to say, I'm surprised you have the balls to step into Taliville." Cal rooted around the desk and found one of the inn pens.

"Why?" Zack asked.

"Because it's a supernatural hotspot. I wasn't sure the rumors were true, but that coffee girl's got to be a shifter. You realize that, don't you?" Cal made a swipe motion across his face. "Her scars are a dead giveaway."

Hearing Cal say exactly what Zack thought when he first saw Blake made his stomach churn. He folded his arms over his chest. "I've never read anything about Taliville in the HIN."

"Because some of the site's moderators are shithead deniers who think there's such a thing as a moral supernatural. To get the real info, you got to hang out in the right bars. Something you've never done." Instead of picking up a pen, Cal opened one of Zack's notebooks. "Looks like you have been doing more than getting fucked."

The notebook in his hand was filled with research Zack had done for Roger. It held names and places important to him and the GLC, and the research Zack had done on Nell, Josefina, and any other names he'd learned while sitting in Sugar Moon the first week.

In Cal's hands, it would be a guidebook to murder.

"That's mine." Zack lunged for the notebook, but Cal kept it high over his head. Tackling his brother had never worked out for him, and that was before Cal had gained field experience.

"Whoa, touchy, touchy." Cal laughed.

"It's fanfiction," Zack blurted out. "Not real research."

"You said you've been working on a bigger hunt." Cal tossed the notebook at Zack's face. "Where is it?"

Zack scanned the desk for the one he always brought with him. Every Gladwell descendent knew the story of the family massacre in 1755. Anton and Seamus and their coven were responsible. *Don't think about how old Roger is and how you haven't asked him about it.* Zack clutched the ring binding as he pulled it free from the stack. He'd been adding to the notebook with the bits he'd learned about the ancient vampires.

Cal wouldn't agree with the method, but Zack could distract him with the intel. He didn't have to breathe a word of the plan.

"Here." Zack held out the notebook.

"What's this?" Cal took it and flipped it open.

"I'm on Anton and Seamus's trail."

Cal laughed and laughed and crossed the room while looking over the pages and still laughing. "You think that's some big unknown? We know where Seamus and Anton are. Duh."

"Yeah, well. I think I can kill them."

"Might have some competition for biggest balls in the family after all." Cal tossed the notebook onto the bed. "But a hunt like that's going to get you killed. Drop it."

"I thought you weren't scared of anything," Zack replied.

"Oh, I'm not scared, but I'm not a fucking idiot." Cal motioned at Zack's neck. "Did you get the fucker who bit you?"

Zack slapped his hand over the scar. "Yeah. Same guy who beat me up. Put him down a couple nights ago."

"Congratulations on your first solo hunt." Cal clapped him on the shoulder.

Instinctively, Zack ducked out of his touch and backed away. When Cal frowned at him, Zack rolled his shoulder. One lie stacking on another, he said, "Got nailed in the shoulder pretty bad too."

"Well, okay, then," Cal said. "Why don't we settle in for some research? Pick a couple of soft targets before we blow out of town."

"Yeah. Guess I could use the backup," Zack replied.

"That's the spirit."

A month ago, Zack would have been over the moon with the prideful look Cal shot him. Now he was begging his stomach not to throw up. He grabbed his tablet from the bed and hunkered down on the floor in the shadows.

Cal took his knife and a few round pieces of wood from his duffle bag. He set up on the balcony and began to whittle the wood down into stakes.

Minutes crept into hours. Zack pretended he was doing research, though his eyes glazed over the posts on the HIN. One of his top competitors had started a thread about Zack's recent absence. He made a quick post saying he was alive and fine. The crawl of time was agony.

But finally, *finally*, the sun sloped toward the horizon.

"How's it going in there?" Cal called out.

"Having trouble picking," Zack replied. "Just so many, you know?"

"Yeah," Cal drawled. "Yeah, I know plenty."

"That sounds ominous." Zack stood.

Cal had his feet propped up on the balcony railing. He let one drop at a time, each a resounding thud. There was a maliciousness in his cold eyes that Zack had never seen in person. "What about werewolf girl from the coffee shop? Know where she lives?"

"She's innocent."

"How many have her pack killed?"

"There's no werewolf pack in Taliville," Zack said, not sure if he was lying or not. No one had mentioned a pack structure around him.

"So she's some omega bitch," Cal replied. "Makes her more likely to be dangerous."

"That's complete bullshit. I've run the numbers and researched the lore." Zack pulled up a spreadsheet on his tablet. Once he had it open, he turned it around for Cal to see. "I've been tracking werewolf attacks in our region. Tennessee is just inside my zone. If you look, most attacks are carried out by groups of four or five who typically have the Malcoeur curse, which is one of the more violent strains. And besides, there's no such thing as an omega werewolf. That's all hyped-up alpha-hierarchy bullshit that most modern werewolf packs don't—"

Cal smacked the tablet out of Zack's hands. It crashed into the wall with a loud crack. "How many more supernaturals are you going to suck up to, you little blood bitch?"

Ice settled into Zack's veins. Cal didn't sound like the brother he'd grown up with. But this was who he was underneath the brother Zack had adored. He'd seen it on the security video Quinn showed him. *Roger realized it before meeting him.*

Josefina's words from their most recent sparring match came back. *Keep as still as you can and watch your foe as subtly as you can. You don't want to give your enemy any advantage.*

"You've had a long day, Cal. Get some rest," Zack said levelly.

"Rest."

"Yeah. You're confusing shit. Not thinking clearly."

"Oh, my head's on plenty straight." Cal pointed the tip of his knife at Zack. "You're the one that's fucked up."

"I don't know what you're—"

Cal slammed his knife onto the desk. The sound made Zack jump, and in that blink of an eye, Cal grabbed his left wrist. On reflex, Zack rotated his wrist and popped free of Cal's hold.

"You think I can't tell the difference between a forced bite and a consensual one?" Cal grabbed Zack's wrist again. His fingers clamped into the healing fang marks. "You don't even have a bruise on this one. I always figured you were into some vile shit. But this, *brother*, is disappointing."

Any minute, Roger would show up. Zack wouldn't be alone. Should he try calling for help? Was Roger close enough to hear? What about Teddy? The innkeeper had offered aid before. But Cal's blade could do real damage to Teddy. At least Roger knew what he was walking into.

Zack had to buy time.

"I know you've killed people," Zack snapped.

Cal loosened his grip, and it was enough for Zack to slip away from him. "That so."

"You got caught on security footage." Carefully, Zack circled around him, heading for the door.

Cal matched his step and stayed in his path. "Footage, huh? And who showed it to you? That dick who's been fucking you?"

"Quinn Turner." Zack took a step back. He could stay between Cal and his knife. That would work.

"That fucker?" Cal smiled broadly. "Security footage from his house? Did he show you what he had going on in his basement? Those blood bitches lived in his house, ate his food, and he was feeding them people, Zack. He's a serial killer who's done some of the most fucked-up shit I've ever heard about. And if you're believing him over what you know is right, then you're more gone than I thought."

Cal was going for the shock value. Like always. Zack could sift the truth from the lies later. "He's dead. I shoved my dagger in his chest and burned out his heart."

"Maybe you're not hopeless."

"You are. You slit a sleeping human's throat. He wasn't a threat."

"Little bro, I got to admire the pair on you, but it's time we ended this little charade," Cal said.

"I have no clue what you're talking about." Zack shifted his weight so one shoulder was further back. He needed to make himself a smaller target.

"I *heard* you, shit for brains." Cal motioned at the door. "Making your plan with your undead dickhead. I know you're hoping he'll come save you. He's not going to get here in time."

Zack's eyes widened.

Cal's glare hardened.

A bird flew past the open balcony door, the only sign of movement in the tense stillness.

Cal moved first. He came in with a big swing for Zack's jaw, which Zack easily dodged. Another swing, another dodge. With a frustrated growl, Cal picked up speed. But Zack had been training with a vampire, and he'd been fighting Cal his whole life. Ducking and weaving, he countered and landed a few punches.

I could win this. Zack grinned.

Cal returned that grin and clocked him between the eyes. "You always get cocky."

Blood ran out of Zack's nose. He wiped at it.

In that time, Cal grabbed the desk chair and swung it at Zack. Zack managed to catch it before it came down on him. They entered a tug of war over the chair, like they'd done over toys and books and a million other things.

And Cal always ... Zack remembered too late. Cal grinned more widely and released the chair. The strength Zack had put into his pull became a weakness, and he toppled over with the chair.

Cal knocked the chair off him, grabbed him by the shirt, and slammed his fist into him.

Keeping hold of reality became a struggle. Zack sagged onto the floor when Cal let him go. Cal stalked over to his duffle bag.

"Don't worry, little bro. I'll get you home. Couple weeks without vampires and your head'll clear. You'll thank me for this at some point."

Cal came back over and flipped Zack onto his stomach. Zack struggled, but he was still dazed. With cold efficiency, Cal zip-tied Zack's hands behind his back, then did his ankles. When he was done, he dragged Zack into the bathroom and put duct tape over his mouth.

"Hang out in here a couple minutes," Cal said quietly. He patted Zack's knee. "I'll take care of that dickhead, then we'll clear out."

Zack screamed into the gag, but Cal kept walking.

The click of the bathroom door shutting was louder than thunder.

CHAPTER 31

While there was a television in the room Roger shared with Zack, they'd never used it. Zack insisted on streaming "live" TV. The inn offered up a variety of channels, but nothing caught Roger's attention. Sometimes he had difficulty telling what the channel was for. Everything seemed to be advertisements for prescription drugs. He settled on a program where a couple was renovating their home.

His phone dinged and brightened.

Door's open. Come on up, said the text from Zack.

Roger swung his legs off the side of the bed as he sat up. He checked the window for the sun's progress. There wasn't much light in the sky. He could survive it. Quickly, he sent a text to Josefina warning her that their confrontation with Cal was imminent.

She replied, *Give me five minutes to get people in place. Need to make sure he's contained.*

Waiting was agony, but she was right. If the situation with Cal worsened, Roger would wish she was close. Better to wait.

Where are you? came the text from Zack three minutes later.

Waiting for reinforcements, Roger sent back.

A second later, one word came through. *Help!*

Would Cal hurt Zack? Roger wasn't willing to risk Zack's safety. He flew off a jumble of letters to Josefina, trying to tell her that he had to move, but they were nonsense. He didn't have time to correct it.

Using a burst of vampiric speed, he hurried up to the room. He threw open the door. The lights were out, but the last few rays of sunlight caught the glint of the gold trim around the room. Cal and Zack weren't in sight.

But there was a pale silver illumination coming from behind him.

Roger rolled forward, going into a somersault. A rush of air went through the space he'd been in. He spun and called on his power. The darkness of the room faded as if he'd turned on an overhead light. His eyes would be bright red, but he didn't care what Cal saw. The bastard had tried to stab him in the back.

"Fucking knew it," Cal growled. "Fucking vampire."

"Fucking hunter," Roger snarled.

Cal aimed the tip of his blade at Roger. "I'll give you one chance, bloodsucker. Release the spell you've got on my brother, and I'll make this quick."

"Zack is under no spell." Roger clenched his fist. "I'll offer you one opportunity. Tell me where he is and walk away."

"Ultimatum against ultimatum." Cal lifted his hands and shifted his weight into a ready stance. "I'm thinking we're both declining."

"Where is he?" Roger shouted.

A muffled noise came from the bathroom. For a split second, Roger turned his attention to the door. In the corner of his eye, he could see Cal coming at him. With a hiss, Roger caught Cal's wrist. The knife in his hand glowed white, but not with the brightness Zack's had the first time they'd fought. Roger didn't have to look away from it. He yanked Cal forward, but Cal came in swinging.

The first blow landed against Roger's cheek. Physics demanded that his head turned with it, but no pain followed the strike. For the first time since he'd woken, Roger truly relied on his power. His hunger sharpened. He wouldn't be able to move at full strength for long.

But he had enough for the moment.

After the blow hit, he slowly tilted his head back in Cal's direction. He tightened his grip on Cal's wrist until the hunter cried out. "Is that all you've got, little boy?"

"D-d-don't hurt me," Cal said. He warbled his voice.

But there was no plea in his eyes. The words were a distraction. Roger shoved Cal away just as he dropped the knife into his free hand. The push caught him off balance and gave Roger space to maneuver.

The fight fell into instinctual moves after that. Roger had speed and experience on his side, but Cal fought fiercely. The knife flashed again and again, rarely finding purchase in Roger. Where it did catch him, it burned. Even getting caught with the edge smarted. Roger attempted to disarm him. Cal dropped the damned weapon once. Before Roger could kick it away, he had it in his hand.

Relying on his vampiric nature was burning away what little reserves he had. Roger punched forward, and Cal easily dodged. Roger couldn't compel his limbs to move faster, and he could feel his strength starting to give. He needed blood.

Cal had plenty of it.

Instead of fighting to keep Cal distant, Roger switched his tactics and brought him in close, too close for the knife to do any good. They traded blows. Roger spun Cal around, grabbed him by the back of his head, and wrenched his head to the side.

"Don't you fucking dare," Cal snapped.

Roger bit down. Blood poured into his mouth. He closed his eyes and drank in deep, not giving a damn about Cal's struggles in his arms. Power was flowing through him. He could drink and drink and drink.

CHAPTER 32

The zip tie handcuffs cinched Zack's wrists together tighter than jump rope ever had. With his wrists separated and locked into the central piece, he couldn't wriggle free. He attempted to break the binding through sheer strength, but it held.

The murmur of voices in the other room meant Cal wasn't alone anymore. Had Teddy heard them fighting?

Zack rolled onto his back and shimmied his wrists down as far as he could. Then he brought his legs up as far as he could. The plastic dug into his wrists, but he worked the handcuffs past his ankles.

"Where is he?" Roger shouted.

Hands shaking, Zack reached for the duct tape on his mouth. It was hard to peel off, and he shouted in frustration at it.

The sounds of a fight threatened to freeze him solid. Cal and Roger were going at it, and Zack had no idea who he wanted to win. *That's not true, traitor,* the Cal-like voice in his head whispered.

He needed out of his bonds before something terrible happened. After pulling the duct tape off, he tried to gnaw on the handcuffs and then pull them apart. It wasn't working. Fumbling and hurrying, he got onto his feet and hopped over to the light switch. The bright light blinded him for a second.

There had to be something useful on the counter, but he scanned over it three times without seeing what was before him. The fight in the other room was a series of grunts coming from both Cal and Roger. Zack could tell the difference. It sounded even.

One of them was going to kill the other if he didn't stop them.

"Breathe," he whispered to himself. "Panic's the enemy. Breathe. Okay. I've got toothbrushes. Way too much hair product. Makeup brushes. Wait, wait. Roger made me buy a straight razor. Where the fuck is it?"

Lying in the bottom of Roger's new toiletry bag was the folded straight razor. With a triumphant exclamation, Zack nabbed it. Unfolding it and getting it under the first cuff was the tricky part. In his haste, he grazed his thumb.

But he got one wrist free. The rest was easy.

He ripped open the door to the bedroom.

Roger had Cal in a hold from behind; one hand was in his hair, while the other was latched around his wrist and pulling him taut. Blood spilled down Cal from the wound in his neck. Cal groaned and struggled, but Roger had his fangs in him.

It would serve him right to die like that, an insidious voice whispered inside Zack's head. It was the voice he'd been learning to trust. The one that sounded like him. Some cold part of him didn't care if Cal died. *But he's my brother.*

He's a monster.

"Roger, stop!" Zack called out.

For a second, Roger continued feeding. The sounds of slurping etched into Zack. Each pull was taking life from Cal.

But Roger ended his drink and shoved Cal away from him.

Cal stumbled forward, crashed into the end of the bed,

and used it to help him spin around. He latched one hand on top of the bleeding bite wound. With his other, he pointed at Roger. "I fucking told you. He's a fucking monster."

Roger wasn't looking in Zack's direction. He kept his gaze on the floor. Zack wanted to run to him, but Cal was the threat. Zack had to keep an eye on him.

"You tied me up," Zack said to Cal. He pivoted so he squarely faced his brother. The straight razor in his hand would have to work as a weapon until he could get his hands on his dagger.

"Break free of the spell already," Cal snapped. "You're stronger than that bastard's magic. You're a Wright. Live up to the—"

"First, vamp magic doesn't work like that. Second—" Zack lifted the edge of his tank top and showed off the hunter's tattoo on his hip. "I'm protected, jackass. My mind is my own."

Cal turned red, then scarlet, which meant he had plenty of blood in his body. He wasn't on death's door, and that was a small relief. But that also meant Cal was a very real threat. As he stood, Cal dropped his hand away from his wound. The coldness in his eyes was almost as shocking as the handgun he pulled from behind his back.

"I knew you were weak. You know, Mom actually started feeling sorry for you while we were on the road this time. She was all 'Zack packed a bag,' and, 'He must be so discouraged. He's not posting as much.' She checked our security cameras every day. I had to convince her you were probably at a friend's or hanging out in your room, or that she just wasn't checking at the right time of day to see you." Cal sniffed derisively. Then he wiped his nose. A bit of blood came away on his hand, and he gave Zack a manic grin. "At least when you went full blood bitch, you chose a strong one. I always figured I'd find you in the middle of a nest."

"Cal, you're my *brother*," Zack said.

"Brother, huh? Fine. I'll give you one more chance. Since we're *family*." Cal tossed a stake at Zack's feet. "Prove you were scratching some itch and the fetish is out of your system. Drive that into your boy over there, and we'll go home."

Slowly, Zack picked up the stake. The edges of it were rough, but Cal had made a decent point on it. If he turned the weapon on Roger, he could have everything he once thought he'd wanted. Cal would show him respect. Zack might even be able to convince him not to tell the rest of the family what he saw in Taliville. He could go back to spewing information on the internet all day and staying up way too late. Maybe he'd finally get to go on the road.

That had meant so much to him.

But he'd been lying to himself since Detroit. Letting the girl go hadn't been a sin. He hadn't been wrong to spare Roger. He'd been wrong to break into a house in the first place. A piece of Cal's soul had to be missing to kill people like he did.

Roger made Zack feel whole. Like he wasn't a fuck-up. Like he didn't have to wait to be good at something.

In his peripheral vision, Zack saw Roger go still. Zack didn't dare look his way. If Roger was scared or angry, Zack didn't want to know. He would deal with Roger's feelings once he'd gotten rid of the threat.

"Last chance, Cal." Zack threw the stake back at Cal's feet. "Leave."

"Ungrateful shit." Cal started to squeeze the trigger.

Too fast for human sight, Roger moved. By the time Cal finished firing the gun, Roger had shoved his wrist up so the shot went high. Their fight started anew. Roger blurred with the speed of his strikes, but Cal was used to fighting vampires. He countered Roger.

Zack made a swing at the back of Cal's head, but Cal ducked it and slammed his fist into Zack's stomach.

Roger grabbed Cal and threw him toward the balcony. He

followed that with a push. Cal caught onto his arms and held on tight. With a crash, they tumbled over the railing.

"Shit!" Zack ran to the balcony.

Below, both men were scrambling to their feet. Just when Roger was about to gain the advantage, Cal knocked him off balance with a kick. Blow for blow, they kept going.

The blaze of Roger's eyes began to dim.

He's losing his strength. That was why he had to bite Cal. He can't keep up. Zack glanced around. Cal's gun was on the floor, but he didn't want to kill him. No matter what Cal wanted to do, Zack wasn't him. He wouldn't pull the trigger on family.

All he had was his dagger and himself, and he didn't have time to rush back for the dagger. He climbed over the railing and held on to the edge. He was on the second floor. The fall would hurt, but he had an idea how he could break his fall.

As soon as Cal stepped close enough, Zack dropped down on him. The direct impact drove Cal to the ground with Zack on top of him. Zack landed on his right leg, and a jolt of pain made it impossible to move.

Cal shoved him off, then climbed on top of him and struck. "You've lost your fucking mind!"

Roger kicked Cal hard enough to send him rolling into the grass where he stayed. He bent down to Zack's side. His eyes were brown and filled with a strange, happy emotion. "Hey there."

"Ow," Zack said. His sides hurt and his ankle screamed in agony. He struggled to see where Cal was. Taking his eyes off his brother wasn't a smart move. "Cal …"

Roger lifted his head and frowned. "He's gone?"

But Cal was behind Roger. Stake in hand, anger hardening his features, he drove it downward.

Sitting up, Zack shoved Roger out of the way with every ounce of strength he had. He tried to catch Cal's wrist, but Cal was too fast and too strong. Cal drove the stake into

Zack's left shoulder. A wide-eyed flash of surprise made Cal look like the brother Zack had loved.

Surprise turned to shock, and Cal scrambled away.

For all the talk, he didn't really want to hurt me. That's nice. Zack put his hand around the stake. He had to keep it still, though it didn't really hurt. Or it hurt a lot. He was having a hard time telling. He began to slide back to the ground.

Roger caught him and propped him up. "Zack, darling. Keep your eyes open."

"They are." Zack grinned at him. "Completely open."

"Keep the stake where it is."

"Duh."

"Shit," Cal said. He slid to his knees in front of Zack. "Shit, shit, shit. Why couldn't you listen to me?"

Roger growled, and it was deep enough that his chest reverberated with it. A primal, angry protectiveness was in that growl.

And it's for me. How nice. Zack was having trouble keeping his head up. Why was it important for him to keep his eyes open?

"Run," Roger snapped.

Cal clenched his jaw. "Not until you give him over."

There were shapes in the growing darkness. Zack raised his right hand and pointed to one that vaguely looked like Josefina. "Cal. You really want to start running."

Cal made a weird noise and sprinted toward the parking lot.

"Zackery, I need you to look at me," Roger said.

Black clouds floated in front of Zack's eyes. Fighting them was hard. Closing his eyes was easier, though he couldn't see Roger's worried frown. "Your shoulder's comfy."

Roger swooped him up off the ground. "Hold on. Please, Zack. Hold *on.*"

Zack put his hand on Roger's other shoulder. He wanted

to tell Roger he'd hold on forever, but moving his mouth took too much effort. All he needed was a little nap.

CHAPTER 33

"Zack. *Zack.*" Roger jostled Zack in his arms.

Instead of rousing, Zack went limp, his hand falling away from Roger's shoulder.

The walls in Roger's heart shattered, and a torrent of emotions flooded him. Rage at Callum Wright slid beneath the growing screams of alarm ringing through him. Zack was losing blood. Short of turning him into a vampire, there was nothing Roger could do. His mind short-circuited.

But he wasn't alone. Choking down a sob, he screamed, "Josefina!"

In a blur, she rushed to his side. When she raised her hand to touch Zack's skin, he nearly bit it off. He had to remind himself she was trying to help.

Josefina swore softly. Then she pointed at one of the vampires who had accompanied her. "Get Micah in his clinic *now.*"

The vampire nodded and ran.

"An injury like that, we can't move at full speed. We can't risk that stake going any deeper or falling out," Josefina said calmly.

How could she be so calm when the world was falling apart?

Pull it together. Roger nodded. "Lead the way."

She jogged away at a speed around a human's, with a long, smooth gait. Roger had to fight the urge to zoom past her. He didn't know where they were going, and she was right. The worst thing that could happen to Zack was losing the stake from his shoulder before he had medical help.

A stake Cal had meant to drive into Roger's back.

Reality became a confused blur. He went through the motions of walking into the clinic with Zack in his arms. Josefina directed him to lay Zack down on a metal table. A man rushed in and started ordering people around: Josefina, him, the vampire sent to get him, another person who barged into the room. They were getting closer to Zack. Someone touched him. Roger growled.

Josefina yanked him out of the room and slammed him into a chair in the waiting room. He started to stand, but she pushed him down. "I know you're scared." She cupped his face. Her thumbs brushed through tears on his cheeks. "He has the best care in there."

"If he dies ..." Roger stopped the sentence. He didn't want to picture the world without Zack, not when he had learned how wonderful it was with him in it.

Josefina knelt in front of him and rested her hands on his knees. "If—and that is very unlikely, given the doctor and witch we have in there—but *if* he dies, we will take the nearest vehicle, drive his bastard brother off the road, and then take three weeks to murder him slowly."

"He was trying to kill me."

She squeezed his knees. "This isn't your fault."

Roger held on to Josefina's hands. Having a point of contact brought him to the whirlpool's edge instead of falling into it. "Zack *saved* me. Cal gave him the chance to turn on me, and he threw it back at him. And then he pushed me out of the way with no regard for his own safety."

"He'll pull through," Josefina said.

But Roger had felt Zack growing limper and limper in his arms. He tightened his hands, and Josefina tightened in return. The touch was comforting. A sign of friendship. Something he'd never been able to count on.

The clinic door swung wide open. Kit and Blake rushed through it, Reed on their heels.

"What are you doing here?" Roger asked.

"This vampire came in talking about a showdown outside the Sleepy Bear Inn," Kit replied.

Josefina stood. "Reed—"

"I've already told Steven that he has to stop spreading gossip before he instigates a panic," Reed said. "But when I heard who was involved, I thought these two should know. They wanted to come."

"Is he going to be okay?" Blake asked.

"It will be a few hours before we know the extent of the damage," Josefina said.

The word reminded Roger of the shout Zack had given during the fall. "His leg. Josefina—tell them to check his leg."

"I will. Give me a moment." Josefina pulled her hands from him.

He was reluctant to let her go, but before his hands could feel empty, Kit and Blake had settled next to him, one on either side. Kit put their head on Roger's shoulder. "We'll stay until they make us leave."

The hours dragged on, but once past, the time felt as quick as the snap of fingers. Reed took call after call, sometimes stepping outside. Roger extended his hearing and eavesdropped anyway. The brick wall blocked large chunks of the conversations, but he caught enough to guess what they were about. Reed was ensuring Callum Wright drove out of Nell's territory. Apparently, Nell had a highway cop on her payroll.

Blake fell asleep on Roger's shoulder an hour into the wait. Her warmth was a comfort even though Roger didn't know the girl personally. Zack had spoken of her often. They were friends, and Roger's heart broke into a few more pieces thinking she might lose a friend because of him.

Kit found a blanket and pillow and stretched out on the floor. They tried to coax Blake to the floor with them, but she was sound asleep against Roger.

During the third hour, Nell arrived. Roger had recovered enough of his ability to speak to go over what had happened with her. "I understand if you want us to leave. As soon as Zack's stable, we'll—"

"You'll go nowhere until you're ready," Nell said quietly. She laughed softly at Roger's confusion. "You have one of my werefoxes curled at your feet, a visiting werewolf asleep on your shoulder, my lover hovering over a medical procedure for a human who I wasn't sure she liked, and my favorite man coordinating a multistate chase just hoping we'll give him a go signal to kill the asshole responsible for this misery. You and Zack may not be in my coven, but I care."

"Thank you." Roger managed a ghost of a smile. "You might feel differently when the Wrights come calling."

"The Wrights might remember that taking on a community is harder than coming after a single target. I doubt we'll have trouble from them. A hunter killed by a vampire at an extravagant party is grounds for a war. A boy hurt by his own brother outside of a hotel is much more difficult to sell."

"They could spin it."

"I already have one of my best spin people telling our version of the story to the right people." Nell put a hand on Roger's shoulder and squeezed. "Worry about your boy. The world waited thirty-two years for you. It can wait a little longer."

"Thank you."

Nell nodded and left.

Roger settled in, thoughts drifting to-and-fro. Adrenaline, or whatever stood in as the vampire equivalent, had completely worn off and left him exhausted. He had almost drifted off when Josefina reemerged with the doctor.

"He's tough," the doctor said. "His shoulder will take some time to heal, and his ankle's sprained. We gave him a transfusion. I say this with respect and for the care of my patient, no feeding on him until I give clearance. Magic can help, but his body still has to do the work."

"Can I see him?"

Blake roused when Roger spoke. She rubbed her eyes. "Zack's okay? Kit, Kit."

"I know," Kit said softly. "Can we see him, doc?"

The doctor sighed and looked them over. "I will allow you all to peek in on him, but he needs his rest. I want to keep him here a couple of days. Then we can move him to wherever you'd like."

"The mansion," Josefina said. "Our security is better. I'll have Reed prepare a room."

"Rooms," Roger said. *I can't afford to accidentally hurt him.* "Next to each other, if you can."

Josefina frowned in confusion but nodded and sought out Reed.

Kit and Blake allowed Roger the honor of checking on Zack first. He was glad they did; he didn't want to fight his new friends.

Machines were attached to Zack, monitoring his life signs. Roger could smell his mortal, living scent without a hint of death to it. He could see the rise and fall of his chest.

The tightness in his own chest eased.

Over the next few days, Roger spent most of his nights at Zack's bedside, though Zack mostly slept. He gathered their belongings and prepared new rooms for them in Nell's mansion. On Blake's suggestion, he bought every book in an ongoing series called *From the Grave*. He added in a smattering of other new books that he hoped Zack hadn't read yet and a leather journal. Kit and Blake decorated the room with flowers and balloons. Reed gifted him a stainless-steel travel coffee mug. Josefina brought a rainbow-colored teddy bear.

Due to his shoulder injury, Zack couldn't use crutches to get around, and he lacked the energy to propel himself through the massive mansion. Roger convinced him to close his eyes before he wheeled him inside the room for the first time.

"Now you can look," Roger whispered.

Zack took in the stacks of books and various gifts and decorations. "You did all this?"

"Far from it," Roger replied. He helped Zack from the chair to the bed and made sure the pillows were piled comfortably behind him. "You have friends."

"Oh no. I must be in a magical coma," Zack groaned. "Friends? Me? How?"

Roger kissed his forehead. "You're not funny when you're dismissing yourself like that."

"But I'm cute."

"Perhaps," Roger teased.

Zack picked up his phone from the nightstand. "What the hell?"

"It should be fine. I kept it charged."

Zack scowled. "Where's my tablet?"

"What's going on?" Roger asked as he handed it over.

"I can't fucking believe this." Zack grabbed his tablet and opened it. He tapped on the screen. Each tap became progressively harder. "No. No. No."

"Isn't it working? I had the screen replaced—"

"They locked me out!" Zack threw the tablet off the end of the bed and screamed at the top of his lungs. After one long scream, he did it a second time. As his air ran out, he broke into a sob.

Roger climbed onto the bed with him, grateful when Zack curled in toward him. He held him and waited for the sobs to subside before he asked, "What does that mean?"

"I can't get into anything. I left my laptop at home, and it was logged in, and they changed the fucking passwords on me. They disconnected my phone. They cut me off. Cal got home. He talked to them, and they cut *me* off. He almost killed me and ..." Zack sobbed into Roger again.

All Roger could do was hold him. His own heart was ground into dust. "Maybe there's some way, if you want to go back to them—"

"Fuck them," Zack said fiercely. "Quinn said Mom knew what Cal did, and I don't doubt it. None of these flowers or gifts are from them, are they? If they cared about me, they wouldn't have disconnected my phone. They would have called. Texted. Fuck them."

The rest of that night, Zack oscillated between crying and staring blankly at the television Reed had hooked up for him. He clung to Roger and his new rainbow teddy bear. Roger wondered if they had enough pieces for a whole heart between them.

The next night, Zack was attempting to move around the house in the wheelchair on his own. When Roger caught up to him, Zack held his head up high. "How long?"

"How long until what?" Roger asked.

"Until we get back on track."

Roger made certain they were the only ones in the hall before stepping around to where he could see Zack's face. "You want to go through with the plan? Take on Anton and Seamus?"

"Why wouldn't I?"

"I thought you were doing it to impress your family."

"I was." Zack looked away, but when he raised his eyes,

steely confidence was in them. "And that was the wrong reason. Roger … You said Chicago's nothing like Taliville."

"That's right."

"It should try to be. I'm a hunter, and my room is overflowing with floral arrangements from people who have known me less than a month. This place is a community. They watch out for each other." Zack held his hand out for Roger to take, and he did. "If we can end those bastards and make something good, we should."

Roger knelt down and kissed Zack's hand, then his wrist, then his lips. "Yes, darling. We should."

"Great. When do we leave?"

~

Zack and Roger continue their story in Vicious Waltz. Be sure to join my newsletter for updates and an exclusive story!

AFTERWORD

Hey there, reader peeps! Hopefully you've enjoyed *Wrong Hunt* as much as I enjoyed writing it! If you loved—or even if you hated—this book, I hope you'll consider doing a review on your fave site so other readers can know the joy/agony you've felt. Readers sharing their opinions is how I've found many a book to read myself. It's fun to share!

If you're eager for more of my stories, check out my Patreon along with my Amazon profile page. You'll find plenty of sweet, spice, and adventure in my tales and I can't wait to share them with you!

Happy Reading!
JS "Jace" Harker

ACKNOWLEDGEMENTS

I've never written one of these before, but this book is a very special occasion. See, when I first started considering myself a Writer, I was thirteen and fascinated with vampires. I'd just finished *Interview with the Vampire* and had way too much time on my hands, so I started writing my own novel. Sometimes I continue on in spite, sometimes by inspiration, but thanks are due to those who've written vampires before me.

A majority of the thank yous go to my mom. After all, she's the one who put *Interview* into my hands. She had to spend weeks convincing me to watch *Buffy the Vampire Slayer* —which I couldn't stop talking about for a decade. She also bought me a word processor when I was fourteen so I didn't have to hog the family computer to write my stories, and she's been incredibly supportive. Thank you, Mom.

My next thank you goes to Sue, my editor. It's entirely her fault I stepped back into this area of the supernatural. To be fair, she was trying to inspire someone to write vampires at a convention we were both at. Sue pushes me to write better and better novels. She's a fantastic editor. I honestly can't be too disappointed with how DSP worked out for me because through them I met Sue. I don't know how long it would've taken me to sharpen up my game without her, and I really don't want to speculate on that either. Thank you, Sue!

Final round of thanks goes out to two of my buddies. When I was worried about how to do vampires and still hold onto my usual themes of consent, one buddy helped me work out the basics of the vampire bite. I've also got a buddy who listens to me day in and day out as I pick my way through words and doubts and over hurdles. She constantly shakes pompoms for me. I hope everyone can find a friend as thoughtful and supportive as her. Thank you, friends.

And okay, I lied. One more round of thank yous. Thank you, reader, for taking the time to read the novel and these few words. Writers are only screaming into the void without anyone to read what they put out. I hope you enjoyed this book and I hope you'll join Zack and Roger in their next adventure. Happy reading!

ABOUT THE AUTHOR

JS Harker loves stories. She was one of those kids who constantly had a book in her hands and spent countless hours adventuring with her siblings. These days she wanders into her imaginary worlds and conjures up tales of magic, passion, and happily-ever-afters. She currently lives in the part of the Midwest that makes Tatooine look interesting by comparison (not that she's ever obsessively thought about becoming a Jedi or anything).

Follow her on Facebook or go to www.jsharker.com and sign up for her newsletter to receive updates!

ALSO BY JS HARKER

The Fang and Dagger Saga

Wrong Hunt

Vicious Waltz

Wicked Games

Tit For Tat Series

Tit For Tat

His Fairy Prince

A Midsummer Night's Party

Also

Keep Me Safe

Soul Bond

www.ingramcontent.com/pod-product-compliance
Lightning Source LLC
Chambersburg PA
CBHW010344220726
48290CB00016B/2624